D0262439

THE DEATH OF LOMOND FRIEL

The Death of
Lomond Friel

Sue Peebles

Chatto & Windus
LONDON

Published by Chatto & Windus 2010

2 4 6 8 10 9 7 5 3 1

First published in Great Britain in 2010 by
Chatto & Windus
Random House, 20 Vauxhall Bridge Road,
London SW1V 2SA

www.rbooks.co.uk

Addresses for companies within The Random House Group Limited can be
found at: www.randomhouse.co.uk/offices.htm

The Random House Group Limited Reg. No. 954009

A CIP catalogue record for this book
is available from the British Library

ISBN 9780701184308

The Random House Group Limited supports The Forest Stewardship Council (FSC),
the leading international forest certification organisation. All our titles that are
printed on Greenpeace approved FSC certified paper carry the FSC logo.
Our paper procurement policy can be found at
www.rbooks.co.uk/environment

Mixed Sources
Product group from well-managed
forests and other controlled sources
www.fsc.org Cert no. TT-COC-2139
© 1996 Forest Stewardship Council

Typeset by Palimpsest Book Production Limited,
Grangemouth, Stirlingshire

Printed and bound in Great Britain by
CPI Mackays, Chatham ME5 8TD

For my parents, Gordon and Sarah Melvin

Hope is the thing with feathers
That perches in the soul,
And sings the tune without the words,
And never stops at all

'Hope', Emily Dickinson

One

ROSIE'S BROTHERS came from the same egg. It was an auspicious beginning to what promised to be a fortunate life, or rather, two lives, although for years they were rarely thought of as plural. They were inextricable, twice as likely together and half-hearted apart. Rosie has heard a full account of their birth and knows all about it. Jacob came first, then William, known to some as Just William because he nearly died, strangled by his own cord – or was it Jacob's cord, or did they share it? Rosie pictures two baby boys dangling from the same string, one of them grey as a dead kitten. She can't believe she hasn't asked about that after all this time.

IT WAS a miracle, according to Aunty Heath.

'A miracle,' she said, shaking her head in wonder and raising her hands, palms up, surrendering to the supernatural forces that were clearly at work.

THE TWINS were identical, the result of a split in one fertilised ovum, an abundant harvest that made both parents cry – the father with joy, the mother with relief. It seemed right after so many fallow years. It was also convenient, since the family plan was to provide the firstborn with a sibling (otherwise who would play with it?). Until Ethel and Lomond were sure about the dyadic nature of their good fortune, the prospect of a sequel had hovered over the difficult pregnancy like a winged crocodile, Rosie's mother lying on the day bed, month after month, failing to bloom. Her blood pressure climbed and her mood sank, then *whoosh* – with a spectacular deluge of afterbirth, the plan was realised.

THE TEN years that followed were chronicled by Lomond through a series of seaside snaps; a mixed collection of portraits (the Friels, stiff as wood) and action shots (blurry boys racing across the sand). Each summer album was dated and stored in an old sideboard, away from the light, so the gum wouldn't perish. The twins grew like sunflowers, tall, straight and golden. They were easy in front of the camera and either ignored it or looked through it with bovine boldness. Their mother featured occasionally in the background, a reluctant floral splash against the vibrant stripes of a windbreak that still lies furled up in the front porch of the summer house, its poles bleached white by the strong north-easterly winds.

THE NEXT baby was called Rosemary. She was not planned and Heath, once more in attendance, did not identify anything miraculous about the birth. Rosie was delivered in the same narrow house as her brothers. She was quickly wrapped in blue and placed in the same basket where, ten years, twenty days and six hours earlier, the twins had basked in monozygotic splendour.

'Your ears were crumpled and red raw – and Rosie,' she paused, 'you never cried. Not a sound.' Heath always maintained this, believing that the mute newborn infant was listening, straining to hear the beat of its mother's heart.

2

ROSIE STILL keeps a small picture of her mother in the back of her purse. Every so often she pulls it out and scrutinises it, close up, her myopic stare looking for something she's missed. The photograph has grown soft and feels like cloth; a black-and-white image shows her mother heavily pregnant, her pinny stretched tight over her stomach. She's standing over the gas hob stirring a pot but looking at the camera and Rosie cannot decide whether or not she is smiling. Her dark blonde hair is pulled back from her face and pinned loosely at the nape of her neck. Some of it has come loose and she's brushing it from her forehead with the back of her hand. It's the last picture ever taken of Ethel Friel.

★

I'VE DRIVEN up to the summer house to think. The house is small and stark, its white harled back facing the sea. The low windows are recessed, their nooks cluttered with shells and candles — and paraffin lamps that work (we have lots of power cuts here). The alcoves run so deep into the stone that it never really grows light, even on the brightest day. It's the price you pay for living with the magnificent ferocity of the great north wind.

There are four main rooms that sit in a line and connect with each other directly, so the only ones that offer any privacy are at the gable ends, the coldest rooms in the house. Each room has a fireplace and very occasionally (on the mornings when frost laced the inside of the windows) every fire would be lit, a full-time job for Dad. His was the west bedroom, and the twins slept in the east. I was lodged in the room next to the boys, flanked on the other side by the living room, so my space was the main thoroughfare for Jacob and William. They would lumber through my room at any hour, day or night — it was a pecking order I never questioned, even when I most needed sanctuary or protected space for my various collections (jars, corks, a few nameless Care Bears and a tiny herd of Little Ponies led by Applejack and Sunbeam, who quickly galloped off somewhere else and were never missed), but I made the most of the dark, the oasis of night and bed, where I could think quiet thoughts and explore myself, my body, and of course, my guilt – the dark hyena in the corner, with its kicked arse and stupid laugh. Hysterical. Ready to nip me, to remind me.

Remember, Rosie. Remember what you did.

COMING HERE is a relief after everything that's happened. Not that I'm running away from it, this is a proactive thing (I'm developing a plan) – and, although Wilson is probably right when he says I shouldn't be alone right now, it feels good. I feel stronger. Anyway, I'm not really alone. Heath is just down the road and there's always Catherine, the ghost – she's the permanent resident here, the rest of us come and go. I first saw her when I was small and couldn't speak. I had barely started talking when suddenly all the words dried up. Dad said it was a sign of genius. Little drawings started to appear, tiny folded messages that were all about the same thing – me. When Dad asked me if I'd done them I shook my head. *Ah . . . it must have been the ghost,* he said, smiling and rolling his eyes, and I knew her name immediately. She took a while to reveal herself. For a time I would wake in the dark with a sense that someone had just left the room – my eyes would be fixed on the door, as though it had closed that very moment, the click of the door latch waking me up. Then, I fancied I saw the latch move and the door close. Eventually I caught sight of a grey skirt hem swinging round the door frame, a pale ankle and small feet in black sandshoes, turning in the blue light.

'Goodnight, Catherine,' I would whisper.

The tiny bones in her feet made bumps in the shoe canvas. She must have been as thin as a rake.

★

When I was mute my father would not guess.

'I don't know what you want, Rosie,' and he would wait for me to show him, looking, not watching, his occasional inattentiveness creating the rhythm of auditory conversations. Sometimes he would drift back to his paper and I had to place my hands on his face and turn his head to look at me, my words lapping over his cheeks. If his back was turned I would tug his trouser leg. If he was talking I would pat him very gently, small repeats, over and over, until eventually I was given a turn. These kinetic dialogues were much like any other. They could be understood or misunderstood, for the usual reasons, but they were never spurious, so I never really acquired the knack for chit-chat. Now I earn my living talking on the radio and the irony hasn't escaped me or anyone else in the family. William says it's why I developed my particular style of reportage, well suited to tight editing and the acute squeeze on air time (I offer them the story, I don't beat them over the head with it). In contrast, my brothers chattered like magpies all day long, especially Jacob, who seemed compelled to fill a room with sound whenever a silence sprang up – usually without any warning, making my older brother very edgy and often agitated. This agitation was fuelled by the disregard of others. If Jacob did not receive the attention he merited things got loud, and if loud didn't do it he was not averse to throwing whatever was handy – cutlery, books, shoes. Plates were particularly satisfying, and the sharp dents made by flying Dinky Toys peppered the walls like shrapnel.

Ignore him, was the wisdom of the day, and so we would take cover and wait until the fatigue of battle overwhelmed

5

him and he fell to the ground, moaning quietly and tracing his fingers across the floor, his once handsome face all pinched and puckered in an expression many would describe as pensive, but which I saw as vacuous. I fancy Dad saw it too, the slightly shrunken head set deep into his chest, pickled in brine and completely empty. There was a shame in seeing it, like catching sight of someone's bare bum as they struggled to change beneath a towel on the beach.

You never mentioned it.

You shouldn't even have been looking.

'You have a salty tongue, Jacob,' was Heath's take on things, and it seemed that nothing would quench it.

The twins' constant yelping and yapping somehow masked my own, temporary dysphonia, which I offered by way of an apology.

Now that Dad has no voice you'd think I'd know what to do.

★

THEY LOOK at Lomond in open curiosity.

'Does he say anything?'

'No. But we still enjoy a blether, don't we, Lomond?'

Lomond's good manners prevail and he gives her a half-smile.

'And what about his therapy? Does he get plenty of exercise?'

This is Jacob's second visit to the hospital since his father's stroke. The first time he just couldn't get beyond the change in Lomond, but today he is prepared. He has formulated all sorts of questions and his wife April has written them down in case he forgets anything. In the event she doesn't need to prompt him. As he works his way through each query she ticks them off. The charge nurse is patient. Her answers are polite but short. She recognises the type – it's the *being seen to ask the questions* that's important, rather than any particular concern for detail. This collusive brevity suits everyone, for different reasons.

'Has he been seen by a neurologist?'

'Yes.'

'And what did he say?'

'She.'

'Pardon?'

'She. Dr Saunders is a she.'

Jacob frowns. The correction feels like a criticism. He doesn't like this nurse. April, on the other hand, looks momentarily startled. She raises her eyebrows and nods, pulling her mouth down at the corners until her chin completely disappears.

'Right. So what does this *Doc-tor* Saunders say about my father's speech?'

'It's too early to say. We really need to wait for the scan results so we can assess the damage.'

'But do you think he'll talk again?'

'Like I said, Mr Friel, it's too early to say. Let's just look on the bright side, eh?'

The nurse tilts her head a little to one side and throws Lomond a wide sunshine grin.

★

THE HOUSE is freezing. I keep my jacket on and start to clean out the stove. The ashes are five months old, remnants of the fire Wilson and I made back in September. He always over-loads the fire, whereas I'm more frugal, I like to think ahead, but I was glad of it that night because I couldn't sleep. Hot milk at three perched on a cushioned hearth, my back pressed against the glass.

Another year gone. Another summer in the city wishing away July.

7

I don't feel like lighting the fire and settling down just yet, I'm too close to succumbing to the dark mood that sidled into the car and sat with me all the way up the road. It takes over an hour to drive here and you can sink a long way down in an hour; you can reach a place it's hard to get out of. What I really need is a drink. I drink when I'm trying to be or not to be the person I am, or the person I'm not.

Or when I am sick.

Or there might be other circumstances.

Depending.

★

HEATH STARES at the phone as though she's never seen it before. Black Bakelite. Ugly-looking thing. Her nephew Jacob has his eye on it. He wants it for his flat in Comely Bank.

It's ringing.

'Hello?'

'Hi, Heath. It's me, Rosie.'

'Rosie?'

'Rosemary.'

Long pause.

'Your niece.'

'Yes.'

'Lomond's daughter.'

'Yes, I know that, eh, Rosie. I'm well aware. How are you, dear?'

'Fine. I'm at the summer house. I thought I'd come round tomorrow at teatime.'

'Tomorrow?'

'Yes.'

'What day is it tomorrow?'

'Friday.'

'I've only got one fish.'

8

'That's OK. I'll bring my own.'

Heath is unconvinced. The girl will forget. She goes to the cold pantry, lifts the dish and contemplates the fish. The brown eye stares up at her, accusing her through crushed ice, its last brutal moment captured and preserved – like those tiny ferns or pieces of heather encased in glass paperweights.

★

WHEN I wake next morning I can smell the sea. It gives me hope. For the first time since the stroke I don't feel I have to call the hospital to check that Dad's still alive.

I just assume.

The air is wet, more mist than rain, made substantial by a gusting wind that only blows round certain corners of certain streets. It's the kind of day when you need to stay alert and ready for the reverse flip if you're going to use a brolly. I don't bother. I just push my hands in my pockets, tuck in my chin and walk quickly into town. I'm heading for Fraser's, the fishmonger's on South Street. The pavements are wide and handsome, audacious for such a small seaside town – more like an *avenue*, lined on both sides by a crowding of old buildings, braced against the weather and sheltered by fine trees. My coat flaps open and the knees of my trousers are wet but my shoes stay dry. My hair lifts and spreads from underneath – like I've just leapt from a plane – yet the person approaching me on this same street at this same moment is dry and intact, as if they somehow occupy a different day (Wilson would have something to say about that, he'd have a theory). I sidestep into the mouth of a cobbled wynd and button up.

NOW, THIS I love. A decent fish shop, pungent and clean as a boiled scalpel. White-slabbed and lovely, the fish lie on a bed of ice, eyes wide and their fish lips gasping against the shock of the cold. I avoid looking at their little faces, focusing instead on their fishy tails, splayed like ballet dancers' feet set precisely in the first position. All the basics are here, cod, haddock, sole, skate, plaice, salmon, tiger prawns, eels (rock or jellied), rainbow trout, kippers, herring, but there are some exotic cousins too – John Dory, red snapper and tuna, whitebait, swordfish, monkfish.

'Do you sell chicken?' asks the woman in front, as I queue, calm and pale as a lemon sole.

I look at the fishmonger and he looks back, deadpan. Not a flicker, and yet – there it was.

Something.

MY AUNT enters the shop. She's fully wrapped, her coat encased in see-through plastic, and she's wearing a rain-mate over a green felt hat.

'Good morning, Cameron. Don't worry, I know it's Friday, but I need another fish.'

'Hello, Aunty.'

Heath looks up at me, astonished.

'Good grief, child. Is that you?'

'I think so.'

'What are you doing here?'

'Um . . . buying fish?'

'Oh, I'll get that. Put your purse away. One more kipper, please.'

'Which one would you like, Miss Friel?' He tilts the tray upwards and we all peer down in appreciation, as though we're scrutinising diamonds on a bed of black velvet. Heath picks one out, small, plump and perfect.

'I'll take that one, thank you.'

He shoots me a glance for approval, so I nod, but only slightly, nothing that Heath would pick up on. As he turns

10

to weigh my tea I find myself staring at the back of his neck. Heath introduces me.

'This is my niece, Rosie. Lomond's girl.'

That's who I am here, 'Lomond's girl'. Not *that woman off the radio*.

'Yes, hello, Rosie.'

Does he know me?

'She has a thing about fish eyes, so if you could take the head off that'll be fine.'

He's uneasy now, uneasy in his own place. I'm trying to think of something to say but I can't seem to make the jump. I've been back five minutes and my aunt is sharing personal information about me with the fishmonger, who knows my dad.

Heath pulls out a Tupperware box and hands it to Cameron. He scoops in some crushed ice and lays the fish on top. The rain suddenly lifts and I help Heath off with her mac and give it a shake outside. I'm about to go back in but decide to wait for her. For a moment there's no traffic anywhere. An old man passes on a black bike and raises his hand to greet me. In the distance I can hear the pound and rush of waves, then the wind drops to nothing.

I SIT down on Heath's chair and pick up a *People's Friend*.

'Still reading this propaganda, Heath?'

'What's that, dear?'

At least she heard something. The delicate smell of kippers in milk permeates from the kitchen, tinged with a gaseous reek. It took Heath a clear thirty seconds (and counting) to ignite the gas, that's at least five shots from the gun – then the muffled explosion of a distant cannon.

Whoom.

'I said you're still reading the Peep Holes End.'

'Oh, yes. I like the stories.'

11

I move to the sideboard and take out cutlery and place mats, then put them on the table by the window.

'Can I turn the fire down?'

'Pardon?'

'Do you mind if I turn the fire down?'

'I don't mind, dear. Help yourself.'

I twist the knob once to the left, flinching from the white heat, and watch the indestructible chrysotile turn grey. The fire clicks loudly as it cools and contracts.

'That fire's really bad for your lungs.'

'Sorry, dear?'

'I said that fire is really bad for your lungs. The room will be full of asbestos dust.'

'Yes, you're absolutely right, dear. That's why I had it put in.'

'What did you say?'

'I said, yes, I quite agree,' shouts Heath. 'These fires are definitely the best for dust. Far cleaner than the open coal.'

She comes through to the sitting room, slightly flushed. She's taken off her pinny.

'I thought we might just eat in the kitchen, since it's just the two of us.'

I turn, mid-sequence, fruit bowl in hand, and look at Heath.

'Oh . . . OK.'

I'm stranded for a moment, a synaptic lapse – then I put the fruit back down in the centre of the table and we continue.

'Good idea.'

I've never visited Heath on my own before and, of course, she's right – how could we sit at the table and not miss his reflection in the window, his napkin tucked over his weekend tie (a knitted one – moss green, with a clip guaranteed for the life of the tie). Heath frowns as we draw up our chairs and face each other across the easi-wipe surface.

'Rosie, I'm a bit worried about your hearing. Have you ever thought of having your ears syringed?'

Two

ABOUT THREE hours after his stroke Lomond was found lying on his kitchen floor by a woman with the unfortunate name of Mrs Danvers. She was able to calculate the exact time of *his event* based on the stage he had reached in his routine. He had just finished buttering his crumpets. The tea was made but not poured, the honey laid out but not yet opened. The radio was playing and the paper was folded open at the crossword. There was a biro, a magnifying glass and a pocket dictionary on the table. Kitty knew all the details of Lomond's morning routine – she had been cleaning for him every Thursday for over fifteen years. Normally she would have arrived much earlier and started in the bathroom while he ate breakfast, but on this particular Thursday she had arranged to come in at twelve because her daughter had asked her to watch the baby in the morning.

KITTY WAS the best sort of person to be found by – she was kind and practical, with a calm disposition, and she'd seen this once before. The first thing she did was call for an ambulance.

'I think he's had a stroke. He's not had his breakfast yet so I'd say it happened before nine this morning. I didn't get here till now.'

Lomond lay on his side with his shoulders leaning against the oven door. He'd stumbled rather than fallen, a prolonged teeter across the room which made him giggle, then a clumsy attempt to grab onto something before his uneven descent to the carpet tiles – quite a gentle collapse for such a big man. He watched his own amateur movements and was struck by how silly he looked, a dancing hippo with a self-conscious smile that stayed on his face, fixed and even (its slow down-ward slip would come later). In order to rest his head on the floor he had to bend it at an obtuse angle, his parallel legs and splayed feet achieving incongruous symmetry, and there he lay – like a seal on a rock – carefully assembled in coquettish pose.

THEY PUT Kitty's call straight through, which she hadn't expected. Now she had to talk to Rosie in her studio, which meant she was talking to that other Rosie, the famous one that she was careful not to mention to her friends (she was naturally discreet when it came to the Friels).

'Oh, Rosie, it's Kitty here. I'm so sorry to call you at work. I thought they'd just take a message.'

'That's OK, Kitty. How are you?'

'Oh, I'm fine, thanks. How are you?'

'Fine.'

'You must be so busy.'

'Well, yes, Thursdays are always a bit hectic.'

'Yes, I can imagine.'

Something fluttered up in Rosie's stomach and then fell again. She could feel it quivering.

'So, Kitty – are you calling about Dad?'

'What?'

'I wondered if you were calling about my dad.'

'Your dad, yes, well, it's Lomond. I think he's had a stroke. I've called the ambulance and they should be here any minute.'

'Oh, my God. Where is he?'

'What?'

'Where is he? Is he all right?'

'He's fine.'

'Fine?'

'He's quite comfortable.'

'Can I talk to him? Put him on, Kitty.'

'I don't think he's able to talk to you right now.'

'Why not . . . is he conscious?'

'Yes, but . . . oh, there's the door. I'd better go, Rosie.'

'Kitty? Kitty!'

★

LOMOND LOOKED on as Kitty and the ambulance men did everything that needed to be done. Actions were executed around him and seemed to follow a sequence, which implied a certain predictability about what would happen next. This felt reassuring, as though there was still a natural order to things, something that could be played out, and with the exception of Lomond himself, all the actors were well rehearsed and entirely convincing. Their proficiency contrasted to his own amateur performance, which felt stagey, and could have proved embarrassing, had he not been cast in such a minor role.

As they carried him down the hallway Lomond noticed Kitty's bag lying open at the bottom of the stairs. He could see her red purse, the old-fashioned kind with the central clasp that you twisted to open. This was her coin purse, the one she used for her bus money until she got her bus pass last month.

'Oh, aye . . . it's all exact fare only these days – that or you're off.'

Kitty always checked her purse before she left the house. She would open it, look at the bus pass she'd put there just

15

two hours before, and close it again. *Snap.* The sound reminded Lomond of his mother, and now − as his frozen smile hit the cold February air − he could see her again, propped up in bed, her purse in her hand.

Snap.

'There you go, son. Don't tell your sister.'

And off he did go, down the stairs and out the front, buoyed up by the thruppence in his pocket.

King of the hill.

★

I JUST walked out of the studio as soon as I got the news. It was exhilarating. If I'm honest, I'd been looking for an excuse to do this for a while. I'd been dreaming about it, and somehow I knew it would happen, I just didn't know how or when. I should have guessed that Dad would be the one to bail me out. Who else would? I'm not exactly popular (except with the people who don't know me, the ones who listen to the show every week), but that's OK − I've been studying this 'learn to love yourself' stuff with some success. 'What's to learn?' was Wilson's response when I told him (I had to − he caught me off guard one day when I was working on my essence shift). Wilson sees me as self-obsessed, and he may be right − but what he doesn't appreciate is that self-obsession does not equate to self-love.

'I'm such a phoney.'

'True.'

'I don't know what to feel.'

'Try feeling this,' he said, dead serious, pressing my hand against his balls.

I live with Wilson. I believe that's the right way round, the way things are. *I* live with *him.* He lives, and I am with him. I can't say exactly when he moved into my flat. It

16

happened inch by inch – shirt by shirt – then about eighteen months ago he lost his mobile and I rang his number so we could track it down. We stood in the middle of the hall like a couple of leverets, listening for his ring tone. He traced it to the bedroom and called back.

'It's OK – I've found it. How the hell did it get into my sock drawer?'

And there it was – Wilson had a sock drawer. When he came back through he held up his phone and grinned. It was still ringing.

'Aren't you going to answer that?'

I had kept hold of the receiver. He put his hand on my buttock and pulled me in, pressing against me as he answered his phone.

'Sorry,' he said, 'I can't come to the phone right now. Leave a message and I'll get back to you as soon as I can.'

'It's me. Call me as soon as you get this. I want you to come home.'

We hung up.

'I love you, Wilson, you're so real,' I said, in my sweetest voice-bubble voice.

'Ya better believe it, baby.'

PERHAPS I was in shock. I hope so. It would explain the fact, THE FACT, that after I took Kitty's call I felt a huge sense of release. I walked out of the office with a new legitimacy, my responsibilities slid off me, scattering in all directions like beads from a broken string. People patted me on the arm and threw me that chin-up smile. They called me *love* and made way for me. They held the lift. It probably looked like straightforward sympathy but it didn't feel like that, nor was it an act of solemn celebrity. On my way down to the basement I looked at my reflection in the steel doors of the lift and I was reassured by what I saw – an absence, a disconnection, just the way you'd expect someone to look in these particular circumstances. I was thinking, maybe I'll be needed now – and the thought put me in high spirits for a few moments, then I felt guilty as hell.

★

THE RED linoleum floors shone like raspberry toffee. Cleaners moved slowly through the hypnotic arc of their polishers, the low hum of revolving machinery softening the ecclesiastical silence of the hospital. When I arrived Dad was still in A&E, waiting to be taken *up*. I wasn't allowed to see him.

'Up where?'

'They're just preparing a bed for him in the stroke unit.'

'But isn't any delay dangerous? Is he being treated now?'

'They know what they're doing, Rosie.'

Rosie? Have we met?

'It's our policy to get them here as quickly as possible and then we know what we're dealing with. The best treatment is the right treatment. Scoop and run we call it.'

'My name's Rosemary.'

'I'm sorry?'

'My name's Rosemary. You called me Rosie but my name's Rosemary. Rosemary Friel.'

FROM THE RADIO I wanted to say.

THAT'S ROSEMARY FRIEL'S DAD YOU'VE GOT IN THERE SO YOU'D BETTER GET IT RIGHT OR I'LL BLOW THIS SCOOP AND RUN POLICY RIGHT ACROSS THE AIRWAYS.

★

JACOB WAS the first person I called.

'Why didn't anyone call me?'

18

'I'm calling you now!'

'Why did they call you first? Didn't they have my number?'

'It was Kitty who called me.'

'Doesn't she have my number?'

'I don't know. For Christ's sake, Jacob, what does it matter?'

Three

B EING A twin had its downside. Whilst Jacob and William
enjoyed great popularity and were generally favoured
over other, disappointingly singular children, their elevation
was entirely contingent on their duality. They could sing and
do card tricks, one picking the card, the other shuffling the
pack, and although William was the more dexterous of the
two, it was always Jacob who held the wand. He was, after
all, the firstborn. Together they were splendid, but not so
splendid as to offend God. William had one leg slightly shorter
than the other, or as Aunty Heath insisted, one longer than
the other. She would light-heartedly blame Jacob, her voice
laughing as if she didn't mean it.

But still.

'He's pulling your leg again, William. Just you ignore him.'
And William would obligingly turn away with a slight limp.
'See what you've done, Jacob?'

Despite Heath's assertion that this asymmetry was a post-
natal development, there was some evidence of a pelvic twist,
and a curve in William's left leg. Calipers were discussed, and
Lomond was keen, but when Ethel realised that this would
involve wearing an ugly metal splint for years rather than
weeks the idea was quickly rejected.

'I think we should consider it, Ethel, think in the long term. After all, you wouldn't deny a child braces, would you? What's the difference?'

'There's nothing wrong with his teeth.'

'I'm not saying there is. I'm saying it's the same principle. Why won't you think about it?'

'It's not the same. It's not the same at all. He would be laughed at, ridiculed.' Ethel shuddered. 'No, I'm not putting him through that. I will not have my son humiliated.'

Lomond sighed. It was a conclusive statement and there was little point in returning to it, although he did wonder quite who it was that would feel humiliated. He recognised this as an uncharitable thought and tried to forget it, but every so often it would stir, like a small creature sleeping under a pile of leaves.

★

'HELLO? Is that the stroke unit?'

'Yes.'

'Can I speak to the person in charge, please?'

'I'm Charge Nurse Johnson.'

'Are you in charge?'

'I'm the charge nurse.'

'Yes, but are you in charge?'

'Who's speaking, please?'

'It's Jacob Friel. I'm Lomond Friel's son. I'm his next of kin.'

'Oh, hello, Mr Friel.'

'Do you have a note of that?'

'Yes, we have your name and contact number.'

'Yes, but am I down as his next of kin?'

'Yes.'

'Good.'

THE WORST thing that can happen to a person is that they lose their mind. That is the opinion of many, and Lomond was no exception – until now.

'There's nothing wrong with his mind, you know,' was frequently stated by the insightful and well-intentioned, as if this somehow compensated for the dribbling mouth and the drop-foot. He had always considered his mental life to be his life, believing it was his thoughts, not his actions, that defined his experience. He lived in his head, an unseen, unsung existence, and assumed this to be universal, the commonality that defined what it meant to be human. This assumption gave Lomond a natural affinity with people; he was at ease with them and expected little from them, believing them to be busy with their own thoughts, just as he was with his. This was not to say he lacked curiosity. In fact, he listened exquisitely, and in doing so unwittingly encouraged intimacy, and sometimes love. It was love that Lomond often failed to recognise, in part because he did not seek it – and did not seem to need it. He was popular with his students; they wanted to please him and in consequence many of them did well, surpassing all expectations. There were some marked exceptions to this, particularly among his female students, some of whom perceived him as solipsistic, or tragic (a widower with three children!), or seductive – for there was no doubt that Lomond was good-looking, his tall frame slightly stooped in quiet apology, his face wide with a strong jaw and resolute chin. His movements were graceful but poorly executed and things frequently broke around him. This clumsy Goliath could awaken dormant emotions in those who had struggled to find a suitable conduit for their affections. A big man, ascribed with a stoicism that he did not in fact possess, Lomond had little notion of his effect – the Ted Hughes of

22

the maths department, his tutorials imbued with a transference more associated with the analyst's couch than an exploration of the quadratic. He was not blind to the clear-eyed stare of youth, but interpreted the dark dilated pupils of his students as a sign of their love for algebra. His long and moderately successful career in academe was littered with the casualties of powerful attractions, all different in their way both in nature and effect, but all entirely unrequited.

It was a sweet oblivion, for Lomond had grown accustomed to a life devoid of intimacy. He settled down with the small steady sadness that took up residence after his wife died nearly thirty years ago. It became his familiar, and lay in the hall like a sick cat, softening his footsteps as he passed.

*

NOW THAT the need to rally was over, Kitty was inconsolable.

Disproportionate, thought April.

'At least he's not in any pain, are you, Father?'

April took Lomond's hand, the right one – the one without any feeling – and rubbed it gently with her thumb.

*

HIS LIFE flashed in front of him, in the postmodern sense – discrete reels of selected scenes, running in no particular order. It seemed paradoxical to Lomond that he found clichés so enlightening – common templates of truth that we all knew and could share.

Finding Ethel was like coming home.

And it was true enough. She felt familiar to him, comfortable. She seemed to know what she wanted and there was something compelling about her surety. He felt secure with her. She gave him focus and helped him realise that life needn't be difficult. She could be relied on to map out their course – and thereafter it was just a matter of following the directions. If there had ever been questions about the actual destination, they had already been answered and were long forgotten.

The thing was to press on.

'Forget the past, that's what I do. It's gone.'

She said it with such confidence, made it sound so easy, that he just fell in, ignoring the doubt. (It seemed neither wise nor possible to forget the past, but Ethel appeared to have achieved it. Whatever happened to her before, she was free as a bird now.)

He met Ethel at a time when he was generally at sea, with the exception of a few moments of clarity when he felt something vital course through his body. These were moments when things felt right, and they occurred in all the usual places – at the top of snow-capped mountains, or on a hillside of springy heather. Lomond could see that even his epiphanies were clichéd, so he didn't mention them, despite their profundity (better not to call attention to his swollen heart, or the hackneyed tears that sprang from nowhere when he least expected them – when he was shaving, or polishing shoes).

LOMOND WAS almost eccentric, but not quite. His self-awareness held him back, robbing him of the confidence to be entirely himself. He felt obscure, and clung to things rather than people, finding cardigans, toasters and bone-handled letter-openers much more reliable and comforting. Lomond could draw great pleasure from the shape and functional beauty of a good cheese knife. He liked to read, not so much books – he found fiction rather pointless – but broadsheets, everything from the leader articles to the acknowledgements. Cover to cover might take him three or four hours, which is a fair whack of an average day. He loved listening to music and was keen on numbers (a common coupling), which he found aesthetically pleasing, seeing them in colours – bright cardinals that varied in aspects of density and luminosity. Lomond had always excelled at maths but wasn't sure what to do with this and his other sensibilities. He liked being outdoors, and held a long-standing interest in birds. He was fascinated by the whole conundrum of migration – but how to reconcile his exceptional numeracy with his love of mucking about outside? He spent years giving this thought, and had come up with a few ideas that sploshed around in his cranial sea.

Then he met Ethel, and after a few candlelit suppers and fireside fumbles, he dropped anchor.

Ethel. *His compass.*

'All I want is your happiness,' she said, and once again Lomond was caught in the full glare of cliché, mesmerised by the steady brown of Ethel's eyes. He had not shared his ideas with anyone before, but now, he poured them out – diffident and brave.

'I thought about becoming a composer.' He faltered for a moment, unable to read her expression. 'When I hear a black-bird singing I can see it on the page. It stays with me, you know? I can build on it, play around with it.'

'Really . . . but composing, isn't that more of a hobby than a career? How would you make a living?'

And of course she was right, she was only confirming what he already knew.

'Well . . . my other plan is to become a bookmaker.'

'Ah, now that sounds quite interesting. You mean, like those coffee-table books? On art?'

Lomond laughed. 'No . . . I mean a bookie, an actuary. I've looked into it and with my formulas it's practically risk free. We couldn't lose!'

Lomond grabbed her hands and squeezed them tight, then released them, embarrassed by his own enthusiasm. He could see his outburst had unsettled her. She uncurled her fingers and pressed them lightly against her mouth. She *was* unsettled, not because Lomond's proposal was clearly ridiculous, but because the thrill she felt when he said 'we' – the way it placed them both so firmly in the future – caught her by surprise.

We.

The word seared Ethel's consciousness, as sure as a branding iron pressed to her rump. Up until then there hadn't been a 'we'. This was exactly the 'we' she had been working towards all those years – a solid, respectable 'we' that would transform her and erase the past. The possibility had dawned on her the day she was taken from the chaos of her mother's bedsit and delivered to the front parlour of 'Mr and Mrs'. 'Mr and Mrs' were devoted to each other. In particular, 'Mr' was devoted to 'Mrs', and young Ethel could hardly believe her eyes – 'Mr' holding 'Mrs's' hand. 'Mr' asking 'Mrs' if she'd like more tea. 'Mr' doing the washing-up, having thanked 'Mrs' for the perfect poached egg, and the toast, which had been made in exactly the right way – well browned and slightly cooled before buttering.

'Timing is everything,' 'Mr' said – as Ethel watched him dry plates and cutlery and systematically put them away where they could be found again (almost as if each thing had its own special place). 'You must grab your chance, Ethel, it only ever comes once.' And she had wondered if her early transportation to 'Mr and Mrs' *was* her chance, so she held on to it, even though she missed her mother (such a dreadful ache – 'Mrs' said the best way to get the feeling to go was to ignore it, so they all agreed to never mention 'it' or Ethel's mother again). Living with 'Mr and Mrs' felt like wearing shoes that were too tight, but they made her feet look so pretty she just couldn't resist, and she prayed that one day she'd have her own 'Mr'.

Now that she'd found him she didn't want anything to spoil.

SHE GATHERED herself and smiled sweetly.

'Lomond, honestly. A bookie,' she laughed. 'Come on, be serious.'

'OK, well, my other OTHER plan is the one I want most.'

'Which is?'

'Which is . . . pigeon racer.'

'Pigeon racer!'

'Yes, pigeon racer. One who races pigeons. One whose pigeons race.'

'Ha ha, very amusing.'

Although patently not. She went on to apply logic and reason to Lomond's dreams, and quickly came up with the obvious solution. He would teach, preferably at a university – with the eventual securement of a chair, if not a Deanship.

Which is what happened.

It was the first and last time Lomond shared his dreams with his wife. He never again spoke about the pigeons, their beautiful eyes and smooth necks – how he would stroke them in his sleep and hear their velvet voices murmuring.

Who are you? Who are you?

Four

WILSON HAPPENED to be watching her when she nearly chopped her thumb off.

'Ahhh. Christ. Shit shit shit . . .' Rosie ran round the kitchen shaking her good hand furiously.

'Oh, God, not again.'

He grabbed her arms and led her to the sink.

'Stick it under there.'

She stamped her feet.

'It's freezing.'

'Keep it under.'

She complied in a mood of helplessness and overt self-pity. Wilson pulled a plastic box out of the cupboard and emptied the contents onto a table already cluttered with unread newspapers and unopened mail. He found some old Elastoplasts and peeled one open.

'Dry your hand and squeeze it at the wrist,' he said, matter-of-factly, holding the plaster up ready.

'Oooooh. Ouch. OUCH.'

He ignored her protestations and stuck the fabric plaster round her thumb, pressing hard.

'OUCH!'

'You need to put some pressure on it to stop the bleeding.'

'I thought that's what platelets were for.'

'Come on – sit down and have some water.'

'I'd rather have a proper drink.'

'At this time in the morning?'

'Please,' she whined, 'I need some anaesthesia.'

'No. Come on, drink your water and I'll make some tea.'

'Tea,' she muttered. Then suddenly, 'Oh, God, Wilson – what's going to happen?'

He assumed this to be rhetorical and began filling the kettle. Rosie slumped in her chair and looked at her thumb, pouting.

'I think I'll phone Jacob. See if he's heard anything.'

'Heard anything?'

'About William.'

'You just phoned him last night. If there was any news he would have called.'

'Not necessarily. You don't know Jacob. He's so up his own arse.'

Wilson stirred a tea bag round in the pot with a wooden spoon.

'And as for April,' she sighed. 'My God . . . can you imagine William risking his cover to call from the middle of a war zone and getting April.'

Rosie put on a supercilious face, but couldn't think of anything else to say.

'She's an easy target, Rosie, it doesn't become you.'

She looked up, annoyed at herself more than him.

'You always defend her.'

He placed the teapot on top of the papers and found a mug, then sat down facing her. She looked tired and her hair was dirty. When she moved she released a faint acrid smell, a burst puffball of stale sweat that made him sniff involuntarily through flared nostrils.

'What?'

'Nothing.'

'WHAT?'

'NOTHING!'

Rosie stared at the teapot. She couldn't stop thinking about William. About six weeks ago she'd heard he was in Ethiopia working in the northern province of Tigrai. He was holed up in Mekele trying to interview Eritrean exiles, but was having difficulty making contacts (people were not willing to talk to *faranjis* and he understood their diffidence). News from William was always sporadic – months could pass, and when there was news it was always by proxy through their father. That was William's only enduring relationship, as far as anyone was aware. His sole correspondent. One of the things Rosie found most distressing about Lomond's stroke was the fact that William didn't know. She found that difficult to bear.

Jacob did not share his sister's concern.

'Do you really think he'd come home if he did know?'

She rejected Jacob's scepticism, more out of habit than anything else.

'Of course he would, Jacob. God, don't you even know your own brother?'

Now two weeks had passed. They'd agreed early on that it would be Jacob's task to track him down, but nothing seemed to be happening.

'Let's see you do something useful with all that influence you're always telling us about.'

(Rosie bit her tongue when she said that, but it was too late. She could hear herself, her famous voice delivering snide unforgiving phrases, its much coveted languor set hard and brittle.)

All she could think to do was write a letter to the Mekele Post Office in Tigrai. She didn't even know if they had post offices in Ethiopia, but it was worth a shot, and it gave her something to do.

25 February
Dear Manager

  I am writing in the hope that you will be able to pass this letter on to my brother William Friel, possibly known as Bill. We think he is staying somewhere in Mekele town. He is a writer from Scotland, age 39 but looks younger. He is about 6 feet tall with blonde hair. He is a quiet man who walks with a limp. I have enclosed a photograph (taken two years ago) and my telephone number. If you have any information please call me. I will pay for the call. Thank you.

  Yours faithfully
  Rosemary Friel

For the attention of William Friel:
Dearest William

  We've been trying to contact you. I have some bad news. Dad had a stroke two weeks ago. He's stable, but they say he might have another. Please contact us as soon as you get this so we can arrange for you to come home.

  Don't worry about the fare.

  Love Rosie

Her thumb had started to throb. Rosie peered at the bandage, which was already damp and grubby with newsprint from Wilson's fingers.

'It'll probably get infected.'

Wilson cleared a little space for her mug and poured the tea.

'Milk?'

'You know I don't take milk.'

'Sugar?'

'Cut it out Wilson you're not funny.'

'Splash of whisky?'

'Now you're talking.'

★

THERE WAS something regal about Heath's visit to the hospital. As an ambulant, clear-headed eighty-four-year-old she cut quite a swathe, attracting the gaze of patients and visitors alike. Rosie felt proud.

'Everybody's looking at you, Aunty Heath.'

Heath ignored her.

'Look, Dad. Doesn't she look fabulous?'

Heath sat down, irritated by Rosie's theatrics. She always hated a fuss.

'How are you, Lomond?'

Heath did not look at her brother any shorter or longer than usual. She opened her bag and pulled out something wrapped in tissue. It was a lime, glossy and dark.

'Rosie tells me you've been sick a few times. Try sniffing on this when you feel it coming on.'

Lomond took the lime in his left hand and squeezed it under his nose.

'Remember, Ethel used to put them in her gin? They were so hard to find then. Now you can get them anywhere.'

She turned to Rosie.

'Your dad used to search high and low for those limes. When he was a student they lived above a greengrocer's and he gave the grocer's boy free maths lessons in exchange for a bag of whatever was in, as long as he got first option on the limes.'

Rosie tried to picture her father as a student with his young wife, living above a shop and making ends meet.

'Aaah . . . sweet.'

She clasped Lomond's arm and rested her head on it, resisting the temptation to suck her thumb.

'Tell me something else about them, Aunty.'

Heath was just about to put the wrapping away when she

paused, her actions interrupted, hands raised and poised, bag in one, tissue in the other. She looked at her brother expectantly – seeking his permission to tell Rosie something else. He returned her gaze with equal directness and shook his head once. She smiled, knowing from his subtle refusal that nothing had changed – he was still in there, digging in his heels.

'What's this – story time? Come on, Rosie, there's an old woman here in urgent need of a cup of tea. As for her sick brother – well, he doesn't look very sick to me. I think I've been brought here under false pretences.'

Lomond relaxed as Rosie disentangled herself.

'OK, so what's everyone's order?'

When she left, Heath searched Lomond's face, taking in the crooked mouth and the slight slip of his right eye.

'You should talk to her, you know, tell her what happened. She's a big girl now. It would be better coming from you.'

Lomond smiled at his sister – pleased that she'd come. All she could do was smile back.

'You look like you've been left out in the rain.'

'Mmmm.'

He managed a quiet chuckle.

'Don't give me that look.'

She'd seen it before, so many times – a gratitude that she never wanted.

Lomond was forty-one when Ethel died. Heath had come down to help with the birth and it just seemed natural that she would stay on to take care of the twins and the baby. She wanted to do it, and kept telling him there was no need for thanks. She saw it as a hiatus, and part of her was glad (although in the circumstances she couldn't say that). Taking extended leave from the library was unprecedented, but Heath and the head librarian went back a long way, and he owed her. (His promise to her stretched over twenty years, and although not technically broken, he still hadn't delivered. At fifty-five she got tired of waiting.)

Heath already knew how to care for a newborn. When Lomond was born their mother plunged into a state of deep depression. The effort of carrying such a late baby had completely exhausted her and somehow she could barely bring herself to look at it. For months she lay, aimless in a bleak landscape. By the time she emerged from it her son was able to sit on her bed, straight-backed, and smile each time his eyes found hers. She could see no reproach in his bonny round face, nor on the face of her daughter, who at fourteen had to bend through 60 degrees to create enough hip to balance a baby on.

It was this absence of blame, this innocent love, that turned her despair to guilt. It seemed fitting to her that the phys-ical trauma of the birth had jiggled her insides to such an extent that her legs no longer followed her head. Paralysed and all square, she accepted her fate with good grace and few complaints. Hers was a condition rather than an illness, requiring no medical intervention other than a good rub down with an emulsifier every second day to preserve the skin. Heath was the obvious masseuse. Slowly, through careful rest and a diet of boiled chicken, Mrs Friel enjoyed a partial recovery and was able to walk the few steps needed to reach the window seat and the bathroom beyond.

It was what they had all been praying for.

Mr Friel had readily agreed to move into the attic room, away from the camphor and the calamine, and the arrange-ment eventually stuck. He was content to call on his wife each evening and play with his son as she poured the tea. This gave Heath some daily respite, which she spent haphaz-ardly doing anything she fancied. She might visit friends or go to the town library (she later worked there not because she loved books, but because it was close by – handy for keeping an eye on mother). In the summer she would sit on the beach and hone her scepticism listening to the evangelists. Although the time was short it was regular and truly her own. Her parents demanded no account of it – and in this sense she was freer than most. Sometimes she would cycle right round the bay and into the forest – her skirts tucked under her seat, and her cheeks slapped pink against the wind, just like any other girl on the brink of womanhood.

★

'COME ON, Lomond, you must try. I can't do it for you.'

The physiotherapist stood in front of him with her arms folded.

'Just hold onto the bar with your left hand and pull yourself up. That's all you need to do today.'

She looked at her watch.

'If you want to get out of here you need to learn to transfer.'

He considered his right leg, willing it to move.

Nothing.

'Just ease yourself forward and put your weight on your good leg the way I showed you. Don't think about anything else.'

But he did. He thought about his right leg and his right arm, not because he wanted to but because his body demanded it. How could he not? He sat in his elastic stockings and thought about the clot that might be forming in his paralysed limb, despite the rat poison. He thought about his brain and wondered what happens to the damaged tissue. His thoughts tumbled around a bit but were mostly coherent. He knew that with sustained effort he could learn to walk again and talk again, but he couldn't see the point. As each long sorry day limped past, his dysphoria grew and he developed a morbid interest in his body. When he looked in the mirror something looked strange. He could see that his body was intact, but there was something different, something small but of defining significance, yet his sustained scrutiny failed to spot the mistake. He could hear himself think, and worried at first that in rare moments of quiet others could too. He hummed tunes to mask the faint crackle of his thoughts.

Noel, Noel, The Angels Did Sing.

'He's getting ready for Christmas, aren't you, Lomond? Only ten months to go!'

'Ha ha. What a character!'

Then one morning, during an unexpected lull, all that stopped.

I can't hear myself think, he shouted (but in his head, so no one heard him).

Lomond stared at his reflection in the mirrored walls of the physio room, but he *wasn't there* – wasn't in that body, and this time all the clichés failed him. He was not 'trapped' inside his own flesh, nor was he 'locked in'. He didn't feel frustrated or angry or frightened. He felt something else, something altogether more base – a feeling he must have learned before his memory began.

He felt like a fool.

It was a sensation that sharpened whenever he smiled.

Somewhere along the line someone must have taught him how it feels to be an idiot.

Five

A LMOST AS soon as I got back from the summer house I
couldn't wait to get out of Edinburgh again. I couldn't
breathe in that hospital and I couldn't breathe at home. Here,
the sea holds me, the way a mother holds a crying child.

Shush . . . I listen to her breathing and the sound stills me.

I'm having tea at Heath's again, but before I go I need to
fumigate every room. The whole place stinks of old fish. It's
the kind of stench that breeds flies, and I think if I sleep in
it I'll wake up with gills. It's coming from the bag of crab
sticks I bought when I was up last weekend. It was an inexplicable purchase (I don't even know what they are). Maybe
I was showing off to the fishmonger with the green eyes?
I'd gone back to the shop the day after the fish-head thing
and bought a smoked haddock. Then, out of the blue, 'Oh,
and I'll take some crab sticks, please.'

I'd said it casually, but I wasn't sure if they should be
weighed or counted so I just chanced it.

'Eight will be fine.'

I wanted him to know that I can find my way round a
fish counter – only I can't, but I seemed to get away with
it (although he looked like the type of person who wouldn't
make anyone feel embarrassed). The crab sticks tasted horrible,

maybe you're supposed to cook them? I do like fish. We've always eaten it at least twice a week, sometimes more, but we tend to stick to the reliable breeds (if that's the right word) – haddock or sole. There has been the odd exotic departure, usually at work functions, or at that dinner party April held which I couldn't get out of because she'd approached Wilson first and he'd accepted. That was in the days when she considered me to be a bit of a celebrity. Inevitably, they served John Dory. It was brought in on a huge platter, too big for April to carry herself, and we all stared at it as if we had just been presented with the Ark of the Covenant. (If I were a John Dory I would assume that *Wow* was the basic greeting call of the human.) The seared fish was tasty but tepid due to the inordinately long period allowed for admiration, thankfully broken by Jacob, who is always keen to take the lead.

Ah, the good old Zeus Faber. Tuck in!

The dinner had gone well until Dad proposed a toast. William had just got back from somewhere (I think it was Mozambique) having spent ages abroad with very little news reaching any of us. I assumed he was about to toast the twins. It was so good to see them together. By this stage of the evening people had started to break ranks and mussy up April's seating plan. I was sitting beside Dad and William sat opposite with his arm around Jacob's shoulders. Dad stood and raised his glass, tilting it towards them.

'To Jacob and April.'

'To Jacob and April,' we said.

I think it took us all by surprise, except Wilson (who doesn't share my view on this). William quickly removed his arm and joined in the toast. It was a seamless recovery, but there was a moment, a definite flinch, when something dismantled, then reconfigured – and that was all it took to show his hurt.

Inside, Jacob and William are different in almost every way, but their relationship always seemed symbiotic. It's what's expected of twins. Heath told me that when William was tiny he said he wanted to marry Jacob. I can tell it's not something either of them like to be reminded of.

I love William. He's been such a lifesaver. Once, he actually talked me down from a rooftop. (I wasn't going to jump, I was going to freeze to death, an experience I thought would be the same as falling asleep – or falling into sleep – the way you do after a half-bottle of ten-year-old malt. Like a milky baby falling from the breast.)

★

THIS IS a perfectly balanced meal. Heath and I have eaten our kippers with caution and are enjoying the sheer friendliness of trifle. We are more familiar now and know what to do, dining behind closed curtains in the easy quiet of the kitchen.

'I can't bear the thought that William doesn't know about Dad yet. I don't know why it seems so important but it does.'

I scrape the last of the cold custard from my plate.

'Mmmmm. That was gorgeous, what can I taste?'

'Amontillado.'

I put the serving spoon in my mouth and leave it there for a moment, frog-lipped – then pull it out slowly, 'How could I forget about trifle?'

Heath gathers in the plates.

'Cheese?'

'No, thanks. I'm stuffed.'

My mouth feels slack. I'll probably get chapped lips now.

'Can Jacob not contact him?'

'He doesn't have a number. He can barely remember when he last spoke to him.'

'Have they fallen out?'

'Not exactly, but things haven't been good between them. I don't think William ever quite recovered from the shock of Jacob marrying someone like April.'

'And who is someone like April?'

'Well . . . you know, someone who's sort of . . . flimsy.'

'Flimsy?'

'Yes, you know, a bit silly.'

'A bit silly?'

'Why do you keep repeating everything I say? I'm trying to be as charitable as possible.'

I don't need this.

'I'm sorry, dear. I'm just trying to understand. You must know that nobody was ever going to be right for Jacob in William's eyes. You can't blame the poor girl for that.'

'No.'

But I do blame her, and normally I would take the trouble to debate my point of view, but my analyst (Wilson) has suggested that there's something irrational about my feelings towards April. He says my depiction of her as a whited sepulchre is a laugh. Apparently, the more I speak about her the sillier I sound – my contralto voice rises in pitch and goes all reedy. Why I feel so brattish about April is not something I care to examine too closely, but I suspect I've got it tangled up with the sorrow I feel about William (the way his sadness follows him, as though he's carrying all our ghosts on his back). Although he's been travelling since he was eighteen he always comes home regularly and we all quickly pick up where we've left off. Communication is somehow easier when William's here, perhaps because everyone loves him – and he's the only one who loves everyone back. It's William who's held us together, and as far as I'm concerned it's April who is behind his current prolonged absence. She has wriggled her way into our lives like a maggot, severing the bond between the twins as sure as if she'd physically cut them apart. They spend less and less time together, and sometimes, when William only has a day or two before he's off again, Jacob might not see him at all. Even when they are together he shows no interest in William's work in Africa. He's more interested in talking about property prices and April's bloody shop.

It is a careless neglect. Why can't Heath see April for what she clearly is – a skelf buried deep under the skin? But this is not what I want to talk about (how typical of April to highjack my thoughts when I've got something much more important to discuss).

'Aunty, I need to talk to you about something. I'm going to ask Dad if he'll consider moving into the summer house with me.'

'What . . . you mean you two move up here, together?'

'Yes.'

Heath frowns.

'Well? What do you think?'

'I don't know,' she says.

★

'HI, WILSON. It's me. Can you hear me OK?'

'Hello?'

I shake the receiver.

'It's ME. I'm on Aunty's Bakelite.'

'I'm sorry, I don't know anyone called Onantees Bakelight.'

'What?'

'I said, I don't know anyone by that name. Who is it you are looking for?'

'I'm looking for Mr Goodbar.'

41

'Slut.'

'Has anyone called?'

'No.'

'Is there any mail?'

'Something was hand-delivered from your work. Feels quite bulky. Do you want me to open it?'

'No. I'll call them on Monday.'

'When are you coming home?'

'I'm not sure. I might stay on for a few days. Jacob and April can cover Dad till Wednesday.'

'What about the show?'

'What *about* the show?'

'Will that give you enough time?'

'I'm not doing the show. I'm off sick, remember?'

'But you're not sick.'

'Well, compassionate leave then . . . whatever you want to call it. I can't go in. I've got too many things to sort out here.'

'What do you mean, sort out?'

'In the house. I've made a decision. I'm going to take care of Dad up here.'

There was a loud silence.

'Hello? Wilson . . . are you still there?'

'Yes.'

'What do you think?'

'What do I think? Well, let's see . . . what do I think. I think you might have at least had the courtesy to discuss this with me first.'

'OK, I accept that, Wilson, and I'm sorry, but that aside . . . what do you think?'

'That aside? *That aside?* God, Rosie, you're unreal. Sorry . . . I can't talk to you just now, I've got something cooking.'

'Oh? What are you cooking?'

'Aw, Christ, Rosie, I'm not cooking anything. I'm just . . .'

I can hear Wilson getting all choked up and I hate the fact that I've done that.

'There's some curry in the fridge.'

'I don't want any curry. I want you.'

★

NOT LONG after I first met Wilson I described my mother to him and he looked at me like I was crazy.

'Are you winding me up?' he asked.

This is where I first started to think about her, here in the summer house. For years my parents used it as a rental, taking it for the whole of July. That was before I was born. Then my mother died giving birth to me and the family stopped coming here. When it came up for sale about four years later Dad bought it and we stayed for the whole of the summer holidays five years in a row. After that the twins wanted to do their own thing and we never really used it again except in the winter or for the occasional weekend.

I think the boys associate this house with their mother. My mother. When I began to really think about her I would try to conjure her up properly, bring her to life, and at first I just couldn't see anything but slowly she started to take shape until eventually I could see her clear as day, fussing over the boys like the mums in the old storybooks – baking bread and hanging out the washing, always wearing an elegant dress belted in tight at the waist. Shiny red lips and hair smelling of roses (this is where Wilson looks at his most incredulous).

I never spoke to Jacob or William about our mother. I waited for permission to do that but it never came. All I can recall is asking Jacob about the photograph.

'Is that your mum?'

I think it was almost the last thing I said before I lost my voice.

Is that your mum?

'Yes,' he said, and gave me such a look.

That night, when Dad had finished my bedtime story, he called the boys in as usual to say goodnight. William kissed me on the cheek and blew a raspberry in my ear. I was still laughing when Jacob bent over me smiling and whispered, 'I'm going to cut your tongue out, Rosie. I'm gonna slice it right off. Night night.'

I've just remembered that now, and I remember other things too.

Other girls smacked their dollies and cut off their hair. They would sit them in the corner facing the wall.

She's been bad, they'd say, *smack smack smack.*

I would watch, horrified. I had a baby doll, three Sindies and a Pippa. In 1983 I adopted a Cabbage Patch doll called Muriel. I still have Muriel's birth certificate, but her whereabouts are unknown. Maybe she's found her real mum.

When my voice came back I tried to lie at school but I wasn't any good at it – the lie stuck in my throat like a gobstopper, making me gag – so instead of using words that weren't true I used words that might be true. My capacity to embellish is now one of my best skills; it has served me well in life and brought benefit to others (though I don't list it on my CV).

'I don't have a mum.'

'Everyone has a mum.'

'Mine's dead.'

'What did she die of?'

'Cancer.'

I also learned about nuance, and how to be disingenuous. I noticed that trotting out 'my mum's dead' in a matter-of-fact tone did not go down well with teachers or peers, so I tried to say it differently. I would emphasise the 'dead' and turn my mouth down in a sad pose, nodding my head up and down to indicate that I understood the gravity of what I'd just said.

But I was only pretending.

AND THEN there's truth.

'Why aren't you adopted then?'

'I don't know.'

★

IT HAD been a long time since April walked through the park, and although the day was bitterly cold, she thought it was an appropriate thing to do. She'd arranged to meet Jacob on the north side so they could go into the hospital together. He had suggested they just see each other in there but the thought of being with Lomond on her own unsettled her. She looked at her watch and tutted, annoyed that her time management had gone slightly awry. She'd spent too long in Peckham's deliberating on what to buy her sick father-in-law. Unsure about the protocols, she found herself hopelessly torn between Mulberry fruits and organic humbugs, then at the last moment she decided to trust tradition and bought a whole pound of black seeded grapes and added a bottle of Lucozade from the newsagent's next door. As April hurried across the park the wind picked up slightly and gusted round the naked trees. It wasn't a very strong wind, but brisk enough to make her hunch and hang onto her Cossack-style hat. A squirrel sprang from nowhere and shot up the trunk of a nearby tree, causing April to scream. Too late, she clamped her gloved hand over her mouth. Her knees had locked together, as if the squirrel might try to run up her leg. It was a sudden fuss.

She glanced up anxiously and saw her husband waiting at

the end of the path. This wasn't the scene she had pictured, the contemplative stroll from which Jacob would watch her emerge, pale and soulful, bearing up well in the circumstances (like that woman in *Dr Zhivago*).

'Come on, Ape, I'm freezing.'

He took the bag from her and walked briskly to the road-side, flagging her back to let a car pass, then – eyes straight ahead – he strutted across the road, wildly waving his free arm three times, up and over, beckoning her to follow. The urgency of Jacob's gestures told her the terrain was dangerous and they needed to move quickly and quietly. April trotted behind. She was all sixes and sevens, but at least she was safe.

★

IT TROUBLED Kitty to think that had she not changed her schedule that day things might have turned out very different. When her sister's husband had his stroke just a few months ago they managed to dissolve the clot quickly and he was back to normal in no time at all. Now he's just the same as before – never lifts a finger because the part of his brain marked 'bone idle' was not affected. When May called her in a state of distress to tell her all about it a part of Kitty couldn't help hoping, but despite the promising start – *Oh, Kitty . . . he looks terrible* – it all seemed to come to nothing.

Now she's thinking about Lomond and how broken he looked when she visited. It caught her out, like a sudden punch in the stomach, and unfortunately there was no way of masking it (she let herself down there, all that weeping and wailing – her cheeks burn just to think of it). She'd expected him to be at the very least a wee bit brighter than when he was admitted. She can picture his face as they closed the ambulance doors, he looked much as he always did, hand-some – like Clint Eastwood in *The Bridges of Madison County* (her favourite film) – but now . . . oh, Lomond! He can't speak or eat or walk, and his beautiful face is collapsing in segments. If Kitty had her way she would give up all her other clients and look after him full-time, whatever it took. She'd seen worse – where there's a will there's a way, she thought – but now it looked as though he was heading for Craigmalloch. She could hardly bear to think of it. Kitty knew lots of people who ended up there, including her own mother, and she could put a spin on it as well as anyone. *The food's lovely. The staff are lovely. The rooms are lovely. The garden's lovely. Lovely. Lovely. Lovely. Everything's bloody lovely.* Just don't even *think* of putting me there.

Life, it seemed to Kitty, was either meaningless or cruel, she did not know which. If the audiologist who lived in the next town had not caught flu last November there would have been no need to reschedule her grandson's appointment, and Kitty would not have had to watch the baby that morning. If she'd arrived at the usual time they could have treated Lomond right away. He would be home by now, fully functioning, or at worst taking a bit of bed rest, his brain intact.

Such a wonderful, beautiful brain.

She kept going over the antecedents, realising that they stretched back and back – a limitless sequence of events. How did the audiologist catch flu? Where? It was a collision of circumstances that relied on a million other events, everything connected to everything else. Kitty didn't know what to make of it, or what to do with it. Had she led a random life? Or had everything – the whole journey of the world, from way before those creatures crawled out of a murderous sea on fin-bone legs – had it all been leading to this?

Kitty's inner fish stirred.

She just couldn't fathom it, but now that she realised she was in love with Lomond, it didn't seem to matter.

Six

C AMERON FRASER had been down at the harbour since
daybreak. He rubbed his hands against the cold then
rolled a cigarette as he watched the creels being hauled up.
The catch was good and the quayside was brimming with
shellfish. This morning he was preoccupied and was paying
little attention to his order. His family had been involved in
the fish business for generations. Their tradition was very
much as the hunters – nearly all the men had been fishermen, although there were some notable exceptions and inter-
ruptions, such as the war and bold emigrations to America
and Canada. And some other splash-marks; a gay cousin, a
circus performer, some bloke who wrote poems – their stories
almost completely obscured in the gathering haze of select-
ive memory. There was just enough not talked about for
Cameron to see the diversity of his own lineage. It made
him feel less of an outsider, and he felt a pang for his dead
ancestors – all those men who ran away from sea.

His relationship with the sea had always been complicated,
and with the exception of one notable incident, it was a
liaison conducted from the shore. Feeling the spray on his
face and tasting the salt round his lips was pleasing, but close
enough.

He was the youngest in his family by far (the mark of a mistake, or a faltering marriage, or worse), and still at primary school when his two brothers first started going out on the boats with their father. A quirk of demography meant Cameron was the only boy the boats left behind. Land locked and with no male counterparts, he spent the long summer months hanging around the harbour on his own, or – with increasing frequency – tagging along with the older girls. They were delighted to have such an even-tempered boy to fuss over, tease and experiment with, someone entirely compliant who could be dismissed at a whim only to return the next day, ready to give whatever was required of him. For Cameron it was an exotic world. He was happy just to be in their company. He marvelled at the smoothness of their skin and the scent of patchouli oil, its sweetness rising through the wet brown smell of kelp. For a while they adored Cameron, and he adored them, accepting the equal measures of kindness and cruelty they meted out to him (washing and tweezing his hair one day, and the next a salty whipping with knotted wrack). He seemed to please them, and although he didn't always understand them, there was no other place he would rather be.

One summer their shrill quayside capers caught the attention of a keen-eyed offshore skipper who spotted Cameron roped to a large cart that bore three pubescent girls and a dog sporting a baby's bonnet. Cameron was heaving his load up the steep hillside, his body thrust so low to the ground that at first the skipper thought he was a small quadruped, maybe a sheep? When the Fraser lad was recognised it was clearly time for the fishermen to intervene. With a sense of urgency his first place on board the largest vessel in the fleet was arranged and he rose with the others the next day. Within moments of the boat reaching the open water Cameron's ruddy glow faded to distemper and his eyes took on the grey of the sea. He was continually sick, vomiting with such violence that the crew (who had seen many a man retch and still go on to embrace the swell) worried the young lad's stomach and throat might tear. He was returned to shore in a small rowing boat, having nearly been lost over the side twice as he writhed in any direction that might bring relief. It was a short and ignominious sailing, and he vowed it would be his last.

Clinging firmly to land, Cameron avoided the harbour area and instead took to spending his days up at the Friels' house, where he hovered round the golden twins like a third shadow. His resistance to any suggestions that he try the fishing again did not falter, despite the continued pressure from his parents and siblings.

Then one day, under a flat solemn sky that belied the ferocity of a distant storm, his father, uncle and both brothers drowned, and the matter of Cameron's future life at sea was never raised again.

'YOU'VE NO signed the chitty.'

'Eh?'

He was thinking about Lomond's daughter.

'The chitty . . . you've no signed it.'

'Sorry, mate . . . miles away.'

'Aye, well, chance would be a fine thing. It's no a bad day though.'

'No,' Cameron raised his eyes to the pale blue sky and smiled. 'It's grand, isn't it?'

'Aye.'

The two men stood silent for a moment, their gaze rolling out to sea. Cameron wished he could go and lie in the soft yellow dunes for a while and give way to his thoughts. He would watch the sky through a sway of marram and lyme, and listen to the grasses whisper above his head. He tried to remember the last time he'd felt the immortal sands beneath him or watched the sandpipers tidy the strandline. It had been too long ago to recall with any accuracy and he realised that at least one whole summer had passed since he'd walked through a forest or climbed the mossy slopes that obscured the bay beyond. Cameron couldn't pinpoint when this withdrawal from life had begun – but he felt sure things were about to change. The morning light grew brighter, reaching the honey-hued stone of the buildings on Market Street, and as the sun warmed the cold bones of the old town he felt an optimism rise in him, as strong and high as a spring tide.

★

LOMOND'S FEAR of all things medical had never been a problem, so there had been no need to understand it. It is not necessary to ponder over a fear of spiders the size of dinner plates unless you are contemplating a move to the Antipodean outback. Straightforward avoidance had been easy for Lomond until he reached his late sixties and began to experience a few troubling sensations, most of which he managed to keep to himself – but falling in front of Rosie was not something he could easily explain away. She cajoled him into going to see his GP by promising not to tell anyone else about his fall (a promise she broke within an hour of making it). Luckily he had a GP who was more than happy to collude with him and they both ascribed the high blood pressure to white-coat hypertension. It was a theory that seemed to fit given the absence of any other symptoms. Lomond had chosen not to mention the headaches and the dizzy spells, and preferred not to recount out loud the time when Kitty spoke to him and all he could hear was nonsense.

'Drax shmee lac vorty scan dee lichen?'

'Pardon?'

'Drax shmee lac vorty scan dee lichen or nut?'

'Yes.'

51

There had been other things, too.

Now Kitty is at his bedside, applying the Sodium Quiz that her sister had given her. The questions are thoughtfully designed to require only yes or no answers, and the guidance suggests that for those with no control over their bodies they could consider using the blink response – once for yes, twice for no. Lomond is lucky, he can move his head.

Nice to know I can rely on the perseverance of the blinking reflex, he thinks as Kitty fires away, questioning him about a diet that already seems distant and impossible.

'Salted nuts?'

Nod.

'Tinned beans?'

Nod.

'Pizza?'

Shake.

'Tacos, enchiladas, burritos or tostadas?'

'Mmmm?'

Kitty looks up.

'Tacos, enchiladas, burritos or tostadas?' she says, speaking slow and loud. Lomond watches her lips. This time they appear to be in synch with her words.

Shake.

Another voice joins in. A beautiful voice that makes Kitty jump.

'*Buenos dias*, Kitty. *Que tal?*'

'Oh! Hello, Rosie . . . you're back. I was just checking your dad's sodium levels.'

'And? How's he doing?'

Rosie kisses Lomond on both cheeks and sits on his bed.

'Hmm. Not too good, I think – he seems to be heading for a really high score.'

Kitty starts gathering up her things.

'I'll be getting off. I have a client at three. It's good to see you, Rosie. We didn't expect you back until tomorrow.'

Rosie's plan to stay on at the summer house till Tuesday changed after her phone call to Wilson. Her feelings of guilt grew over the weekend (of course they did, but not in a straightforward way, her guilt is endogenous – it springs from obscure origins).

'I know, I've come back early.'

'Well, that's good,' she says, pausing for a moment to smile at Rosie. Kitty likes Lomond's daughter, but she always goes a bit tongue tied when they meet.

'I think Jacob's coming in today. We'll finish this later, Lomond.'

Kitty waves the quiz in the air as she leaves.

'Bye,' calls Rosie, then she turns to Lomond.

'Later? Is she coming back today?'

Kitty has been visiting twice a day. Lomond shrugs.

'Anyway, Dad, I have something exciting to tell you.'

She pauses, as though he needs time to brace himself.

'I have a plan.'

She looks round, then draws herself closer in.

'I've thought about this a great deal and I want you to say yes.'

She's twiddling about with his fingers, sorting them out into some kind of order.

'I want to take care of you, Dad. When you're ready to leave the hospital I want you and me to move into the summer house. There's no way you can manage at home with all those stairs, and the layout in the cottage is perfect. Look . . .'

She pulls a folded sheet of A4 from her pocket and smoothes it out on the bed.

'I've measured all the doorways and there's room for a wheelchair – not that you'll need that for long, well . . . you might, but I think you'll do brilliantly once we get you out of this place and into the sea air. There aren't any steps and

53

that whole stretch between the house and the town is really flat. We'll have Heath nearby and once you're on your feet again I can start picking up some freelance stuff. It'll be great. Think of it as a kind of Victorian convalescence.'

She stops, interrupted.

'Why are you in bed, it's nearly lunchtime? Anyway, I know you probably think I haven't thought this through but I have and I'm doing it for me, Dad, not just for you. It's what I want. Please just think about it.'

She turns the sheet of paper round so it's the right way up for Lomond and they look at it together. A wonky floor plan, everything out of scale, then a gap and a wavy sea with a boat sitting on it. A flat sun in the right-hand corner, exactly where she always puts it.

His frozen face saves them both.

'I'm going to find us some tea and give you a minute to get used to the idea. Just think it through, Dad, please. We can bumble along together just like we used to, only this time I'll do the talking. I've been up and spoken to Heath about it but that's all. I haven't told Jacob yet and we're still trying to get a hold of William, but, och . . . they'll be fine.'

She exhales, lighter now, able to breathe properly.

'That's the plan. At least we can give it a try.'

And she leaves quickly, not waiting for his reaction. He can tell from the way she walks that she's excited. He recognises that slightly jerky gait, just an inch short of a skip. It gives him such an ache to see it. She disappears through the open doorway, turning sharply sideways and off to the left, then appears again, heading right. Her back is straight, her body stiff as an Irish jigger. Lomond stares into the space she leaves behind, blinking twice.

He feels exposed, propped up proud like a giant teddy on a neatly made bed. He tries to move himself deeper down into the covers by thrashing around on his left side. He manages to throw one of the pillows onto the floor and his supine position somehow gives him more purchase. Then he drowns in starched cotton. The old man opposite him watches without expression, his face partially obscured by an oxygen mask. Their eyes meet but both refuse to acknowledge the other. It is a careful indifference between two men who are determined to have nothing in common.

A young woman comes into the bay. She's wearing a heavy mohair coat flecked with lavender. It looks expensive and much too old for her, suggesting maybe it has been handed down, or is a gift. Her pale neck pokes out of the generous butterfly collar like a hyacinth forced in the dark. The old man turns his face away from her and closes his eyes. Neither of them speaks. She sits down, removes her gloves, and cries softly for a few minutes, then puts her gloves back on and leaves. When the old man opens his eyes he resumes his blank gaze. Lomond looks away, embarrassed and anxious to conceal what he has witnessed. He would have shut his eyes too, but he forgot.

He forgot himself. Forgot he was over here, watching.

It's so easy to let things slide through. Lives are left outside, like a pile of muddy boots, and every so often a visitor comes, dragging in the dirt.

WHEN ROSIE comes back she seems calm, her sanguine demeanour suggesting that she's assumed Lomond will agree to her proposal.

'Where's your cup?'

She casts about for what she calls his funnelled cup. ('Oh, cute!' April exclaimed when she first saw it. 'Nurse, do you have this in any other colours?') Lomond tracks Rosie's gaze and they simultaneously locate the beige plastic lid, half concealed under a pile of damp tissues.

'Have you been crying, Dad?'

He shakes his head and smiles. A frown sets across her forehead as she pours some of her tea into his cup. *My baby cup,* he thinks. All objects used by Lomond are now defined by the possessive adjective: Lomond's cup, Lomond's plate, Lomond's spoon. He feels like an evacuee, all labelled up. Even the stroke is particular. *Lomond's stroke.* It's always 'after I had *my* stroke' or 'since you had *your* stroke'.

'Every one is different,' the nurses say, knowingly, as if they have somehow been designed for that particular person, and have been accepted, conferring ownership. 'You never see two the same.'

Only, Lomond won't accept it. He wasn't about to get cosy with his.

Oh, sorry – excuse me but this isn't mine.

Despite his high score on Kitty's sodium quiz there has clearly been a terrible mistake. He could see that the damage was done – that, unbelievably, the thing had happened, but he too had a plan. Something very different from what Rosie had in mind.

'Dad, do you remember someone called Cameron? He owns Fraser's, the fish shop down from Heath's.'

Lomond tries to throw Rosie a quizzical look but isn't sure how it turns out.

'He seems to know you. He says you're one of the few customers who ever gave a tip.'

And she leaves it there, keeping things light – savouring the fact that her dad is the type of man who tips the fishmonger.

Seven

WILSON LEANED back in his office recliner and looked out of the window. He couldn't read the sky, which seemed clear but might have had a thin cloudy wash running through it. He was stroking his troll's hair. It gave him great pleasure to hold the little pot-bellied figure in his hand and smooth out its dark strands into a thinning peak. It had occurred to him that if he grew a long beard he could do this all day and experience the same effect in a more socially acceptable way. His department liked to think of itself as liberal, but the particular rule about 'not stroking the hair of small inoffensive plastic trolls during meetings or tutorials or any other public gathering' was not one that could be broken. The Head of Department had pointed this out to Wilson not long after Rosie had given him Plug (so named because it reminded him of his old maths teacher).

'They've asked me not to bring Plug to the Board of Examiners meeting!' he lamented.

'Aw, that's rotten.'

'Apparently there's been a few complaints, mostly from colleagues, but one from a student who said Plug put her off during an exam.'

'God, any excuse these days – poor wee Plug, whatever happened to diversity?'

'Exactly. I pointed out that Richard Titmuss was well known for his gonk collection when he was head of LSE.'

'Was he?'

Rosie looked up from her paper, briefly interested.

'I don't know. Anyway, I reminded old Hargreaves that all policies have unintentional effects, particularly the reactive ones. He could end up with a backlash.'

'A backlash?'

Wilson ignored her.

'I bet that unnerved him,' she said, yawning. 'He probably can't sleep at night.'

'You can jest, Rosie, but let's just see what happens at Academic Standards next week. I think you might be *very* surprised.'

And he remembers pouncing on her when he said *very*, crashing through her newspaper and snarling into her neck like a wire-haired terrier, and Rosie groaning – a sound that his memory interprets as ecstasy.

HE HADN'T slept well after Rosie's phone call and was completely caught up in thinking about how to play things so that she would reconsider her plan to take care of Lomond. He could start with the obvious.

IT WILL NEVER WORK.

To support this assertion he'd begun writing a list of the reasons why – Rosie is lazy; Rosie can't cook; Rosie can't make beds; Rosie feels sick at even the thought of blood (he wasn't sure if there would be any blood involved but it seemed indicative of a general unsuitability); Rosie is unable to clean up anyone's sick except her own (ditto); Rosie repeatedly forgets to feed the cat; Rosie is selfish; Rosie is a child.

When he reviewed his list he couldn't judge whether or not it held any sway. He extended it, rephrased it, rethought it – and generally worried it to death. He didn't flinch from applying the full glare of his critical eye. He stripped her bare, sat her in a cold room under a blue fluorescent light and cut her hair to the bone, then stood back and looked at her bumpy head and her silly ears. There was no shortage of things he could say about Rosie and her weaknesses – the list just kept growing – but his blunt words fell flat on their true little faces, failing to convince, and no matter what he wrote, it still felt as though he was penning a love sonnet. Perhaps it would be better if he appeared to support her decision, then scared the hell out of her by exaggerating the sort of things that were likely to arise. He turned his thoughts to Lomond. He sat him in a corroding iron bath, put him on a toilet, laid him on a soiled bed – the smell of faeces and urine pene-trating the house despite daily boil washes and sheets blasted dry by a cold north wind. He could see Lomond's pyjamas blowing on the line, full and stiff like an overstuffed guy.

Look, Rosie – look at you pegging out the washing, look at your red hands. Now look – see yourself exhausted, ignoring your father's calls in the middle of the night as his skin cracks and weeps.

Wilson thought this would be more effective, it would be quite easy to scare her (it certainly scared him, and he was always the last to scare). *You're so brave, Rosie,* he could say, that would unsettle her. *Rosie, you're so good.* That would unsettle her even more.

But he knew he couldn't do it. His thoughts about how to break her made him feel sick. Their lives were about to change irrevocably and the only thing he could do was figure out where he fitted in. He wasn't even sure if he wanted to.

Someone knocked on his door.

'Come in.'

'Sorry, I'm a bit early.'

'That's OK, Fiona. Take a seat.'

Wilson slipped Plug back in his drawer and picked up the essay that was lying on his desk. He skimmed through it quickly while the student unravelled her scarf. She sat back and watched him pull out a sheet of paper and pick up a pencil.

'How are you?'

'Fine. A bit tired. Had a lecture this morning.'

'Oh, good. What was it about?'

'Well, I'm not very sure to be honest. I didn't really understand it,' she laughed.

'What was the subject?'

'Virtue ethics.'

'Ah yes, ethics.'

Normally he would probe further, but today he couldn't be bothered. He didn't give a stuff about Aristotle.

What about me, Rosie? I've had a stroke too. Look – I'm having one now!

'OK, Fiona, let's have a look at your essay. Have you read the feedback?'

'Yes.'

'And . . . what do you think? Does it make sense?'

'Umm . . . some of it, I suppose.'

'Good . . . let's start with the bits that make sense. Tell me what you might do differently.'

Rosie – I didn't want to tell you this but I've only got six months to live.

'Well, I don't actually have it with me.'

'Right.'

The student looks at Wilson and waits.

'Would you like to look at this copy?'

'OK.'

Fiona accepts the essay and looks at it, impassive.

'Can you see why the essay has been marked as a marginal fail?'

She scans across each page, her eyes flitting up and down rather than left to right. All those words!

But Rosie, you can't go — I'm having your child.

'Not really. I'm not sure what they want.'

'OK, so let's talk a bit about your own thoughts on the question. What is it you're trying to say?'

'Ehmm,' she murmured, then smiled and began to chew her nails. 'What was the question again?'

Wilson read it out.

'Let's break it down a bit.'

He wrote the question out in the middle of his blank sheet and began sketching out a Venn diagram to highlight the main elements, narrating his own efforts. The student smiled but made no comment.

'Speak to me, Fiona. Tell me something, anything, about poverty in Scotland today.'

'Well . . . some people just don't want to help themselves.'

Wilson sighed.

'And why do you think that is?'

Don't go, Rosie. Don't be so selfish.

'They're just lazy, I suppose.'

'Right, so . . . what evidence can you cite to support that?'

'Well . . . my uncle's on the sick and there's nothing wrong with him.'

Wilson looks at Fiona a little bit too long. She breaks from his gaze and stares out of the window.

'What reading have you done for this essay, Fiona?'

'Websites mainly. All the books were out.'

At that moment Wilson can go no further. He winds up the tutorial with a few pointers on the multifaceted nature of social divisions, reissues the reading list, then takes it back again and thrusts a book into Fiona's reluctant hands, advising her that she must read the prescribed chapters and draw up an essay plan for discussion next week. As she drifts out of the room – slowly rewinding her scarf – Wilson can feel her despondency, but it is nothing compared to his own.

★

JACOB WAS a mass of psychic bruises. He had a knack of taking everything personally, including the fact that Rosie had come back a day earlier than planned. He growled at her.

'I had it covered, you know. Everything was arranged.'

'I know, I wasn't worried about that. I just decided to come back early because I've got something to discuss with Dad . . . and with you and William. Have you heard from him?'

'No. I've only just put out some feelers.'

'But . . .'

She stopped herself. There was no point in berating him for the delay, he'd just bite back, and anyway she was on a roll having come straight from the hospital and just wanted to get this bit over with as quickly as possible.

'Do you think they'll lead to anything?'

'I've no idea.'

'Who did you contact?'

'The TDA.'

'What's that?'

'It's a development agency in Tigrai. It's the only lead we've got but I wouldn't get your hopes up, quite frankly.'

Rosie decided not to mention the letter she sent last Wednesday. April came into the room sideways carrying a huge wooden tray with silver handles. The weight of it pulled her shoulders into a little-old-lady stoop and she looked as though she might buckle at any moment. Jacob watched her struggle across the open-plan dining area. He was bearing the look he reserved for his wife – an expressive mix of incredulity and horror.

62

'Cup of tea, Rosie?'

'Haven't you got anything stronger?'

Unsure how to react (they had only just had lunch), she laughed politely, and – to the relief of all three – placed the tray on the low white beech table. Then she sat down, pressed her knees together, and rested her hands on the lid and handle of the teapot.

'Shall I pour?'

The black crockery was already laid out – tall cups on tiny saucers (too small to accommodate a teaspoon), a matching milk jug, a plate of shortbread triangles neatly broken from a round.

'Cream?'

'With tea! No, thanks. Haven't you got any milk?'

'Oh, I'm afraid we've run out. I could pop out and get some?'

'It's OK, I'll take it black.'

'No, you're quite right. I'll pop out.'

Suddenly she was heading for the hall and Jacob looked furious.

'April, for goodness' sake sit down!'

Not quite a shout, his voice was loud and he was looking straight ahead at nothing at all. She stopped immediately and smiled, one hand raised to Jacob.

'It's all right, darling, I don't mind, really.'

And she turned to go.

'SIT DOWN, APE!'

Rosie thought she heard a whimper, then April came back and sat down again, smiling as she poured the tea.

'I'm so sorry, Rosie. Perhaps you would prefer lapsang souchong?'

'APE!'

'Black tea's fine.'

'You see? She says it's fine.'

Jacob couldn't bear it when April made a fuss, especially over someone like Rosie.

'Biscuit?'

'Ta.'

Rosie dunked her shortbread in the tea and held her free hand under her chin as she quickly transferred the soggy biscuit to her mouth, only just catching it in time. It seemed to Jacob that the more refined the surroundings the coarser Rosie became, and there was no doubt about the refinement of their newly refurbished three-bedroomed terrace in Bruntsfield. They had recently moved from their small but charming one-bedroomed flat in a nearby brewery conversion, and they still had the flat in Comely Bank, which brought in a healthy rental and more than paid for itself. It was all part of an equity plan that was geared towards their ultimate goal – to ascend the nearby hill and reside in leafy Merchiston. Their destination was rarely far from their minds, rendering the journey towards it long and exhausting. The road to Merchiston involved several crucial connections if they were to make it in time, and those connections were impacted by the vagaries of market prices, booms and slumps, interest rates, the price of oil, Middle East politics and the worrying growth of the Asian economy. It was a lot to keep an eye on.

Rosie drank the hot tea. She was inordinately thirsty after her visit to the hospital, which always left her feeling desiccated and in need of a good soak. She planned to go home and have a bath before Wilson got back – he wouldn't be expecting her so he'd probably work late.

'I spoke to Dad today about what happens next.'

'Next?'

'Yes, after he leaves hospital.'

'And . . . what did he say?'

Rosie looked at Jacob, giving him a moment to think about his own comment.

'He didn't *say* anything, Jacob.'

'Oh? Oh . . . of course.'

'I want him to move into the summer house with me.'

'WHAT!'

There was a brief rattle of cup on saucer.

'You're mad. What about the show?'

'Why does everyone say that? The show doesn't rely on me.'

'The show will go on!' piped April, delighted to have thought of it.

Jacob stood up and paced around the room, then sat on a leather chair and buffed up the chrome with the sleeve of his yellow cashmere. The women waited. To Rosie's great surprise he said nothing – she had expected an outburst, had hoped for it, it would give her the excuse she needed to walk out. (She'd kept her coat on specially, distressing her hostess and causing such protestation she thought it might end in a tussle.) Now she and April were watching the tiny protruding vein that had appeared on his right temple – a small blue threading, familiar to both.

'April, I think perhaps you should get that milk.'

'Yes, of course, darling. Quite right.'

She got up and smiled at Rosie.

'Shan't be long.'

April made haste and consequently took an age to gather whatever it was she needed to buy a pint of milk, popping in and out of rooms, opening drawers, and searching handbags – and all the while there was Jacob's little blue blood-worm, engorged now, and Rosie wondering if it was feeding into the brain or feeding from the brain, and which part, and to what effect? Finally the kerfuffle subsided and April left, pulling the heavy door quietly behind her.

Rosie rubbed the back of her neck, which had begun to ache.

'I don't agree with your proposal.'

'Why not?'

'Because it's completely mad. The house is a dump and you're certainly not capable of taking care of anyone. It wasn't so long ago you needed care yourself.'

'Who told you that?'

'Never mind, you know what I'm referring to.'

She felt confused. It had never occurred to her that William would betray a confidence, even to Jacob.

'I don't know what you're up to, Rosie, but get this,' he said, pointing his finger and wagging it at the start of each measured phrase. 'Whatever it is, it's Not Going To Happen. You've done enough damage to this family already and I'll see to it that you don't do any more. I am the next of kin and I will decide what happens to Dad. He needs some sensible long-term planning, not some half-baked proposal from a dipsy, unhinged daughter who has never – NEVER – been responsible for anything or anybody other than herself. There is no way you're whisking Dad off to that freezing house. He's an old man and he's just had a serious stroke – the whole idea is utterly ridiculous. Now . . .' he took a long breath, as if something were finished, 'you go back and you tell Dad you've changed your mind. You tell him you realise he's going to need proper nursing care. Tell him, Rosie, because if you don't I will.'

She thought she was ready for this – she'd constructed a response – but her arguments fell apart and her words slid away like tiles from a Scrabble board, landing in an inarticulate heap.

'Fuck off, Jacob.'

It was the best she could muster.

★

I'M SMALL again, made small and stomping off – a small, ridiculous person rushing from the flat – my ideas not worth

66

tuppence. At the front gate I collide with April. She's clutching a pint of milk in her gloved hands. A mist has descended and droplets are forming on the top of her furry hat. We both apologise profusely.

'Are you all right, Rosie?'

She sounds genuinely concerned and presses the milk carton against her creamy wool lapel so she can touch me gently with her other hand – a brief resting just below my shoulder that lifts again before I can flinch. I'm aware of it, and I'm aware too that the wet carton of semi-skimmed is bound to mark her coat.

'I'm fine. I just remembered I have to be somewhere.'

Then I notice something April's already noticed.

My stupid eyes are weeping.

'Something in my eye. Got to run, see ya.'

I keep my head down and go, walking quickly with my hands in my pockets rather than pressed against my mouth (which is where they want to be). When I reach the corner, about twenty yards or so from the house, I hear the gate closing and I realise she must have stood there watching me, despite the rain.

YOU'RE NEVER far from a graveyard in this city and it's turning out to be just the day for one. The fine mist has developed into a smear that clings but doesn't penetrate, not quite coagulating until there's contact with another solid – a park bench or a brush from the sleeve of a passer-by walking blind behind a lowered umbrella. I cut through by the church on my way home and visit a few old friends: Wilhelmina, Herbert, Oswald, Jessie, young sailors and old maids, sisters of brothers long dead, soldiers, sea captains, beloved wives and much loved fathers, mothers sorely missed. When I lean forward to climb the steep brae I can feel rain drizzling down the back of my neck. Deliciously cold – it makes me inhale sharply and straighten up quick, shaking the kinks out of my spine. I can taste the wet on my lips, sweet Highland cloud water that has rolled across the scree. I pass a man selling the *Big Issue* and briefly wonder why he's chosen such a quiet pitch on a wet afternoon. Maybe he's got a funeral to go to? I don't have any money with me and can only give him an apologetic look, which he accepts graciously. He must get those I've-no-change/I've-already-bought-one looks all the time, but he knows his market, knows that those who don't give today might give tomorrow (depending on what life throws up in between), and he remains gracious, proferring blessings in this holy place.

I walk through the first section of the churchyard where the stones are glossy and flecked. Here lie the new dead people – their lives remembered – marked by tight little bunches of variegated carnations that can last for weeks, impervious to cold or drought. (If anyone puts nasty little flowers like that on my grave I'll die.) In this part, at the front of the church, the bodies are still flesh, worms excreting in brains, eyeballs shrivelling up like non-germinating chick-peas. The paths narrow and the gravel turns to old stone, smooth and ancient black – not quite cobble, not quite slab. I weave through headstones and flagstones, reading the inscriptions, calculating ages and life spans, relationships and circumstances (although here my knowledge of social history lets me down and I wish Wilson was with me – or Dad). I pay my respects to the missing names – the loved, not joined by the loving; beloveds lying alone (like Gala at Pubol, waiting in vain for Salvador – her bones perfectly arranged in a red Dior dress).

A stone angel is watching me, smiling, and I smile back, feeling something akin to envy. The mist rises and there is a slight warming that makes my ears tingle. Churchyard moss shines iridescent green under the grey sky. (Creeping dead man's blanket they used to call it – I can remember William pulling me away from it. *Oh no, Rosie, don't touch that – it's poison!*)

My feet are freezing in thin cotton socks and I'm starting to shiver – it's too cold to linger. I walk quickly to the side exit, needing a drink now, and a long hot bath. As I walk I run my hand across the mossy drapes that hang over the small headstones nearest the gate, then I press my fingers under my nose and take in the scent of a thousand wet February days.

WHEN I get home Wilson is there and I don't quite manage to hide my disappointment.

'Oh! You're here.'

'That's nice – I've missed you too.'

'It's only been a few days.'

I take off my coat, feeling huffy and thwarted. I was really looking forward to that drink (Wilson has become a tad prim about daytime drinking).

'That's right,' he says. 'Just a few days, and even fewer phone calls, and then when you do call . . .'

I push my shoes off – heel to toe – and sit down to rub some feeling back into my feet. They're damp.

'Shit, my shoes are leaking. I only bought them last month.'

'Take them back then.'

'I can't, they were in the sale. Bugger!'

'Of course they'll take them back, use your fame. All it would take is a throwaway line about going on air with wet feet.'

He's probably right. I do enjoy a modest celebrity, although enjoy isn't really the word, far from it. My job is easy compared to the work done by field reporters or current affairs producers, or pretty much anyone else involved in the programme. If I can use my little bit of fame I will, but never without feeling a complete fraud. Wilson has helped me with this. He says we don't get to bask in the sunlight for long so we may as well enjoy it, and anyway, he maintains that everyone else is a fraud too, including him.

But not Dad though, he's not a fraud.

OK, not your father, I accept that.

And not Aunty Heath . . . she's not a fraud.

OK, not Heath.

And not William, he's . . .

Oh, for God's sake, Rosie, OK. Everyone's a fraud but NOT including the Friels.

Except me.

What?

Except me . . . I'm a fraud.

Correct, except you . . . but you're the exception to the rule.

We could call it Friel's Second Law.

True.

And I could be the proof! I could be the one black swan that proves that swans are white!

Eh?

Probability, my dear Watson. Surely that's the closest we get to the truth?

I peel off my socks and examine my toes. They're red.

'Oh, no . . . I think I'm getting chilblains.'

'Good.'

Wilson is giving me one of his pity-poor-me expressions that only dogs can carry off.

'Anyway, how come you're home so early?'

'I don't feel well,' he says, the dog hanging in there.

'What's wrong?'

He screws up his face and holds his stomach.

'I think I've got cancer.'

'Really? What kind?'

'Ovarian.'

'I know just what you need for that.'

I go into the kitchen, take out a bottle of whisky and pour two drinks, taking a mouthful from one and topping up, then I carry them through. Wilson is still playing the dying man on the sofa. 'Here, drink this.'

To my surprise, he drinks without protest, throwing it down in one swift action then banging his empty cup on the coffee table.

'Hit me again,' he says.

'Hey! You better slow up there, cowboy – think of your ovaries.'

'I am. That's why I need another drink.'

Eight

H E HAD more or less decided to die as soon as possible. He wasn't sure how he might achieve this – clearly it would be difficult unless he regained more control over his body – but considering death as a viable option brought him great comfort. Lomond had, of course, thought about death more and more as he grew older; it became familiar to him, a benign consequence of an unremarkable life. He thought of it as a tender thing, a blissful sleep after a long and tiring day. Lately – before the stroke – he had started to look forward to bedtime, he would desiderate sleep the way a smoker craves the next cigarette. His night-time ablutions were like unhurried foreplay – always filling the basin and enjoying the lap and splash, listening intently to the sound of washing, the rub of wet hands against rough skin. He brushed his teeth thoroughly, up and down the way his sister had taught him, but always finishing with a renegade sideways sweep. He liked to lie in the dark and listen to the familiar noises of the house – the sigh of the boiler, the radiators knocking. The sound of his cistern hadn't changed in fifty years. Like him, it took its time and recovered slowly. The ancient mechanism wasn't designed for frequent use, and guests invariably had to pump the handle furiously, as if drawing water from the very core of the earth. This laborious flushing gave rise to a strange acoustic — a loud and prolonged clunking, an industrial symphony that reverberated through the house. Casual users would emerge from the bathroom looking culpable (despite Lomond's reassurance — *Ah . . . there's a knack to it),* and to those unfamiliar with Edwardian plumbing the noise was quite alarming, and surely indicated that something wasn't right? But to Lomond, it was right. Without noticing, he had grown to love his tall, narrow house with its elegant eaves and long back garden that stretched like a shadow, barely wider than the house itself — then dipped to the bank edge of a low-lying stream. He could not contemplate a move.

He would rather die.

But he would need to call upon all his mathematical and analytical skills to figure out exactly how he might achieve this.

It would be his last great calculation.

★

LOMOND'S STROKE seemed to be losing some of its allure. He had no means of tracking time but it felt as though no one had approached him for hours. Could it be hours? He wasn't entirely sure what an hour felt like in the post-stroke world but he had lain a long time undisturbed, without needle or pump, nothing recorded, no measurements taken, his busy chart unread as the nurses passed to and fro, their fickle attentions now directed elsewhere — drawn by the bright patina of newer strokes. No longer acute, he had quickly become uninteresting, a dull lump of a man who now occupied the less glamorous world of para-medicine. He wasn't sure why there had been no physiotherapy today but he was unconcerned — glad of it, in fact — and was content to watch the uneven rhythm of the day play itself out. He wanted a cold drink but his buzzer had fallen out of reach. All he could do was moan in his best Boris Karloff voice; the louder he got the dafter he sounded – *thuth . . . thuuuth*. The effort made him swallow hard and he felt as if he might choke on his own tongue.

He tracked the movement of the nurses intently, his arm poised and ready to wave as soon as a gaze turned his way. It reminded him of waiting to be served in his local tea room, where large middle-aged ladies in flouncy aprons and Bo-peep caps assiduously ignore the thirsty customer, attending instead to tablecloths that need straightening and jams that need replacing. Their tired unsmiling faces are the colour of uncooked dough – bearing testimony to their thin wage packets and their aching feet. Lomond would often pop in for a cup of tea and a cake. He liked waiting and enjoyed those purposeful pauses that killed time gently and painlessly, like a slow sedative easing the ache of an empty afternoon. He would read the menu carefully from cover to cover, savouring its contents.

His throat seemed to be closing in – swallowing required thought rather than reflex – and he wondered if he would ever again feel the crumble and melt of an apple charlotte in his mouth, or the sweet flaking sugar of a yum-yum on his tongue.

Strange, the things you miss, thought Lomond – those rude waitresses, engaged in harmless rage, cheated of the life they once dreamt of, when just to walk along the street made men whistle, hungry for sex. They could turn heads all right. They were courted and stalked like deer in heat. They believed anything might happen, and for one or two it did – events took them elsewhere, to London or Australia, some even moved to America, reappearing occasionally to get their teeth fixed. *It's so good to be back*, they'd say, as their relatives stared at their glowing faces and their bright white smiles.

Now, the tea-room women had thickened and sometimes couldn't even stop a bus at a bus stop. They had become invisible, but not to Lomond. He could still raise a smile and make a heart beat skip.

AT LAST he caught the eye of a tall nurse. *Thuth thu thu.*

'More water, Lomond?'

She briskly removed his jug and replenished it, then filled his cup with water.

'Here's your feeder.'

He took the cup and sucked the cool water through the spout, taking in air and belching loudly.

'Ooh, that's better,' spoke the nurse.

She picked up his wrist without explanation and checked his pulse.

'Is there anything else I can get you?' she asked, her eyes fixed on her watch, then without looking up she noted something in his chart, straightened his pillow, and was gone, leaving Lomond to concentrate.

Every drink is a brain teaser. He's coaxing the cold liquid down his throat and can feel the water running along his jawbone and into his ear. At that moment – perilously close to choking – it suddenly occurs to him that drowning might be a possibility. He pictures the classic stones-in-the-pocket stuff – the seaside suicide – and he knows he'll never be able to engineer it (he's pushing away the image of himself, white naked in the sand, hauling his half-dead body towards the sea with all the grace of a walrus). But there are other ways and other circumstances. With enough incapacity a person can drown in less than two inches of water.

He could drown in a bucket if he had to.

The bath is the obvious solution. Once in, all he needs to do is convince someone (the someone who has just lowered him into the water) that he is safe enough to be left alone for a while, which surely – in the interests of dignity – would be considered sympathetically?

As he struggles to swallow, Lomond realises that his best bet is to convert his losses and play to his new strengths. He thinks of it as his eureka moment, and the simple mathematical allusion pleases him. He will take an Aristotelian approach, embracing the elements of water and air to produce a warm, moist death. A simple matter of physics will trigger the final chain reaction, and although there will be a lot of work to do before his plan is realised, at least now he has a goal – The Unsupervised Bath (or T.U.B. for short, he thinks, evoking further pleasure from the brief playfulness of his soft, cauliflower brain). From now on everything he does must be carefully calculated to edge him closer to TUB and the noise of a bathroom door closing. Water lapping gently round him, and the sound of wet lips parting as he slides under, tiny kisses dripping from the tap.

'Cup a tea, love?'

Lomond doesn't notice the WRVS lady poised at his bedside. He is fully occupied constructing a whole new reference framework of choking reflexes, carbon dioxide levels, a constricting larynx. She touches his arm.

'Tea, love?'

It must be about two thirty, trolley time. Soon the visitors will start to flow through the wards and begin their vigils, conducted through quiet evasive chatter about *the outside*. Lomond has no appetite for it. During visiting time he feels almost glad that he can't speak – what would he say?

I am going to drown my sorrows. And again, the sweet smack of kisses falling on water like rain, but whose kisses? He ponders this, and with eyes closed inhales the smell of ginger laced with lime. And then he knows.

★

I CAN'T seem to find anyone that I can have a sensible conversation with. Jacob is being his usual vile self and Wilson is being Wilson, adorable and puppy-like, too forgiving for his own good. Heath has become uncharacteristically laconic when it comes to my plans for looking after Dad, and I can't speak to anyone from work, for obvious reasons. I haven't told them I'm resigning yet, I need to think about how to do that so it doesn't look like I'm happy to leave, but I will be oh so happy to leave. I can't wait to get away from the office and the studio with its carefully arranged chaos, and I hope I never have to enter the hospitality room ever again, except maybe as a guest to discuss my latest book – *How to Teach Stroke Victims to Speak Again* by Dr Rosemary Friel (PhD).

Q. Tell us, Dr Friel, your father was severely dysphasic, how easy was it for him to follow an untested rehabilitation programme designed by his own daughter – did he experience role reversal?

A. Ask him yourself!

MOST PEOPLE are under the misapprehension that my work is interesting, but really I'm just a mouthpiece – I say what I'm told to say and regurgitate other people's ideas. The shows are tightly scripted and I don't get to choose the topics. I don't even do the research any more, it's all sent to me beforehand. I follow someone else's bias and I don't seem to learn much. Everyone thinks I must be so erudite but I'm not. I know little bits for a little while and then they're all edged out by the next pile of little bits, retroactive interference they call it, and I end up with nothing. It's like eating a Big Mac and fries and then thinking – wait a minute – where did *that* go? It's not something people admit to in the business – they like to think of themselves as journalists – but the truth is you've just covered a feature on nuclear power and you still end up not knowing anything about it, so you dodge the topic. You lead an evasive life. Everything is temporary, talk the talk and move on – yakety yak, don't look back. There's no chance to engage with the material properly, in fact the producer discourages it, he says it affects the relationship. 'We don't tune in to hear your views, darling – just breathe shallow and give your guests all the air.' And he's right, of course. The time I did *engage* it cost me dear (two weeks' leave and a formal apology), so I've developed the knack of sounding interested when really I'm not – can't afford to be – but the ephemerality gets me down.

Now I have a chance to do something *substantial,* something that matters, and if that sounds like a juvenile flight from anomie then fine, let's put it all down to arrested development.

Hello? Did you say something?

What?

What?

I thought you said something.

No.

Well, say something now.

Why?

Because I love your voice.

Of course you do.

Some voices get into your head and they nestle down and stay there. Their power is underestimated. People can fall in love with a voice – they make assumptions based on the characteristics of two small muscles at the back of the throat. I've done it myself, and it has been done unto me (I've had more than my fair share of phonophiles). My voice is melodious, like treacle Wilson says, and although I'm not musical I have what I think is called a good range, a wide Octavian span – I can swing high and low with ease and have lovely tones (which I take as a reference to my Scottish lilt, but I might be wrong about that). I've always loved listening to voices. The house was full of them as I grew up, a radio in every room.

A good voice can render me speechless.

This [pause] is the BBC.

I have been told many times that my voice is beautiful.
Someone on the production team once described my voice
as 'incongruous' and when I asked her what she meant her
throat turned red as a cockerel's wattle. I spared her any
further discomfort by dropping the issue – I knew what she
meant anyway. My voice belies my appearance. It makes me
feel dishonest. When I meet the guests before the show I can
see the disappointment in their eyes.

Nine

HEATH FELT perfectly composed until she boarded the train at Haymarket. The carriages were full and she struggled to make her way through to her seat.

'I'm terribly sorry but I've booked this seat,' she said to the young man who sat in it.

He removed one of his earplugs.

'There's no booked seats on this train. They told us to sit anywhere.'

'Oh.'

He plugged himself in again and slumped down, his arms folded and legs outstretched between the feet of the woman sitting opposite, who looked at him and shook her head slightly as she gathered up her things.

'Take mine. I'm getting off soon anyway.'

Heath was grateful and thanked her profusely. She didn't think she would be able to stand for much longer, her body ached and she was feeling worse by the minute. As the other two passengers stood up and moved to let Heath change places she could feel the resentment – their reactions reminding her of her age (there is a particular look reserved for the old – cursory, but with an edge to it). The light was starting to fade outside, fields of purple kale disappearing in the twilight of a late February afternoon – blue on blue. A vaporous hologram of her own tired face appeared at the window, looking in. It gained substance, an ancient exhibit illuminated behind glass. Heath searched beyond and through her own reflection and was surprised to reach the broken face of her baby brother. Pieces of his life were strewn amongst the dark hedgerows, like pages torn from a book. It seemed then, in that precise moment, that Lomond had been taken from her, wrenched away by busy strangers who have no knowledge of him; who don't know about his fear of passing aeroplanes or his dislike of fruit and American films; who don't know to open the window at night, even when it's below freezing, and to draw back the curtains to soften the dark; who might not respect his need for privacy, his shyness, the awkwardness he feels when others expose their emotions. Heath feared for Lomond. She worried that his worth would remain concealed under his dead limbs, that his self-effacement would mean he was overlooked.

That they would lose him.

They'll see him sitting there in his pyjamas, his mouth all twisted and unable to speak, and they'll think he's just an old man who's had a stroke.

She felt agitated and needed to concentrate on her breathing for a bit. *Pull yourself together, girl.*

It was clear to Heath that her baby brother was irretrievably changed, so badly broken, but in a strange, clean way, as though he'd been laid under a tea towel and hit with a toffee hammer. She was reminded of those early asymmetric drawings the children did for Father's Day – the fantastic giant eye and twisted mouth, the arm swinging out from one side, long and unjointed. She still had those drawings, stored up in a box with other remnants of previous summers, but she never looked at them. The children had all been encouraged to draw, and when Ethel died the boys' pictures became less elaborate. In particular, Jacob went back to his stick-and-circle drawings, whereas William's people still had their bodies. They both drew X-ray figures of their mother lying flat, her limbs visible under the bedclothes. As time passed the twins returned to their battle scenes and spaceships and daggers dripping with blood. This was considered to be a good sign. They seemed more comfortable with gore and violent death. Of course, it was a boys' thing, Heath recognised that, but some of Jacob's drawings were troubling and failed to elicit the adult appreciation he had come to expect. There was no snuggling up together to admire his growing collection of baby pictures: Baby with shark's teeth, Baby in open coffin, Baby impaled on a stick.

'ARE YOU all right?'

The woman who had relinquished her seat was still standing nearby and spoke over the heads of the younger passengers, her voice raised enough to attract attention. For a moment everyone within earshot looked at Heath, her skin distempered under the carriage lights.

'I'm fine, thank you,' she said, more sharply than she had intended.

This was an example of the kind of fussing that occurred more and more frequently when she was out these days. There was always a middle-aged woman hovering about – keeping an eye on her. This well-intentioned vigilance was deeply annoying. The train rocked momentarily as if they'd gone over something on the track – a small rodent perhaps, or a shoe. It was dark now, the windows had become mirrors and the man opposite Heath was staring at one of her reflections (or so she thought, it was difficult to tell amongst all the brightly lit symmetry – people facing forward looking back). She pulled out a white monogrammed handkerchief and blew into it, then flicked it neatly under her cuff and turned further in toward the window, her head almost touching the glass. She had often thought about her own death, but never Lomond's.

Now it looked as though he might beat her to it.

His quiet strength was gone, his presence different. He held a certain look that Heath had seen before in her father's eyes after their mother died. It was a calm look that he'd carried until everything was done – the funeral, the sorting of affairs – then he turned his face to the wall and wouldn't turn back. His death surprised everyone; it was eloquent, and spoke not of love, but of despair, telling them that she and Lomond weren't worth staying for.

The prospect of losing her brother pushed her towards panic. Despite the fact that for years their contact had been restricted to holidays and overnight visits, the centrality of Lomond in her life felt unaltered, and she wasn't sure if, without him, she would be able to find any pleasure in the world.

She didn't want to be the one left behind.

She played with the loose skin on the back of her hand, examining the faint, translucent blue with a benign curiosity (she liked her tissue hands, and sometimes viewed them through her magnifying glass, fancying she could see her cells). When she looked up at the window again an old woman with no lips looked back at her, surprising her for a moment, but then familiar – her eyes obscured by a thin clouding, like drops of milk on water.

THE NEAREST station to Heath's was located several miles out of town, in a much smaller place, where fewer people lived. She completed the last leg of her journey by taxi. The driver didn't speak, even when she paid. She waved him off, grateful, and waited until the noise of the engine had completely

83

disappeared, then listened to the mood of the sea. The walk from her small house to the edge of the rocky shore was short, yet the sound of the North Sea had softened over the years, almost as if the tide, not her, were growing tired. When the wind blew from the west she had to strain to hear the waves hitting the rocks, but tonight there was a clear regular booming, like the faraway strike of a dozen kettledrums.

Heath unlocked the back door, put down her bag and turned on the lights in her kitchen. Still wearing her coat and hat, she leaned against the sink and let the cold water run for a while, her hand resting on the tap, before filling a cup and straightening to drink. She looked out of the kitchen window and suddenly felt uneasy. She sensed that someone was standing outside, equally still, just beyond the reach of the illumination coming from the house. After a frozen stop of two or three seconds she drew the curtains across the full length of the window and switched off the light. She could feel her heart pumping, too fast she thought. Sitting in darkness, she listened with ears that had grown so slack they could no longer screen out extraneous noise, sounds she could have ignored when she was younger – traffic, canned music, the sudden boost of a boiler. It meant she was always interrupting her own conversations.

What's that noise? What noise? THAT!

Rosie said it was her Broadbent filter losing its tension – like tights that grow baggy at the knees. It wasn't something you could undo. The only thing that lessened the impact of losing her ability to discriminate sound was her deteriorating capacity to hear in the first place. Now she listened, but there was nothing audible coming from outside. She set about closing more curtains and switching on lights. She turned the gas fire up high and finally took off her hat and coat before going back into the kitchen to make tea. As she moved from one room to the other she turned on the radios, filling the house with chatter – a repeat nature programme about the urban fox (she saw foxes regularly on the foreshore, but no one believed her). Then she sat down in front of the fire with her tea and a plate of bread and butter. The anxiety she'd first felt on the train was still there. She got up and re-tuned the radio to classical music. As she took her first mouthful of bread she heard a short, terrible scream and froze again, then remembered that she hadn't re-tuned the radio in the kitchen. She recognised the noise as the scream of an owl, or a fox barking, and she laughed – just a single, unconvincing note. *Huh!*

★

IT SEEMED to April that her husband was increasingly tense. He never found it easy to relax, but ever since his father had his stroke Jacob had become more and more difficult, criticising most of her efforts to help.

'Black seeded grapes – for God's sake, April. First of all, you know Dad doesn't eat fruit and secondly how's he going to get the seeds out with only one working hand and half a mouth? He can't even spit properly never mind swallow. Didn't you see the bloody great Nil By Mouth sign hanging over his head?'

It was true. What upset April was knowing that he would consider this to be a sign of thoughtlessness, whereas in fact she had thought about it a great deal – she'd just got it wrong. April made a lot of mistakes, always had, but she could never be accused of not thinking. She believed it was her errors that made it difficult for people to understand her and appreciate how thoughtful she in fact was. She led a pensive, internally busy life; unfortunately her meditations were rather slow, which meant she rarely had the chance to reach any kind of conclusion before the next thing came along. In consequence, her remarks were often non sequiturs – but

85

how can a person think about one thing and listen to another at the same time? She asked Jacob about this once but he just laughed and told her not to worry her pretty head about it. She appreciated the compliment, but it did preoccupy her. She was thinking about it now, as she followed her morning beauty routine. April believes that looking good is important. She takes care of her skin and always makes sure her hair is cut and coloured. Her daily treatments are so long-standing she can think and tone simultaneously. Jacob had lost patience with her this morning even before they were out of bed. They don't usually talk before breakfast, but today when he woke his mind picked up exactly where it had left off the previous evening.

'You know, I can't even remember Rosie ever making a proper meal. It was always Heath or Dad who did the cooking. How the hell does she think she's going to cope?'

He lay on his back and put his hands behind his head, staring wide-eyed at the ceiling and looking alert. April moved over, shielding her left eye from his elbow.

'In fact, that's right . . . the one time Dad and Heath both had flu at the same time it was William and me who kept everything together, not her. All *she* did was make some bloody awful get well cards.'

He shook his head in disbelief.

'Hopeless. Absolutely bloody hopeless.'

'Is there a freezer in the house?'

'What?'

April repeated her question.

'Is there a freezer in the summer house?'

'No. Why?'

'I was just thinking, you can buy some very good frozen meals these days from Marks and Sparks.'

'What? What are you talking about? There isn't a Marks and Spencers in St Andrews, and anyway, that's got nothing to do with it. Why are you encouraging her?'

He threw the duvet across the bed and rose angrily.

'Just keep out of it. You don't know what you're talking about.'

Before April could answer he had disappeared into the bathroom.

'I'll tell you another thing,' he shouted through the walls, 'she's bloody unstable. I don't think Dad would be safe with her.'

April didn't say any more. The conversation was moving too fast. When Jacob left she had a chance to catch up and think about what he'd said. She smoothed some almond oil round her delicate eye area and pondered over the substance of her husband's tirade. Deep down, she didn't always agree with Jacob, but she felt it was her job to support him, and besides, although she believed Rosie wasn't as bad as he made out, listening to Jacob attacking his own family made her feel more secure about their marriage. She applied her make-up carefully, enjoying each moment, and practised a few facial expressions before she got dressed. She was expecting some deliveries at the shop today and there were two fittings booked for this afternoon, so she wanted to look her best.

Ten

KITTY LIVES in a brick house, an old one, like the ones in England. She had thought of it as quite rare – there are only a few brick streets in the town – but then she crossed the border and they were everywhere. Her eldest daughter lives in Carlisle now and Kitty flits across quite regularly, thinks nothing of it. She considers herself a traveller, having also visited Yorkshire and Arran. Sometimes she commutes into the capital for work, and although there is much that she likes about cities, she prefers the town. She always wanted to travel abroad, see something of the world, but her husband Dave wouldn't budge once he was off shift. He drove lorries all over Europe and he assured Kitty she wasn't missing much (although she had the sense to know that his assertions said more about him than Europe). There are things Kitty would like to do, and, at sixty, she realises her life has been full of possibilities – things that she could have done but didn't, for reasons less clear to her now. She climbed a Munro once, as part of her friend's fortieth – just borrowed some boots and up she went (all that hoovering and floor washing had kept her fit). She stood on the summit rock and exposed her face to the sleet, enthralled even though she couldn't see more than thirty feet in front of her. On the way down she saw a herd of red deer grazing on the lower slopes, there must have been over a hundred. It was almost the best moment of her life. She looked through binoculars and counted the branches on the antlers of a huge stag.

Twelve! she uttered.

The guide encouraged her interest and they chatted for ages, laughing sometimes, and stopping to point something out that the other one had missed. Then, when he held out his hand to help her over a stile, Kitty felt that fierce sense of loyalty that came with being married – a sensibility that drew a clear bold line at her feet, a line she could not cross, so she turned back and rejoined the group.

There was so much to talk about when Dave got home. Kitty had been feeling bad about having fun while her husband was stuck on the autobahn, and it helped her to share it with him, try to make him feel a part of it. Her account of the day on the hill moved from the descriptive to the metaphysical.

'I felt so small, so insignificant, but wonderful at the same time. It made me think about the whole earth, the universe, and the universe beyond the universe!'

'Hmmm.'

'And you should taste the water up there! I took a drink from a wee stream and it was delicious. I never knew water could taste so good!'

'You drank from a stream? My God, woman, don't you know that water's probably contaminated?'

'Oh no, I don't think so, it was crystal clear.'

'That doesn't mean anything,' he laughed. 'There's probably a dead sheep lying upstream and you've just drunk water that's run through its innards!'

Kitty put her hand on her stomach. Surely the guide would have told them if there had been any danger? She carried on, undeterred, telling Dave about the deer and all that she'd learned.

'Why do you think we don't have bears any more, or lynx or wolves?'

'Because they've died out.'

'No . . . they were hunted out, not died out. Killed by man.'

She paused to let him think about that.

'So why do you think we still have deer?'

'Because they're protected.'

'Yes, but *why* are they protected?'

'I don't know – you tell me.'

'For hunting!'

Her pitch was high, driven up by the irony of it.

'How long's that gonna be?'

She was checking the pies in the oven.

'Ten minutes. It was the Royals that protected them, you know. If it hadn't been for them the deer wouldn't exist now.'

'Well, I'll no exist either if I don't eat soon. Hurry up.'

Kitty sighed and began setting the table, working round him without disturbing the paper he was reading. Dave was relieved that she'd been so easily discouraged from blethering on about that bloody walk. He'd noticed her flushed cheeks, her enthusiasm blowing round the room like a summer squall. It was important to keep Kitty's feet on the ground, she could be a bit fanciful at times, but he wasn't a hard man and there was a slight niggle of guilt that was in danger of spoiling his tea.

'So, does that mean you're a bloody royalist now?'

'No,' she said whimsically, stirring the beans.

What it meant to Kitty was that things were not straight-forward, that the world wasn't always what it seemed – but she kept that thought to herself.

She remembers that walk still, how the feelings the day evoked had turned from fantastic to just plain silly when she tried to articulate them to Dave. She knew his eyes were sharper than hers, he'd pointed this out to her many times over the years, showed her how naive she could be.

Dave rarely engaged in conversation, but when it came to Kitty's foolishness he could be quite loquacious. He could see her revelations for what they were – fool's gold, panned from that wee burn with the dead sheep in it.

★

KITTY SAT in her sister's kitchen while May heated up some milk for their hot chocolate. It was their mid-week tryst, a long-standing arrangement that they had always held in Kitty's house until Dave retired last year. His presence had stymied the whole thing. Of course they had politely offered to include him, but with the full expectation that he would turn them down. Dave, however, accepted the invitation, tasted the hot chocolate, and found that he loved it – so the two became three, and the sisters, realising how important their meetings had become (despite the fact that they usually spoke about nothing in particular), felt entirely displaced. Their sense of loss took them both by surprise, and without any specific reflections on why they felt the way they did, they switched to May's house and equilibrium was restored.

'Here, Kitty, bit of an upgrade.'

May stirred the drinks with a tiny electric swisher, then she sprinkled chocolate powder on top of the milky froth.

'Try that.'

The sisters cradled their mugs, each reflecting the movements of the other. Kitty was quiet. She put her mug back down on the table, picked up a teaspoon and began playing with the foam, which was disappearing fast.

'You still worrying about Mr Friel?' asked May.

She was thinking about him, and felt caught out.

'I suppose I am a bit. I still feel so bad about going in late that day.'

'Oh, come on, Kitty, not again. You know it could have

91

happened any time. What if I'd felt like that about Alan's stroke?'

'You were at work.'

'Exactly. I was at work, and you were somewhere else too. It's not your responsibility to be watching over him. He could have his next one anywhere.'

Kitty looked at her sister, startled.

'His next one?'

'Well, you know, they don't come in ones, do they? What you gonna do – move in?'

She hadn't thought about the possibility that there were more to come.

'I would if I could.'

'What d'you mean?'

'I mean, I think he could manage if someone was with him. I could be a sort of live-in housekeeper.'

'And what about Dave?'

'I know.'

Kitty couldn't make sense of her husband's behaviour. He'd switched overnight from working sixty-hour weeks and more (way beyond the tachograph limits) to doing absolutely nothing. She had hoped that they might have one of those modern retirements where people take up new interests and go on holidays, things like that – but it was a faint, dreamy hope. There was a moment, when Dave stood in the middle of the living room, clapped his hands (once), rubbed them together and said 'Right!' with such purpose – but then he sat down in his armchair and had barely moved since. At first she put it down to tiredness, the accumulative fatigue of working non-stop for fifty years in jobs he hated; then she assumed it was a period of adjustment, something time would take care of – but time passed and nothing changed except the sleeve protectors of his chair, which grew thin as a result of regular boil washes. She pondered over depression, but

Dave didn't really fit any of the profiles (other than low activity), and over the months Kitty came to realise that her husband's inertia was not a change but a continuation – an ongoing disinclination to do anything other than sit.

May saw her sister drifting off again.

'So, what do you think of the chocolate?'

'Lovely.'

There was another long pause during which the sisters lightly touched hands and felt grateful for each other. Their lives had not been so very different, but both knew that Kitty had somehow missed her turn.

'Well, at least you've got the name for it.'

'Uh?'

'Housekeeping.'

They both chuckled, hugging their drinks close to them so they could smell the cocoa.

'What is it about this Mr Friel anyway?'

Kitty smiled and tilted her head to the left, then told her sister all the things she loved about Lomond, giving detailed descriptions of his habits, like the way he marks his place in a book by pleating the page so that part of it protrudes out of the top.

'It makes such a mess of the page. I asked him once if he had any books that needed ironing.'

May didn't hear what reply he gave to her sister's attempt at wit, for Kitty – who, as far as May knew, had never looked at another man – was now lamenting the state of Lomond's collars, and the way the hair on his strong neck grew in kiss curls that got trapped underneath if he buttoned them too tight, and she was further perplexed by his unfortunate inclination towards yellow, which apparently was the worst possible shade for his complexion.

★

ROSIE SAT on the window seat, drawing circles in the condensation.

'What's it been?' he asked. 'Two weeks?'

'Nineteen days.'

'Really? My God.'

'They're moving him to rehab tomorrow.'

'That's good.'

'Yeah − he'll get to do a lot more there. I'm setting him
a goal − walk and talk by Easter or no egg.'

The room was like a sauna. Rosie had switched on the
gas fire about an hour ago because it was easier than re-
setting the central heating, which had gone off ten minutes
before Wilson normally left for work. That was how long the
flat could hold the heat before it escaped through the hastily
stripped floorboards and the old sash windows. The drafts
were terrible. He said that's what windows were for − to let
air in. She said their function was to keep air out. Meantime
the frames rattled in the wind as if Boreas himself were
tapping on the glass.

Wilson had brought back a pile of marking yesterday so
he could stay home and keep an eye on her. He still wasn't
sure how to handle the situation but he could sense that
things were shifting. Last night there was almost a pre-stroke
atmosphere. They drank red wine and watched *Small Time
Crooks*. Occasionally they laughed (even at the stroke joke −
but only after a cautious *shall we?* glance), then they fell into
bed quite drunk, and when he kissed her she cupped his face
in her hands and smoothed out his eyebrows with her thumbs,
then kissed him and turned onto her other side. He pressed
into her, his knees against the back of hers, his hand round
her breast. He moved her hair away from her ear and nuzzled
into her neck.

'Please . . . don't.'

She pulled her hair back over her ear and turned onto her

front. She was probably crying very quietly, which meant there was nothing he could do (it wasn't unusual, particularly after she'd spent time with Jacob), and Wilson found it easy to roll over and sleep.

By morning he had no idea what she was planning, but he still suspected she was beginning to reconsider the move to the summer house. Hopefully her change of mind – her *coming to her senses* – had begun. He decided to treat the day with care and proceed stealthily so as not to upset the reframing he believed was going on inside her head.

She spoke into the window.

'When is Easter anyway?'

'April.'

'Is it always in April? How come it moves?'

'Rosie, we have this conversation every spring.'

More precisely, they'd talked about it once before, last year when they were planning a trip to Poland. It was their first Easter as cohabs, a spring when blossom shouted out – brazen and splendid – and the pale face of the moon stopped them in their tracks. Wilson, still keen to impress, had explained the relationship between the sun and the moon and the equator, how they all transcend our futile attempts to chart time as an ordered concept that follows an even progression, edging its way across a flat temporal plain. Not so!

'Calendars – pah!'

'Pah? You're so archaic, Wilson. Old before your time.'

'My time is whenever I choose,' he'd said, narrowing his eyes and thrumming his fingers across his cheeks. Wilson used melodrama to conceal his deeply held convictions about time travel and parallel universes (it was a kind of double bluff). He understood the staggering consequences of quantum mechanics, but he knew that some things were best kept to oneself.

The trip to Poland never happened. By the time they'd

worked out the when, the where and the how – spring had passed. There were many such journeys, vivid and virtual, construed enthusiastically but nevertheless driven by convention rather than desire. They almost went to Orkney in September, Venice in the winter, and France just before the sunflowers. The planning of holidays was one of many social mores that had not quite been displaced by the low-key, studiously unsung thrill of living together.

The fact was they were content.

As the months passed into their second year the essentially irresolute nature of their lives began to trouble Rosie, but it was a low-grade, intermittent troubling, and Wilson was good at dispelling it. Whenever she worried about all the interesting things her colleagues did that that they didn't do – walking the Great Wall or cycling across deserts – he would summarily dismiss it by turning it on its head. Simply put, the more eventful the life, the duller the person – which, if true, rendered them quite the most dazzling couple around.

'Do you think Sartre and de Beauvoir went on holidays?'

'Well, yes, I think they probably did. Didn't she go to China?'

'No. They were too busy creating their own meaning by cheaper, less complicated means.'

Wilson rarely felt confined by the need to be accurate. He preferred to paint with a broad brush. It seemed to him they had a good life, but Rosie couldn't quite shake off the feeling that there was something else she ought to be doing.

'Colin's going twitching in the Alpujarras this spring,' she'd said recently, clearly unsettled.

'So?'

'Well . . . it's interesting, isn't it, it's an interesting thing to do.'

'Not really. It's classic displacement. He's obviously not getting enough sex.'

Now, Wilson wondered if he should have taken Rosie's

discontent a bit more seriously. Perhaps she just longed for a change. The thought cheered him – it suggested that if he could think up a big enough distraction it might knock all this nonsense about taking care of Lomond on its head. He looked at her, still dawdling by the window, her head resting against the wet glass, cooking up God knows what. He checked his diary.

'Easter Sunday is on the eleventh so that's – one, two, three, four, five – five weeks and five days away. Do you think that's long enough for Lomond to learn to walk again?'

'I'm not sure. They'll know more after his next assessment.'

Five weeks and five days, plenty of time to get her back on track again. Rosie was rubbing the condensation from the inside of a shape she'd drawn. When she turned round he noticed that her hair was damp and lumpy where she'd been leaning against the glass. She walked out of the room without looking at him, leaving her bleeding heart dripping on the window.

Eleven

T HE FOCUS had moved in a sure-footed, well-rehearsed
way, from Lomond's *stroke* to Lomond's *discharge*, even
though, to anyone looking on, he seemed to be worse – his
hemiplegia pulling him sideways like a tall plant straining
towards the sun. This new curvature seemed to accentuate
rather than diminish his physical stature. He experienced
spasms, extraordinary contractions that bolted through his
long, renegade limbs, sending crutches and tripods flying
across the room – great noisy pronouncements of his useless-
ness. His body took on a new moral order, a simple dichotomy
of good bits and bad bits – his good hand missing his unreliable mouth, the bendy straw pranging against his cheek.
Invariably, Kitty was there to steady and guide him, as assured
as any nurse – whilst Rosie floundered at times, overwhelmed.
She knew she needed to toughen up and be more like Kitty
– not that they were so entirely different, both bereft at the
sight of him stumbling on, crashing through the briar like a
great bear buckling under the effects of the hunter's dart.

'Right, Rosie, give us a hand.'

Kitty held onto Lomond's right arm, bending and turning
towards him to put her other arm round his waist.

'Make sure his feet are straight,' she strained. 'Now, give

him your arm. No . . . you need to let him hold onto you, not the other way around. That's it. Now . . . after three, Lomond, let's just rock you up and swing you onto the chair.'

They rocked him gently back and forward to build some momentum, then he was up on three with nowhere to go. Kitty eased him to the left but Rosie pulled him forward and he let go of her arm, pushing his hand against her shoulder to break the inevitable fall. Rosie's other shoulder hit the floor and Lomond managed to roll himself to the right, avoiding her and landing on his back, his feet coming to rest in a nonchalant twist – as if he were only wanting of a cheroot and a cloudless blue sky.

'Oh, God . . . sorry,' laughed Rosie. 'Are you OK, Dad?'

'Sshhh.'

Kitty had managed to break from the chain and was standing by the empty wheelchair, her hands over her mouth. A nurse with a straight back and a grimace appeared.

'Oh, dear – what's happened here then?'

The tone was interrogative, its slight quaver a trill of annoyance. She was joined by another nurse, in a different uniform, who was carrying what by all accounts looked like a cummerbund. Together they swung Lomond up and round, landing him back onto his chair as if he were weightless. Rosie, meantime, lay on the floor, giggling helplessly while Kitty clamped her own mirth behind her capable hands. The nurses looked at each other, the older hankering after the days when, in these circumstances, she could have legitimately issued Rosie with a good slap across the cheek to break the hysteria.

'Right, lass, that was rather silly, wasn't it?'

Rosie managed to swallow and nod in agreement.

'Sorry, Sister,' she said, momentarily contrite, then breaking into laughter again.

'Shall we get up?'

She tried, but her hand slipped and she banged her head

on the lino. Overwhelmed again by the indignity of it – legs akimbo and hair splayed across the floor – her laugh, far from subsiding, grew more raucous. The nurse sighed and bent down to Rosie, catching the distinct smell of alcohol as she helped her to her feet. Rosie wiped her tears and assumed the mantle of humility so clearly proffered, listening attentively to the brief lecture on visitor–patient protocols and responsibilities.

'It was my fault,' insisted Kitty. A plea from the sidelines, ignored.

'Yes, well . . . thankfully there are no bones broken. I don't think a broken femur is going to help your father's rehabilitation, is it?'

'No, Sister.'

'I'm not a sister.'

'Sorry, Sister . . . I mean . . . Charge Nurse.'

'I'm not a charge nurse either, this is Charge Nurse Reid,' and she gestured toward her much younger colleague.

'Really? I just thought, at your age . . . I mean, with all your experience. What I mean is, you carry great authority, Sister. Sorry, ehm . . . Nurse.'

The charge nurse intervened.

'I think Mr Friel needs to rest. Shall we call it a day?'

The nurses waited, clearly expecting Rosie to comply. They were looking only at her, so Kitty, seemingly exempt, sat down. Rosie apologised to Lomond and kissed him, then brushed herself down, put on her coat and said her goodbyes. She didn't want to feel sheepish, but she did. The nurses walked with her to the exit and one of them held the door open.

'Bye, now.'

'Bye.'

As she walked across the car park she had the unshakeable feeling that she'd just been escorted from the building.

★

THE DISTANT legacy of cheap fish had long since faded, but the palate remained altered for ever – white flesh on the tongue, sweet and juicy, cheap at any price in Heath's book. Saturday's small chicken lasted for three days, the soup stretching for five in the winter when the larder was cool, and Wednesday was a lamb chop with a tin of baby food (Heinz low-sugar apple sauce) and a boiled potato. These habits could vary with little upset – if the fowl were too large or the chops all bone Heath could let it go – but Tuesday, Thursday and Friday were reserved for fish. She might have more – the soup might occasionally be replaced with a chowder – but never less. Their immutable position was secured not by reason of religion or caste, but by those core, defining habits that defy rational account.

Lately, things have changed. Each time Heath goes into the fish shop, Cameron Fraser asks about Rosie, and each time Heath's answer is the same; she doesn't know when she'll be back, it depends on work and what's happening with Lomond. She's noticed that the Fraser boy (he's nearly forty, but seems so young) has acquired a new curiosity, which is perplexing, and a new solicitous attitude, which is annoying. She would like to avoid him altogether, and could take her trade elsewhere (there is always Neptune's Larder round the corner), but for one thing – Cameron's fish is the fishiest. There is no doubt in Heath's mind, his whitefish is the most delicate (yet resilient), and the thickest cut (which it has to be if it's to cook properly). Why this should be so she's not sure, but she is aware that he is always one of the first local buyers down on the quayside for the market (still held regularly, despite the dark hand of Brussels twirling its fingers in the cold waters of the North Sea).

The walk to Fraser's Fish is ingrained in Heath's routine and stretches her just enough to pump the heart and oil the joints. She nearly always takes another walk just before dark, whenever that might fall, to help her sleep. In winter she sleeps more, but her summers are full of white nights. Insomnia runs in the family. She can remember the sound of her father crossing the attic floor at night, the same boards creaking, loud but slow, as if he were trying to be light-footed. He would stand under the skylight and gaze out; his astronomical knowledge being, well, astronomical. Heath wasn't aware of this until he came home from the war and started to teach Lomond how to read the stars. She would eavesdrop on those father–son conversations, held out in the garden under a black night sky. She thought he'd acquired this knowledge during the war, when, as an older conscript, he was trained in navigation, but her mother later told her that he'd been selected as a navigator because of his knowledge of astronomy, which had been passed on to him by an uncle who farmed in the Cheviots.

When Heath heard this she felt shut out.

She never knew why her father hadn't taught her the constellations, and did not have the audacity to ask, but assumed it was because she was a girl. She never minded not being included in the fishing trips and the joinery sessions, the building of ships in bottles and the meticulous construction of model aeroplanes that could neither fly nor glide. She held no interest in football, in the merits of a good racehorse, or in how to work out the best odds, but oh . . . the stars!

Whenever she can't sleep, she thinks of all those times they could have stood together, stargazing, perhaps with the scent of honeysuckle creeping through the grass.

CAMERON WAS asking about Rosie again. There was something about his persistence that shifted from being irritating to being troubling.

'I haven't heard her on the show for a while.'

Since there was no explicit question Heath ignored the comment.

'Not well, is she?'

'Oh, no, she's fine. What about your mother, Cameron? How is she?'

'Oh, she's fine.'

'And yourself?'

'Fine, thanks.'

'Good. So we're all fine.'

'Aye.'

He at last surrendered the fish.

'Does Rosie like turbot?'

'Pardon?'

'Does she like turbot? It's nice with some coriander and garlic.'

'I really have no idea.'

'Could you ask her?'

'Ask her what?'

'If she likes turbot.'

She looks directly at him, pausing before she puts her purse away. She feels it's time to rein this in. Suddenly she remembers Cameron as a young boy, always hanging round the twins when they stayed at the summer house. They were the same age. He appeared almost every day, seemingly content to wait until dusk on the off chance that the twins might let him play. It became so regular that none of them took any notice. He became part of the landscape. Heath would like to think that she had at least greeted him when they passed, but she couldn't be sure. She certainly recalls seeing him there, swinging on the gate with a long stalk of grass in his mouth, always keen and polite. She can see that same eagerness now in those green eyes.

Even before she says it she feels harsh.

'No, Cameron – I'm not going to ask her. Sorry.'

She leaves the shop and is inordinately glad to reach the fresh air. Her heart has quickened again. As she walks home she thinks about Cameron. She pictures him rising in the darkness and moving stealthily through the house, then out to market — soundless as a fox. She thinks about the night she came home after her visit to Lomond and wonders if it was him she sensed hanging about outside, watching the house. Maybe he was out there, standing in the dark, chewing on a piece of blonde seagrass?

★

ROSIE HAS centred herself down the middle of the kingsize bed and is lying neat, her legs straight and arms tucked into her sides. She smoothes out the duvet cover so it follows her form like a snowfall, then pulls it tight across her chest and slides her hands back under, resting them on her thighs. Her shoulders stick out in bony symmetry and she keeps her chin proud, consciously aligning her head to her spine and enjoying the sheer precision of it. She stares at the ceiling — it's square and ornately corniced, and looks like a Christmas cake. The phone rings and she hears the answer machine click on, then the caller hangs up. For a fleeting moment she thinks it might have been William and regrets not picking up. It's three weeks since she wrote to the post office in Mekele so there's a good chance that someone has read her letter. If they don't know William they'll probably return to sender, and even though it's a bit soon to expect anything back, it is technically possible, and her mental flag is up. Two days ago she started checking the post, scanning for an African postmark. There is a backlog of mail on the kitchen table and Wilson keeps urging her to tackle it, particularly the stuff from the studio. He says it's important to keep going.

Where? she asks.

It's not reasonable. He can't expect the mundane to be priv-ileged over the bigger issues, such as lost brothers and dying fathers – and she so completely unable to change anything.

THIS TIME the phone wakes her up. It's Wilson.

'I called you earlier but you were asleep. Are you still in bed?'

'No.'

'Come on, Rosie, get up. It's nearly twelve.'

His entreaty, delivered gently, is like a smack in the mouth. Rosie starts to sniff.

'Come on, honey. What is it?'

'Nothing. I'm fine.'

She's not in the mood for talking (much to his relief since he is about to give a lecture on Rawls' Difference Principle).

'What time are you seeing Lomond?'

'Not till three. Why?'

'Just wondering. I thought we might go for something to eat later. I'm about to face sixty first years who'll force me into the role of grumpy old bastard so I need something to look forward to. Fancy it?'

This is his toughest day of the week – two lectures, a tutorial, and a pile of interminable formative assessments – and he can only face it by looking beyond it.

'Are you there, Rosie?'

'I'm going to do it, you know,' she said flatly.

'Eh? Do what?'

'I'm going to take care of Dad. I know you all think I'm incapable and maybe I am but I need to try.'

'Well, we can talk about it later over dinner. I'll book Henry's for seven.'

His decisiveness works.

'OK. I just need you to know I'm not changing my mind.'

Rosie feels better after the call. She gets up and opens the blinds to bright sunshine, diamonds winking on the distant

105

water. She sits on the window seat, pulls off the socks she's been wearing since yesterday and picks out the fluff from between her toes. Each toenail is topped with a ragged band of red varnish. She rummages in the bathroom cabinet and finds four bottles of remover, each barely used. She carries one back to the window and places it on the sill together with four cotton-wool balls, then adds a tiny bottle of cherry-red chip-free varnish, all set out in a line. She stands back and surveys the items, adjusting the position of the cotton balls very slightly before going into the kitchen. There's a sheet of A4 stuck to the fridge with READ YOUR MAIL written in red marker. Rosie mixes herself a drink then goes back to her self-assembled nail bar, where she draws in a deep breath and settles down with a tall gin and tonic – no ice.

Within minutes her renewed resolve starts to falter. She finishes cleaning and painting her nails and walks to the kitchen on her heels, keeping her toes as high in the air as she can, sticking her bum out to achieve some balance. Her mail is piled neatly on the table, ordered according to size. She sits down and sifts through it, tearing up the obvious junk and putting it in the bin, then she re-sorts what remains into a much smaller pile. The breakfast dishes have already been washed and stacked. With no particular intent in mind Rosie takes down a jar of pulses and pours some into a large mixing bowl, then she covers them with water and puts them aside to soak. The sight is satisfying. Once again she stands back from where she is and looks around her. Everything is just as it should be: clean dishes and soaking beans, a fruit bowl with papayas and limes, crusty bread in a wicker basket, wrapped in a tea towel to keep it fresh.

This is the kitchen of a capable woman.

She rinses out her glass and begins to tidy away the gin bottle, then changes her mind and pours herself another. She goes back to the window seat, sits with her feet stretched

106

out in front of her, and looks down on to the back green. Empty washing lines wait in the cold, and the grass leans in clumps, uncut, like a field in winter. Already the snowdrops are beginning to look grubby and the yellow aconites are gone. Rosie drains her glass and wiggles her fresh new toes, but despite her best efforts a film of dust particles has set in the fast-drying varnish, rendering her cherry nails as dull as fusty fruit.

Twelve

THE MAN in the next bed is a well-known trumpet player. Lots of people come to see him. These people are better looking and noisier than anyone else's visitors and bring some colour into the insipid pastels of the rehab unit. Sometimes it sounds like a party, and while the other visitors *tut tut* and surreptitiously complain, the patients enjoy it – they like the vitality of it. It leaves them speculating about the potential richness of a vicarious life.

Which for some is their best hope.

The trumpet player is only fifty-three and it's no accident that both his legs have gone. He was a forty-a-day man with a quiet temperament and a prodigious talent. Loved and respected in the jazz world, his name appears on top album covers, although only true aficionados are aware of his individual career. Jimmy never wanted to headline, preferring the back of the stage, and until a few weeks ago he was still performing, fuelled up on whisky and painkillers and missing his cigarettes more than his right leg (they cut that off three years ago). Now, instead of being a trumpet player, he is a double amputee (right below knee, left above knee). It was rumoured amongst the staff that the old man with slicked back hair who joined the visitors yesterday was Stan Tracey.

He came back again today with a middle-aged blonde who turned out to be Jimmy's wife.

'You never get your husband to yourself, do you? Still, you'll be able to catch up once you get him home. Shouldn't be too long now.' The occupational therapist smiles and breezes past, giving her a reassuring pat on the arm. Jimmy and his wife watch her assiduously as she heads toward the workshop clutching a state-of-the-art foot in need of repair. They each hold their gaze on the spot where she disappears from sight, the faint reek of fear settling between them as they contemplate the resumption of their marriage.

Kitty lowers her paper and openly watches the jazz people, which gives Lomond a chance to watch her, his eyes resting easily on her lovely face. Her eyelashes are dark and inordinately thick, and he wonders if that means she is particularly hirsute. He has often pictured her naked body, always smooth as alabaster, her soft curves painted in a primitive language, white against the deep reds of his quilted bedspread.

'Look at him. I think he must be somebody famous.'

She nods in the direction of the visitors. The scared blonde is talking to Stan, her brave face turned away from her husband.

'I expect he's another musician. Oh, what a pity Rosie isn't here. She probably knows who they are.'

Lomond smiles his daft smile. He knows Kitty believes that Rosie somehow spans two different worlds, the one they all share, and the other one – the one only famous people can access. The fact that Rosie never ever mentions her work only reinforces Kitty's belief that she is protecting something private and can't afford loose talk with just anyone. She always imagined Rosie's frequent visits home as being rather cloaked affairs, conducted almost in secret, and her instinct was to stay in the background and get on with the cleaning. So anxious was she to convey the complete reliability of her discretion that once, when she literally bumped into Rosie in a rather exclusive food-hall (Kitty buys her oatcakes there – it's the only thing that keeps Dave off the bread), she pretended not to know her.

'Kitty! Kitty . . . Hello! How are you?'

'Oh, sorry, I didn't see you there.'

She had orbited round Rosie for years. When she first started to clean for the Friels the girl was only fourteen and the twins had left home.

'Oh, you should see them, May – it breaks your heart. The lassie's never had a mum and she hasn't a clue. She still sucks her thumb but Mr Friel never says anything so she has to wear braces to pull her teeth back. All she does is read and fiddle about with her projects, always listening to the radio. There's one in every room. *And* she reads the papers! They sit there sharing the *Herald*, him pulling on his pipe and her with her thumb – like Tweedledum and Tweedledee.'

'Sounds a bit weird to me.'

'You think?'

'Aye.'

May gave a little shake, as though she was cold.

'She's certainly nothing like Olivia.'

'No.'

Olivia was the youngest of May's three teenage daughters. The two women thought about her for a moment, saying nothing.

'Chalk and cheese.'

'Hmmm.'

Kitty pictured Lomond and Rosie in the kitchen – all that harmonious grazing, barely looking up as they simultaneously reach for the teapot, one intuitively giving way to the other.

'She drinks tea by the gallon. Absolutely loves it!'

'Really?'

'Yeah. Earl Grey. No milk or sugar. At least eight cups a day.'

'My God. Is that good for you – all that tea?'

'I wouldn't have thought so,' replied Kitty. She didn't tell her sister about the sheets she found soaking in the bath, how by the following week she was washing them through and making sure they were pegged out before she left. It just became part of her routine, a routine that saw her ironing Lomond's shirts and freshening them up with a ginseng spray that she'd bought with her own money. She kept it under the sink, not exactly hidden, but pushed right to the back, next to the ant powder and the grate blackener (dated nineteen-oatcake but still might come in handy – you just never know).

WHEN THE showbiz types leave, Kitty turns her full attention back to Lomond.

'Time I was off.'

She switches from a smile to a frown and begins to pack up, looking angry about something, but in a theatrical way. Lomond leans comfortably in his chair, his dead hand placed on his dead leg. He looks on in a state of separateness, enjoying the sight of Kitty doing ordinary things. He appreciates the complexity of everyday actions now – putting the top on a pen or buttoning a coat, the way the eye orders the hand without looking.

Only in his case it doesn't.

His good eyes can't communicate with his good hand. Even though he habitually wrote with his right hand he's always been an ambidexter. He could chalk up equations with either hand, and sometimes used his left one in lectures without thinking about it, usually in a moment of sheer enthusiasm because that was the hand nearest the board. Lomond was ambilateral with other movements too – he could pitch and catch with both and kick with either (he was a bit of a sporting sensation in his day, the early pick of any team). He was also an ambivert, but all his ambi parts have died – starved of the blood and oxygen they need. The scans show the superficial detail of what looks like a very small death, but the records fail to note that this dark withering has occurred at Lomond's epicentre, and that he has lost his point of origin.

He cannot will his hand to write an x – it comes out as discrete little threads, skittered across the page like spiders' legs. He looks at them in astonishment, having felt sure he'd drawn the perfect x. Clearly the relationship between inputs and outputs has changed; he has entered a disordered world, and for Lomond, whose life has been spent amongst axioms, it is hostile territory.

HE WATCHES Kitty feeling her way through the contents of her huge bag. She occasionally peers into the seemingly impenetrable darkness of its fully lined, washable interior, her frown set firm as she speaks. He watches as though he is allowed to, as if it's his job to look. He knows it is making her flustered, but he doesn't feel a part of that; he has lost all sense of culpability and watches her because he enjoys it.

'I was thinking . . .'

Rummage.

'When it comes time for you to go home I could change my lists. If I knew the dates, I could work for you full time . . . kinda thing . . . I could come in every day . . . so to speak . . . just whatever suited, you know . . . depending on how things are.'

She was scowling now, looking for goodness knows what.

'I know there's a lot to think about and you're having meetings and all that but I thought I'd offer . . . just so you know that's an option.'

Rummage.

'I'm, eh . . . well, it would suit me, to be honest . . . save me scheduling all those different folk. I wouldn't want to give up Mr McKendrick, though . . . not for a while, anyway. I don't think he's got long to go, poor old stick. He's as thin as a rake and they don't seem to be bothering. Oh, God where have I . . .'

Rummage.

'I suggested Complan and the district nurse just shrugged and said I could give it a try but really, I don't think it's up to me. I was thinking of writing to his daughter in Canada but that seems a bit intrusive as well. What do you think?'

Stops rummaging. Crumples bag down on lap. Looks up expectantly.

Lomond blows out of his mouth. An unlikely bubble of spit fails to burst.

'Hang on . . . I've got a tissue somewhere.'

She plunges back into the bag and pulls out a black comb.

'There it is! I knew it was in there!'

He wipes his chin with his sleeve and watches her run the comb lightly over her hair and smooth it down with her other hand, closing her eyes for a moment and tilting her head upwards and to the side. It feels very intimate, not the sort of thing she would have done before.

She is either flirting with him or has ceased to see him as a man, he doesn't know which.

'I could easily get the 22 between you and George. He only lives down Victoria Park.'

She's up now, doing amazing things with her buttons.

'Should I talk to Rosie about it?'

He nods.

'OK. I'll see you tomorrow.'

She bends over and lightly wipes his mouth with a tissue she found in her coat pocket.

'Take care of yourself, and remember to use that buzzer when you need to.'

She points to the device, then leaves without another glance. There is an unexpected moment of quiet in the unit and Lomond fancies he can hear Kitty walking all the way through reception and out the front door. She is still rummaging, this time for a scarf, and he can hear the silk and nylon mix slide across her pale neck as the wind hits her skin. He closes his eyes and tracks her all the way down the drive until the connection is suddenly broken by the noise of Jimmy releasing the brakes on his wheelchair. By the time he has propelled himself from the room Kitty is gone – every last sweet note of her.

Whatever it is that has died in him, his senses have not abandoned him. He can still feel the wing of a bee falling on his cheek – and on a clear dark night he could still spot a candle burning a mile away.

Thirteen

WILSON FINDS her asleep on the sofa. She's wearing one of his jumpers over her pyjamas. Her feet look cold and her slack mouth gapes slightly, her hand resting on her chest in the thumbs-up position. He doesn't know whether to rouse her or tuck her white feet under a blanket and leave her until dinner. He whispers her name and she stirs, slipping her thumb back in her mouth, her eyelids trembling and her eyeballs agitating from side to side at an implausible speed, reminding him of the old family dog who'd slept for the last three years of his life. His eyes did that; Wilson's mum said he was dreaming of chasing rabbits. Eventually he wouldn't walk beyond the garden gate. He'd stop and wait until Wilson eventually turned round and called him, his tail still swinging at the thought of it, but the legs too tired. *Just let him sleep*, Mum said. It didn't seem to bother her, but Wilson could hardly bear to look at him lying there – farting and whimpering, his mouth pulling into a weird Mutley grin. They had grown up together – a boy and his dog. Even in his sleep his tail would move at the sound of Wilson's voice, sometimes managing just one faltering flick upwards before thumping back onto the floor. *Thud*. He could hear it now, that last heart-wrenching ball-breaking eye-stinging eloquent *thud*.

'Who's Rory?'

'What?'

Rosie was awake.

'You just said Rory.'

'Oh . . . I was just thinking about my old dog. I saw you lying there and . . .'

'Christ, what time is it?'

She sprang to the edge of the sofa.

'Umm . . . nearly quarter to four. I left early, couldn't stand the . . .'

'Oh, shit. Shit. Shit. Shit.'

Rosie put her head in her hands and pulled her hair back, her eyes closed now, her neck stretched.

'What is it?'

'Dad. I was supposed to see Dad at three . . . and I'd arranged to see his keyworker or his named nurse or whatever they're called to talk about plans for his discharge.'

'Discharge? But surely that won't be for ages?'

'Plans, Wilson, I said *plans*. You know − those things we make all the time then do bugger all about?'

She was rubbing her face hard, as though she was washing it − and talking behind her hands.

'Oh, God,' she moaned, 'my plan. My plan. My plan stinks.'

'Rosie?'

'He'll be there now. They'll be listening to him. He won't tell them my proposal because he thinks it's a joke. He thinks I'm a joke.'

She started to sob.

'Who?'

'Jacob of course, who do you think?'

'Aw. I'm sorry, Rosie.'

He gave her a pat.

'Don't pat me, I'm not a dog. Why are *you* sorry anyway?'

She stood in front of Wilson, confronting him.

'What are *YOU* apologising for?'

He has no idea, but the intent was good.

'Well, I'm just saying . . .'

'What? WHAT are you just saying?'

She pushed him out of the way and he stumbled backwards a few feet then regained his balance.

'Christ sakes, Rosie, what did you do that for?'

She looked at him, shocked, as if *he* had just shoved *her*.

'Oh!'

She covered her mouth and nose with both hands, then fled from the room, slamming the bedroom door. This was something new. He could hear her crying but daren't approach her (a tigress with toothache came to mind). She was moving about and quickly re-emerged fully dressed, then flew out the front door, shielding her face as if a look might blind her or turn her to stone.

'That's assault, you know, Rosie Friel . . . I could prosecute!' he shouted after her, feeling piqued and ridiculous. Wilson undid his coat and stared at the open door. It had been a long hard day and he was glad that she'd gone.

★

JACOB THOUGHT the meeting had gone rather well. He'd sweated his way through it, expecting Rosie to arrive at any moment and sabotage what proved to be a sensible discussion. They'd brought out all their key personnel (with the exception of the speech therapist, whose apologies were met with resignation and pursed lips). They'd looked squarely at the facts and drawn sound, practical conclusions. It was evident from the speed of the discussion that they clearly knew what they were talking about. Remember they're only *recommendations*, added the young social worker, rather spuriously he thought. She suggested it was too early to expect Mr Friel (everyone else called him Lomond — why couldn't she?) to be able to formulate, or find the means to articulate his *aspirations*. She twittered briefly about his *abilities*, *preferences* and *strengths* (strengths! Get real, woman — have you looked at him lately, wilting in his chair like a May Day daffodil?). Her perspective drew a range of silent responses — pinched nostrils, narrow eyes, those pursed lips again. She mentioned something about proxy decision making (eh?), that he might *fall under* the Incapacity Act (hah! Incapable. Exactly! She's making her own noose now). She said the main issue was one of *communication*, and that Mr Friel's wishes must be ascertained by whatever means available, be it human or mechanical (what's she on about?). It was unfortunate, she suggested, that the speech therapist had not been able to attend the meeting, given the centrality of our (our? — speak for yourself, dear) communication difficulties. With full respect to Jacob, she believed there was another son (missing in Africa), a sister (eighty-four and counting) and, of course, a daughter (absent and probably drunk), who should all be consulted.

The professionals doodled on their notepads, drawing little houses, stars and squiggles, faces with square jaws. The consultant checked his watch and began to read the case notes of the next patient. Jacob stared at the social worker, frowning and willing her to shut up, his little blue vein worming round the side of his temple like a tadpole breaking through spawn. April stared too. She was working hard, trying to take notes, but her brain deflected all clinical details automatically, and she found the paraphernalia discussed by the other girl, the wee thin one in the flat shoes, quite baffling; hoists and drinking cups, non-slip mats and pressure-reducing cushions, helping hands and wobble-boards. She perked up slightly at the mention of a new and complete bathing range, wondering if her knowledge of corsetry might at last come into play, but the discussion moved on too quickly and her notes just couldn't keep up (she was having to spell phonetically or sink without trace – *kolestrol, newmonia, iskeemik*). April listened intently to the social worker, who was by far the most stylish in a green Nicole Farhi sweater and brown shoes by either Paul Green or Arche, she wasn't sure which. The social worker had a lovely, calming voice, a bit like Rosie's, and somehow she was easier to follow. April stopped scribbling and watched her intently, slowly nodding in agreement as she started to experience the tantalising feeling of *something making sense*. Jacob moved his foot on top of hers and pressed down hard. She stopped nodding and looked round but he wasn't looking at her, he was still staring at the social worker. He pressed harder. The gold shoe-buckle compressed against her bone and she let out a small yelp and pulled her foot away, tucking it safely round her ankle. The doctor looked up briefly and snapped to, gathering his papers and clicking his ballpoint several times before placing it back in his top pocket and barking out some instructions which passed April by completely. One of the nurses said something in reply, equally incomprehensible. April was completely transfixed. She had never seen so much cleverness in one small room. It was all very reassuring. As the meeting broke up she moved to catch the social worker and ask about her shoes, but Jacob gripped her by the elbow and firmly steered her through.

HE'S TREATING her to a small celebratory glass of pinot noir. April finds the curios that clutter the gantry distracting (there's just no theme to them). She tries to rise above the sticky surfaces and concentrate instead on conversing with her husband. She feels uneasy drinking in a bar, and her foot hurts – she thinks it might be bleeding.

Jacob is triumphant. He's talking about the meeting with confidence and authority, so much so that April wonders if she should be noting things down.

'Shall I take some notes?'

'Notes?'

'Yes. Shall I write these things down?'

'What things? What *are* you on about?'

'Well, it's all just so complicated, darling. I thought it might help if we jotted things down as we go.'

April is a great believer in notes – and lists. She compiles lists within lists and has lists which direct you to previous lists: single-column lists; lists with sub-sections; draft lists; multi-topic and single-topic lists; essential lists; dream lists; checklists. An unchecked item on a list can keep April awake for hours, particularly if it is the only remaining thing to be ticked off, scored out or highlighted (green for 'must do', orange for 'done'). When something needs to be added to an existing list that cannot be accessed immediately, she writes it down in one of her notebooks.

'There's nothing complicated about it. Weren't you listening in there? Obviously he needs twenty-four-hour care and all the proper equipment etcetera etcetera.'

'But surely,' April hesitated slightly, 'with more of this re-habilitation business, he'll get a bit better?'

She was thinking about all the cleverness in that room and what use might be made of it. She was also wondering what had happened to Rosie. When Jacob confirmed her absence from the meeting as 'disappointing but entirely typical' the 'chair' had written something down and April couldn't help wondering what. 'My sister means well but she has her own issues. She's really very vulnerable,' he'd said. April had never heard him refer to Rosie (or anyone else for that matter) as vulnerable before. It wasn't one of his words. Nor did she recognise the tone. There was a compassion in his voice that suddenly made her feel very proud of her husband.

'Better? How can a piece of dead brain get better? If anything he's going to get worse. You heard what the doc said about the risk of another stroke.'

April nodded. She thought she'd heard that something could be done about that, change of diet, that kind of thing. She's one of the you-are-what-you-eat brigade and had jotted down a few notes at this point in the meeting (which meant she missed the next part – the part Jacob was now reminding her of – about pressure sores and seizures and urinary tract infections).

'Poor Lomond.'

'Absolutely.'

'And poor Rosie.'

'Poor Rosie? She can't even be bothered to turn up. She's the one that called the bloody meeting in the first place!'

'Yes, but as you said, darling, she's vulnerable.'

'Vulnerable! Drunk more like. When are you going to get it into your head April, my sister is bad news, always has been, always will be. She's caused nothing but trouble from the day she was born, now come on, let's go. I have some calls to make.'

He stood up and held out April's coat. She moved to the very edge of the seat and lifted her wine, half full, to her lips.

'Leave that, come on.'

They parted quickly in the street, Jacob hailing a taxi to take him back to the office. April pulled her coat around her and for a moment wondered where to go. It would have been nice to pop in and see a friend, grab a coffee and tell her all about the meeting and this dreadful business with Lomond. She might even share her worries about Jacob, how the pressures all rest on his shoulders as next of kin, just when the business is heading for its busiest period (spring is hectic in the property market). The friend might ask about Rosie, her celebrity sister-in-law, why she hadn't done the show for the past couple of weeks, and April would need to be careful what she said and not mention the drinking. What she'd really like to talk about is her own father, how he'd died when she was fourteen and the first thing she'd thought was thank God he's not coming back to stink up the house with his smoke. It had been so peaceful through all those weeks he'd been in hospital. No more waking up to the sound of him coughing up phlegm at six in the morning. The last time she had visited he'd shrunk to about half his size, huge eyes encased in such a tiny head, more like a sheep's head, his pyjamas all bunched up where his shoulders used to be, tubes everywhere and his breathing short and light – like a series of small frights.

Now here he was again, a resuscitated memory.

April would like to express her regret for refusing to pull her chair closer to his bedside so that he might see her, and for being so very irritated that his funeral fell on the same day as the school dance. A friend might be able to listen over a coffee and still like her, might not judge her as harshly as she judged herself. It was something she'd never tested out. Of course, she could always talk to Margaret, but she'd be closing the shop now, and, anyway, as the owner she needed to keep a careful eye on professional boundaries (Jacob had reminded her of that more than once). April pulled on her tiny kid leather gloves and mentally sifted through her contacts – as if she might have misplaced a soulmate – but there was no one she could call. She tried to oust the image of her father by thinking about other things, but he kept coming back, lying there without a fuss, so flat his bed looked empty, just a head placed on the pillow with ears that seemed to grow as the rest of him turned to husk.

She's sorry she refused to hold his little mouse hand. Being a teenager no longer seemed a reasonable excuse.

★

SITTING UNDER a monkey-puzzle isn't going to solve anything. Rosie lies under the branches of the giant Chilean pine and stares up through the strong dark whorls. She's trying to decide whether they are spiky leaves or leafy spikes. The gardens remind her of the psychiatric hospital she used to go to once a month with Lomond – skipping past the high gates and up the drive, jumping over her own rope. She could double skip, her rope cutting through the air fast enough for her to hear the sound of speed, which Rosie equated to skipping at the speed of sound. She liked the crack against the tarmac, a pitch even higher than the bang of her brothers' cap guns.

hurr-ee-scurr-ee-had-a-worr-ee-no-one-liked-his-chick-en-curr-ee

She enjoyed her visits to the hospital and the time she spent with her dad. Everything was easy when she was with him. They occupied the same space, travelling together like time lords who could see the strangeness of ordinary things – leaves turning to fishes and swimming in shoals across forest paths. They could just as clearly see the ordinariness of strange things, and were neither frightened nor impressed by the bravado of the exotic.

Rosie could feel things, too, just as Lomond did.

WOULD YOU say she was sensitive, Mr Friel?
Yes.
Perhaps too sensitive?
No.
Then how sensitive? Give me an example.
Well – she became very distressed at school when someone brought

in a glass box full of stick insects. They were placed under a spotlight
and the children were all required to group round and look at them.
And?
And Rosie was distraught.
Why?
Why? Dr Bird . . . if your raison d'être is to achieve complete
camouflage what's the worst thing that can happen?
Ah. I see.
Indeed. As far as Rosie is concerned she was witnessing a tragedy.
Quite.

THE GROUNDS of the hospital stretched beyond its own
horizon of trees. Rosie remembers the last part of those slow
drives, following the contours of the high wall and crawling
round bends (not literally, that's car-speak). *Dad, you're driving*
me round the bend, she wanted to say – but of course she
couldn't. Even though Jacob wasn't with them he would
know just by looking at her if she'd been talking.

Not a word, Rosie, or the tongue goes. Think I couldn't? he said,
slicing into a peach and pushing the bruised fruit into her
mouth.

THEY'D LEAVE the car at the gates and break the rules by
walking through the rhododendrons, scrunching across wood-
bark and ducking under boughs of pendulous pink pearls.
When they broke through the undergrowth onto the drive
Rosie would race on ahead. She'd worked hard at perfecting
her skipping and wanted Lomond to see just how very good
she was, her straight gait finding its place under the enchanted
rope as it turned through its arc, stiff as a hula-hoop, with no
help from her. Rosie kept time by chanting in her head.
The game was for five people – two to turn the rope and
three to skip, each running in and out in turn – but she made
do by whipping the rope round twice on each breathless

chant of 'in' or 'out'. It meant doing six double skips, which is easy when you're at your peak – that prestigious time just before you hang up your rope for ever.

> *Mother, Mother, I am ill*
> *Call for the doctor over the hill.*
> *In came the doctor,*
> *In came the nurse,*
> *In came the lady with the alligator purse.*
> *Measles, said the doctor.*
> *Mumps, said the nurse.*
> *Nothing, said the lady with the alligator purse.*
> *Out goes the doctor, out goes the nurse,*
> *Out goes the lady with the alligator purse.*

She could even skip up the wide stone steps, her magic rope carrying her right to the front door where she would stop and wait for Lomond to catch up before pressing the buzzer, then together (it took two), they would push through the heavy doors into a capacious circular hall of cream and green with shiny floors and a domed glass ceiling so high it made Rosie dizzy to look at it. This was the perfect space for skipping. She imagined the crack of her rope reverberating from tiled floor against tiled walls and all the way up to the glass dome. It would sound magnificent, the way it should sound, each whip just lasting a millisecond, but so clean, and sharp as a pin – a wincing prick of sound that would set the rooks screeching and flapping from the rooftops. Folk from the surrounding buildings would look up at the commotion – a dark cloud of scruffy black birds heaving themselves up in gunshot panic and shooting off in all directions. Eventually they'd get to know the cause – *that's Rosie's rope,* they'd say, *whipcrackaway whipcrackaway whipcrackaway.*

She knew it wouldn't be allowed. People moved through

this perfect sound auditorium in silence, sticking closely to the wall. Rosie and Lomond would whisper their arrival at reception then take the diameter route to Child Psychiatry. The straight tangential corridor that led to Dr Bird's office was more dead space, long and wide and perfect for speed skips and cartwheels. Rosie would fall slightly behind and follow Lomond, holding his hand – trunk to tail like a baby elephant – even though there was more than enough room for her to walk beside him. Despite their restrained pace Rosie would arrive for her therapy tousled and pink-cheeked, with twigs in her hair. When she moved she released a smell of peat, as though she'd tunnelled her way in.

SHE LOOKS at her watch. It's late. She's been lying under the monkey tree on her back like a tramp. No, no one would think that – she's too pale, her skin is too smooth and she has good teeth. She sees herself through the eyes of the three men who love her, the three whose love she knows of, whose love has been declared. *I love you, Rosie*, each has said, yet here she is lying on the grass in a public park, wiping her nose with her sleeve. People who notice her look the other way. The ground is damp and she can feel the cold stabbing at her buttocks. She comes out from under the tree and a yellow dog barks at her then runs off sideways. She walks slowly through the park. There's no reason to rush, the meeting would have ended hours ago, or perhaps it was postponed? Anyone who might have been expecting her will have given up by now. She brushes the back of her skirt and generally straightens herself out as she goes, pulling her hair back tight from her face in an attempt to *buck up*. She hasn't decided what to say yet but an excuse will come to her, she won't be stuck for words, not like back then, playing cat and mouse with Dr Bird – only who was the cat and who was the mouse?

Richard Bird was handsome, even a little girl could see that. He had dark curly hair and very white teeth and Rosie liked his colourful jumpers. They were the sort of jumpers that nice people wear, people who don't take themselves too seriously. They might have stripes or Aztec symbols on them, or penguins, that kind of thing (there's a knack to non-threatening knitwear, a fine twine between nerdy and cool). You could tell the psychologists from the psychiatrists by their clothes. The psychologists wore baggy knits and corduroys and the psychiatrists wore suits. Dr Richard Bird was a conundrum. He believed in the power of the sub-conscious but his main clinical tool was a jar of Smarties – more colourful and effective than Fluoxetine (or so he thought). He would offer Rosie a sweet every time she communicated and of course, she had him conditioned in no time, pulling faces and stockpiling sweeties for the journey home. She was smart and brought her own tube, sharing her booty with Lomond in the car. He loved the brown ones best and always chanted the same thing before popping them into his mouth.

Buy some for Lulu.

She had no idea what it meant.

Rosie saved the alphabet tops from Smartie tubes and kept them in a little cloth bag. For a while she took to carrying them around with her, shaking the bag like a castanet (one shake for no, two for yes, three for look-at-me, four for don't-look-at-me, rattle-snake shoogle for go away), but she never took the talking bag with her to the hospital (Dr Bird made such a song and dance about the Smarties that she didn't want him to know she could have one at home pretty much any time she wanted). Over time their sessions changed – instead of crayons and paper Rosie was given poster paints and big brushes and was put in front of a large easel so she could work on a vertical surface. Every so often Dr Bird would provide Lomond with a vague and – it seemed to him – alarmingly intuitive, uninformed analysis of her 'work'. When she drew a large pumpkin with a mouth full of huge square teeth he suggested that Rosie might be frightened of 'oral aggression'. He called them her *Gobble-Gobble* feelings.

'But it's Halloween,' Lomond protested, but only mildly, already feeling judged for his resistance.

Generally, though, each session began much like another.

'Anything since last time, Mr Friel?'

'Not a dickie bird,' Lomond would say, without anyone laughing.

It was their own private joke.

Fourteen

THE ACTIVITY room is empty. Rosie searches the obvious
places and finds Lomond and Kitty sitting at the picture
window in the dining room, each with a cup of tea – one
sipping, one sucking. The light is fading fast but the top of
Arthur's Seat can still be seen beyond the rooftops, rising from
the Salisbury Crags, looking high and grand and much more
distant than it actually is, like a far-off mountain. They are
watching weather gather on the summit, both thinking themselves up there, bracing themselves against the wind as they
pick out the Bass Rock some thirty miles beyond. Each
unaware of their synchronicity, they ponder over the notion
of all those gannets gracing the skies and plunging, black-
tipped and arrow-straight into the sea. Eighty thousand blue-
eyed blondes crammed on a rock, their ostentatious babies
zipped up in little lambswool suits, all white and fluffy like
they've just been teased out with a comb.

Thus preoccupied, they sip and sook and don't notice
Rosie – but she's noticed them. She's noticed the way their
shoulders are touching – merging their silhouette like a paper
chain – and the way they both seem to be focused on the
exact same distant point, as if they've turned towards a shout
or a loud bang; the way they're not talking; the way she's not

talking; the way Kitty doesn't search for things to say.

Lomond noisily drains his cup and leans back, struggling to disengage from his bendy straw. It's a blue and white straw – not hospital issue, and Rosie assumes Kitty has brought some in. Lomond is supposed to practise raising his cup to his mouth, but his hand won't cooperate. She watches her father manoeuvre the tenacious straw with his tongue, which looks bigger now, as though it's grown into a bull's tongue – the kind you see resting on a platter in the butcher's window surrounded by plastic parsley (like that somehow softens the fact of it being a *tongue*, for God's sake). It is not possible to look at a disembodied tongue without feeling something, whether it's coiled in a jar of jelly or straight on a plate, it makes no difference; cold pressed, unsalted, boiled or braised, no amount of spice or Worcester Sauce can change the essential fact of eating tongue.

Mouth eating mouth.

Chewing tonsil tissue – flesh marbled with sinew, severed from the throat and laid out with a slap.

Rosie shivers. She needs to find a toilet, which means passing the nursing station. She leaves Kitty and Lomond to continue whatever it is they're doing undisturbed and approaches the open office. There's a nurse with her head bowed over a clipboard and another peering closely at a computer screen, her face screwed up as she wiggles a mouse and clicks at the scroll bar. A young man in a white coat, probably a junior doctor, is standing next to the computer eating a bag of crisps and flicking through a copy of the *Sun*. None of them looks up as Rosie walks past. She feels relieved, as though she's got away with something, and her confidence grows as she marches past again, heading back to the dining room to break up the tryst.

'Hello, Kitty.'

'Oh, Rosie. How are you?'

'Late. Very, very late. I'm so sorry, Dad. For some reason I decided to take the car and the bloody thing broke down. I tried to phone but I couldn't get through so I left a message. Did you get it?'

He shook his head. She sat down in front of him with her back to the window.

'Mmm. Mmmmm.'

'Did you have the meeting?'

Lomond nodded then shook his head.

'Not good, huh?'

He shook his head again and worked his mouth, but instead of opening it clamped shut, tight as a money purse, his lips turning white. He was blowing out of his nose like a bull just before the charge, then he threw back his head with a jolt and his mouth opened. The wanton tongue lolled about, then retreated to lie unswallowed – but only just. Rosie looked across to Kitty, who shrugged and smiled.

'Have you heard anything?'

'Not really, no. There was no one here when I arrived about an hour ago but Jacob has been in with his wife, hasn't he, Lomond?'

'Mmmm.'

Rosie nodded slowly, stopping on an upward turn as though she was expecting Kitty to say more, but she didn't.

'Right. Well, I'd better have a word – find out what was discussed. I'll be back in a minute.'

She patted Lomond's hand then withdrew it quickly as if it was hot.

'Oh! Sorry, Dad. I didn't mean to do that.'

Kitty wasn't sure why Rosie was apologising, but whatever it was it made Lomond smile.

Ah . . . that's rapport, she thought, pleased with the word and wishing she could say it out loud. This is when all that time they spent together counts, father and daughter mulling over the papers and building weird contraptions – megaphones and mousetraps, a wooden rack to hold Rosie's skipping ropes – they even built a crystal set once, but she can't recall whether it worked or not. They would both dedicate all their time to a project and be completely engrossed then suddenly abandon it without a second glance and move on to something else. Kitty never knew what she could tidy up and what shouldn't be touched. It all looked like junk to her but she learned to 'leave well alone' until the dust just couldn't be ignored, and even then she'd check before she moved anything. Every so often Heath would come and stay for a few days and the clutter would be disposed of without permission or ceremony.

Kitty envied Lomond's sister. She would have liked Heath's independence, and she often thought about what her own life might have been like without marriage and children. Unlike May, she found the prospect attractive. When Kitty looked at Heath she saw a kind of freedom. In different circumstances they might have been friends.

She resisted the urge to straighten Lomond up again and smooth out the neckline of his jumper. He wasn't wearing a shirt underneath and his neck looked thin and exposed, a stark showing for a man who always wore a collar and tie. She knew he wouldn't feel properly dressed like that and it troubled her. She'd been doing his washing since he was first admitted and there were two fresh shirts folded in his locker, never worn. She'd complained to May about it over the phone.

'I've put clean shirts in his locker . . . you'd think they'd surmise from that.'

'Well, they don't bother, do they . . . all those buttons.'

They both mused for a moment over a line of tight white buttons and a double cuff.

'I love a man in a collar . . . especially a dog collar.'

'May!'

'Why don't you offer to dress him?'

132

'Me! Oh no. I couldn't.'

'Why not? They do it in China. Cook by the bed and everything. Why don't you ask him?'

'Oh no, May . . . I couldn't.'

She'd thought about it, though. She'd moved through the sequence of bending him forward and carefully pulling his charcoal cashmere over his head, then leaning him back again, his shoulders still broad, his white vest stretched across his chest and the hair on the back of his head all ruffled and sticking out like a sleepy-headed boy. Kitty's blushing thoughts had forced her to stand up and fan herself with a Constable place mat – glad that she was on the phone and not sitting in May's kitchen with only a cup of hot chocolate to hide behind.

WHEN ROSIE came back she had her boyfriend with her.

'Look who I found lurking in the corridor!'

It was the first time Wilson had visited Lomond since his stroke (he doesn't do hospital visits unless he absolutely has to, finding the company of the sick too doleful). In truth, he wasn't visiting now – he was worried about Rosie and wanted to make sure she came home. The *good riddance* moment he'd savoured when she left the flat turned out to be just that – a moment. He'd tried to really sink his teeth into it but when he did, when he bit down hard – swearing and slamming the front door so she'd hear it before she reached the bottom of the stairs – it was gone, displaced by something generous, the sense of concern that he so often felt for her.

He'd been waiting in the car park, watching the entrance and planning to catch her as she left. As more time passed he began to wonder if perhaps he'd missed her, then just when he'd decided to give up and leave he saw her walking up the drive looking like a dog's dinner. He was going to call out but decided against it. She had a feral look about her that suggested any sudden noises or movements might send her running off into the undergrowth. Instead, he watched her as she reached the double doors and pushed one side open. She was about to move through when a small side flank of visitors forced her back out again, her long arm stretched to her fingertips as she struggled to keep the door open. The family trundled past her, oblivious to the fact that their exit had pinned Rosie against the door and forced her into a very awkward stance. When they were clear she descended off her toes and once more began to move through before again having to retreat, this time to give way to a small flock of white-capped nurses, all talking across each other like chattering geese. *Don't ignore her. Let her past, you bitches*, he muttered under his breath. Rosie held her position for a moment or two after they'd gone, then tentatively moved forward, first slow then fast, giving the impression of a surreptitious entry – as if she'd seized the moment to steal through unauthorised. Wilson was left with her after-image still pinned against the door, tiptoed on muddy boots with her coat open and her skirt skew-whiff. Suddenly he felt an overwhelming urge to rescue her. He just wanted to save her, but he wasn't sure from what.

LOMOND ASSUMED from Wilson's face that this was the first time they'd met since the stroke. He recognised the look.

'Hello, sir. How are you?'

He moved forward to shake Lomond's hand but the antici-pated palm didn't move, leaving both men feeling wrong-footed. Instead, Lomond managed to raise his left hand and Wilson held it loosely in his – more of a waggle than a shake, as though he was about to lead him onto the dance floor.

'Good man. Yes. Very good to see you.'

Wilson blustered his way through his discomfort, letting go of Lomond's fingers rather too quickly.

'Excellent.'

'You know Kitty, don't you?'

Wilson turned enthusiastically to Kitty and in a stiff angular motion touched her shoulder. His pomposity was increasing by the minute.

'Ah, yes . . . the famous Kitty! Pleasure to meet you.'

'Hello, Wilson. Nice to see you again, although I have to say I'm not the famous one of the party.'

'Well, that depends how you define famous, Kitty. Your reputation precedes you, or rather, the repute of your border tart. In my book that's a strong claim to fame. Anyone who can create cake deserves to be noted. The celebrated Mrs . . . oh, I'm so sorry, I can't remember your second name.'

'Danvers.'

'Danvers, that's it! Well, there you are – the celebrated Mrs Danvers. Purveyor of cakes and all things—'

'Shut up, Wilson, for God's sake. Sorry, Kitty. I need to explain that Wilson is a time lord. He does his best to conceal this but occasionally he slips up. Clearly he has just slipped into the nineteenth century and is in fact Mr Micawber, for which I can only apologise.'

Kitty briefly continued to be the centre of attention and was thrust from domestic obscurity into the spotlight, her life suddenly a source of great interest. She wasn't sure why such a bright successful young couple should be so interested in the details of her life – when she was born, the demographics of her family, the exact location of her house, what she puts in her border tart, her views on trans fats, the reliability of the local bus service, anything really – but she suspected it was so Wilson didn't have to talk to Lomond, and if she was being used, she didn't mind. It was clear that Wilson had not been prepared for the changes in Lomond, the torpid body and the slack jaw, some muscle wastage already apparent where his right trouser leg has ridden up his calf, the exposed flesh too white and entirely hairless. The wet chin had not gone unnoticed, but it was the slip-slide of the right eye that was Wilson's final undoing. There was something particularly poignant about the loss of a familiar face.

He just couldn't look at him, not yet.

That's the thing about very clever people, thought Kitty (continuing to oblige with a detailed account of route 32), they're not always good at the practical things.

Sticking to the emergent theme, she asked Wilson how he'd got to the hospital.

'I pinched Rosie's car, I'm afraid . . . too lazy to walk.'

'Oh.'

'It's all right, I'm insured.'

'But I thought . . .'

'Well done, Wilson, you've just blown my cover.'

'Cover?'

'Yeah. I told Dad that I was late because the car broke down.'

'Oh yes . . . well . . . yes, it *did* . . . it did break down, *but* . . .'

There was an expectant, benign pause.

'I fixed it! I've not had the chance to tell you, Rosie, but I fixed it with one of your stockings. It was sheer hell (ha ha) but I did it and it worked. Running sweet as a nut now. Strong things, stockings, we should use them more often.'

The unlikely image of Rosie in suspenders hung in the air.

'Hmmm . . . any particular denier?'

'Denier?'

'Thickness.'

'Ah, thickness. Well, the thinner the better, so long as she holds. It's the tensile strength that matters.'

'And size?'

'Depends entirely on the driver. In your case Rosie I'd say short, whereas Kitty here might tend toward a longer length.'

'Colour?'

'Not crucial.'

'So, what are you saying . . . that beige is OK?'

'Yes. Absolutely.'

'American Tan?'

'Well, yes, I'd say so, any colour would do really – although I would suggest there is still a place for aesthetics in motor mechanics.'

'Ah.'

Lights were being switched on, their fluorescence extinguishing everything that was pleasurable – the luminous red of the evening gone, together with the forgiving light that Lomond had watched play across Kitty's face. More visitors were arriving and the trumpet player was wheeled in. Wilson was aware that pockets of hospital air were stirring, releasing God knows what. He was trying not to breathe through his mouth. Kitty announced that the wind was getting up and she needed to go. She pulled a tightly tied Tesco bag out of her giant shopper. Inside was a clean cardigan for Lomond, the one with the square buttons. She reckoned they'd be easier for him to do, and she hoped that if he wore a cardy they would have to sort him out with a shirt. Even they wouldn't leave him with his vest showing. She gave the bag to Rosie and left quickly, having pledged to collect his jumper tomorrow for the wash.

★

ROSIE AND Wilson bowed their heads into the treacherous wind. Just when it seemed to heave a final gust and roll out over the Forth it came back, sending the fresh new daffodils into a blind panic. A nearby tree moved towards the last moments of its antiquity, letting out a long satisfying creak, a sound too dry to emerge from anything living. Its trunk was clad in ivy and there were thick creepers either descending or ascending from ground to highest branch. Wilson rested

137

his hand at the small of Rosie's back and guided her towards the car.

'Come on, let's get out of here before the whole place gives.'

He had to yell a bit to carry his voice over the wind, but not that much; he was overdoing it. He wished he was wearing an overcoat and hanging on to a trilby hat, pressing it against his head the way they do in the old movies. When they reached the car Rosie got in on the passenger side, which was unusual. Normally she would prefer to drive. They each slammed their door shut at exactly the same time, on so precisely the same moment that if you were listening you'd swear only one person got into that car. The thought of that raincoat had slid Wilson into sleuth mode and it occurred to him that such unlikely simultaneousness is the sort of thing that could throw a crime investigation off track completely. There might be circumstances in which it would be useful to engineer that again, maybe during a getaway, although the likelihood of contriving such synthesis was low.

It's the sort of remarkable thing that just can't be recreated.

They drove home in silence, Wilson respecting Rosie's preoccupation. She was dwelling on two small but significant realisations that had arisen from the visit. The first was that she hadn't even *thought* about Lomond's washing, the issue had just never occurred to her. The second was that Kitty had a key to Lomond's house, whereas she didn't. Not only that, but Kitty seemed happy to use the key, and appeared to know the exact location of her dad's knitwear.

Wilson parked the car and turned off the ignition. They sat for a moment, listening to the wind.

'Good-looking woman, that Kitty,' he said.

'Do you think so?'

'Oh yeah, definitely. She reminds me of someone.'

'Who?'

'Oh God, I can't think. She's so like someone.'

'Methuselah?'

'She was in that Graham Swift movie we got out – the one about the bloke's ashes.'

They made a dash for the front door, Wilson's face set with the strain of continued concentration as they climbed the stairs. He opened the door and Rosie followed him in as though she was dragging a great weight across her shoulders. She immediately flung herself on the sofa without removing her coat or boots and clasped her hands neatly underneath her chin, as if in prayer. Wilson was still standing in the hall when he suddenly yelled out.

'Helen Mirren!'

He came through jangling the keys and looked at Rosie – still as a tomb, her eyes closed.

'Helen Mirren. She's *exactly* like Helen Mirren in that film.'

'What film?' she asked, eyes still shut.

He scratched his chin.

'*Last Orders!*'

He got it at last, but she was unimpressed. Only her mouth moved.

'Mine's a gin – just as she comes, babe, no ice.'

Fifteen

L OMOND WATCHES his life like a voyeur. There he is, sagging like a poorly constructed lean-to on the brink of collapse. The question no one seems to pose is whether it would be better to prop him up (which is technically possible), or let nature take its course. All that's needed to finally dismantle him would be a good strong wind blowing in the right direction. He could be wheeled out to Rannoch Moor and left (perhaps attached to a small windsail – just to catch the wind). What better way to go than to lie amongst the sweet-smelling bog myrtle and feel the rain lashing against his cheek, the call of the curlew above his head. In his stillness red deer might graze at his feet, or he might see a mountain hare fleeing from a dangerous sky. As he slips into sleep his last sight on earth might be a golden eagle.

Who could deny a man such an ending?

He might put it this way.

$x - (d + i + p) = y$ (where x = life, d = dignity, i = independence, p = privacy, y = death).

It's not complicated. There are no corollaries or algebraic conditions, yet the option of y is ignored. It is only the 'propping him up' scenario that is discussed, and Lomond is expected to strive towards $x - (d + i + p)$ with the instinct of a spawning salmon.

It's not much of an offer.

His resolve grows stronger with each encounter; every time he's required to interact with something or someone it's his commitment to death that helps him find some small volition. Only now there are some who suspect his efforts are superficial.

You're not really trying, Lomond.

Prove it.

But really, the onus of proof rests with him, just as it always has. It's for him to convince them that he is progressing towards that longed-for journey home, back to his own bed, his beloved chair, and his bath, with its little claw feet.

★

THE DAYS were beginning to stretch after a long benign winter of brief afternoons, cold and bright under a sky of north-east blue, sometimes so short they passed unnoticed. As the young sleep their way through winter, straining towards the dark in a kind of heliotropic inversion, the old wake just the same. They lie in the darkness waiting for dawn. Bright 100-watt bulbs illuminate familiar kitchens, hot gas heating milk, kettles boiling for tea, the low murmur of the World Service, then the click back into darkness.

Heath woke more suddenly than usual (that's how it felt – as if something had woken her). It had been a restless night of gusting winds and inexplicable knocks and bangs, some distant, some close – noises that you just needed to trust. She'd learned long ago to let the night get on with its own business, which it did, posing no threat to her. In fact, Heath believed that night creatures chose to be near folk who lived alone. They made less fuss. They didn't throw on the outside light and peer out the window, urged on by partners who call out instructions from the perceived safety of their beds. Heath could turn over and fall back into rational sleep without giving the noise another thought. It took a lot to unnerve her.

Now she froze. It was the same kind of freeze that befell her last week, only this time she could actually feel her heart, not just the pump of it, but the actual organ; she could feel the whole thing sitting there inside her, surprisingly small and so close to the hand that she pressed against her chest. Her breathing was short and fast and it struck her that she might be about to die. She had never felt quite so precarious. Then, somehow, the pumping eased up slightly – she could feel her heart deflate and relax and she knew the moment had passed.

She looked around the room. The light rose perceptibly and her morbid thoughts came back. The dawning of her brother's death.

Lomond!

Did she say it?

She wrapped herself in lemon candlewick and put on her slippers, then she sat on the edge of the bed and took a small sip of water before getting up and going to the living room. She stood at the open door, turned on the light and looked, searching her memory of the room. Something was different. Her book of phone numbers was lying open beside the telephone. The alphabet pages were held in a spring-action metal casing with a telephone dial on the front. The dial had fourteen holes – one for the index and the rest for the letters. The book was old, full of contact numbers for the dead, but it still worked. When you dialled a letter the book would spring open with a loud *creak*. She liked the noise, it sounded like a corncrake calling from the long grass. *Kkrrexx krexx.*

She crossed the room and looked at the open page; it had Rosie's number on it. She dialled.

ROSIE SNATCHED the phone and drew the receiver back under the duvet. Wilson sat up and listened, expecting the worst.

'Hello?'

'Rosie?'

'Heath?'

'Any news, Rosie?'

'News?'

'About Lomond.'

'What time is it?'

'I don't know.'

'Hang on.'

Rosie heaved herself up from under and peered at the clock radio, her face puckered – baring her teeth.

'Christ.'

She looked again to check.

'Heath, it's . . .'

She lifted her head and looked again.

'It's five o'clock in the morning. In fact, it's not even that. It's night-time.'

'I'm sorry. I was just thinking about Lomond. There isn't any news, is there?'

'No.'

'Did you see him yesterday?'

'Of course I did,' said Rosie, too snippy.

Heath felt relieved, but it was qualified.

'Would they phone you if anything happened . . . or do you think they'd phone Jacob?'

'Jacob, I suppose.'

'And would he phone you?'

'Yes, of course he would!'

She needed to finish.

'And would you phone me, dear?'

'Aw, Heath, please, I need to sleep. Of course I would phone you. Dad's fine. Don't worry. Go back to bed.'

'Promise you would call. It doesn't matter when . . . I don't sleep.'

'I'll call you tomorrow.'

'Do you mean today, or Sunday?'

Rosie sighed audibly. By this time Wilson was asleep again but more bits of her were beginning to wake up and soon she would be in a serious state of consciousness.

'I mean later today, whatever day that is.'

'That's fine, Rosie. I am sorry I woke you. I just needed to check. You get back to sleep now. Night night.'

'Bye.'

Heath replaced the receiver and closed the book.

Krrrrex krexx.

She couldn't remember leaving the book open like that, and she wondered if that was the noise that had woken her. A night noise that couldn't be trusted.

★

ON SATURDAYS Cameron shuts the shop early (it's that kind of town). Usually he goes home and makes cauliflower cheese, which he and his mother eat in front of the television. He cooks, unfettered and without criticism, while Mrs Fraser pursues her own routine. She helps in the lifeboat shop until four o'clock (her relationship with the RNLI is complex and ambivalent, but she keeps that to herself), then she tends the graves of her husband and sons, preferring to do this alone. She cannot tolerate standing by the graveside with Cameron, a great wave of resentment wells up inside her – that she should lose her man and her fine strong boys and be left with the weak one, the late baby that brought bad luck right from the start.

Ina Fraser has no head for facts, but she knows what she knows. *I know what I know,* she says if anyone tries to contradict her version of events, and that's usually the end of it. She says it in such a way as to suggest that there are things that only she knows, but can't reveal. It makes it difficult to argue. The fact that everything had been going well when the family boat went down is a detail long lost in her account of things. Her life was a chain of continuous calamity, and as such, a multiple drowning seemed almost inevitable. If it was going to happen, it would happen to her. In fact, Ina felt chosen. She was married to the sea and her family were a kind of late dowry, built up through her own hard work because her parents had left her with nothing. Despite her misfortune she feels secure in the knowledge that the sea will always provide. Ina holds no truck with notions of overfishing. She believes the sea's bounty is infinite, and has no sense of any connection with the world that lies beyond the horizon (a world that stretches as far as the eye can see is world enough for Ina). *The fish always come back.* She says this with complete conviction – and when others lament the wanton plundering of oceans Ina does not take sides, but she is always clear about where the problem lies.

I blame Albert Finnie.

It's not Albert, Mother, it's Ross.

Even Ina cannot attribute decimated fish stocks to her only surviving son, but she believes that Cameron is at the root of all her misfortune.

She should have realised from the way he cried and cried as a baby. He would not accept comfort, and refused to take her milk. His wailing was enough to turn it sour. When he did suck, his tummy would grow tight as a drum and his screams drove them all demented. The best she could do was swaddle him tightly to stop him flailing about and keep him in the back room so they could at least have some respite from the incessant noise.

He cried like that for nearly a year, then a quietness descended over the house. It took them a while to notice – indeed, Ina forgot all about him. It was only when she opened the door to the room and the pungent smell of Cameron's nappy hit her that she remembered. The stench worsened when she picked him up. He twisted in his pupa, his mouth opening and closing in a noiseless mewing. She often thought how strange it was that the thing she most yearned for, some peace and quiet, could sidle in unnoticed and re-establish itself as if things had never been any different. The baby no longer protested. His little hot face smoothed itself out and his features settled in quite a pleasing way, drawing comment from others, including, for the first time, his own family. Cameron's father tried bouncing him on his knee and Ina clapped her hands and sang 'ally bally', his brothers shook rattles and played *boo*, but their efforts drew little response. They grew irritated at the baby's impassivity and soon lost interest.

When Ina loosened the swaddling the infant failed to emerge from his chrysalis, his unbound arms remaining tight against his body, their preferred arc of movement (when it happened at all) being forwards and upwards. It was Cameron's perpendicular bearing, his way of holding himself in as he moved, that earned him the name of *Cyberman* – a nickname applied without affection to the small humourless automaton whose only redeeming qualities were a handsome face and a compliant nature. Without those, things might have been much worse.

THIS DOESN'T feel like a routine Saturday to Cameron. The day is taking on a new shape and he is moving through it more urgently than usual, propelled not by habit but by a new sense of purpose. Despite chasing for more time he takes an indirect route home so he can pass Heath's house again, just in case Rosie has come back. There's no sign of her car (he's sure she can afford much better than the old black Golf and loves her all the more for having it). He looks through each window as he walks past, turning his head only slightly. The old woman has been less than helpful lately and he's keen not to make his relationship with Rosie too obvious. He marches – his walk starchy and even-paced, feigning nonchalance – but there's nothing to see. When he reaches home he goes straight to his tiny bedroom and closes the door. The atmosphere is stuffy. He un-snibs the window and pushes the lower frame up hard. It jams quickly but leaves an opening of about an inch or two, enough to let in a slice of cold air. He picks up yesterday's underpants and wipes some of the condensation from the glass then tosses them into a corner. The room is still quite dark and will stay in shadow until the last mean hour of daylight washes across the grey harling of the back wall. The frost has cleared but it will be another two months before any warmth penetrates the stone walls, and late May before there is enough sunlight to dry out the window frames. Cameron crouches onto his knees and opens the cardboard drawer of his divan. He takes out a plastic bag and lays the contents neatly across the bed. It's not much of a collection – a few copies of the *Radio Times*; some thin tellin shells, glossy pink and delicate; a yellow-brown scallop shell; a postcard of Edinburgh rooftops and a crumpled five-pound note (the one Rosie used to pay for the crab sticks the week before). He surveys the artefacts briefly, then puts them away again and brings the hall phone into his room. Then he pulls a piece of paper from his trouser pocket, smoothes it out carefully, and dials the number that he's written down.

'Hello?'

Cameron's heart gallops at the sound of her voice.

'Hello?'

147

He can hear her swallow.

'William?'

He puts the phone down and retracts, letting go quickly, as though the receiver's hot. He wipes his mouth with his hand and takes a deep breath, slowing down his pulse. Just as he turns towards the kitchen the phone rings. He flinches, realising that he's forgotten to withhold his number. She must be using the last number redial. He watches the phone until it stops, smiling at the thought of her dialling his number and waiting for him to answer. He imagines her listening to the ring tone – *his* ring tone (not that she knows it) – she's twisting her finger round a lock of her hair and staring into space, as if with enough concentration she can will him to pick up, and he nearly does, but it's not the right time; he needs to see her face to face. Their lives are undeniably connected, he knew that from the moment she gave him that look in the shop.

There's no going back from a look like that – it's the only real thing there is.

★

THERE HAS been a misunderstanding. When Rosie called Heath, as she promised she would, she found herself saying that she would travel up the next day for an overnight, and Wilson made the assumption that he was going too. He was looking forward to it, seeing it as an opportunity to progress the gentle dismantling of Rosie's plan. (If they could survey the house together he would be able to point out all the things that wouldn't work. As a sign of his support he'd throw some creative solutions in amongst all the insurmountables. He was quite good at being devious. It was an underused capacity, one he put down to his strong feminine side, along with his emotional intelligence and a penchant for chocolate.)

He'd thrown some things in a bag and was standing at the window surveying the sky. He rubbed his hands together vigorously in the pre-emptive *I'm the Captain* way that he always did before a journey. Then he made his usual meteorological pronouncement.

'I can see some nimbostratus gathering from the east. Better take the brollies.'

But Rosie didn't want him to come.

'I was thinking I might stay up there tomorrow as well and make a proper start on the house.'

'Oh.'

Wilson dropped his hands, completely deflated. He had a tutorial tomorrow at eleven o'clock and could only go with her if they came back early in the morning.

'I suppose I could catch a train if you took me to the station straight after breakfast,' he mused. It wasn't a question.

'The thing is, Wilson, I think Heath might be a bit thrown if we both go. She's already in a thinly disguised flap about what we're going to eat tonight.'

'Don't you want me to come?'

Rosie shook her head.

'Did I say that? I'm concerned about Heath, that's all. That middle-of-the-night phone call isn't like her. I think she's really upset and worried and I don't want to stress her out any more than she already is. You can't just drop in on an eighty-four-year-old without any warning, you know . . . surely you can see that?'

'I can see that I'm not wanted . . . by either of you.'

'Oh, Wilson, stop being so childish.'

He laughed briefly.

'Fine. Let's turn this on me.'

Neither of them said any more.

The tedium of petty argument swept over them, over-whelmed them, and both wondered in silence if this was a new stage in a process of disintegration. They went into the bedroom and Wilson pointedly unpacked as Rosie packed.

Socks in socks out pants in pants out.

Not too long ago one of them would have broken the impasse, probably Wilson – he was the more generous of the two. He did consider it. He could just throw her on the bed, growl and speak in a French accent, pinning her down so she could feel his strength – but he knew it wouldn't work. She was like a different woman, always flying out the door wearing the wrong clothes and coming back cold and wet, not wanting to talk, or at least not until she'd had three belts of whisky (and counting). She would fall into bed and crash, sleeping with her mouth open, no movement until something woke her – a dead limb needing blood or a lip stuck fast on a dry tooth. By morning her breath was sour. Wilson told himself he didn't need to settle for this. He had options, like that new research assistant from Canada with the red hair and the slightly small but very pert breasts. She always had that zingy fresh smell that you only smelt in other people's showers, never your own. She definitely fancied him; they had a bit of a cryptic email thing going on. Also, she got his jokes. He could bed her no problem.

By Christmas he might be headed for Vancouver and a new life.

Why not?

Here's why.

Rosie from the radio dancing the fandango in a tight black dress.

Rosie clicking her pinkie joints at the scary bits in a film.

Rosie fielding a debate on Voltaire and the theory of optimism.

Rosie's face when she looks at a baby.

Rosie sitting in the kitchen looking at pictures of fairy cakes.

Rosie's fairy cakes.

Rosie being sick.

Rosie crying when ET is found in a ditch looking like a pickled colon.

Rosie's head bent over a book.

Rosie telling him to fuck off when he spies on her through keyholes.

Rosie waving from the window of a train as it pulls out, taking the world with her.

SHE ZIPS up the bag and eventually finds the car keys.

'Abyssinia.'

'Yeah.'

Wilson is pointedly unhurried. He looks up from his paper and notices she's forgotten the umbrella, but it's too late – she's gone.

Sixteen

I MAKE myself look to the right. More than once I've forgotten, then realised I've just passed one of the engineering wonders of the world without so much as a glance. Huge sections are under wraps and it's hard to distinguish where the scaffolding ends and the bridge begins amongst the lattice-work of girders and great steel struts. In the past I have even failed to notice my own passage through it on the train, rattling about in a great metal cage high above the guillemots and gannets without so much as raising my head from yet another bright new superfine, eximious book, which is – according to a range of gushing, prize-winning authors – dazzling, extraordinary, moving, magnificent, exquisite, unsparing, compassionate, profound. Yeah, right. Over-hyped but well dressed in a quirky jacket with ballyhoo stitching. Read and weep. If it wasn't for the fact that I am myself complicit in peddling the stuff I'd go straight to trading standards.

I feel a bit like a teenager again, peeled bare and sore to the touch. When I met Wilson I wasn't looking for anything. Well, actually I was, I was looking for my coat after attending an illustrated talk by someone from a family of famous explorers. It was a Saturday night. I hadn't realised that my coat had slipped through the back of my chair and I was caught in a tight circular search. Wilson said I looked like a cat struggling to commit to the perfect spot.

'Is this yours?'

He'd held up the coat, a heavy camel thing with brown acetate lining that sagged below the hemline, and that was it – one impostor rumbling another amidst what was generally an authentic gathering of like-minded people who no doubt had all climbed Kilimanjaro. We were immediately bound by the certainty that neither of us would ever do anything like that. After a few drinks he walked me home and I invited him in for a cuppie before his long walk back to Leith. He held his teacup with two hands and I could tell that we were both quite excited. There was a sense of something happening that didn't need to be rushed. He didn't seem interested in my flat – there was none of that scanning the artefacts and making judgements – although his last comment as he was leaving suggested he'd at least made some observations in the bathroom.

'I see you're a bit of a conchologist.'

'Yes.'

And then he left.

I was ridiculously pleased that I knew what the word meant. I'm not really a conchologist, although I do collect shells and I like to arrange them in groups. I find great comfort in a jam jar full of striped limpets. It seemed extraordinary that only the week before I had read the word *conchologist* for the first time on a headstone when I visited Highgate cemetery (I could even remember the name of the deceased – George Brettingham Sowerby). At the time the connection excited me. It felt like there was an inevitability to Wilson and me.

Now as I drive north I can feel all the bits of my life disconnecting.

Maybe that's inevitable too.

THERE'S SOMETHING gradual about the way the bridge ends that tells me there's rain ahead. It starts less than a mile into Fife, and by the time I reach Heath's it's pouring. I turn off the ignition and watch it through the window. In the east a downpour such as this is given the respect it deserves. Now this *is* dazzling, extraordinary, moving, magnificent, exquisite, unsparing, compassionate, profound. I want to stand in it with my face turned up and my mouth open, but I know it'll be cold and I haven't brought my hairdryer. I don't fancy my chances with Heath's Morphy Richards, even if it is still intact (complete with hose and hood for hands-free drying). I remember the first time I brought Wilson here, a spontaneous visit on a sunny bank holiday in May. There was no answer at the front door so we walked round the back and saw Heath through the window. She was wearing a pastel-blue hood that was connected to a remote dryer unit via a flexible hose. The hose was slung over her shoulder like a handbag. Her singed ears stood proud and pink and the radio was turned up very loud to counteract the noise of the 'noise-less' induction motor. She was chopping rhubarb.

'If I ever get like that, shoot me.'

Wilson commented that in such circumstances at least my hair would look nice for the funeral.

I suppose that indicates some kind of commitment – talking about old age as if we'll still be together. Back then the notion thrilled me.

THE NOISE of the rain on the car roof is overwhelming, fixing me to the spot. If I looked in my rear-view mirror right now and saw a juggernaut thundering towards me, or a tsunami rolling over the horizon, I don't think I could move; it would be more pressing to stay put. I'm having an ontological moment, a slight jarring of the senses that needs a few quiet minutes to smooth itself out. These might be the most important moments of our lives, monastical moments of change where we come out slightly different. As I interrupt myself with this unoriginal thought something outside catches my eye. I wipe the side window and peer through. There is a man looking at me from the other side of the road. His arms pressed neatly down his sides, like a soldier standing to attention. He's wearing a heavy jacket but his head is uncovered and his hair is glistening wet and so dark that even from here I can see a bold fringe of cows' licks framing his face. He waves at me then lightly jogs across the road to the car, his arms still incongruously tucked in and straight. I roll down the window and he shakes his head to clear the water from his face and neck, his hair springing into little rats' tails.

'Hello, Rosie. Some day, eh?'

I'm surprised that he knows me, then I recognise him from the fish shop.

'Oh, it's you! I didn't recognise you with your clothes on.'

Seventeen

DESPITE THE clammy heat of the ward, April kept her coat on. She wanted to keep her gloves on too, and would have preferred to wrap her scarf across her mouth in a kind of makeshift air filter, but she knew this might not be acceptable hospital etiquette. Lomond was lying down, apparently asleep, and April was poised on the edge of a plastic chair, appearing to pivot on the tiny kitten heel of her left boot, like a spinning top at rest.

She watched her father-in-law in silence, smiling at him with the kind of smile she would give an unattractive baby, then she eased back slightly and quietly pulled out her notebook from her bag. The leather notebook creaked as she opened it. She bared her teeth and looked up, but Lomond did not stir. His mouth gaped, quite widely, and there was no colour in his lips. Some crusty deposits had silted up around the edges of his mouth. April edged forward an inch or two and peered at his face, her flared nostrils on guard. He unexpectedly exhaled and when the stench of his breath hit her she recoiled quickly, covering her mouth with the notebook.

This was April's 'shift' within a carefully drawn-up timetable that she now examined closely, just for something to do. A few unintentional bed-side collisions with Kitty had led Jacob to suggest that what was needed was one of April's Charts. She was beginning to regret the colour coding since Rosie was proving unreliable and Kitty attended even when she wasn't scheduled to, rendering the chart awash with orange (Kitty) and splodges of drab yellowy-brown (should be Rosie but Kitty attends instead) where it was originally green (Rosie). It was all turning into a bit of a mish-mash. April scrutinised the fluorescent tartan, ruing her decision to use highlighters when pencil and rubber and a numerical or alphabetical key would have done the job better.

A sudden bold stroke of white swept in front of her.

'Oh!'

'Sorry, hen. Did I give you a fright there?'

April wasn't sure if the woman was a nurse or an auxiliary. This was one of the most frustrating aspects of the hospital – no one declared themselves. Half the time you didn't know who you were dealing with. It seemed reasonable to ask, but Jacob's habit of insisting on name and status had caused considerable rancour. The rules were so different here, radically so, and in consequence, offence was easily and unwittingly caused. Each encounter between the uniformed and the ill-informed held the potential for varying levels of resentment, expressed ultimately through the sometimes protracted claws of patient care (a tight grip, the small shove – voices too loud and curtains left open, shaming the sick).

It was best not to rattle them.

This one seemed to know what she was about, her stentorian voice rousing Lomond from sleep – eyes open, and seemingly alert, yet still the gaping mouth. April moved out of the way, perching herself on a chair right at the end of the bed, casting about for a focus while the nurse propped him up and began to do something using bits and pieces from her little tray. She had the nonchalance and competent air of a busy senior stylist, the type who can command compliance without resorting to eye contact.

'Let me take you through this so you can do it yourself.'

April looked up, puzzled, and was alarmed to realise that the nurse was talking to her. She pressed her hand against her clavicle and raised her eyebrows.

'Don't look so worried, it's quite simple really.'

The nurse smiled, her hand poised in mid-air. She was holding a wet swab and beckoning April to come closer. But April couldn't move. Her expression was fixed and her hand stayed on her chest. The nurse carried on.

'There's nothing to be scared of. You just have to be really gentle and make sure that his mouth is clean. It's important not to let it get dry and sore, otherwise it could become infected. Once I've cleaned away all this nasty dry stuff from round the edges I'll get you to put some Vaseline round his lips. We'll have him looking lovely again in no time at all – eh, Lomond?'

The nurse had turned her back and was speaking as she worked, which gave April a chance to recover herself.

'When we've done this and sorted him out I'll show you where we keep the crushed ice cubes to keep him refreshed, then you can just help yourself. Right . . . now, there we are. Your turn.'

She stood back with her arm outstretched, like a lollipop lady.

'But I'm not a blood relative.'

'Oh, that's all right. It's not a requirement, we're not that fussy, are we, Lomond?'

He could close his mouth now, but it was painful. The surface of his tongue felt as though it had been shredded with a fine mesh cheese-grater. He longed for some relief, but the impasse between the two women was complete. Lomond looked away, emitting soft gulps and clicks from the back of his throat.

'I'm sorry, Nurse, but I'm not very good at this sort of thing. I'm going to have to leave him in your extremely capable hands.'

April stood, still with her notebook, and glad she hadn't taken off her coat. She grabbed her bag and gloves and left, holding her determined smile and impassive expression for as long as she could. (She had rounded several corners before the hot tears turned her eyes pink, drawing compassionate glances from passing strangers.) When she stopped to pull out a hankie someone touched her on the shoulder, making her jump.

'April? Are you all right?'

'Kitty! Oh, thank God you're here.'

Kitty's eyes widened.

'What is it? Has something happened to Lomond?'

'Um. Oh, no, he's fine, he's just the same.'

'Oh,' she blew out a long breath, 'thank goodness. You had me really worried there for a minute.'

April blew her nose and rubbed it vigorously.

'You seem upset. Is there anything I can do?'

'No, no . . . I'm fine . . . just being silly. Are you on your way in, only you're not on the rota?'

'No, well, May and I have been up visiting a friend of ours – gallstones – so I thought I'd pop in while I'm here. You haven't met my sister, have you? May, this is Lomond's daughter-in-law, April, Jacob's wife. April, this is May.'

At that precise moment April suddenly realised that she hadn't even said goodbye to Lomond when she left. Her hand shot to her mouth.

'Oh, God!'

She stared at Kitty, unseeing, and the sisters watched and waited, unable to predict what might come next. April closed her eyes and sighed.

'Oh, no.'

She dropped her hand but kept her eyes shut and shook her head as she pulled on her gloves.

159

'Oh, well. It's done.'

When she opened her eyes she thought she was seeing double. They all paused in mutual confusion, the sisters not knowing what had been done, and still alert to any possibility.

'I need to rush. I've got to cover the shop for the next hour and a bit. Nice to see you, Kitty – oh, and thank you for coming.'

She touched Kitty's sleeve lightly, then, having unwittingly insulted each sister in a particular way, she left.

WHEN SHE reached the shop she closed the door behind her by facing inwards and leaning her back against it, letting her head rest on the central wooden panel for a minute. This wasn't the first time she'd fled to her sanctuary of freewheeling corset rails and a precisely ordered stockroom full of neatly boxed bras.

It was nearly twenty years since April began her training as a corsetière and for most of that time girdle was a dirty word. Now it was coming back. Women had found pride in their shape again and suddenly there was a market for contemporary versions of the Waspie and the All-in-One. At last there was a call for all the skills April had to offer, and her clientele were getting younger every day – graduates of the Wonderbra with a growing interest in old-fashioned underwear. Not that there was anything old-fashioned about April's stock. She still kept a decent line of high-control support garments for her merry widows, but things had moved on. She did a brisk trade in waist nippers and mini-slips with built-in briefs, and Truform's elasticated bone belts were flying off the shelf since she put that notice in the window about pulling in the waist by a clear two inches (it's true).

The shop was a present from Jacob to mark the new millennium and to help April take her mind off things (she'd just withdrawn from IVF at the last minute). In market terms the timing couldn't have been better, and what had been created as a distraction became a small business success. It was, quite literally, a dream come true for April. She'd been transfixed as a pre-pubescent girl by the vivacity of the woman on the television who wore the eighteen-hour girdle. Each Playtex ad was like a little story – snapshots of the life April wanted – and she still considered them as great performances (oh . . . the shock of going out to dinner without wearing a girdle then realising that she *was* wearing it after all!). She had toyed with the idea of tracking down the actress for the opening of 'April's' until Jacob pointed out that she would probably be in her fifties at least and what happens if she's fat as a Christmas goose with sagging breasts and a huge arse?

Jacob!

April thought it unlikely, and she didn't necessarily see being over fifty as a problem, but she supposed he was right. In terms of body re-shaping there is a limit to what Lycra can achieve (although those limits are much wider than most people realise – and comfortable too, insists April – things have come a long way since latex). In the event, the shop opened to a near-deserted street on a cold wet day in March with a slate sky that turned the pink bunting grey and a wind that played the striped awning like a timpani drum. The local beauty queen was Jacob's idea. When Miss Prestonpans (38–24–36) cut the huge ribbon it hit the pavement with a slap, like an old floor cloth slopped from a bucket. Five people looked on from a nearby bus stop, their umbrellas jostling for air space as an accordionist wearing an anorak and a flat cap squeezed out a few bars of 'The Campbells are Comin', then a bus came along and uplifted the whole audience, together with the lone reporter from the local paper, who seized the opportunity to leave on the number 19 (having asked only one question – *Why not wait till April, April?*). The final straw occurred when April's satin shoes were doused by the spray thrown up from the rear wheels of the departing bus.

'Stop! Stop!'

Everyone thought she was calling after the bus.

'Stop playing!'

The accordionist stopped squeezing, unhitched his hands and pulled his hood up over his cap.

She turned to Jacob and pointed to the musician.

'*You* said he was French!'

Jacob looked at the man in the anorak.

'Pierre?'

'Ah never said ah wis French.'

'But you're called Pierre.'

'That's just ma stage name, pal.'

A small tailless dog trotted across their path and cocked his leg against the potted box hedging.

'Oh!'

April ran into the shop, crying. She should have stuck to her guns. She knew the Playtex lady was a brilliant idea. It would have given the whole thing a media-savvy slant. Maybe Rosie could have swung a plug for them on the show, or might even have considered doing a retrospective piece. She felt confident that the lady, whoever she was, would still look good. *Class lasts*, thought April, and it would have been a great product promotion for the eighteen-hour girdle range. Most people didn't realise that they were still being made, still with a fantastic woven rubber fabric that made them unique. April had included them in her stock and could have extolled the virtues of Spanette to the adoring crowd that would have undoubtedly turned out to see the actress (look at the Bisto lady, everybody loves her).

She could have made it happen.

Standing in the empty shop, sniffing and squeaking, she stared at the black and gold balloons bumping and bobbing in the draught that she'd stirred up when she slammed the door. Someone tried the handle and she quickly snibbed the lock, then pressed her back against the door, keeping her hand on the handle. Her head began to ache and the skin around her eyes and across the bridge of her nose felt tight. Slowly she released her grip, unbuttoned her coat and smoothed out the creases in her skirt.

She hadn't meant to turn on her heels – she wanted to be more resilient – but having done so it frustrated her, it really did, the way some things always seemed to outrun her.

Like infertility, loneliness, and death.

Jacob paid off Pierre and Miss Prestonpans, then leaned into the door of the shop, tapping gently on the glass and waiting for the sound of the snib.

'Please, pumpkin. Let me in.'

★

WHEN ROSIE tumbled through the door her cheeks were red even though the bolt from the car was only a few yards. She hugged Heath, babbling, but didn't mention Cameron, which Heath thought strange since she'd watched them (quite openly) from the living-room window. She'd been looking out at the downpour when the car drew up and she saw it all – Rosie sitting stock-still behind the wheel in one of her trances, and him emerging from the trees opposite like the third man. Heath wanted to say something about her growing unease around the Fraser boy – all those questions, and the way he'd stalked round the house yesterday, looking in the windows – but because her niece had obviously chosen not to mention him she felt she couldn't either. To disregard Rosie's discretion would be like exposing her. Strange, though, there was a strangeness to it – and when she looked at Rosie she saw the silent child who would sit in the dust and play for hours with just a few pieces from a yellow plastic tea set, mouthing all the parts and speaking to no one.

Reluctantly, she said nothing.

'It's freezing out there. Any chance of a hot toddy?'

Rosie opened the dresser and began to make herself a drink. Although she was smaller and slighter than Ethel there were times when she looked and sounded just like her. She could make a movement so evocative it would throw Heath completely. Now, seeing her there – the way she poured the whisky, with a certain brightness in her eyes – it was as if Ethel were back. Lomond would still be outside, gathering up the bags and unstrapping the babies from the car.

IT WAS clear to Heath that Rosie was drinking again. That night she finished the whisky off with a sherry chaser. At nine o'clock her eyes were bright with hope and mirth, at half past nine she loved Heath more than she knew (but would say no more about it, her hand raised to indicate it was a feeling beyond words), quarter to ten brought optimism, then ten o'clock despair.

By bedtime she was drunk and there was nothing left except guilt, a dark sediment that stuck to the bottom of her glass like threads of blood.

Heath helped her to bed then made herself some hot milk. The phone rang, but when she picked it up the line went dead. She was worried about Rosie and wanted to call Lomond, but couldn't, or didn't (and felt bad about it, treating him as though he's already gone). There was no one else she could contact. Jacob was out of the question. His advice would be to do nothing, a position he would describe as caring rather than abdicant – 'tough love' he called it, but the gloat would play across his lips, shut tight against a mouth full of poisonous frogs.

She considered phoning Wilson but was unsure. Had they

been married things would be clearer, there would be a husband instead of a boyfriend. As it stood, Heath didn't know what was happening there, things seemed to be on the wane. Rosie had made no mention of him when she talked about moving Lomond to the summer house. Heath shook her head then quietly opened the door of the spare room and looked in. She thought the sound of the phone might have woken her but Rosie was lying on her front with her cheek against the mattress, still asleep. She was snoring lightly, breathing somewhere between her nose and the roof of her mouth, the pillows discarded and the duvet pulled well up against the cold. Heath picked up some clothes and a pillow from the floor, an action that echoed through the last three decades – tucking in the little girl who spoke with her eyes and veered between impetuosity and wariness, more dual-istic than her twin brothers. Both quickfired and cautious, you never knew with Rosie what you were going to get.

It was a particular crowding that Heath thought might be resolved when Rosie began to speak again, an event that occurred without warning, and that was met without fuss (for fear that to acknowledge it might be to destroy it). Her voice thrilled them – it was a blessing, too sacred to stare at. They responded of course, but calmly, assiduously declining to look, ignoring it the way you ignore a blackbird that has just hopped into your kitchen.

She chattered and sang – so quick – high notes and low, but still as changeable as ever, confident one minute and diffi-dent the next, her doubts rotating round her exuberance like a small companion star.

It seems the mutism was a red herring.

Heath quietly closed the door and went back to the kitchen. Her milk had grown a skin. She tipped it down the sink and paused to look through the window. She was trying to decide what to do for the best, but it was difficult when there was no one to talk to. If only William would come home and bound through the door in wet boots, trailing mud across the carpet.

Ah, William – where are you, my sweet?

Eighteen

CAMERON WOKE at dawn and there she was in his head, as though she'd been waiting for him all night without moving. He resumed thinking about her even before he opened his eyes. She had become a steady presence, his intimate, observing everything he did and listening to everything he said. This meant of course that he must do things well and carefully consider what to say.

He made his mother a cup of tea, laid it out on a tray with a folded napkin of kitchen roll under the mug, and knocked gently on her bedroom door.

'Mother?'

'Uh?'

'Can I come in?'

'What is it?'

'I've brought you some tea.'

'Why?'

'I just thought you'd like a cup.'

He opened the door and placed the tray on the bedside table.

'What's this in aid of?'

His mother eyed him suspiciously, her thin mouth turned down at the corners, her hair flat under a brown tight-mesh net. She looked like an old man.

'Nothing. It's just a cup of hot tea. Save you getting up.'

'You never make me a cuppa tea.'

'Well, there's always a first time. Isn't there? See you tonight.'

He looked up and smiled at her, leaving her to wonder what was going on. Ina turned the napkin over and reinforced the neat fold, then sipped her tea. It was just the way she liked it, sweet and black, but she couldn't enjoy it. It occurred to her for the first time that he might be planning to leave her, but she dismissed the idea. Where on earth would he go? Cameron pulled on his boots and went out, taking care to close the front door quietly. The neighbour's cat sat on the wall and tracked him with a lazy, unimpressed gaze. He stopped to stroke it and the cat arched its back in a reflex action, its electric tail twitching in a high-voltage surge. He walked on and the cat hunched up again, tucking in its front paws, each precisely placed, and its eyes half shut but still watching.

Already Rosie was making him a better person.

BY ELEVEN o'clock he realised he was the last man on earth. Something catastrophic had occurred in the forty-five minutes since the last customer had left the shop – he just knew it. The key to the catastrophe (there is always a key, usually a single element, or a form of energy, which is paradoxically essential to life) was heat emissions, and Cameron was the sole survivor because at the exact moment when the heat-seeking reactor sought and found every warm-blooded configuration and destroyed it, he'd been standing in his walk-in freezer sorting out the seafood salads.

Cameron stood behind the front door of the shop and stared out of the small glass window on to the grey, lifeless street. The window was high set, beginning just below eye level, and his disembodied stare had frightened off many an occasional browser (drawn in by that very window, the stark authenticity of it, and the ancient wooden door – bolted and strapped).

168

If this were real he'd turn the lights off and pop back into the freezer, just in case there was a second strike. Cameron played out the 'last survivor' scenario more than most, working it through further than the average Joe. He wasn't afraid of solitude, and believed he could be content with a simple life. He would turn his back to the world and live on the coast, facing the sea. It would not be such a huge adjustment.

Only today it felt different. Today it was a most unwelcome scenario and he wanted rid of it.

Peering from his porthole was like peering from the belly of a great fish that lived on the ocean floor, where the darkness remained impenetrable and infinite. He felt trapped. Cameron could no longer hide in his freezer during Armageddon. Now he had someone else to think about, someone to save, even if it cost him his own life. How can the very thing that makes life worthwhile also jeopardise it so seriously? He had never borne witness to love – but clearly it was a very dangerous thing.

★

I WISH people would just say what they're thinking. I woke with a blinding headache and scant sympathy from Heath. A distinct frosting on the cornflakes, I'd say, and a few looks that I just couldn't read.

'What is it?'

'Nothing, dear. How's the coffee?'

'Lovely.'

Which is where I contradict myself about saying what you think. What is she using – Camp? I could show off and try to redeem myself by encouraging a bit of reminiscence (it never fails with anyone over forty). Recently we did a piece on retro foods – Jammie Dodgers and Marmite, that kind of thing – so I happen to know a bit about Camp. I don't usually remember anything we cover but for some reason I do recall a statistic here, which I think I can now taste – sugar flavoured with chicory and a few drops of coffee (4 per cent to be exact). I move to the window by the sink and stand with my back to her, looking out and pretending to drain my cup before I rinse it under the tap.

That's when I spotted it.

'There's a bag of something hanging on your front gate.'

'Really?'

She comes to the window and we both stare at it. Heath has no idea what it might be.

'I'll get it.'

I bring it in and place it on the table. We sit down and look at it. I'm waiting for Heath to open the bag, but she doesn't move.

'Aren't you going to open it?'

'It'll be for you, Rosie.'

'For me? Why would it be for me?'

'It'll be from the Fraser boy.'

'How do you know? Did you see him?'

'No. I just know.'

We play out the moment, looking at the Co-op bag and wondering what kind of kill it might hold.

'It can't be fish on a Monday. Maybe it's a rabbit?'

'Open it.'

I pull something out about the size of a brick. It's wrapped in old newspaper. I pick it up and weigh it on the flat of one hand.

'Mmmm, heavy. What d'ya reckon?'

'I've no idea.'

I unwrap it carefully, as though it's my favourite piece of china, something irreplaceable that has tracked me across continents.

'Cheese!'

We both gasp loudly and laugh with such evident relief that I wonder what on earth we were expecting. I look back in the bag for a note, but there's nothing.

'Are you sure this isn't for you? Maybe from one of the neighbours?'

'Positive.'

'Mmm . . . how sweet.' (Sweet is not quite the word I'm looking for.)

The cheese is in a cold sweat. We look at it with disdain and I know we're both thinking about Cameron. There is a faint tracing of newsprint on the waxy surface that gives it a slight gorgonzola look, but that doesn't disguise its true character – a very yellow, very wet, grubby, processed cheddar.

The thought of eating it makes me gag.

Heath cups the paper back round it, carefully, as if it might release deadly spores, then she puts it back in the carrier bag and drops it in the bin. She washes her hands, saying nothing. I've agreed to meet him later but I can't bring myself to mention it. We're going to see *Goodbye Lenin*.

I must be mad.

Technically, the rain has stopped, but the haar has thickened into a damp fleece, dimly illuminated by an obscured, weak sun. Birds gather and wait, cormorants and dark shags brooding, hunched up and miserable, unable to fish through the cloud. The gulls move inland, barking and laughing across the cabbage fields. There's nothing else moving except a few curlews wheeling blindly through the air, calling out as the world closes in. Visibility can only be a matter of 20 or 30 feet. It is a familiar kind of day, but still extraordinary, a day that demands to be watched.

I can tell that Heath still feels unsettled about the cheese.

'I'd guess that's going to last a day or two,' she says, then draws back from the window and sits down beside me at the table, still looking out. I'm reading the pets column in the local paper.

'Have you ever had a dog?' I ask.

'No. Mother was allergic, or so she claimed. I suspect it was an excuse to dissuade me and Lomond from any hopes of getting one. I always wanted one, though. I used to dream of getting a Dandy Dinmot or whatever they're called. Don't ask me why. I think I just liked the name – Dandy Dinmot. It became one of those things that represented something else . . . independence probably, or growing up.'

'So why didn't you ever get one?'

'Oh, I don't know. The right one never came along, I suppose. Or perhaps I never quite grew up.'

'You! You are the most grown-up person I know.'

'Well . . . life has a way of running off in directions you never planned for.'

'Hmm.'

Now I'm thinking of all the things Heath's done for me. It's never occurred to me that she might have preferred another, different life. Heath stretches in her chair, bending her elbows and flexing her arms in a classic yawn. Usually she would take a nap at this time in the morning, a travel rug wrapped round her knees – like an old woman. It must be awkward sharing her little house with me, even for a day or two. There's really just room for her and a Dandy Dinmot.

I go back to the paper.

'Look, here's one . . . listen to this. *Nine-year-old Jack Russell looking for his final hearth. Good nature. No children, cats or other dogs.* How can a dog that doesn't like children, cats or other dogs be described as good-natured?'

'You're not looking for one, are you?'

'I've been thinking about it, for when Dad and I move into the house. I'll have the time and it would be company for him when I'm out. I'd need you to help me, though, take it out and stuff if I'm away. Would that be OK? Not that I plan to be away.'

'Of course.'

Heath's looking at me now, trying to figure me out (as am I. I don't know why I said that about the dog).

'Rosie, do you think you've really thought this through?'

'Well . . . it would be nice to have a pooch, and look what happens if you procrastinate. Nothing. It doesn't happen. You could have just gone out and got one. Why not? You still could. You could try for some decrepit three-legged thing, or go for the good-natured-but-keep-him-away-from-kids Jack Russell and dedicate your time to teaching him some new tricks.'

'I wasn't talking about the dog, Rosie, I was talking about Lomond.'

Ah . . . here we go. Et tu?

'Oh. Don't you think I can do it?'

'That's not what I said.'

'But is it what you think?'

Heath doesn't answer straight away. We both look out the window at nothing, and behind that – somewhere in the fog – there is me and Dad living in the summer house, a series of impossibilities defining each day.

'I don't think this is about you, Rosie. I just can't see how anyone could manage him at the moment.'

'But in time, Aunty. It's not even been a month yet and they say that rehabilitation takes at least six months. Personally I don't think it ever stops. I don't think there's a limit to what the brain can achieve if you just keep trying. I know he has a long way to go but the brain can regenerate.'

'No, it can't, Rosie . . . that's the thing. Brain tissue that dies in a stroke can't regenerate. I'm the last to be discouraging, God knows I want him back, I can't bear to see him so hopelessly dependent, but you have to be realistic. It doesn't help anyone to deny the obvious. Jacob thinks that maybe—'

'You've spoken to Jacob?'

'Of course I've spoken to Jacob. Just as I've spoken to you.'

Just as? There's nothing just as about it. How can she equate speaking to Jacob with speaking to me?

'Has he been here?'

'No, but we keep in touch over the phone.'

'Well, that's news, isn't it? He never phoned you before.'

She gives me a look – a frown, and lips pressed in disappointment rather than disapproval. I immediately feel churlish and try to get back to the point, but it's difficult with my saboteur brother smirking in the background.

'OK, so maybe regeneration is the wrong word. But the brain can learn to do things differently. There might be things that will come back with a bit of practice. We just don't know what we're dealing with yet.'

Now she looks sorry for me. I need to stop looking at her. I stand up and automatically go and fill the fancy retro-style kettle (a Christmas present from Jacob and April – it has a silver whistle over the top of the spout and looks daft in this kitchen).

'So, what does Jacob say? That I'm hopeless, I suppose.'

'He's worried.'

'Ha! I bet he is.'

Worried about wagging tongues.

Tongues that tell.

I switch on the kettle and rest my hand near the base, waiting for it to warm.

'He thinks the best thing would be a move to Craigmalloch, at least until we're clearer about his recovery.'

'And you think Dad'll recover in Craigmalloch? You think he'll find the inspiration to recover in *Craigmalloch,* sitting amongst demented old women who can't even recognise their own children?'

'It would only be for a trial to see if he likes it, and then—'

I start to laugh.

'To see if he *likes* it! To see if he . . .'

I can hear my voice – high and thin, then it gets squeezed out altogether. Even though I've got more to say there's just no room for it; something is surging up from my chest and I have to close my mouth and my throat to keep it down. I screw my face up tight. It's all in my throat now, pressing behind my ears, and there's a terrible pain somewhere, and my shoulders are shaking, really shaking, and Heath puts her arms round me and I pull my hand from the kettle because it's too hot and that nearly knocks us over so she has to grab me tighter and then there's a long persistent cry somewhere and I don't know whether it's me or the kettle and it climbs and climbs until it's too high for us to hear it but you know it's still going on, screaming in another stratosphere.

★

I'VE JUST been put to bed, clothed and sober, my face wiped with a warm damp flannel. My hairline is wet and there are crystals of salt under my eyes, irritating the skin. My eyelashes feel crusty at the roots and my body is hollow. For some reason I feel like one of the Railway Children – the *Daddy my Daddy* one – tucked up with a temperature and tended to by a mother in a high ruffle-necked blouse, having just tried (and failed) to do something terribly grown up. Something brave but futile that I only partly understand.

I can hear Heath. She's in the kitchen trying to be quiet – closing cupboard doors very slowly – and I picture her flinching at every sound, creaking hinges and the inevitable last click of the catch.

Why doesn't she just leave them open till we're done with this?

Nineteen

WHEN THE phone rang he leapt on it too quickly.
'Rosie?'

But it wasn't her. It was her producer, Frank.

'I take it she's still AWOL?'

Wilson resented that. He responded calmly with a description of Rosie's bedside vigil, fibbing for her again. It must have sounded convincing because Frank apologised.

It's been over three weeks since Rosie left the studio and she's still not responding to calls from work. She never talks about it (it's as if she's had a phantom stroke – she can't remember that she had a life before). Contractually she's OK (the GP has it covered), but it's the kind of business that expects more. Her audience expects more. They want to know where she is and when she'll be back. They miss her throaty laugh.

He misses her throaty laugh.

The new anchor is a young presenter from Motherwell. She comes with good credentials – a journalist and field reporter, the daughter of a famous crime writer who has herself featured on the show many times – and you can tell she's hungry. Marina seems at ease with any and every type of guest or topic. She's clearly doing her homework. Wilson has grown to appreciate the signs of a well-prepared link, or rather, the signs of an ill-prepared one – poor research and over-reliance on a brief. In the two broadcasts he's listened to since Rosie left he's formed the opinion that Marina, if anything, over-prepares. He thinks having too much background can get in the way of listening, so the interviewer sometimes fails to hear what the guest has just said. They're too busy formulating the next clever question, and sometimes complete gems slip through their fingers.

Rosie understands this. They talked about it not that long ago.

'You're us, Rosie. That's your job.'

'Us?'

'Us. Us. The provincial listener who feels ambivalent about their place in the world. We don't want to be talked down to but we don't want too clever either. Yes, we want some social conscience stuff that raises a good cause, but then we want to settle down to something we're really interested in . . . like the truth behind Lena Zavaroni's lobotomy.'

'Leucotomy.'

'Leucotomy. You sure? Anyway, wielding a scalpel through the brain of a wee lassie from Rothesay . . . that was brilliant.'

'Yeah, that was a good one. Hard to do, though. There was a lot more to that story that they didn't want us to touch.'

'Like what.'

'Mmmm. I'm not supposed to say.'

'OK. Don't.'

'They wanted to keep the focus on the illness, not the cause.'

'Which was?'

'Well, put it this way, it was nothing to do with the pressures of being famous at the tender age of ten.'

'But surely that was the main argument?'

'Exactly. That's what I hate about my job. At the end of

the day the decision makers aren't really interested in the truth, which I wouldn't mind so much if they didn't dupe the listeners into thinking otherwise. Its fundamental business is deception, which is different from story telling. I wish they'd just . . .'

She'd trailed off. Wilson never put pressure on her to discuss material that wasn't used. Sometimes he'd listen to a show and suddenly understand the mood she'd been in, but she never really talked about it. He knew she pulled out of a retrospective about Jamie Bulger last year – just refused to touch it, irrespective of consequences. She struggled with anything to do with children's suffering, it was her blind spot (quite a weakness for a journalist). A thought suddenly crossed his mind.

Maybe she jumped before she was pushed?

The speculation pulled Wilson out from the fugue state that had kept him on the sofa for most of the afternoon.

He was determined not to call her this time. Why should he?

The pile of marking on the coffee table had not been touched. He really needed to get on with it. He was hungry but couldn't be bothered making anything. He was cold but didn't want to light a fire. All he did was go to the window and stare out at the rain and the distant hillside necropolis. Everything ground to a halt when she wasn't there. She wouldn't believe the empty space she left behind each time she flew out the door with nothing but a pair of pants and a toothbrush in her bag.

★

ROSIE GROANS and opens her eyes. Heath is sitting on the bed.

'That's the phone for you. Will you take it?'

'Who is it?'

178

'Wilson.'

'Oh, I can't . . . not right now.'

She turns her face to the wall, pulling her knees up almost to her chin. Heath notices the way her back curves into an almost perfect round, like a kind of boneless crustacean, her little prawn fingers waving briefly from the covers, gathering the quilt in to half-cover her face.

'What shall I say?'

'I'm sleeping,' murmurs Rosie.

'At four in the afternoon?'

'I'm sleeping. I can't hear you.'

Heath sighs and goes back to the phone, leaving the door half-open.

'Hello?'

'Yes.'

'Is that Wilson?'

He swallows all the things he might have said in answer to such a daft question.

'Yes, it's me.'

'I'm afraid she can't come to the phone. She's in bed.'

'Oh, no! Is she sick?'

'No, she's just tired . . . nothing to worry about, but I think we should just let her sleep for a while. Can she call you later when she's rested?'

You mean when she's sober?

'Of course. Tell her I'm at home.'

'I'll do that.'

'OK. Bye.'

'Yes, thank you. Bye.'

Wilson reluctantly hangs up the phone. Being out cold by four in the afternoon is unusual, even by Rosie's standards, but when he thinks about it, what does he know? They hadn't shared that many afternoons – her hours were irregular and he didn't usually get home till about half six.

179

Maybe she has another life?

He'd come home early to phone her, having resisted the urge to call last night. He'd slept well but woke from a Rosie dream, then – round about mid-morning – the need for real contact was suddenly there. Someone had thrown a switch and flooded the room with her. Now he was going to have to hang on for God knows how long. He certainly wasn't going to phone again. He'd give it an hour, maybe two, then that was it. If she hadn't phoned by six he was off out.

'OH, WHAT a shame, you've just missed her.'

'Missed her?'

'Yes. She's gone out.'

'Oh. Where's she gone?'

'I don't know.'

Liar. Even thinking that of the revered Aunty Heath made him feel uncomfortable.

'Has she taken the car?'

'No.'

'Do you think she might have gone to the summer house?'

'Perhaps. I shouldn't think she'll be long. Shall I ask her to call you?'

'Yes.'

'Are you at home?'

'Yes. Did you tell her I called earlier?'

'I did, yes.'

'Thanks. What's your weather like up there?'

'Terrible. We've had fog all day and it still hasn't lifted. How about you?'

'Yeah, it's pretty miserable here too. OK, well, sorry to trouble you.'

'It's no trouble.'

'Bye.'

'Bye.'

It was nearly eight o'clock. If he'd just called earlier instead of this ridiculous holding out he might have caught her. He's been dancing the tango alone, now all he can do is wait, or try not to wait – that's what he really wants to do. *Not wait.*

When you're in love with a drinker (he can't say the 'A' word, not yet) and their whereabouts is unknown they can only be doing one thing. Wilson leaned forward with his elbows on his knees and his head in his hands.

Fuck you, Rosie. Do what you want.

★

ROSIE HAD been gone since six. She'd slept for a few hours, then had a bath and left without eating anything. Heath hadn't asked her directly where she was going, expecting Rosie to tell her as she left, but all she said was she wouldn't be long.

Two hours – was that long? It seemed long in this weather. The fog was still there, concealed by darkness. Heath settled back into her chair and began listening to a play on the radio, but the voices sounded too shrill and the sound effects remained just that – sound effects, she didn't believe any of it. She turned the volume down and walked through the kitchen to the pantry, where she lifted an upturned plate that was covering a ham salad. She looked at the carefully arranged food then covered it up with the plate again. It was too cold for a salad, such a wet, dark night – she should have made something hot but the ham was a kind of protest. She regretted it now. Rosie was bound to be cold when she got back. (No matter what it is Rosie actually does on any given day she always traps pieces of weather and place and brings them back, like small prey. When Rosie was growing up, Heath was forever tipping sand from her niece's shoes or plucking leaves and twigs from the back of her jumpers.

She remembers pulling straw from Rosie's hairbrush, how the long flat stalks of yellow made her bright blonde hair look brown.)

Heath checked her cupboards. The contents were set out randomly – like a pensioner's Christmas box. She started to reorganise a few obviously misplaced items, clustering sweet with sweet as she scanned each shelf: orange jellies and Angel Delight placed alongside a packet of Pearce Duff blancmange powder. Every so often she pulled down a tin of Spam (there were several) and stacked it in the tinned meat tower next to a Fray Bentos steak and kidney pie. Things seemed to be shaping up nicely but the task quickly brought its own complexities, leaving Heath in a state of indecision as she clutched a jar of sandwich spread.

'Oh, for goodness' sake!'

She plonked the jar next to the Bisto and closed the cupboard. The phone rang and she answered. This was the third time he'd called and neither she nor Wilson bothered to disguise their disappointment at the sound of each other's voice. Heath had no update to give but managed to effect nonchalance in the hope that this would calm him down. When she put the phone down she felt as if she was covering up. It was a feeling she recognised from the past, all those times when she didn't tell Lomond about Ethel, the way she'd shaken Jacob by the shoulders with such sudden force – and him standing neatly before his mother, stiff as a peg, her face so close to his pinched little mouth that his cheeks were sprayed with spit.

She could still see it, all the loveliness gone from Ethel's face, the violence a small, vivid eruption from something hot and dangerous – a rage so entirely shapeless that tackling it was like wrestling with the wind.

Twenty

LIGHT FLOODS over the nurses' station. Warm and comforting.

'Do you think she'd say something . . . maybe do a wee interview for the patients' radio?'

'Oh, aye, ah think she would. Why would she no?'

'You're probably right. She seems awful nice. She's always cuddling her dad and laughing. Who do you think should ask her?'

'No me anyway. How no you?'

'Me!'

'Well, at least you're a nurse. She'd listen to you.'

'She's not how I imagined her.'

'No. I know what you mean. Funny how you think of somebody. I saw her as tall with dark hair like Jane Russell.'

'Who?'

'Jane Russell . . . the actress. She was in *Gentlemen Prefer Blondes*.'

'I don't know that one.'

'Course you do! Marilyn Monroe?'

'No.'

'"Diamonds are a Girl's Best Friend"?'

'Ah!'

Helen had just moved to nights. It was the quietest time

of the shift and Betty had come up from cleaning the physio rooms for a chat and a cup of tea. Somehow word had got out about Lomond's daughter. Helen knew she shouldn't really be discussing any patient-related business with the ancillary staff, but it was only Betty. She'd been here longer than anyone and you could rely on her discretion. They paused under the soft fringes of the anglepoise.

'Wee biscuit, Betty?'

'Ta.'

'Did you hear the thing she did on Lena Zavaroni?'

'Oh aye, that was good.'

Betty dunked her custard cream in her tea.

'They had to sell the family business, you know . . . something to do with the brothers.'

'Did she have brothers? I can't remember?'

'Oh aye, brothers and uncles galore. Ran a big ice cream business.'

Helen looked confused.

'Are you not thinking of the Nardinis?'

'Oh aye, maybe you're right. Whereabouts is Nardinis again?'

'Largs.'

'Oh aye, Largs, that's it . . . and where was Lena again?'

'Rothesay.'

'Rothesay? Och, so she was, that's right . . . poor wee thing.'

Betty drained her tea.

'I heard she likes a drink.'

'Who, Lena?'

'No. Rosie Friel. I heard she's aye drunk. I could hardly believe it but then that's often what they folk are like.'

'Who told you that?'

'Sam. You know Sam, the porter – walks funny, aye whistling. Mother died last year and left him with two parrots. Anyway, he says he saw her lying in the bushes down by the bridge.'

'Are you sure?'

'Oh aye, completely sure. Sam's not one to gossip. Bit like ma'sel.'

They laughed with their mouths closed, the sound of their muffled mirth penetrating the morning light, like the distant call of an exotic bird.

★

A GIRL dressed like a commis chef has instructed Lomond to remain upright and seated for at least half an hour. What, he wondered, did she think he was going to do? A frivolous slouch, perhaps? She was hatless, thin and emphatic, and had a wagging finger – but he could see that her intentions were good. She had several wart-like growths on the side of her knuckles – probably verrucas – and had just fed him with a teaspoon, occasionally missing his mouth because she was worried about her horse. He can remember the name of the horse but not the name of the girl. She'd sought to elicit sympathy for Flash, who was being temporarily housed in a frost-covered field with earth like broken brick, but it was the girl he felt sorry for. Earlier that day he had passed his suicide ideation test, or at least he thought he had – the results hadn't been conveyed yet, but he was quietly confident.

Doctor. In the last two weeks have you ever thought that you would be better off dead?

Patient shakes his head.

Doctor. So you haven't thought about hurting yourself in any way?

Patient shakes his head again.

The doctor left, pleased.

There's been a lot of talk lately about depression. The nurses have been asking him about his mood (in a methodical kind of way) and for a while he was worried that he'd been talking in his sleep, ideating his suicide out loud. Then he overheard the staff talking about drumming up referrals for a new service.

'Clinical neuropsychology they call it.'

'What's that?'

'Expensive conversation. Nothing clinical about it.'

Now, sitting nice and straight, he's been thinking about Archimedes' Principle, how it used to tie him up in knots as a boy. He would float himself at every given opportunity: in the bath, on the river, out at sea, hot days down at the old quarry, filling his lungs and lying in God knows what. Buoyant. It took a while for him to understand the distinction between volume and weight, but when he did everything fell into place in an unshakable, asymmetric way, like a limerick. He became fascinated with rules and explanations that rendered the usual unusual (and vice versa of course – there was always a vice versa). Lomond began to speculate that everything – the whole universe, everything in it and upon it and beyond it, everything that existed and everything that happened, the future and the past, all that can be observed and everything that can't, everything known and unknown, all of it – that all of it followed the same basic rules, of which there were only a few, five or six maybe, ten at the most. By the age of eleven he was unwittingly expounding chaos theory to his mother, a semi-invalid who could follow none of it. He was dazzled by logic and furnished his mind with it. To Lomond, reductionism was poetry – the quintessential quest. He was a very modern boy.

An auxiliary refreshes his water jug, placing it just out of reach. The solid sound of ice bumping against the sides of the plastic jug reminds him of a picnic somewhere, a very refined one, with creaking wicker and warm cucumber sandwiches. He can't remember where they were or who he was with, but a bee stung him on the head and he remembers feeling he couldn't mention it.

His memories are growing older and sharper but losing their context. Does that mean they're unreliable? He closes his eyes and wills himself away from the sting of the bee and the urgent need to remain quiet. The ice in the jug has already started to melt and the water will soon be tepid and unpalatable, like cold tea.

Back home, in his thin, ectomorphic house, the metal ice tray he and Ethel were given as a wedding present is still in the ice-box at the top of the fridge. He must have pressed the lever to dislodge ice from that tray a thousand times. He would pour her whisky into a tall glass crammed with ice to create the illusion of a long drink.

But Ethel was not fooled.

She would hold the glass up to the sunlight and shake it, squinting through pale gold as though she was looking for the end point of titration. All she saw was displaced liquid. She'd drain what was there, throwing her head back to straighten her lovely throat, then shake the glass again and hand it back to him.

'I prefer my ice to float,' she'd say, smiling as she warmed up.

HE WILL use his brain, the only part of him that's damaged; it will be a question of mind over matter. Negative buoyancy wasn't going to be an easy state to achieve; he knows that when the water enters his airways he'll try to cough it up. His larynx will go into spasm and the vocal cords in his throat will constrict to seal up the air tube. Water will run into his stomach and he will fall unconscious. But it will need to be quick; if he is found too soon, before any water reaches his lungs, the chances are he could be resuscitated, and there would be absolutely no hope of a second attempt after that. Taking a bath will for ever be a shared activity. It has already become quite a social event for the women (always women) who wash him, expertly and systematically – babbling across him as if he wasn't there, like they're down the laundrette. He's grateful for their indifference, and relieved that he can't talk. What would he say as they lather his shoulder blades and paddle water between his naked thighs, brushing against his mercifully flaccid penis?

Lomond is aware that his attempt will be a one-off, now-or-never opportunity. It's essential that his larynx relaxes and the water has time to reach his lungs while he's unconscious. Time alone will kill him, but he'll need to earn it. There are some things he will never be able to do again, but he might be able to manoeuvre a wheelchair the few short feet between the bath and the door (which, since last year, has an easy-to-use snib lock, Kitty's suggestion after years of knocking on the door and calling out, *Is anyone in there?*), and he might – with hard work and the right 'Aids to Daily Living' – be able to heave himself from a wheelchair onto a bath seat. In other words, he might be able to convince Kitty to let him go it alone. Locking the door will give him the extra time he needs. With luck, he will be safely gone by the time she comes back, or at the very least his face will be fully submerged and his ears so full of water that all there will be is a slow stopping. The water will drown out the sound of everything else, including the wild beat of Kitty's heart as she stands on the upstairs landing, beating her fists on the door.

★

TIME RUMBLES past like a distant aeroplane; he can hear it, but he can't measure it. After an incalculable spell of dead sleep Lomond has started to dream again. He's floating inside a space capsule, only it's not quite floating, it's more of a swinging (he is suspended by a calico sling that wraps round his buttocks and holds him in), his trajectory stopping just short of the walls. Something has been scooped out of him and he feels light. Gradually the swaying stops and he's sinking into warm water. His bare legs are turning white; they're straight with no knees, like fluorescent tubes of light. There are dead flies embedded just under the skin round his ankles. His thin pubic hair has trapped hundreds of tiny rainbow bubbles. He can't see his chest. His arms float off like drift-wood. The water is still warm and he can feel it lapping under his chin and pool-dipping into his ears — then a tick-ling over his face as a line of baby spiders marches across his cheeks. His eyes close and he surrenders, listening to his heart-beat: intermittent, sporadic, spasmodic — then still. He opens his eyes. Vitreous fluid bathes his corneas and his vision clears, revealing a sharp young world. It is a distinct effect — like the peeling away of thin gauze. Lomond looks through a porthole. The moon is pulling him in for the last time, its luminous beauty making him weep into a sea of dead men's tears.

'Lomond.'

Kitty shakes him gently by the shoulder until he wakes.

'Lomond.'

A mermaid with a pale moon face leans over him, singing his name.

'Penny for them?'

Kitty is looking at him, smiling, her hand resting across his wrist. His eyes settle on her, going nowhere, and she matches his gaze for a bold, fleeting moment, then pulls her hand away and rubs the back of it.

'Oh, sorry. My hand must be freezing. It's really miserable out there.'

He's looking at her in a way that makes chit-chat un-necessary. Kitty gestures towards a leaflet lying on his tray.

'Can I have a look?'

He nods without checking what it is she's pointing to.

She picks up the leaflet and starts to read 'Tips for Safe Swallowing'.

'Have you had a chance to think about what we talked about?'

She asks the question without looking up, but then she does and they both laugh at the notion that he's just been too darn busy to give it a thought.

'You know what I mean.'

He nods.

'So? What d'you think . . . I mean about me coming in every day, maybe with a few overnights as well?'

She's smoothing imaginary creases from the leaflet, taking in Lomond's smile as it stretches up one side of his face. He looks like an old moulding of himself, his gum the same pallor as his lips and skin.

He nods again, and when he catches her eye directly, he holds it, and his expression becomes serious. He nods more slowly.

'Mmm hmm.'

'Mmm hmm?'

'Mmm hmm.'

'Good. Well . . . that's good.'

Now she's nodding as well, scanning the leaflet with raised brows.

'Well,' she looks up again, 'that's good. We just need to decide when to tell the family.'

He doesn't know whether she means his or hers.

She returns to the leaflet and looks at it closely, giving herself some time. Her heart is beating very fast. She places the leaflet back on the table and continues to smooth it out, surveying its position with a critical intensity. Lomond leans forward and manages to reach her, his warm hand falling with a thud over her fingertips. His touch closes her eyes, like sleeping grass folding under the heat of the sun.

★

ALL APRIL could see from the window of the manager's office was a wall of grey harling and a single Jews Mallow, its early flowers closed tight against the cold. Harling depressed her. She stared at it, her posture slipping, and thought about her parents' bungalow. The front beds of the small garden would be full of yellow and cream primroses about now (unless the new owners had dug them up). She could never understand why they were called that since they struck her as being neither prim nor rose-like. Her mother had always been too busy to take any notice of the garden, but her father loved it. When she was small he gave her a tiny trowel and a tiny fork, each with a pale wooden handle that fitted perfectly into her hand.

Where would he get such things?

She wondered this for the first time. As a child she had so many miniature things; a miniature ironing board, a miniature chair, a little carpet sweeper. She could put water in her miniature washing machine and agitate it, washing teeny-weeny clothes that she would peg out on string with the tiny pegs she kept in the front pocket of her apron. She'd hold an extra peg between her teeth just like the grown-ups did, then one day she swallowed one. Her father rushed her to the hospital even though the peg was tiny and she felt fine. They told him it would just work its way through in its own time – which is exactly what happened.

When it did April pretended she had given birth to a little blue baby all of her own.

'Sorry to keep you, Mrs Friel. That was one of our GPs. There's a bit of a winter bug on the go just now and some

191

of our residents are not too well. Now, how about I find someone to show you round?'

The woman smiled brightly and waved someone else into the office. April looked at her red lipstick and the dyed black hair and tried not to judge.

'Thank you, Matron. I'm sorry to be a nuisance.'

'Not at all. That's what we're here for. Of course, we'd arrange for your father-in-law to visit if you want to proceed, and we'd like to meet his next of kin as well.'

'Yes. I'm sorry my husband couldn't be here. He was called away at the last minute. He sends his apologies.'

She could feel a hot blush climbing up the front of her throat and igniting her ear lobes. *They may as well flash while they're at it,* she thought. She was annoyed that Jacob had asked her to visit Craigmalloch on her own, it didn't seem appropriate – after all, she wasn't a blood relative. Someone else should be doing this.

'Like who?' he'd said.

Like you, she'd wanted to say.

A young girl led her down a corridor of open doors, each one a bedroom, each with a bed directly opposite the doorway. Some of the beds were occupied; ghostly faces too slow or disinterested to catch April passing.

'Are these the ones that are unwell?'

'What?'

The girl hadn't a clue what she was talking about. Suddenly April felt a bit guilty about having looked in the bedrooms at all. She wished she hadn't asked the question.

'The people in their beds. Are they unwell?'

'Sorry, we can't discuss the residents.'

'I didn't mean . . .'

'This is a single room.'

She had unlocked a door and walked in, switching on the light. April followed.

'They're all the same but they can bring in a few favourite bits and pieces if they want. It's up to them. They can have their own telly if they want. Most of them do, except Mr Cargill. He's completely institutionalised. He came from Strathavon, ken, the long-stay hospital, and he'll no go into his room through the day. Just sleeps and washes in it. He thinks he's still in the army.'

'I thought you didn't . . .'

April stopped and decided it was best not to point out the girl's indiscretion. No point in getting their backs up on the first visit. She'd leave that to Jacob.

'Didn't what?'

'Oh, sorry . . . I thought this one didn't have an ensuite but I see there is one.'

'Aye, every room has one. It's the rules now.'

She pushes the internal door wider, revealing a small windowless bathroom with rails and long-armed taps and one of those raised toilet seats that look like a potty. There's a strong smell of urine in both rooms and each movement releases more odour.

'We'd get the fan fixed, of course. What does he prefer, a bath or a shower?'

'I don't know, actually. You'd need to ask Kitty about that.'

'Right. Well, that would all be done when he comes in anyway.'

April pulled a hankie from under the cuff of her blouse and held it to her nose, blowing gently. She needed to get out into the fresh air.

'That's fine. Thank you.'

'No bother.'

As they walk back down the corridor April tries to be personable.

'So, are you on day release or whatever they call it?'

'Eh?'

'Day release . . . from the school?'

'Ah'm no at the school. Ah'm a senior care assistant.'

'Oh, sorry, I do apologise . . . you just look so young!'

'Aye well, that's what the residents are aye saying . . . why are you no at the school, Marie? I've been here nearly two years.'

'Gosh, and already a senior?'

'Well, acting senior. There's a lot are off sick.'

'So you like it here?'

They've reached the office and Marie taps on the door. There's no answer so she knocks again.

'Come in.'

'That's Mrs Friel finished.'

'Right.'

The manager is peering through her gold-rimmed glasses at the computer screen. She wiggles the mouse and leans even closer towards the screen, raising her chin as she closes down the window.

'Thanks, Marie.'

Her attentions stay with the computer and April laments the lack of good manners. She's desperate to go and is tempted just to walk out, but she's determined not to let her own standards slip. The manager shakes the mouse again. 'Come *on*,' she says, then she sighs and removes her glasses before turning to April.

'Blooming thing . . . have you seen enough?'

'Oh, yes . . . thank you. '

Enough to feel extraordinarily lucky when at last she leaves the building and walks into thick freezing fog without a hat.

Twenty-one

'MY FATHER always promised us that we would live in France.'

'Really?'

'No. Not really.'

I was testing him out, but even before I said it I knew he'd fail. It was like the lobster scene in *Annie Hall*. I had woken up in Heath's spare room missing Wilson and wondering why the hell I'd agreed to meet Cameron, but there was no time to think about that; I had to concentrate on getting myself out of this situation without hurting anyone. (I couldn't just not turn up, something told me you shouldn't play around with the feelings of a man who steals through the fog in the middle of the night to deposit a lump of cheddar on your gatepost.)

'I really like your dad.'

'Yeah, me too.'

We had arranged to meet outside the cinema. The New Picture House has been here since the thirties and still feels like an old theatre. I queued here in the summer when I was little, sometimes as an embarrassing tag-on with my brothers, but more often just me and Dad sniffing our way through weepies like *Annie* and *Greystoke, The Legend of Tarzan*, and of course, *ET* (who still hasn't come back, despite his promise and the fact that I was good). We would always arrive in good time to be sure of a ticket (you still can't book in advance), so arriving early today was just force of habit, but when I got here Cameron was already waiting. I was going to just say something right out – make my excuses and go – but as soon as I spotted him I could see that he'd made an effort and for a millisecond something lurched inside me, a kind of unbidden pang.

His dark hair was uncharacteristically flat, as though he'd brushed it carefully and maybe added some kind of gel. It wouldn't last long in this weather, but for now it glistened, black as a raven's wing. He was sheltering under the stone canopy, holding a large umbrella in a rather awkward way, slightly out from his body, maybe to keep it from dripping on his shoes.

Aw . . . another pang.

I'm sure Cameron isn't an umbrella type of guy. It must be for me.

When he saw me he forgot to smile, or didn't know he was supposed to, he just looked at his watch and smoothed down his hair, frowning then turning his back on me and muttering something about the doors not being open yet. I couldn't just leave, not right at that moment, so I suggested there was time for us to go for a drink across the road and he agreed. We moved out into the rain and stood for longer than it would have taken us to cross the road and reach the pub while he grappled with the brolly. Eventually it opened and he held it over my wet head.

Now we're sitting side by side in a mock Tudor booth and my glass is empty.

'He used to always test me out.'

'What do you mean?' I said, worrying my glass and staring at his (which wasn't even halfway empty).

'Well, like he'd ask for all different kinds of fish, fancy stuff that no one's ever heard of.'

'Like what?'

'Oh . . . lots of things, I can't really remember now. I just know he seemed to know more about fish than anybody else. If he was buying tuna he'd ask what kind it was. He'd say, "Cameron, is this Blackfin or Skipjack?"'

Cameron spoke in Dad's voice and the similarity threw me a bit, which must have showed because the next thing is he's apologising for upsetting me.

'No, no, it's fine. It's just been a while since I heard Dad's voice. He's still not got his speech back.'

'Really?'

I notice he seems to say that quite a lot, not in affirmation but as a question. I don't want to be noticing Cameron's inflexions, I just want to go home.

I need to leave − now.

'Would you like another drink?' he asks.

'OK, thanks.'

I watch him walk to the bar. He seems to be holding his shoulders up slightly although without knowing how he normally holds himself I can't really be sure. It's a stance I associate with someone who's trying to conceal the fact that they're a bit pissed, only he's hardly touched his beer. He orders a double measure for me, without asking − which I don't like but it would be churlish to mention it − and when he holds out the money to pay I notice the tenner is shaking. He sits back down beside me and I have to swivel a bit to get some eye contact. We've already agreed to skip the film and as I drink my whisky it occurs to me that maybe he's pacing himself, thinking we have the whole evening ahead.

Come on, Rosie, get yourself out of this.

I can feel my clammy hair rising into a lumpy, mid-length wave as it dries out. Cameron's is starting to spring into action too, but in a much more attractive way, with little curly fronds appearing behind his ears. He's looking at the decor and reading the menu board, and my usually assured ability to create a link in any direction I want seems to have deserted me completely when suddenly he creates the opportunity I'm looking for.

'Are you hungry?'

'Not really, no – Heath is cooking a chicken and I promised her I'd be back for dinner. I need to go.'

'Oh.'

'Sorry.'

'That's OK.'

His reaction is unflinching, almost as if he saw it coming, which of course he probably did. It's probably been obvious from the start that I've changed my mind. He smiles and looks at me briefly, breathing quite loudly, then downs his half-pint, his face scrunching up as though he's drinking Gaviscon.

'Can I get you another drink before I go?' (I felt I had to ask, didn't want to add insult to injury.)

'Yes, thanks. I'll have a pint this time if that's OK.'

Bugger.

I can feel him watching me as I call up the drinks. I should really just order his pint and leave it at that but the situation still feels delicate and I don't want to offend him. He looks away as I walk back to the table. I sit opposite him, making sure that our feet don't touch.

Then he says something out of the blue that I didn't expect.

'So . . . how are the twins?'

'The twins? Umm . . . they're fine, thanks. William's in Africa. We're still trying to contact him about Dad.'

'Really?'

Shit!

I wish I hadn't told him that. I don't want him to know

anything. I don't want to talk to him about my family – I didn't even realise that he knew the twins, but of course he does, they're probably the same age.

'Yes. It takes a while to reach him. There's no internet access where he is.'

'Where is that?'

'Ethiopia.'

'Really? Wow . . . it's always the quiet ones, isn't it.'

'What do you mean?'

'Well. I always thought Jacob was the brave one. He was the leader, wasn't he, always ordering folk about. What does he do now?'

None of your business.

'He's in property.'

Whatever that means. I don't feel sorry for him any more. He's toughened up ever since I mentioned the chicken. He's looking at me more directly now, but maybe that's because I've changed seats. I start to gather my coat.

'I saw him with the knife, you know.'

'What?'

I stop.

This is very confusing.

'I saw him threaten you, more than once. You were terrified. I think it's terrible the way he treated you.'

'I don't know what you mean.'

'William saw it too, but he didn't do anything. Nobody in your family seemed to do anything about it.'

'I really need to go now.'

I'm standing, putting on my coat, a chill crossing my shoulders as if the fog has penetrated the bar. Just as I begin to turn, Cameron grabs my wrist. I wrench it free.

'Hey!'

'I'm sorry, I was just—'

'*Don't* touch me.'

Creep.

He holds up his hands like he's in a stick-up.

'Sorry, I didn't mean anything. I can understand why you're upset and I'm sorry. I shouldn't have said anything. I know how hard these things are, and I know how hard it was for Jacob too. I think it was all just terrible and I'm really sorry.'

'What do you mean, all just terrible? What are you *on* about?' I square up to him. 'This is nothing to do with you, none of this is any of your business. What do you know about my family anyway?'

'Quite a lot, actually. Don't forget I was a friend of your mother's too.'

'A friend of my mother's! What are you *talking* about?'

He raises his eyebrows, trying to look smug but not quite managing it.

'I knew Ethel before you were born – well, obviously it had to be before, sorry. We were close, you know. She used to sleep in the sand dunes near my house. She used to let me brush her hair.'

This is incredible. I don't know what he's talking about. My mother lying in the dunes. Creepy Cameron brushing my mother's hair.

I don't know how we reached this point of weirdness so quickly. I can't move and my mouth is open and I'm trying to tell him to shut up but all I can do is open and shut my mouth like a guddled trout.

'I felt sorry for her. I was the only one who didn't laugh at her.'

Laugh at her? What does he mean?

I've managed to start moving towards the door.

'In fact . . . I really liked her. She was very beautiful and she always treated me with respect.'

His voice was rising now, calling out after me as I leave.

'Respect, Rosie . . . she was a real lady.'

He shouts something else but I can't make it out, I think because I'm making some kind of noise myself. I push the door harder than it needs and end up tumbling onto the street like someone's thrown me out. I run down the street towards the sea, glad of the low cloud and the rain against my face. When I reach the foreshore I take off my scarf and open my coat, then pull the neck of my jumper out and away from my body, as far as it will go. I offer my bare throat to the moonless sky and the cold water cleanses me. I can smell the brine and feel it seeping through the worn-out soles of my boots. I try to embrace the darkness and fancy I can see a glimmer of spume bursting over the rocks. When I lick the corners of my mouth I can taste salt, and I realise it's seawater and not rain — I must be closer to the rocks than I thought. The sand begins to give under my feet so I sit down and pull my hair back tight from my face and look to my left. I'm within about twenty yards of the sand dunes but I can't see anything. The darkness hangs solid like a heavy black cloth, and I picture my mother lying behind it, warm in sunlight, and sleeping on white sand — like a child of nature.

IT'S TOO cold to stay here. My best plan is to go back into town and take the long way home. I'm worried about bumping into Cameron but at least I'll have the streetlights and the distraction of roads and crossings and the occasional passer-by. I need distraction — something that will help me break the images in my head. Jacob has tied me to a chair and is trying to push a pair of scissors under my chin to prise my head up off my chest. I give way, frightened he'll cut my throat.

Stick out your tongue, Rosie.

But it won't break through. It bunches up between my teeth and the inside of my lips, pushing up towards my nose, pushing that skinny sinewy bit that runs between my gum and the little gutter of skin that sits under my nose. Jacob is flexing before me like the great long red-legged scissorman.

> *Snip! Snap! Snip! the scissors go;*
> *And Rosie cries out – Oh! Oh! Oh!*

When William comes back Jacob tells him we're playing a game from Straw Peter. He puts down the scissors and the twins look at me curiously as I try to wriggle free – my mouth plump and pouting like a kissing fish.

★

WHEN I see Heath's front light glimmering through the fog, weak and yellow, I feel heroic and calm, much as Grace Darling might have felt when she finally tethered the coble and scaled the rocks back to the lighthouse.

'You're absolutely soaking! Where have you been?'

'Down on the beach.'

'The beach! For goodness' sake, Rosie, go and get dry. I'll run you a bath.'

Heath tutted and sighed, gathering the neck of her Fair Isle cardigan and pulling it up to her chin as she surveyed me from head to toe. If only I could say I had been out doing something courageous, saving lives – like Grace. But I couldn't. I couldn't account for myself.

Other than to say I'd been out drinking with a weirdo.

'No, I don't want a bath. I need to get home.'

'Home? You can't go back to Edinburgh tonight, surely? Can you drive?'

She looked at me more closely, sniffing discreetly and taking in my eyes.

'I'm not drunk, if that's what you think. I just need to

change my clothes and heat up a bit before I go. Any chance of a cuppie?'

★

I FEEL as though I'm getting nowhere. The headlights thicken the fog and I keep switching them from dip to full to dip, flickering through the cloud like Tinkerbell. I'm thinking about life before me. There are so many questions I want to ask Heath about my mother – prenatal questions – but I need to clear my head first. My neck and shoulders ache by the time I reach the bridge and I realise I've been clutching the steering wheel tight and driving with my chin practically on the dashboard. I loosen up and move my head in a slow circular motion and the relief is immediate. The water is beneath me now. When I roll down the window to let in some air I hear the horn of an ocean liner heading out to sea, two long notes of farewell, then the steady heartbeat of a slow-moving freight train rolling over the same track, the beat muffled soft with cloud. When the beating stops I can still hear a deep subterranean *whoosh*, the amplified rush of my mother's blood flowing around me – and her heart somewhere, pumping it through.

Twenty-two

H E WASN'T dreaming. He was awake, and Rosie was sliding her cold hand under his arm and fitting herself into him, her legs following his, her feet stroking his ankle. She smelt of snow. Wilson lay still and let her warm herself, then clasped her hand to his chest as she kissed his back, her cheek wet against his skin.

'Sorry,' she whispered.

'Me too.'

The light was beginning to rise and the curtains stirred, but only slightly. She must have opened the window a little before she got into bed.

*

FOR THOSE trapped in the present by a limited imagination, Tuesdays were just another weekday, but to busy time travellers like Wilson they were key portals. His Tuesdays carried an edge, where the chances of a slight convergence occurring between parallel lives increased, close enough to risk a collision. This potential instability existed between early morning and early afternoon. He would invariably wake early, and from six a.m. was aware that he might be pulled through the portal into another time zone. This was highly unlikely (but more likely than winning the lottery), and the effect was that he would try to get things right during these periods of charged possibility, just in case there was a perseverance of memory in the other world. Also, he wanted to leave a good impression, so on Tuesday mornings he always tried to say something clever and memorable, something that would be recalled with fondness after he'd gone (last week, for example, he'd managed to declare that art was no longer ruled by the imagination – it was effective within its context). By two o'clock the orbits would change and veer off again, and Wilson could relax.

He looked at Rosie. She'd slunk home like a cat in the middle of the night (he had no idea when she actually got to bed) and would probably sleep all morning. Maybe she was the one slipping through portals? He was beginning to question how well he knew her. Her hair was matted and wavy, spilling from her head like old stuffing. It seemed darker than usual, and her face paler. In winter her freckles faded, giving her skin a dull, unwashed look that only a day in the sunshine could put right. He propped himself up on one elbow and gently blew across her eyelids. They started to twitch, or rather, her eyeballs started to move; she must be dreaming. He peered at her neck – such a pretty neck, slim and sinewy with no Adam's apple to speak of, just the tiniest of bumps, whereas his was like a gnarled old crab apple.

It's bigger than your balls, she'd said, looking at it as though it was some kind of malignant growth. *What is it anyway?*

When she touched it with her fingertips he'd explained it was made up of cartilage and testosterone and was a sign of virility and strength, then, just as he thrust his chin up for better display, she'd rolled out of bed and shuffled into the shower, leaving him all toffee-nosed. He'd called after her, shaking his fist and squeezing his voice through clenched teeth – *Curse you, Pansy Potter* – then froze his expression and caught himself in the mirror. It was an impressive sight (he thought), like a Peter Howson, hewn from a tree. Rosie had quickly developed a healthy respect for Wilson's crab apple. She reckoned it was somehow responsible for his Sam Peckinpah voice, which was what she fell in love with in the first place. He'd played to his strengths right from the start, wooing her over the telephone until she weakened and finally agreed to meet him again.

It was a sonorous affair. With such a voice, everything else was secondary. If traces of helium ever leak into the atmosphere he'll lose her for sure.

Her eyeballs have stopped. She'll sleep for at least another two hours, maybe waking at eight – the time when children wake – stirred by the late winter light. He relishes the chance to lie with her and pretend they are married – husband and wife, with a baby lying in its cot at the foot of their bed, gurgling in its own sweet voice.

★

WHEN ROSIE wakes, Wilson has already gone. The note on the fridge reads:

> DE
> ARRD ONTBO
> THERW
> OR
> KING THI
> SOUTITDO ESNTS
> AYANYTHI
> NG.

She runs a deep bath and lies in it as long as she can, relishing the sound the water makes when she pats it – a primeval cleansing that makes her feel she could be anywhere. She lies first on her back, then turns onto her side, pressing her hands between her knees, then rolls onto her front and stretches out.

She's trying not to think about the things Cameron said to her. Keeping her face submerged, she watches her hands moving in the clear water. They look like crabs caught in a bucket.

Twenty-three

I N NOT much more than a week's time it will be spring, Kitty's busy season. This is when she dislodges colonies of dust mites from their opulent velvet cities of blue and cream. For the less well-off client, winter cling film (stretched tight under the heat of a hairdryer) is removed from the windows and nets are thrown in the wash.

May watches her sister, intrigued by the sight of an accessory. Kitty is wearing tiny pale blue earrings (barely perceptible, like flecks of dust) that match her turtleneck jumper.

'Is that new?'

'What, this? Not really.'

It would appear that she doesn't want to discuss her knitwear in any detail, but May persists.

'It's nice. Very flattering.'

'Oh. Thanks.'

The soft wool folds beautifully, caressing Kitty's curves, and the neckline covers the fine lines below her throat.

'It's a really fine knit, isn't it?'

'Yes, it's really comfy.'

May strokes Kitty's sleeve lightly.

'Is it merino wool?'

'I think so.'

'It feels like there's a bit of silk in there too, and maybe even a wee bit of cashmere. You'll need to hand wash it.'

May lays her head on her sister's chest and puts her arms around her.

'Ooooo . . . you're so soft.'

They stay quiet for a moment, each gazing at nothing in particular, Kitty stroking her sister's hair. When May straightens up she starts making the chocolate, moving around the small kitchen for pot, milk, mugs. Her sister tucks herself out of the way, squeezing into the cramped space between table and chair. Her eyes are noticeably blue, more than usual May thinks, perhaps because of the earrings and the jumper.

'So . . . what've you got on today?'

'Absolutely nothing! I'm having a day off today and I can do whatever I want.'

She lifts up her hair from her neck and immediately lets it fall, stretching her arms in a yawn, then straightening her back. Her posture has always been good and she's never had any problems with her back, whereas May has always had a tendency to slouch, and now her lower spine aches most of the time.

'I thought I might go up the town and look for a new laundry basket. Our one's falling apart.'

May keeps her eye on the milk.

'Then I'm going up to the hospital to see Lomond. I need to take his washing back.'

'But I thought you said you were off?'

'Well . . .'

There was a pause, brief, but long enough to cause May to turn round.

'I am, but I don't mind going up. I think Rosie's out of town again so it seems a shame not to pop in. Did you get that new shaker thing you were on about?'

May's eyes widen and her mouth forms an O before she speaks.

'Oh, God! Well done.'

She carries the mugs to the table then swings round, opens a cupboard and takes out a glass shaker with a silver top. May sits down opposite Kitty and puts it in the centre of the table, pulling her hand away quickly when she's sure it's stable. She continues to look at it, smiling and clasping her hands.

'What do you think?'

May is still admiring it as she asks the question, and doesn't look up.

'Aah. It's lovely.'

The sisters shake the shaker, May first, then Kitty – both smiling widely now, showing their teeth and pulling up their shoulders in mutual delight – then it's carefully centred back down on the table. As they survey it, May leans forward with her lips parted in concentration and moves it forward a quarter of an inch towards Kitty, just to make sure that the pleasure is equally shared.

'Do you remember the jelly babies?' asks Kitty.

'No.'

'Yes, you do! If we had an odd number you used to cut the last one right up the middle. You never just cut the head off like most folk.'

'Oh, yeah,' said May, shaking her head, 'jelly babies. I could murder one right now.'

When her sister left, May watched her from the window as usual, and as usual Kitty turned at the gate to wave, only today it was an excited, circular wave and she was pointing to the corner of the garden.

'What?'

'Hellebores.'

'WHAT?'

'HELLEBORES.'

May opened the window.

'Hellebores! I can see your hellebores poking through already! Bye!'

She left in great excitement, and as she passed an old man walking the other way she said hello and he doffed his hat, his day brightening. May's scrutiny picked up a lightness in her sister's step and she could see she was happy. She wanted to call after her, *Be careful, Kitty Kat* – but why should she? May didn't know why she felt her sister's happiness was fool-hardy, it seemed mean to think of it like that, and anyway, she was quite far up the road already, and her head was bowed into the wind. She'd never hear her now.

★

KITTY'S DAY just got better and better. She found the perfect laundry basket, shaped a bit like an urn with a weave of riotous colour – bold primary stripes of red, green, yellow and blue.

Made in Africa!

Goodness knows what Dave would think, but she didn't care, she was feeling reckless, confident. The basket was strong but light as a feather, with handles woven into the rim in just the right places. Best of all it was in the sale at a huge reduction (she couldn't *believe* the original price, it was only straw after all). It felt portentous and she couldn't resist, even though she knew it would knock everything else out in the bedroom. She bought it from a little place down Stafford Street that she'd only ever browsed in. It was her favourite shop. She loved everything about it, the little bay trees by the door and the huge mirrors, crowned with sumptuous gold mouldings of cherubs and angels. There was always a delicious smell of, what – vanilla, ginger? During December customers were even offered a drink of mulled wine! They had a machine that made it from sachets and poured it into tiny paper cups. The aroma of cloves was so tempting, but of course, since she had never actually bought anything over the years she felt she couldn't take a cup, even when pressed.

But maybe this year she would – now that she'd purchased the basket?

It was an awkward thing to wrap but the assistant managed to fashion a handle with some thick string (natural hemp – organic). She tied it to the existing handles so that Kitty could carry it with one hand. It was slightly awkward at first, but once she had popped her own handbag and Lomond's bag of clean washing inside it she found it easiest to clasp it in front of her with both arms.

More luck followed – no rain and lots of space on the bus, so the basket got its own seat all the way up to the hospital.

★

IN THE day room three men on four legs are playing catch with a beach ball. Dad isn't there. I say hello and one of them waves, the ball landing at his foot. I check back with the nurses, who think that Dad's wife has been with him since lunchtime.

'He doesn't have a wife,' I say, and leave it at that.

I find him in his bay, sleeping, his face smooth and handsome, his features almost even – as if nothing has happened. Kitty is asleep too. She's in a high-backed chair at the side of his bed, and there's something odd about the positioning of it. The chair is facing the foot of the bed, so they are side by side rather than face to face. Dad's sleep is bone-deep, whereas Kitty's appears light. A passing fly might wake her. Her head is tilted towards his, her arms folded, like someone dozing on a train. They're sporting the same colours, she with a caramel scarf over a powder-blue jumper and he wearing the striped pyjamas I bought him at Christmas. His bedside table has been wheeled to the end of the bed and on it stands a large woven basket, bold and brassy. I stand behind it and rest my hands on the rim. It's big enough to hide behind, and I need to lean round the side of it to see the sleeping pair. Kitty stirs but settles again and I can't quite bring myself to wake them.

I go back to the nurses' station and chat to an inordinately forthcoming doctor, someone young and clear-headed who's happy to browse through Dad's notes. I recognise this as a rare opportunity; it's as though I've penetrated the inner vault where they keep the classified information and I can't help feeling that any second now the doctor will realise I'm not who I claim to be and slam the file shut. There is still no sense of sequence to what happened after Dad's stroke and I'm going to make the most of this and glean as much as I can. But I mustn't set the pace too fast; one question too many might stall him completely.

Why wasn't he put on aspirin?

Why wasn't he seen by the neurovascular clinic?

Why isn't he getting speech therapy?

Isn't there more to rehab than physical workouts – what about re-training his brain?

What about communication aids?

(And then there are the less sophisticated questions, the ones rarely asked because it's not as simple as that.)

Will he walk again?

Will he speak?

Will he do the crossword again?

What is it, *exactly*, that he's expected to do?

THERE IS so much I don't know.

'Weren't you at the meeting on Friday?' he asks, looking to see if there's a minute on file.

'No. I couldn't make it.'

But so what if I had. I don't want to read the minute, I want to read the *Don't minute this* minute. The one that minutes his move from A&E to a geriatric ward for assessment because there were no beds and no trained staff in the fancy high-tech stroke unit. The one that minutes the scramble to find someone who can see him when they examine his smile and realise he can't raise his right arm. That'll be the same minute whose records reveal that he didn't receive any aspirin for three days because the ward didn't receive the report from his CT scan. And why is he here and not in a specialist rehab unit for brain injury?

All the little (un)minutes.

And as we talk I begin to see a sequence emerging at last, a sequence where events derive from their predecessor according to the laws of *being old*.

But still − so what.

So what if, in the highly complex world of gerontology, the strategy logo is *Fits, Falls and Funny Turns*. What's wrong with that? (A bit of wry humour never hurt anyone, and let's face it − if you didn't laugh you'd cry.)

THE FRESH new doctor is responding well to the interview technique I have selected (I've developed many over the years − this is one I call 'soft soap'). He's expounding his views on all sorts of policy issues when we are interrupted by a nurse who seems to be in charge.

'Excuse me, Doctor, but I don't think Miss Friel's interested in that kind of detail. The main thing is her dad's doing fine and I'm sure he's waiting to see her.'

She stood between us and began scrolling down the computer screen using a mouse with a clickety wheel.

'Oh, no, that's OK. He's asleep, and I *am* interested! What do *you* think of the approach to thrombolytic therapy − too cautious?'

'I . . . we're very busy here, Miss Friel, as I'm sure you are. Look, is this some kind of interview?'

She looks at the doctor.

'Miss Friel works for a radio programme, *Today Matters*. Have you heard it?'

'No, I don't think so. When's it on?'

'Friday mornings. It's very um . . . contemporary. Is that what you'd call it?'

She looks at me and I smile but say nothing. There is no hope of retrieving the conversation. The file is closed.

★

KITTY WAKES.

'Oh, Rosie, how are you? Good to see you.'

I drag a chair over, scraping the feet across the floor. I'm making as much noise as I can to break up the sleep-in.

'You too. How's the patient?'

'He's fine. Feeling tired, I think.'

I sit down and lean over Dad, touching his good arm and yelling (not quite) into his ear.

'Time for your medication, Mr McMurphy.'

He opens his eyes and frowns, the way he's always done.

'He usually takes a couple of minutes to register,' says Kitty, and we watch him, enjoying what we see. When he finds his focus it is fixed on something beyond the foot of the bed; Jacob is strutting towards us wearing his signature suit, a grey double-breasted style that would appeal to a much older man.

'Well now, if it isn't the man himself. Don't get up, Kitty, it's only Jacob.'

I wave Kitty to stay in her seat. She stands up, then sits down again. Jacob stops when he reaches the basket (beside it, he looks like a segment from a Gilbert and George montage).

'Hello, Kitty. You're looking well.'

'Hello, Jacob.'

She smiles and casts her eyes downwards, like a girl. He raises his voice.

'Hello, Dad. You're looking well.'

Dad nods and there's a pause that could turn awkward so I speak next. We all look at Jacob.

'And me – am I looking well?'

'Not really.'

'Thanks.'

I hadn't expected any other answer, but I can see that Kitty is feeling a bit awkward so I try to lighten things up.

'I've just found Kitty sleeping with Dad!'

Kitty looks up briefly, her eyes wide, then she twists herself round in the chair and starts pulling her coat down. There's a long gash in the lining and she grabs the material and quickly covers it up.

'Oh, I know, I'm so sorry about that . . . it must be the heat in here, it's so stuffy it just sends you right off, doesn't it? Well, it does me anyway.'

As she apologises her cheeks turn bright red and the skin above her cheekbones puffs up, making her eyes look small and evasive. It's a straight flush – a pink shock – and so sudden it even catches the attention of the men, who stare at her, witless. She doesn't look so good any more and I wonder if she's having a panic attack. I make a point of not looking, unlike the men, who continue to stare – transfixed by her rubescent cheeks – as she flusters her way into her coat, fanning herself with her hand and waving Jacob towards the chair. He doesn't move so she has to manoeuvre round him, then she reaches into the laundry basket and pulls out Dad's washing.

'I've brought back your underpants, and there's two vests and a fresh pair of pyjamas in there. Could you pop these in his locker, Rosie? Sorry, but I really need to go. I'm running late.'

She wraps her arms round the basket, glad of it I suspect, hugging it as though her life depends on it.

'Bye now.'

We make bye-bye noises in barbershop harmony, and Jacob regains some movement, enough to give a little wave.

'Well,' I say, 'there goes something.'

★

SITTING ON the bus, Kitty keeps reliving her embarrassment, and every time she pictures it she blushes again. She knows she needs to keep thinking about it until she can recall it without going red, so she doesn't try to think about anything else, she just lets the thing replay over and over again – setting herself as though on a repeat rinse cycle that will eventually flush out the colour completely. Now that Rosie's back she's decided to give herself a break and not to go up to the hospital for a couple of days, let the family get on with it. She tells herself he's probably sick of the sight of her anyway, but she doesn't really believe that.

When she gets home she plonks herself down on the sofa and puts the basket on the floor.

'I'm all washed out.'

Dave looks up from the television.

'What the bloody hell's that?'

'It's a laundry basket. Don't you like it?'

'Where'd you get it?'

'In town. It was in the sale.'

'You paid money for that?'

'Of course, it's handmade! I think it's lovely.'

She held on to the *lovely* as long as she could.

'They saw you coming, hen.'

He shakes his head and turns back to *Countdown*, pen and paper to hand, ready for the conundrum. She looks at the basket that has made her smile so much. He's right, it does look out of place against the pale bamboo wallpaper and the russet tones of the carpet, the colours are too brash – maybe it would be better suited for a kiddies' bedroom? Oh, she just doesn't know now, the certainty has gone and her bright mood is dimming faster than the African dusk. She unbuttons her coat and pulls off her scarf.

'I'll put the kettle on.'

She carries the basket out into the hall and puts it away in the cupboard under the stairs. When she snibs the door it feels like she's locking away the sun.

Twenty-four

THE FRASER boy has opened the front gate and is knocking on Heath's door. He's carrying two smoked haddock in a small white freezer bag. She opens the door slightly

'Yes?'

'Hello, Miss Friel. I brought you some fish since you didn't come in today.'

'No thanks, Cameron. I'm not needing any fish at the moment.'

'Oh, go on. They'll be perfect in a bit of milk.'

He holds out the fish and she opens the door a bit more. It would be rude not to.

'That's very kind of you, Cameron, but really I'm fine for the moment, thank you.'

'Please take them, Miss Friel, I can't take them back to the shop now.'

'Why don't you and your mother have them for tea?'

'Mum doesn't eat fish. Please.'

He's looking over her shoulder, into the house. She takes the bag. It's cold and she can feel the plump slippery meat of the fish.

'I can only use the one. Let me put one in another bag for you.'

'No, you're fine. Is Rosie not in then?'

'No.'

'I thought she was maybe out when I saw her car was gone.'

'I'll just get my purse.'

'No, no, you're fine, please.'

'But . . .'

'When will she be back?'

'She's not here. She's gone back home.'

'Ah, right. She gets about, doesn't she? When will she be back?'

'I don't know. Now let me pay you for the fish.'

'No, I don't want any money, please. Just tell Rosie I was round asking for her.'

He scratches his jaw and all round the back of his neck. There is a line of brown underneath his fingernails and when he raises his arm a faint smell of fish blood is released.

'I'll do that. Thanks again.'

She has no such intention, but is keen to shut the door as quickly as possible. It was the first time that he'd called at her door, and she was hoping it would be the last.

She lays the fish on a plate in the pantry and covers them with another plate, a tin one that has someone's name painted on the back. *B. Nish.* Who is *B. Nish*? She thinks about it, but draws a complete blank. This is a new kind of blankness, more absolute, a sense of something gone rather than just misplaced, so there's no point in looking.

Later, it comes back to her. She realises that the plate is one the twins brought back from Scout camp (they were always mixing up their gear, claiming as much as they lost). She remembers marking the boys' names on cups and plates using leftover silver paint from their Airfix kits. Those enamelled plates are indestructible; there must be thousands, millions of them still in circulation. Where do they all go? She imagines someone out there, piling cat food onto a cream-coloured plate with a blue trim; they're reading the inscription, *W. Friel*, trying for the life of them to remember someone they never knew.

★

'WHAT THE hell are you doing?'
  'Go away!'
  'You'll start a fire if you're not careful. That's all we need.'
  'Shut the door!'
  'But what about yir tea?'
  'I don't want any. I've already eaten.'
  'When?'
  'Go away!'
Ina Fraser is standing in the doorway of her son's room staring at him. He's crouched over the single-bar fire and appears to be toasting a beer mat. She was right to suspect his good mood – it didn't last long. She's about to say something, but changes her mind and leaves. When she closes the door he tests the beer mat again, he needs to be careful not to scorch it – he just wants to remove all the moisture from it and crisp it up so that he can write on it and keep it preserved. It is dry enough. He puts his giant atlas on his knee and places the beer mat on top of it, then leans right down and writes an inscription in tiny square capitals.

ROSIE AND ME IN THE CROSS KEYS: 8TH MARCH.

Straightening up and holding it at arm's length, he checks it over, pleased with the uniformity of the printing, then he blows on it several times to make absolutely sure the ink won't smudge before putting it in the bag and stowing it back under the bed.

★

WILSON HAD bought some brown trout for tea but she couldn't face it, not even Goan curry style.

'I'll just have an omelette.'

She said it as though she was giving her order.

'Cheese?'

'No! Definitely no cheese. Can I have it with those tiny wee crispy potato things you make?'

'Of course, my sweet. I'll make you my special Saggie Goo.'

'Not too hot!'

'Not too hot.'

'And can you make it with a wee bit less garlic?'

Fake shock.

'Can dogs do the backstroke?'

He gave it some smarm, wobbling his head and tightening his apron as he walked through to the kitchen, leaving her with something to think about. While she stayed with her own preoccupations (which didn't include any dogs), he broke eggs and thought about what the impact would be if dogs could move their front legs through the same arc as a human arm. He pictured a black dog sitting on its haunches, completely canine, then nonchalantly raising its front paw and wiping some dust from its eye. The radio was on low, playing the blues, and he moved round the kitchen pulling out ingredients and chopping onions in that clever-dick way where the knife never actually leaves the board. Rosie was curled up on the sofa with an aperitif. She'd been much more talkative since she got back from Heath's and he was trying to be glad about it and ignore the Hail Mary tone, that distinctly reparative edge that told him she was *making an effort*.

Last night they'd talked about things entirely unassociated with Lomond, and for a while it felt like the old days. He'd even managed to mention the show, albeit indirectly, without eliciting any objection or outburst. Encouraged, he'd started

222

to tell her about his latest idea for a screenplay. Wilson regularly shared screenplay ideas with Rosie. They came to him, unbeckoned, on the eve of blue bin days as he sorted out all the unread newspapers that were stacked round the flat in neat little cairns. She usually responded willingly, closing her eyes and thinking her way in. He'd give his pitch (an opening scene, ten lines of story, a closing scene), then watch her closely, waiting.

Can you see it?

And she would breathe in deeply, then open her eyes and answer – a straight yes or a straight no.

I should just send it in.

You should!

But he never does. All those films, unrealised, within days he has forgotten every last detail of them – but he knows they might have changed the world.

'This one is about fish.'

'No, no, no. Sorry. No. I don't want to talk about fish.'

'This one is not about fish.'

'Yes, it is.'

'No, it isn't.'

He takes hold of her wrists and pulls her hands away from her ears.

'It's about the history of Kashmir.'

He lets go and her hands stay in her lap.

'It's about survival and endurance through a savage history of partition and war. A true story, it takes place over a period of one hundred years.'

Hooked.

'The location is a thick forest at the foot of the snow-capped Pir Panjal mountains. The forest is beside the Himalayan lakes of North India and is populated by bears that . . . eh . . . populate the forest. Almost the whole film happens in Kashmir *but* it starts and ends on an estate in

Scotland. How's that for structure? In the first scene it's 1899 and the Duke is writing to the Maharaja of Kashmir. He's about to send him a remarkable gift.'

Reeling her in.

'He sends him . . . ten thousand trout eggs.'

'No! You said it wasn't about fish!'

Letting her out again. She's getting away.

'It isn't. It's about a guy in a Srinagar carpet factory with a dream. OK, OK, there's a bit in the middle where all the fish die and how he saves the second batch of eggs and liberates them into the snow-fed streams of Kashmir, *but . . .*'

'No buts. No fish. Not tonight.'

'Aw, but listen, you wouldn't believe what happens to this fish farm. History closes in but they survive, they survive everything, even a seven-year occupancy by Muslim insurgents.'

'No. Sorry.'

'Aw, but Rosie, forget that it's a fish thing – Kashmiri trout is the sweetest flesh you've ever tasted. So sweet they're sending them back to their ancestral homeland, right back here to where it started. That's the last scene, one river flowing into another, a Kashmiri deer drinking from the stream, then the camera follows a rainbow trout, bright-eyed and glistening through the clear water, then there's a pull-away shot – widening out – and back, back to the deer . . . a whole herd of them, only now we're back in Scotland and they're running across the hillside in their hundreds – cue orchestra . . . or maybe not, maybe just the sound of their freedom thundering across the screen.'

But it's too late. Her ears are covered and her eyes are closed. She's dishing out soul food, singing 'Take My Breath Away' in a voice that would silence Peckinpah.

WILSON IS ready to cook the eggs. As he puts the brown trout back in the fridge he vaguely remembers his idea from last night and thinks he should write something down so he can go back to it. Rosie calls to him.

'Is it gonna be long?'

'Ten minutes.'

She comes through and starts to set the table, clearing away the mess and laying it with a waxed oilcloth she bought years ago at a market in Sainte Foy la Grande. It didn't hang well, the brassy border of lemons sticking out at each corner. She kept meaning to buy clips for it.

'Dad was really down today. He asked me to call Kitty.'

'Did he? How?'

'Well, he showed me . . . you know.'

She flutters her hand, impatient to make her point.

'How?'

'Och . . . he just mimicked making a phone call when I asked if she'd been in today, so I did the twenty questions thing and it turned out he wanted me to call her. I don't think she'd been back in since I embarrassed her in front of Jacob.'

She pours herself more wine and leans against the worktop, one arm folded in and the other resting on it, holding her glass to her cheek.

'It's a bit weird that, don't you think? Why would she not come back after that?'

'The actions of a guilty woman, I'd say.'

He scoops the omelette onto the plates.

'Hmm . . . guilty of what, though? You don't think they have, do you?'

'Have what?'

'Slept together.'

'Maybe. Now come on, eat while it's hot.'

They move to the table and sit down. She picks up her knife and fork and rests the ends of their handles on the table while he spoons some Saggi Goo onto her plate. She watches, looking at the food but not eating.

'My God, maybe they've been at it for years.'

'Well, she's a good-looking woman.'

'What's that got to do with anything?'

Wilson swallows, slightly too soon.

'Nothing . . . I'm just saying, you know, she's an attractive woman, for her age.'

Rosie tuts and shakes her head. He's not sure why.

'Come on . . . eat.'

'Sorry.'

She cuts into her egg, more congealed now than cooked.

'I'm not hungry.'

'At least eat some Goo.'

She nibbles on a piece of charred potato then drains her glass and pours another.

'I think they're up to something.'

'Up to something. What the hell could they get up to? He's helpless. Come on.'

She's stares at him as though he's exposed an illusion.

'He is, isn't he?'

She moves her food around then puts her cutlery down the centre of her plate.

'I can't eat this, sorry.'

'S'OK.'

'I'm an idiot, aren't I?'

'No.'

'My plan to take care of him is idiotic, isn't it?'

'No.'

'Is there any ice cream?'

He stops eating and looks at her. That face.

'Ice cream?'

'Yeah. I think I'm entering my Häagen-Dazs period.'

'Eh?'

'It's one of the stages of loss that Kubler-Ross missed.'

(Rosie is thinking of a character from a story she read

about a woman whose cat died. Suddenly she feels just like her and it's a comfort to occupy a fictional world.)

'Oh.'

Wilson puts more food in his mouth and immediately reloads his fork. He has an inordinately vigorous chew, a manly chew that can take a Granny Smith in its stride. She can hear his molars bumping together. The first time he took her out for a meal and she heard how noisy his teeth were she thought they must be false and was ready to walk away. He still doesn't know what a close thing it was – that the fate of their whole relationship hung on what he did with a toothpick. He swallows and shovels in the last of his eggs before he speaks.

'So what comes next?'

'Rage.'

Twenty-five

APRIL IS trying to concentrate on her spring display. She's standing outside the shop looking at the naked mannequin in the window. It's impossible to visualise a new display while the old one is still there, so everything has been stripped bare, but the window can't be left like that; she needs to come up with something today. This year she's planning to go quite minimalist – just a few discreet pants and bras amongst lots of daffodils swathed in thick brown paper and bleached raffia, maybe with some white cardboard boxes, open-topped and crammed with paper roses. There's a daffie delivery due at ten and now she's worried about the maintenance. The slightest sign of wilt would be a disaster. It's at moments like this that she wishes she'd gone to art college (she believes she has a certain receptiveness, a kind of instinctive sensibility towards the arts; inanimate things can move her in unexpected ways, and it's not just the grand designs, it can be little things – a tiny watercolour wash, or a pebble), but there are other moments when she wishes she'd gone to business college, or that school in the borders where they study fabric and fashion. Invariably, whatever the task, she carries a sense of not being properly equipped, of requiring instruction, believing that there is always a right way and a wrong way to do things.

Today feels like spring. There's a messy wind that licks round corners, blowing this way and that. It's darting about like a pinball, keeping everyone on their toes. The air is fresh and smells of rain. She's been dodging in and out between the showers like a little figure popping out from the doorway of a hygrometer.

'April showers already! I'll put the kettle on.'

Margaret is always making tea in the tiny kitchen at the back of the shop. April calls through after her.

'That steam's going to play havoc with the daffodils. You'll need to keep the door shut.'

It is important to keep her relationship with Margaret professional. She is a loyal, reliable assistant and the older customers like her, but she has a lazy inclination and is just a bit too keen on her tea breaks. April has worked hard at trying to strike the right balance of being friendly but authoritative, and generally her efforts have been successful, but there have been some awkward moments – like the time she found Margaret's grandson playing with the garters in the back shop.

It's only for a week. He'll be good as gold.

She wasn't at all happy about it, but couldn't bring herself to say no, just as she couldn't deny him the raw materials for his catapult. By the end of the week he had refined his design and left with quite an impressive weapon. She'd even thrown in a matching thong.

Margaret appears with two teas.

'That's the rain off again.'

They cradle their cups and look out the window.

'I nearly called the shop April Showers.'

'Ooooh, that would've been great.'

She'd thought so too, but no one else liked it. The whole family had discussed it one night after dinner and it was Rosie who suggested an anagram of some kind, but then she and Jacob started arguing as usual and ended up off the subject.

Rosie: How about 'Frilly Pair'?

Jacob: Don't be ridiculous.

Rosie: Why not? It's an anagram of April Friel.

April: And how would you spell it?

Rosie: F-R-I-L-L-I P-E-A-R. It's brilliant!

Jacob: Oh, grow up.

SHE STANDS on the pavement, unsure how to judge her own ideas for the display. There's little point in asking Margaret (when April mentioned the brown paper her face said it all), or Jacob, who is a lost cause when it comes to lingerie. Who else is there? Her sister-in-law? April would love to know her opinion. For all her dull-coloured outfits and her mystifying aversion to a matching bag and shoe, she suspects there might be something quite saucy lurking under Rosie's sable tops, but asking Rosie something about the shop or, for that matter, any aspect of her life was hard to imagine.

The sun breaks through clouds the colour of oysters and April is caught in the floodlights. Lit up in the window, she sees how thin she is beside the mannequin. She looks like her mother, a tiny frame on sparrow legs whose longevity confounded everyone. She outlived her husband by more than twenty years, and as she emerged from his shadow, the two women grew closer and April began to see her as an individual in her own right, with her own history, and a life before her daughter was born. Eventually, she started to enjoy her mother's company, they could laugh at themselves and each other, take risks. April even tried to convert her to a push-up bra — but it all came very late.

Now, three years after her mother's death, she suddenly feels bereft.

A deep pain in her heart threatens to buckle her and she

has to move forward and lean her hand against the window, with her head bowed. Margaret can see that something's not right. She rushes out and brings April back inside, where she sits her down and insists she put her head between her knees. It helps, but when Margaret goes to put the kettle on, April is left an orphan. She realises this is what she'll be for the rest of her life, and she wants to warn Jacob, tell him to love his father more. He needs to make the most of it while he can.

The urgency she feels stays with her all day, and when Jacob comes home she follows her heart.

'Jacob, you can't put Lomond in Craigmalloch.'

She just says it outright.

'It would kill him.'

He is taken aback by his wife's passion, and for once, doesn't know what to say. She immediately wants to soften her tone but the words are out, and can't be unsaid. They shimmer brightly in their own truth – her blunt prophecy ringing in their ears like an acute deafness. Jacob remains silent and looks pensive. His eyes are fixed on the TV news but the sound is turned off and she can tell that the images of carnage in Madrid are not registering. Expressing her opinion so boldly has left April emotionally exhausted. She kisses Jacob on the cheek and goes to bed.

★

I CAN'T believe my ears.

OK, thank you, Simon. Now, we've had loads of emails asking about Rosie and lots of you want to know how she's doing and when she'll be back. Well, we can give you a bit of an update on that. As most of you know, Rosie is taking a break from the show to spend time with her family and her lovely dad, Lomond,

231

who hasn't been too well but we're delighted to say he's doing reeeally well and, if you're listening, Lomond, best wishes from everyone in the studio and get well soon. Now, we will keep you all posted on this one so thank you for all the messages and emails and yes, we do pass them on, but please — no more! Although I'm sure they'll keep coming and I know Rosie appreciates all your kind thoughts and felicitations. Now — do you have a mobile phone, and if you do, how safe is it ? Did you know that in the UK someone's mobile phone is stolen every five minutes, so . . . what can you do to keep yours safe? Here's Hardeep to tell us more . . .

'WILSON!'

'What?'

'Did you hear that?'

'Hear what?'

'Me on the radio.'

I've switched her off. Wilson comes through wearing my swimming cap.

'No. What was it, a recording or something?'

'No, it bloody was not. It was Marina-bloody-what's-her-name talking about me. What a bloody cheek . . . they've got no bloody right.'

The more I think about it the worse it gets.

'Fuck!'

'What did she say?'

'Oh, I don't know, some stuff about me and Dad.'

'What stuff?'

'It doesn't matter, it's not the detail — the point is they've got no right to be discussing my personal life on the bloody radio . . . not without talking to me first. Christ!'

This is where I'd like to grab a packet of Marlboros and light one up, but I don't smoke. Wilson is watching me, waiting to see what I'm going to do next. He thinks I'm going to reach for the whisky, so I don't, even though I could really do with one. We both stand about for a bit.

'AND she said they'd received loads of messages about me which they've passed on. Well, where are they? Where the hell are they?'

I lift my arms and stretch them out wide, holding nothing.

My nerves are really jangling now. I feel like I could hit someone, I really do. I feel like I could march into the studio and smack Miss Motherwell right in the mouth. Wilson goes into the study and comes back with a stack of mail, mainly A4 size.

'They're here.'

He drops the mail on the floor and points to my laptop and the answer machine.

'Rosie, everyone's been asking for you – loads of people, but you're just not communicating.'

I hate that, when someone uses your name like that even though you're the only two people in the room.

'Well, *Wilson*, you may not have noticed but my father's had a stroke . . . a serious, serious stroke. Not one of your take-a-few-aspirin-and-watch-the-salt kind . . . more of a half-your-brain's-gone-may-as-well-have-been-shot-in-the-head kind.'

I need to move around otherwise my head will explode.

'OK, yes – concession. I may have been a bit preoccupied lately, but—'

'Preoccupied? *Preoccupied?* You've been a complete pain in the arse. You've walked out on your job, you've walked out on me, you've walked out on everyone. What are we all supposed to do, Rosie . . . just wait around in the hope that eventually you'll notice us again?'

'I do notice you. I think about you all the time.'

'Think about me? What do you mean, *think* about me, I'm here, look . . .'

He grabs my wrist and presses my hand against his chest.
'Feel that? That's me. Look at me, Rosie . . . look at me.'
'Stop saying my name!'
'Yeah, well – just forget it.'
He lets me go and sits down on the sofa, leans back and closes his eyes.
'This is your show, *Rosie*. Don't let me get in the way.'
What does he mean by that?
There's so many things I need to get back to here – the Rosie thing, the swimwear – but I don't want to lose the main point, which isn't about me, it's about what they said on the radio.
'I'm going to call the studio and speak to Frank.'
'Fine. You do that.'
He's keeping his eyes shut and doing some kind of yoga breathing. His hands are lying limp on the sofa. They look chalk white and fleshy, small squishy hands, creepy handshake hands – I wonder if that's why he's always got them in his pockets? Maybe he's got a thing about his hands? It's not something you ask. He moves beautifully. His long arms hang loose and his hands just kind of fall naturally into his pockets. In fact, when I think about it, if he didn't put his hands in his pockets his arms would probably look a bit too long. They'd probably get in the way. Or swing. He's pushed his hands down between the seats, like he knows what I'm thinking. But he can't possibly know.
If he did he wouldn't be here.
I keep getting distracted and I need to concentrate on what I'm going to say to Frank. He's the one who has the final say on what goes in and what doesn't. He's a peace-maker, like Wilson, he'll try and smooth things out between me and the washboard from Wishaw, I know he will. I take a deep breath and pick up the phone but I have to stop because I can't remember the number.

Wilson reels it off, eyes still shut, which is beginning to annoy me.

'Is that Frank's direct line? Hang on, say it again . . . zero one four one three two what?'

'I've already spoken to Frank.'

'What?'

I put my finger on the receiver.

'Actually, I've spoken to him a few times. I told him it would be OK to say something.'

'You're joking.'

'Nope. Somebody needed to let them know what's happening. You can't just abandon people like that.'

'Why didn't you tell me?'

'I did.'

'You did not tell me. You haven't said anything about speaking to Frank.'

'I did. I told you I was fielding your calls. You just don't—'

'Sorry, can you open your bloody eyes when we're speaking, please. God sakes.'

He opens them wide, then wider, and stands up, then he pulls them open even wider with his fingers and waggles his face right in front of me. I can see that his eyeballs are covered in tiny veins.

'Very eloquent,' I say.

And he says, 'Fuck off.'

Then he turns round and starts to walk away, so I thump him on the back.

'Hey!'

He's crouching a bit and raises his arm as he turns back again, I assume to protect himself from the next blow – and because he made me hit him, I hit him again. This time I smack him across the side of the head and he reels over onto the sofa.

★

235

I DON'T remember how we got onto the bed. I think I might have passed out for a minute. Wilson is propped on one elbow stroking my hair. I like the touch of his soft hands. I'm crying and my ears are full of tears so I have to push hard on those little bony bits above the ear lobes until my hearing pops.

'I . . .'

'Shhhhhhh.'

'But . . .'

'Here. Don't talk now.'

He gives me a tissue.

'I'm so sorry. I just feel so . . .'

I catch my breath.

'I'm so sick. I'm so sick of me. Please . . . cut my throat.'

I shut my eyes and offer it to him, stretching it and spreading my hand across my clavicle. Suddenly my muscles relax and I feel very calm. I imagine this is what it must feel like if someone *does* cut your throat, but almost as soon as I think that I know it's wrong – that in reality it must be like suffocating, or drowning. There might be a moment when you feel light – when you lie on the water with your dress billowing out around you – but soon you'll be dragged down, flapping and flipping like a fish in a net.

I look at him. He's still wearing my beige swimming cap. The colour goes quite well with his maroon cable knit and makes me think of rhubarb and custard.

'You look like a cancer victim.'

'I don't care,' he says. 'It's who I am. I'm never going to wear that wig again.'

★

THE SMELL of hot dust and quick-drying bacterial spray had become familiar in a terrible way, an arid stink that made him boak first thing every morning. Lomond longed to breathe in clean fresh air, cold enough for goosebumps. How sweet it smelt! He remembered, and hoped he'd always known it, the smell of ice, and water, and rock. He suspected there were great swathes of things he had forgotten, but how would he know?

He was parched. His feeder cup was within reach, and there was some water in it, but it was hard to muster up the energy needed to coordinate the action – the sheer *thought* it would take to stretch across and lift it and draw it to his lips. It was a complicated, demanding sequence and he wasn't sure if he was up to it. His thoughts were disparate and discrete, like bits of Lego lying in a box. Separate, they were nothing, but the act of linking one piece to another seemed too difficult.

A hard row to hoe is how Kitty would have put it – rolling her 'r's.

He woke again and immediately felt tired, his eyes heavy and desperate to close. He dipped in and out of consciousness, each time his thirst greater, the water further away. He could hear his tongue snagging across the dry roof of his mouth. Some part of his brain took over (not the pick-up-a-cup-and-drink part, another part, reluctantly filling in) and at last his arm reached out and brought water to his lips. The warm liquid rolled over his tongue like balls of mercury, failing to wet it. He needed to soak his mouth before he could drink, but there wasn't any water left and it was easier to sleep.

Twenty-six

THE FIRST time Cameron actually spoke to Ethel Friel he thought she'd been washed up. She was lying at the foot of the dunes, quite close to the high tide line, and her hair looked damp. That was the first incongruity, hair the colour of wet sand, the next was the unusual way she was lying. On the beach most people lie on their backs, but she was lying on her side, with no blanket underneath her. She was wearing a pale green dress and was curled up like a young fern, her head almost touching her bare knees. In all those camouflage colours – the washed-out frock and skin white as silver sand – he nearly missed her, nearly jumped on her head as he tumbled down the bank. He had to throw himself to the left at the last minute and landed in some sea holly. Spiny bracts pierced the heels of his hands as he levered himself up, and he yelped, but she didn't stir.

As he watched her through the seagrass he was ready to believe she was dead.

He'd just got back from a long and miserable stay in Argyll, having been sent away immediately after his father and brothers drowned to stay with an uncle he'd never met or heard of before (evidently his mother couldn't cope with him *and* the funeral, and anyway, *Argyll was lovely*). His uncle lived in a one-bedroom flat on the ground floor of a low-rise block, and for three weeks Cameron slept under a full-size pool table, zipped up in a blue nylon sleeping bag. Surprisingly, he found comfort in the clack and rumble of the balls above his head, the noise preventing the worst of his dreams from taking hold. It was only late at night, when the balls lay dormant in their nets, that he was forced to swim for his life across deep water, black as treacle and with no horizon in sight.

To take his mind off what had happened Uncle Jack took him to the cinema, where they watched *Jaws* on the biggest screen Cameron had ever seen. Word about the tragedy that had befallen Jack's nephew soon spread, and in the evenings faces would bend down and peer at him as he lay in his bag under the table. He would look back at them, unblinking, and the women would shake their heads and say, *That's a sin.*

It had been strange not to hear the sea, and he was glad to be back.

MAYBE SHE'D been killed by a shark. He was about to prod the sole of her foot with a stick when a cloud covered the sun and she shivered and pulled her dress over her knees. He froze, stick in hand. She opened her eyes without moving her head and watched a tiny bug climb a grain of sand, then she sighed and pulled herself up, rubbing her face and stretching into a yawn. When she saw Cameron she barely flinched, just a short 'Oh!', then she yawned again and laughed.

'What's the time, Mister Wolf?'

He didn't know what to say.

'I . . .'

He lowered the stick and hesitated. He didn't want to say, *I thought you were dead.*

'I think that's the tide turning now.'

He twisted round and looked out to sea, his hand raised as a visor, his stick anchored in the sand, looking very like the lad on the cover of *Scouting for Boys*. She stood up and followed his gaze for a while but didn't reply, then she planted her feet wide apart and started brushing the sand from her dress. When she bent down he could see her breasts, full and cupped in a sweetheart bodice. She wasn't wearing a bra. The veil of cloud parted slightly, revealing a dullness in her skin and a looseness about her upper arms as she ruffled sand from her hair.

She's older than she looks.

It was only when Ethel straightened up and pressed her hands into her lower back that he noticed her swollen belly. How could he have missed it?

Well gone, at least seven months.

(He knew quite a lot about pregnancy, the neat bump of the first baby compared with any that followed, the massive breasts and the spreading arse. He hadn't spent all that time sitting on walls with the girls and watching the world go by for nothing.)

'What's your name?'

'Cameron Fraser.'

He was speaking to her stomach.

'Oh.'

Her face searched his.

'I was so sorry to hear about your dad and your brothers. Can you believe that they're dead?'

He thought about it, square on for the first time.

'Yes.'

No one had asked him such a question, and no one had done what she did next. She put her arms round him and held him for a long time, clasping his head under her chin, half humming, half singing.

Ilka lassie has her laddie
Nane, they say, hae I
Yet a' the lads they smile at me,
When comin' thro the rye.

He felt the thrum of her throat vibrating through him. It was as if he was *in* her, sharing her body with the baby, and he fancied he could feel its tiny feet kicking against his ribs.

The sea was calm, breathing like a sleeping bear, and he breathed with it, inhaling deeply, then a pause and a long gentle exhaling.

★

SHE LOOKED at the back of Dave's head and wondered how such a few thin strands of hair could deposit so much grease.

'Mind out.'

He leaned forward just long enough for her to whip out the stain protector and replace it with a clean one. There was a grubbiness about him that kept her away from him. It was a lazy kind of dirt – the scurf of self-neglect, there were deep crevices running across his neck, as distinct as ink-black lines on parchment. Kitty was used to dirt and had a refined sense of it, a clear system of classification. Her father had been a miner, and she remembered him coming home covered in coal dust, a band of white peeping from under his cap. He had the flat-stare eyes of a returning soldier, the door shut firmly behind him and a 'Don't bother knocking' sign hanging from it. His dirt was clean, a black robe that commanded respect. Her mother would scrub his back and rinse him with cups of warm water drawn from a pail. He sat with his wide hands gripping the sides of the bath and his head turning through an ellipse of sinew and muscle.

It was Kitty's job to clean the bath when he finished, scour away the tidemark and the dull bloom of sacrificial skin that she fancied he left behind.

She moved round to the front of Dave's chair.

'Arms.'

He complied, lifting his hands, and she took away the loose covers and threw everything into the machine, wishing she could do the same thing with him and get rid of every greasy trace.

★

IT WAS to everyone's great relief that the regular Friday ward meeting was cancelled. Whilst the continued absence of the speech therapist could have been accommodated, and the annual leave of the social worker was quietly celebrated, a missing consultant was too much – a vital missing link in an already weary chain.

Instead, meaningful conversations were conducted between parties of two or three, and the charge nurse – fresh from a course entitled 'Personhood Maintained' – broke with tradition and elected to sit in the day room for a while and watch the world through the patients' eyes. She was trying to *get into their shoes.* Her static presence unsettled everyone, each in various ways, with the exception of Lomond (whose abdication had been noted; he occupied neither this world, nor the patient world). After a light puréed lunch he was wheeled back to his bedside, where he rested with his head on his pillow, his eyes closed against a darkening room. He was becoming less vocal, his repertoire diminishing where it should be expanding. He was thinking less and dreaming more, dwelling in a dark cave like an old Paliyan tribesman, living on soft yams and honey. Only occasionally did history hijack the present, usually in the shape of the drunken wife he'd failed to save, or Rosie, the beaming child he cosseted,

242

whose light had been snuffed out early by something he should have protected her from.

She started so bright.

In their efforts to find Rosie's voice, the doctors had interrogated him over the years, compiling a composite picture that cast his life in a very particular light. Certain things interested them – his insularity, Ethel's drinking, a mother paralysed by his birth.

How did that make you feel, Lomond?

And now, dismantled again – pieces falling off him with the slightest prod, like bits of old masonry. Somebody spoke.

What?

He opened his eyes.

'We're just a wee bit concerned, Lomond. It's only natural that you're going to feel a bit down in the dumps at this stage, but we can give you something to help.'

The charge nurse looked as though she was going nowhere. She'd settled down in the chair beside him, cheery and sucking on a Murray mint. He watched her rolling the buttery sweet around with her tongue, her mouth filling with juices.

'I know you've already seen Dr Shaw but I think we should have a wee word with Mr Findley . . . see what he suggests. OK? I expect he'll ask Dr Bird to pop in.'

Slurrp.

Dr Bird? Could it be the same one – Rosie's doctor from way back when? He tried to work out the dates but it was too difficult to think in terms of numbers. Let down by his old allies he fared better with pictures – Rosie just a child, and the doctor young and unassertive, his face boyish, so it was possible that it could be him. Had he been a psychologist or a psychiatrist? Lomond couldn't remember, but either way he surely wouldn't be practising across the whole life span. It must be another Dr Bird.

'Looks to me like you're happy with that.'

He raised his head now and shook it.

'There's nothing to worry about, you know. You'll like Dr Bird – he's one of the old school.'

What did she mean by old school? Did she mean deferential? He remembered now, Richard Bird was a young psychologist with opinions and hope, but he'd buckled under Rosie's persistent silence and the superior prescriptive powers of the psychiatrists. His agreement to the drug therapy was an ignoble act and Lomond always felt that Bird had let Rosie down.

Only – not as much as he had.

The extent of Lomond's betrayal was evident when he showed Heath the pills and saw her face stiffen. He'd been told not to worry, that little Rosie was in good hands, that scientifically the medication was as fully established as antibiotic treatment.

'Child psychopharmacology is leading the way in paediatric psychiatry and these guys are the best. You're lucky to have them, Mr Friel.'

Some luck.

When it came to administering the bloody stuff his references to magic medicine sounded lame and weak, the words hollowed out by Rosie's unshakeable faith in anything he told her. Every time she took a pill he felt shame.

Oh, Rose . . . you are not sick.

Soon her tummy hurt, and she lost her bright-as-a-button shine. Dreams kept her awake at night. And the skipping stopped.

THE CHARGE nurse pushed her chin out, worrying the last toffee morsel between her teeth. He continued to shake his head and raised his left hand.

'Well, at least think about it over the weekend so we can catch Mr Findley on Monday.'

But he didn't need to think. The only circumstance in which Lomond would meet Dr Richard Bird again would be if he still carried a good right hook – and that had gone.

★

LATE SATURDAY afternoon was the only chance he had to do a bit of shopping. He closed the shop at four and was in the stationer's by five past, browsing through the carousel of cards in search of something for Mother's Day. A small boy had commandeered two of the towers and was spinning them like prayer wheels, chanting his own mantra. One of them began to topple and Cameron quickly grabbed it, the back of his hand stopping just in front of the boy's face.

'Poo . . . you stink.'

He screwed up his face and walked back to his mother, who turned and looked at Cameron, then quickly looked away, pulling her son into her side and caressing his head. Cameron rubbed his nose, triggering a fragrant jostling of fish and soap. He bought a card with a bouquet of roses on the front, not bothering to read the verse inside, and left quickly, heading for the gent's outfitters at the opposite end of the street. He was going to buy a new shirt. Rosie might turn up again at any time and he wanted to look good and smell good. Trying to keep up appearances every day when you only owned one decent shirt was quite a strain.

As he marched (yes) towards Henderson's he rehearsed their next meeting, convinced that if he could just catch her for a few minutes he could put things right. Obviously what he'd said in the pub that night was upsetting. She hadn't seen it coming and it just winded her a bit, he could see that now – and no wonder. How does she deal with it? The shame of a mother who *if she's not drunk she's dead*. There were lots of names for her – Martha, Blanche DuBois, Ethel Ethanol; as a boy he didn't understand any of them, but he knew something the others didn't. He knew how lovely she was – he'd been that close. She'd held him and sung to him, and it had left him dazed but feeling as though he was worth something. It was still his most vivid memory, and for the first time he realised that Rosie must have heard her too, they must have listened to the same song. That's why she has her mother's voice. He didn't even know if she could sing.

Of course she can sing – he'd just never heard her, but he knew he would, and the realisation turned his mouth dry.

He had to stop and give his heart a chance to recover. And that's when his dream came back to him, the one that had lulled him to sleep so many times as a boy. *Rosie floating in her mother's womb like a tiny alevin, her space baby eyes looking straight at him.*

Now she was back in his life and this time he needed to make sure she wasn't going to slip away. She wouldn't, not once he'd told her what he'd felt that day down in the dunes, the way her little feet had pushed against his ribs.

'CAN I help you?'

He was standing just inside the doorway, slightly out of breath.

'What?'

'Can I help you?'

'Ehh . . . I need a blue shirt, long-sleeved, seventeen inch collar.'

'Cotton or linen?'

'Whatever's cheapest.'

It turned out that after all that rushing he had thirty minutes to spare before the shops shut. He tried to relax a bit and do some window shopping. Maybe he could buy her something – a wee bracelet or a locket? He looked in the jeweller's window and spotted a silver chain, as fine as

Turkish tatting thread, but would she wear it? Last time they'd met she was wearing a scarf, and although she loosened it she hadn't taken it off so he couldn't be sure if she wore anything against her neck. He smiled at the thought of finding out, and turned towards the beach. There was enough light left for a bit of beachcombing and he was sure to find something for her down on the lower shore – a sea urchin perhaps, or a Cushion Star.

Twenty-seven

THIS IS the kind of thing that gives you rheumatism later on. We're lying on our fronts in the long grass – staring at the Scottish parliament building. Wilson can't decide whether he's a tiger or a sheep. He's spouting something pedantic, as befits the location.

'*The thistle like a rocket soared and cam doon like a shtick . . .*'

'What's that?'

'Disillusionment.'

His elbow slips as he speaks and when his head drops one of his sabre teeth pierces his tongue.

'Ouch! A'ff bit my tongue.'

He dabs at it with his finger then licks his own blood.

'Tastes like an old penny.'

I look back at the unfinished building and sigh, wondering where all the money's gone. (It looked so good on paper.)

I wish we were in a real hayfield – a proper one out in the country. This place puts me in a certain frame of mind where remarkable things lose their power. There is more wonder in the stark exterior of a small kirk than in a great city cathedral or the grand Roman architecture of our municipal halls. I'm never more miserable than when gazing at some splendid neoclassical architecture. I'm particularly averse to the ornamental, and baroque leaves me cold.

Look . . . it's a monumental facade.

You betcha.

Of course, I know nothing about it, but when I look at a magnificent construction I always wonder how many died building it. I don't want to think like this, I just can't help it (Thoreau's dead Yankees just loom up before me, unbidden but impossible to ignore). Wilson says I'm a Calvinist at heart. He doesn't really know what that means but I don't want to be a clever clogs *and* a Calvinist – so I let it go.

There's a Pegasus cloud above our heads galloping from west to east and I swear I can hear it fly. I imagine the last crystals of winter ice melting on its flanks. But the sound is real.

'Can you hear that?'

'Yeah . . . annoying little shits.'

Wilson pulls his old man Muppet face and raises a fist, shaking it weakly at the kids doing wheelies at the front of the building. He's lying low, making sure they can't see him. I raise my head above the pampas grass and watch a group of animated people being herded towards the gates of Holyrood Palace by Desmond Tutu (could be). They're dressed for the weather in heavy coats, scarves and gloves – too well wrapped to be Scottish. The breeze carries fragments of their voices across the grassy plains and the sounds bring thoughts of William. There's still no word and his absence feels like a chasm. Wilson pulls me back down and presses against me.

'Let's have premarital sex.'

His breath is hot against my ear and I can feel him growing in his pants. I pull off my pashmina and spread it over him to blanket his groin, then slide my hand under and unzip his trousers. His hard penis emerges from his pants like a great squirting cucumber, ripe and ready to burst. He's looking at it, keeping the scarf raised like a tent. His white face reddens as I rub, fast enough to start a bush fire – then he moans and ejaculates, our hands wet with seeds and juice, semen trapped in a web of tartan mohair, clinging like dew.

Pegasus has flown. The sky, an implausibly even blue, catches the distant sea. We're lying apart in a state of easy separateness – our fingers barely touching, the tips light as blades of grass.

'We'll have to get married now.'

He stays flat but gives me a sideways look to see how I react. It makes him look fishy. I prop myself up on damp elbows and look at the building again. The longer I look the more perplexed I become.

Como es? it shouts. *What d'ya think?*

I'm not sure. It's too demanding. It makes me sigh just looking at it.

'I could burn it down if you want. It'd be easy – all that timber.'

He's lying on his hip now, chewing on a stalk and playing with the fingers on my left hand – lifting them up and letting them flop back down again like he's checking for signs of life.

'I wish you were happy.'

'How do you know I'm not?'

He rises from his bed of reeds, and, taking my other hand, stares at me, clear eyed, and I think he must be able to really see me now because he says, 'You're so innocent.'

And I want to ask, *of what* – but I'm scared of the answer, because I know it will be incomplete. As we walk back the wind grows cold and the light changes, growing dull but somehow more luminescent. We follow the yellow light towards home. Wilson stops to buy a paper and I go on up. Tonight there is nothing I need to do. Dad has indicated that he doesn't really want evening visits, and Kitty will be with him all afternoon.

On a Sunday?

I know . . . that's what I thought.

I pour myself a whisky and slug it down, then top up my glass and take a warm mouthful. I hang up my jacket and pull out another glass for Wilson. He comes in as I pour him a generous measure.

'I've made you a drink.'

'Uh . . . no thanks. I'll open some wine.'

'You sure?'

'Yeah.'

'OK.'

I look at his glass and shrug before I drink it, then carry my own into the kitchen.

'You know, when I called Kitty the other day a man answered the phone and it really threw me for a minute.'

'Who was it?'

'Her husband, I assume. I never think of Kitty having a life. I just can't imagine it. I realise I hardly know anything about her, this woman who's been with us since I was small. She taught me how to iron a shirt.'

I can see Wilson pursing his lips like a woman (ironing was a skill I worked hard to acquire, then quickly lost).

'When I got my first period it was Kitty who tucked me up with a hot-water bottle and a tampon, and . . . oh, God . . . she made me my first Easter bonnet from an old cornflakes box and lots of pink netting.'

'Your first . . . you mean there were others?'

'It was awful. I felt ridiculous, but I remember Dad clapping and asking me to twirl round so he could admire the back. You know I can't think of anyone I've taken more for granted. I suppose she's been a bit like a mother at times – the little night-mouse type that works while others sleep, putting everything to rights . . . a kind of force for good.'

I raise my glass to her, then empty it. I have a horrible

251

feeling that I have treated her as a kind of 'below stairs' presence. Of course I've always been polite and respectful, but to hold no curiosity about someone's life is a kind of arrogance. There is nothing respectful about indifference.

Wilson has put down the potato peeler and is looking at me in disbelief.

'Night-mouse?' He laughs.

'What? What's wrong with that?'

'Night-mouse?'

I can't be bothered working out his derision and turn away. He's always picking up on the spurious detail.

'I just can't believe your naivety sometimes. A little night-mouse? What are you talking about?'

He follows me into the lounge.

'Don't have another. You haven't eaten since breakfast.'

I feel intensely irritated by that and pour the last inch or two into my glass.

'I'm fine.'

'You've got such a romanticised notion of motherhood. There's no such thing as *little night-mice*. There's nobody like that, believe me there isn't, never mind what Walt said. If Kitty was like that, and I bet she wasn't, then she wouldn't just be the mother-you-never-had, she'd be the mother-none-of-us-ever-had.'

I feel petulant and let it run, wanton.

'Never mind looking like that. I really think you should speak to Heath and ask her what your mother was really like.'

'We've talked about that loads of times. Anyway, I'm going to talk to her, I'd already decided that. She's coming down tomorrow and Jacob's going to meet her off the train and take her to the hospital. I'm going to meet her for coffee later on.'

'Good.'

I move to the window seat, intent on thinking about what I want to ask Heath. I'm going to have to tell her about meeting Cameron so that we can talk about what he said. I still don't know what to make of it. I look out into the garden and watch the high wall move, nestling down and compressing under a sinking sky. The grass is dark but the stone is lit – a moon somewhere. The house shifts, stopping a fox, then she carries on, her belly slung low, her snout glistening when it touches the light, then dipping back down quickly.

It's difficult to read the sky and the grass and the molten stone. Everything is perplexing still – the buildings, the garden. I don't know what to think about the small stirrings that keep catching my eye – like the way Dad reacted when Kitty walked into the day room, his throat emitting a short, low purr, then his eyes quickly settling on her.

There was a brightening.

So much so that I left them to it.

★

THE AFTERNOON is stretching longer than expected, the cold descending before the dark. Lighting stoves in sunlit rooms. Invisible smoke riding a brave west wind. Wilson is lying on the sofa clutching his stomach, complaining of indigestion after a heavy slab of chewy pork.

'Must have been a clapped-out old sow.'

I can tell he's thinking about it, following it through. (Wilson doesn't just imagine, he constructs, he'll be smelling it now – a slack-skinned pig with receding gums and hairs that grow inwards.)

'You've eaten too much, that's all. Take some pepto-bismo or whatever it's called.'

'Aw God, pink chalk – why can't we buy Rennie's like

everyone else, those nice fruity ones that smell nice and taste fruity?'

He's shuffling his way towards the bathroom and as he passes the phone it rings – a one-ring pick-up.

'Hello.'

I watch his face. It's dead set.

'Yes, who's calling?'

He's looking at me.

'OK, Cameron . . . I'll just get her.'

He holds out the receiver and I walk right past and into the bedroom, where I sit down on the floor with my back to the radiator and hug my knees. I can still watch him from here.

'Sorry, but she seems to have popped out. Can I ask her to call you?'

He listens.

'No, I don't think so.'

He puts down the phone.

'He says he'll call back.'

Wilson closes his eyes. He looks tired, as though he knows this isn't going to be straightforward. He's weary of it already and is only going to ask me about it because it would be weird not to. He goes to the bathroom and I hear him open the cabinet, then shiver, then slam something down on the sink (probably the pep bottle). When he comes back out he wipes his mouth with his hand and drags his fingers down to the end of his chin, pulling on the beard he keeps threatening to grow. He looks fortified now, ready for pretty much anything I can throw at him.

Twenty-eight

I N THE field of mathematics there is something known as Friel's Law. It appears in a small scientific pamphlet entitled *The Opposite of Maths*, written by Lomond Friel in the late 1960s. The article draws heavily on an original paper, also by Lomond Friel, which appeared in the *International Journal of Mathematics Education* a few years before. Friel's Law is, *in fact*, not a law at all, but it looks like one, and behaves like one, appearing to deliver everything expected of one, and to some, ergo, it is one (despite the well-executed central argument of the pamphlet, which clearly sets out why Friel's Law fails). This ironic but predictable contention – that Friel's Law *is* a law – gave rise to a further paper, *The Paradox of Friel's Law,* and thus began a long running discourse that featured regularly across the annals of mathematical theory (bringing Lomond the comfortable academic chair that carried him to retirement).

Lomond began his treatise not long after the twins were born. It took several years to develop, and by the time it was picked up by a small independent publisher in 1975 the boys had grown about five feet and Ethel was pregnant and drinking more than ever.

Perhaps irrationally, he believed that the publication of his mathematical rationale would somehow solve their problems. Ethel would see that he was a success, or rather, would see that others saw him as a success – and this would be enough. She would find her way back to him – attracted by a small distant star, a tiny illumination known as Friel's Law.

HE WAITED until the boys were in bed then lit a barbecue under the warm night sky and grilled some trout with skewers of charred peppers and fennel. Then he went back into the summer house and woke Ethel, who was having a lie-down after her daily walk through the dunes.

Sleeping it off.

At first she was reluctant to join him in the garden, but he pleaded with her, and the smell of white meat and liquorice drew her out. He had even poured some white wine, a Riesling, but thoroughly chilled. It wasn't something he ever did, so she knew something good had happened, a sabbatical perhaps, or even better, a permanent move to Boston. An excitement grew and she smiled. In that moment her face was as young as he had ever seen it – so that when he gave her a copy of *The Paradox of Friel's Law* he was crying a little, not because of any mathematical determinants that suggest a predictable world, but because his wife was beautiful – pale as a morning moon, her eyes and nose and mouth a perfect symmetry.

There was a pause when she heard Lomond's news, then she snorted, and again, and soon was laughing and pouring herself more wine.

'Is that it? Is that THE NEWS? Well, here's another law for you. This one's called Ethel's Law. *E* for Ethel minus *B* for another bloody baby equals . . . nothing. How about that one? Ethel's law . . . nothing equals everything plus one minus me. Put that one in the book, Einstein.'

She drank the wine as if slaking a terrible thirst, then picked up the bottle and walked back into the house.

'What about your fish, Ethel? Don't you want it?'

He couldn't even shout at her, his raised voice strangulated. He sat down on a deckchair and rested his head on the cold canvas. His eyes felt small and tired. Crinkle eyes. He pressed his index finger into the corner of his left eye and scraped a grain of sand out with his nail, then examined it, as if it held an answer.

The windbreak caught a punch of air and made a noise like a flag whipping in the wind. Lomond shivered and looked at the pamphlet lying on the table. It was a thin, spineless thing, written in honey (as Einstein might have said) – at first sight wonderful, but now it was all gone. He stood up and walked towards the beach carrying Ethel's plate, then threw the food onto the sand and left it for the gulls. He felt as though he'd played his best hand and lost. Dispossessed, a dead calm settled on him – a strange kind of relief – and he knew it was the beginning of grief.

★

THERE WERE no celebrations when Rosie was born, just a small family funeral and a sombre christening, both held in the same church, a place unvisited by the Friels before or after the ceremonies, and although Lomond has no recollection of the physical interior of the Presbyterian kirk, he can remember the comfort he drew from the plain dignity of it, and the impossibility of love and loss, the way they can accommodate each other, and he remembers too holding his baby, her head knobbly as a pomegranate, her heels exquisite, like water chestnuts. She barely moved throughout the ceremony, just the slight curling and uncurling of weightless fingers – a tiny penitent, limp as a jeweller's rag.

★

HE STIRS, half of him resting on his pillows, the other half gone. Sketched against a white starched canvas, he looks around him, scanning for something of himself. The lime his sister brought him is odourless now and hard as a walnut, difficult to grasp. He would like to smell something from the other world – a lemon, or coffee, or burning toast.

He'd like a jar of blossom honey.

A bag of sherbet.

A string quartet at the foot of his bed.

Of course, there is still a drowning to come, there's no faltering from that, and he wonders if the thing he sees in Kitty's eyes might be the knowing look of a potential accomplice. (She's an intelligent woman, she's bound to understand. He wouldn't expect her to hold him under – but maybe just a strong pull of the feet?)

Meantime, the possibility of small pleasures emerge unexpectedly, like daisies on snow.

BY THE time she finally comes his thoughts are in disarray, blowing about in a gusty alley he's never seen before, a back route that might lead anywhere. He's feeling something but can't find the word for it, a craving perhaps, but for what?

Kitty scrutinises April's rota.

'You've got a hectic day ahead, Lomond. Heath is visiting tomorrow afternoon and it looks like Jacob might be bringing her.'

She hesitates, picking her teeth discreetly through closed lips with the nail of her pinkie, looking at him.

258

'Shall I speak to him if I see him, about what we talked about, you know . . . about when you go home?'

Lomond nods and (he hopes) throws her a wicked look. 'Are you in pain?'

No. I'm in a maze. I want to follow my intuition but it's gone.

He drifts off, leaving Kitty to calculate the when and how of raising their plan with the rest of the family. When he next wakes she's not there any more, but she's left tracks. One glove pressed into a corner of the chair, and the absolute certainty that she will be with him until he dies.

★

HE'S RUNNING his fingers along the railings like a dreamy boy, looking in on the domestic detail of other people's lives. Tall windows, boastful and brazenly undressed, their electric chandeliers turned up high, filling elegant rooms with bright white light. Stark spaces where everything is designed to exhibit something else. Look! A carved mantle, skirtings over a foot high, shutters at half-cock – for no reason other than to ensure that they are noticed. Men and women reading hardback books, their stockinged feet wrapped against raw, unforgiving surfaces – slate and beautiful wood. Living in a picture of a life.

Sometimes Wilson hates it here. He distrusts the professed authenticity of it – the greengrocer and the red and white butcher. He longs for a Scotmid, loathing his penchant for fine cheeses – the way he'll mull over the Connage Clava.

His refusal to buy English apples.

His silly insistence on white soap.

He carries a tall, cast-down look, mistaken for a means of distancing himself from his surroundings, but really the hang-dog look of a shameful life.

When he met Rosie she convinced him he wasn't a

hypocrite and he convinced her she wasn't a fake. That's how it worked. Now he almost wishes she was a fake, or at least a liar. Rosie would rather not speak at all than lie. It's as though she doesn't know how to. After the phone call she told him all about her 'meeting' with Cameron as if she were giving a statement, dwelling on spurious details like the time and the weather, something about an umbrella and what they had to drink. The intent of her flat, even delivery was to underplay the whole thing, but her formality backfired and Wilson read her nonchalance as concealment.

'So why did you agree to meet this guy for a drink?'

'I don't know.'

'I need a reason, Rosie.'

'I don't have one. Maybe I felt sorry for him?'

It felt like she'd done this before. The occasional suspicions he'd held over the past two years – the times when she'd disappear for a day with only vague accounts, her tiredness, the hot nights without sleep, then in the morning a scattering of damp scrunched-up tissues dropped across the duvet like wilted roses, and her at last still, lying in petrified sadness. And now this – a brief, sordid encounter with a man she doesn't know. It all seemed to be part of the same alternative construction, another possible Rosie that was gaining in substance, setting like white fat on his tongue. No longer able to distinguish between his imaginings and those things that had actually happened, and feeling the distinction didn't much matter anyway, Wilson couldn't be bothered listening any more. He'd had it with the depressions and her crises and her dull-edged half-stoned reekie falling into bed. When Cameron called back Wilson waited for her to pick up then watched, callous, before leaving without dramatic gesture or coat. There wasn't anything she could do to put things right (even her telling Cameron not to call again sounded intimate – it's not the kind of thing you say to a casual acquaintance).

He walked the streets, wanting to stay away longer and let her stew, but it was cold and he turned back, desperate to crawl into bed and sleep. When he reached the front door there was something about the sonority of the key clicking through the lock that told him she was gone. The flat glimmered in a blue light, dim city stars weak under a wax moon.

He couldn't be the one to stay again.

Pulling on his coat and longing for dead love, he picked up his briefcase then put it down in the outside hall so he could use both hands to soften the noise of the door closing. It was just a habit – a sensibility that stemmed from all those times when Rosie was inside, sleeping it off. With one hand keeping the key turned and the palm of the other resisting the wood, he closed it, leaving the flat empty and silent while they both wandered out into the night – one going one way, one the other, or perhaps both walking in the same direction, in a line, or parallel, or converging, there was no way to tell.

★

IT NEVER occurred to Kitty that Dave would say no. He'd not shown any interest in her work before, and she realised now that whenever she spoke about it she had assumed he wasn't listening – a collusion of inattentiveness that suited them both. She opened her powder compact and held the mirror close to her face, a slight turn of the head and tender touching along her jaw bone, as if it were mending from multiple breaks.

'I think I'm getting younger.'

May looked up.

'I think you are! You look fabulous.'

'Do I?'

She snapped the compact shut and threw it in her bag, then crossed her arms and gave herself a rub.

'Oh, God . . . what d'you think I should do?'

This was an unexpected visit so they were making do with tea and a digestive. May marvelled at her older sister and the way she could handle a mirror in public, with panache, just like the Americans. Women thought nothing of it over there, she'd seen it in New York with her own eyes, all ages pulling out lipsticks and applying powder in delis and department stores and in the elevator at Macy's, until eventually, it didn't seem so bold. Kitty would have loved it – Christmas shopping in NYC – but she couldn't go with them, and contented herself dreaming about it.

Manhattan!

Kitty never tired of listening to her sister talk about it, and the thought of wee May walking up Seventh Avenue made her cry. Because she'd never been, she could add her own detail – the noise of skate blades turning on ice in the Rockefeller Center, a bird calling across Central Park pond, maybe a thrush or a nuthatch. She could smell the egg-shine of a bagel and hear a saxophone playing in a small bar. She knew she would never have the courage to go into that bar, but this way, she got to go anywhere she wanted.

May put the biscuits out on a plate.

'I think it's your decision and you should do what you want. What's his problem?'

'He says I spend too much time with Lomond already. Thinks it's unhealthy.'

'Unhealthy? In what way?'

'He didn't say. I told him that even though I'd just have the one client – well, except for old Mr McKendrick – it would be the same money, maybe even more if that's what he's worried about, but he wouldn't budge. He just said no and refused to talk about it.'

'Ah, well – it's nothing to do with money, is it?'

May looked at her and raised her eyebrows, willing her to

speak. Kitty raised one in reply, unconsciously constructing that slightly disdainful look that seemed so classy to May.

'Oh, come on. You know what I mean.'

The eyebrow stayed – a warning shot.

'He's jealous.'

'Jealous! But how would he know? He's never even met him. As far as he's concerned Lomond's just another one of my old men.'

'Ah ha . . . so if he *had* met him you'd expect him to be jealous?'

'I didn't say that.'

'Oh, but you did, Kitty, you most certainly did. Maybe not in so many words, but you did say it.'

She sat down and placed the teapot between them, stirring it. The sisters pursed their lips as the tea was poured, then May got up and removed the plate of digestives, returning with a mint Penguin, which she snapped in two with unbelievable precision.

Twenty-nine

DESPITE WHAT everyone says, people are eating less fish. Cameron knows this to be true, and those commonly heard claims of twice or thrice a week should be viewed as suspicious – a clear case of mass posturing. Heath is one of the few exceptions, but even her consumption has started to fall. He blames the rising price of white fish and the introduction of a cold fish counter at the large supermarket that occupies the site adjacent to the abattoir on the edge of the town. The location is where the cottage hospital used to be, and with the exception of the woman who owns the wool shop on the corner, every local shopkeeper on Market Street was born on that site, as were many of the local councillors. Meetings of the Trade Associations are like school reunions, or choral society gatherings, or the Round Table. It's all the same folk.

Cameron did not feel like a member of this business community, but he did feel he was a part of its demise. This sense of collective defeat cushioned each individual from the harsh facts of their insidious decline. It was now, as his mother tallied up the taxes, that the extent of his losses were evident. Of course, with some clever market research he could diversify – focus on the kind of trade a supermarket could not provide. He knew there were possibilities.

The struggle was to find the point of it.

After his call to Rosie he found himself walking round the harbour towards the castle. When he reached the ancient swimming pool he sat on the smooth rock, dull as a toad, and searched the water for the moon. The dark pool had swallowed it like a greedy dog. He tried to pull the cuffs of his new blue shirt down over his hands to keep them warm, but the sleeves were too short. The thing was tight across his chest and pinching him under the arms, making him feel bloated – his body distended – as if there was a great swelling of organs.

It was still painful to breathe, had been since the moment she'd started to speak.

Listen, Cameron . . . you're terribly mistaken about all of this.

His fingers were cold wooden pegs, too stiff to undo his thin buttons. He yanked the material apart and the buttons flew in all directions, their brightness reclaiming the moon.

I'm sorry but I'm not going to apologise if I've misled you.

She spoke more loudly than usual and he knew the other guy was still there, the one who'd answered the phone earlier. He pictured her pulling faces, and him, lowering a newspaper and sniggering, making a throat-cutting gesture – cutting him out. Cutting out their past, the way terrible things are denied. She'd hardly let him speak, and then when she did he couldn't answer.

It's so wrong of you to call here. Where did you get my number?

The moment Rosie had hung up on him his mother had banged on his door. She was lamenting his profit margins and warning him that as his unpaid accountant, she was raising the rent. Then the phone rang, and as she reached out he snatched it.

'Hello?'

'Cameron?'

Within a few seconds – the time it takes to say a name, and the pause to hear it – he was reprieved.

'Yes . . .'

Rosie had dialled the number that she'd written down from the last-number redial service after she'd received the anonymous call. She'd tried it before, but this time he answered.

'Fuck! I *thought* it was you. This is your number, isn't it – you've phoned here before, haven't you? You've phoned and hung up. What kind of creep call is that? I don't know how you got this number but it's without my permission. Do *not* use it again. I *don't* want to talk to you.'

Her voice had lost all its honey, sour words pushing down his throat. He needed to catch her attention before she hung up. It felt like his last chance.

'We touched,' he shouted.

'What?'

'We touched – you just don't remember. Rosie, don't hang up! Listen to me. We touched before you were even born. I saw you in your poor mother's womb. I saw you . . . your eyes were too big for your head and you looked right at me and kinda shrunk back and I think maybe you seen yourself in my eyes and got a fright – I think that's why you're scared of the fish heads – you're just scared of yourself, but that's just so wrong, Rosie, 'cause it wasn't your fault that your mother died like that – it was the drinking that killed her, everybody knows that, everybody said it was gonna kill you too but you lived, you lived, Rosie, and it's like I've just been waiting for you to come back. Come on, Rosie, please.'

There.

An oceanic lull.

'Rosie? I've always known you . . . d'you understand? I'm the one.'

Holding the receiver with both hands, he listened down the line, ear pressed against an unexploded mine – each word snipping a wire. The bedroom door was open and his mother was standing in the lobby. She heard everything.

266

The flock wallpaper of tall grasses closed in over her head and a cold clamp of air penetrated her chest. She raised her hand and covered her mouth completely, the movement drawing his eyes to hers. He gave her a look so sharp it pushed her back. She retracted into the darkness, running her free hand along the wall as though she was blind and having to feel her way out.

'Please don't cry, Rosie. I don't want to upset you. We don't need to talk about it if it still scares you . . . you just need to know it.'

'Oh, God.'

Her voice sweet again, high as a baby monkey's.

'Come on now, it's OK, it's O-K . . . come on . . . that's it, sweetheart . . . it's OK. It's OK now . . . sshhhh . . . that's it, that's better . . .'

Whispering. Caressing her. She felt his breath on her face, his outrageous intimacy pressing her down.

'Stop it!'

'Aw, come on now . . .'

'Stop it! *Shut up*! You have no right to talk to me. You're not involved in anything here. You're just a nuisance caller and this is harassment now. This is just some kind of perverted rubbish . . . some kind of sad lonely distortion . . . it's all rubbish! Look, I really mean this . . . I don't want to hear from you again. Do not contact me. If you do I'll call the police.'

There was a pause.

'Rosie.'

'Just *leave me alone*.'

'Rosie, wait . . .'

She hung up again. This time he banged the phone against the wall then dropped it as he left, a side-fist thumping against the door, then a foot, and out of the house before his mother could open her silly mouth and say something ludicrous.

HE SHIFTS on the black rock to ease the shooting pains in his buttocks and suddenly slips down towards the edge of the pool. Peddling in search of a foothold he realises he's not wearing shoes, his feet – under threadbare heels – are numb and completely useless. He shifts his weight again and throws himself back, braking with his hands and elbows and finally stopping just as his feet dip into the water, its strange viscosity lapping like a tropical swamp. He sets hard against the rock, sculpted in awkward pose, his hands bleeding through seams of coal and sandstone. Rivulets of blood run along the rootlet marks etched in the rock, ancient equatorial tree roots – thin as hair – wisping down to the seabed.

Cameron holds on in precarious balance, the time either long or slow, he can't judge.

Eventually he looks down. His legs stop at the water's edge and his feet have gone under – perhaps eaten by eels, or a catfish. The effect of any movement has to be carefully anticipated since the slightest downward slip will trigger an unstoppable descent.

He will glide like a greased hull into the depths of his greatest terror.

His only chance is to roll himself across the rockface. With enough sideways force he should reach the edge of a natural butt where the stone drops down onto sand. The rock surface is rough, pitted with holes and stigmarian mould, the remnants of a petrified forest. He will need to throw his torso with as much violence as he can muster and hope that his legs will follow. Raising his head back again he rotates it slowly to ease the muscles that burn in his neck. To his right he can just make out a cluster of acorn barnacles nestling together like a bunch of salted alpines, impervious to Atlantic storms. The light rises slightly, catching the electric blue of a young limpet wasting its beauty under his flat gaze.

It would make a perfect cerulean love token for Rosie.

Leave – me – alone.

He dwells on her words, tiring with the thought of them.

Leave – me – alone.

Perhaps he could.

He closes his eyes and wonders if it would be possible to rest here, just for a moment. Blood trickles from his elbows and runs down the inside of his forearms to his frozen hands. A clump of dead man's fingers grows from the rock. He turns his head northwards as far as he can, glimpsing the open sea.

And she's there, resting on a rock. Rosie's mother, unchanged and combing her hair – her belly swollen under her lichen dress, her eyes black and wet.

She looks like a silkie.

The quickening wind blows fragments of song across the water.

> *Gin a body, kiss a body,*
> *Need a body cry?*

The sound of her sweet voice relaxes him, and in a final moment of alchemy his stone limbs melt and spread across fossil earthquakes. A sea spider dips her pincers in his warm blood.

Then he slips into the pool.

Thirty

APRIL JUMPS in her seat at the sound of the doorbell.
'Who on earth?'

She looks at her watch, buffs the tiny face with the end of the yellow silk scarf that is softening the scoop neck of her jumper, then peers at it again. Jacob presses the mute button on the remote and they look at each other, waiting. The bell rings again, longer this time, and still April jumps, moving to the very edge of her seat.

'Who could that be on a Sunday?'

'I don't know.'

'Do you think it's the police?'

'The police? Why would it be the police?'

'I don't know.'

'Have you done something?'

'No!'

The bell is ringing continuously now and they both stand up, April gathering her scarf and clutching her neck. Jacob goes to the door.

'The hole!'

'What?'

She throws out a series of tiny rapid flicks with her right hand and whispers loudly.

'The hole . . . use the hole thingy . . . the peephole.'

He slides the cap to one side and looks through.

'Oh, Christ.'

She knows who it is from his tone and darts back into the lounge to tidy up and switch off the television. She can hear their voices, already raised as they cross the hall. They are both moving slowly, giving her just enough time to grab a magazine from the rack and position herself back on the chair, then scramble up again when she realises she's picked up a copy of *Hello!*. They're in the room before she can reach the rack for another, and she stands − stranded for a moment − then shoves the magazine under her seat and sits down. Part of her knows that she will go unnoticed, that, in fact, rather than read it she could sit and eat it, for all the attention she would draw. She had long considered what it was about Jacob and Rosie's relationship that perplexed her. It wasn't just straightforward hostility or dislike (she hadn't spoken to her own brother for years and it troubled neither of them) − it was more complex than that, and undeniably exclusive.

With some bravura she stood up and greeted Rosie in a voice loud enough to break through their disagreeable, immutable conversation. Rosie managed a wave of acknowledgement, enough to satisfy April, who was content to go off and boil some water.

'Why not?'

'Why should I?'

'Because I'm worried about her. I think that guy is capable of anything.'

'Then call her. I'm not driving you up there on a Sunday night. Anyway, you're talking nonsense. You've got a bloody cheek rolling round here drunk as a skunk − and I certainly wouldn't impose you on Heath in that state. My God, you just don't seem to see how inappropriate that is. You've lost it again, Rosie − you really have.'

'Rubisshh! Sshhh, forget it . . . you don't know anything.'

'I know that you're upsetting everyone, including Dad. You've just completely confused him with your ridiculous proposals.'

His derisory laugh is timeless and strikes Rosie as being so *essentially* him – so *eau de Jacob* – that she imagines it bottled, a tiny sardonic phial, which, if uncorked, even for a second, renders her a child again. But this time she's determined to get her way. The thought of Cameron Fraser approaching Heath torments her, but she knows she's drunk too much to drive. With Wilson gone, Jacob had seemed her best hope.

'Don't bring Dad into this. Listen, I'm telling you he's been watching the house. He must have broken into Heath's and stolen my number.'

'What rubbish! You're deluded, you know that?'

'Look, I don't want to argue, I just want this one-time favour.'

'No.'

'Christ sake, Jacob, come on – I never ask you for anything. Can't you do this one thing? What if something happens to Heath?'

'Then it'll be your fault for creating this mess, won't it . . . as usual.'

'That's so pernicious. When are you going to let it go?'

'Pardon?'

'You heard.'

'If you're talking about Dad . . .'

Something crashed to the floor in the kitchen and April's voice sang out.

'Sorreeee.'

He lowered his head and scowled, then walked towards the door, pointing at Rosie.

'We're not finished here.'

He closed the door so all she could hear was the cadence of their voices. Her eyes battled between shut and half-shut and when she sat down her head immediately rested on the back of the sofa. Quite suddenly she felt a tiredness that drew her legs up and lay her on her side. The anxiety left her, and when she placed her hand on her heart she found that it had slowed right down, almost as if she were already asleep.

★

SHE PULLS her shoulders up and clasps her hands together as if she's about to pray, then repeatedly taps her wedding ring against her eternity ring in a tiny round of applause as Rosie slumps onto a kitchen chair.

'I don't think we've ever had breakfast together. What would you usually have?'

'Alka-Seltzer and black coffee.'

April laughs. She thinks Rosie is joking.

'Well. How about some muesli with blueberries . . . see off those free radicals.'

'What?'

Slowly waking to the horror of having collapsed drunk on Jacob and April's sofa, thus confirming every lousy thing they know about her, Rosie thinks she hears April saying something political.

'They're full of antioxidants and they can actually reverse the ageing process!'

'Great . . . I'll take two.'

She stares at the condiments as April babbles like a happy girl.

'Apparently, the antioxidants break down the free radicals that kill off the cells and damage our DNA. That's why we age. Once the process is stopped the cells will regenerate.'

The coffee percolator is gurgling, perking Rosie up.

April places a breakfast bowl in front of her and she nods as she spoons in a mouthful, then shakes her head when she swallows.

'Where did you hear all this nonsense?'

'It's not nonsense! I read it in the *Daily Mail* last week.'

'Ahh.'

She nods again.

'Where's Jacob?'

'He's gone to work. He's collecting Heath later and taking her to the hospital. Oh . . . can I help?'

Rosie has moved from her chair and is opening cupboards, looking for a glass.

'No, you're OK, I've found one.'

She pulls down a long glass and turns on the cold tap, letting it run before filling and rinsing and filling the glass again. April twists in her seat, straining to intervene.

'We've got bottled, or filter.'

'No, this is fine.'

She tries not to watch Rosie but is compelled by her audacity – her bare feet, the way she opens their fridge and takes a look, then shuts it, pushing it just enough for it to catch, as though she's worked that fridge all its days. She sits down again and drinks the water in a series of diminishing gulps. It makes April want some too. She fancies she can see Rosie visibly rehydrate back to that careless beauty, the kind that doesn't fade with age.

It's in the bones.

Blueberries or no blueberries.

'More?'

Rosie gasps for air and doesn't quite close her mouth again.

'Yes, please.'

April sighs as she fills up the glass. This feels good – Rosie letting her help – but she knows she mustn't overstep her mark, so she puts the water down and leaves the kitchen, snibbing herself into the en suite and applauding again with her little elfin hands.

★

HEATH WOKE up in flight from a phasma that blew across the garden towards her and snagged itself on a lamb's tail. Its inside-out skeleton was delicate, like china bone, and she knew from the pelvic asymmetry that it was William swinging amongst the branches.

It was not a portent; it was a dream, a series of images selected for no reason other than they were handy. (The surviving traces of things she'd done the previous day – cutting some pussy willow for a vase, and later reading an article about a 9,000 year old skeleton that had been discovered years ago on the banks of the Columbia river. These were the hooks she hung her worries on. Nothing odd about that.) Thinking her way clear of all fanciful notions, she ate breakfast and washed up, ignoring the silver birch and any waking possibility of something strange dangling there, paler than the white catkins. But the dream stayed with her, following her to the station, and as the train began to pull her south she wished that she'd looked at that tree and dispelled her morbid fears once and for all.

JACOB WAS at the barrier, making a fuss about requiring a ticket to access the platform. He was querying how they expected old people to cope with such an unhelpful arrangement when Heath came through the turnstile, tugging at his arm as she passed. As someone who placed great measure on punctuality she was keen to press on. The train was late, and she ought to have been with Lomond by now. The thought of her brother watching the clock bothered her inordinately, reminding her of other visits, of the times she saw him waiting for Ethel to come home, pretending not to – then eventually putting the boys to bed.

And years later, waiting again – this time for Rosie when she hit what she now calls her 'navy period' (blue just wasn't dark enough), and Lomond skimming a Dick Francis, white-faced with worry and still pretending.

Jacob has lost his urgency.

'We're going to be late.'

'Don't worry. Dad can't tell the time any more.'

'What do you mean?'

She looked at Jacob, puzzled.

'Well, he can't read, can he . . . he can't read a clock.'

'How do you know?'

'He's been assessed. He can't read anything, and his recognition is poor too. He's OK with faces, but objects are hopeless. If you show him a picture of a chair he doesn't know what it is.'

'But . . . how do you know that?'

'Because he's been assessed.'

'But how can you assess what he sees if he can't tell you?'

'I don't know. He can indicate yes or no, can't he, so I suppose they show him a picture of a chair and say, "Is this a chair?" and he'll indicate yes or no.'

'And if he says no, does that mean he doesn't know what a chair is?'

'Well, yes . . . if he gets it wrong.'

Heath tries to imagine what it's like to not know. What does it actually mean to *not know* a chair? Does it mean you don't know what it is, or just what it's called? How come he can still use one if he doesn't know what it is?

'He doesn't get it wrong. It's the question that's wrong. Have they thought of that in their assessment? Have they assessed the integrity of their own enquiries?'

276

She's pulling on her grey gloves, forcing them onto the wrong hands – the pinkies slip easily into the thumbs but the thumbs refuse to fit the pinkies. Then she yanks at them and tries again. This time she matches the right glove to the right hand but holds the fingers the wrong way round – thumbs inwards – then pulls the glove over her right hand and stares at it, furious. Her thumb has completely disappeared, and the middle finger flops backwards, empty. It looks like a calf's tongue.

'What on earth do you mean?' Jacob asks, completely unable to follow his aunt's reasoning.

'I mean, if they knew anything about anything they'd ask, "Is this a picture of a chair?" Then maybe they'd get somewhere.'

Finally, the gloves are a spent force. She throws them into her handbag, zips them up and squashes them down, squeezing as hard as she can.

*

DAVE WAS a good man. She had often said this. The first time was the night before her wedding when her sister stretched her hand across the twin beds they'd slept in since childhood and whispered.

Kitty, are you sure?

He's a good man.

Yes, but are you sure?

Yes.

Then why can't you sleep?

Kitty was lying on her front, prostrate, her elbows cradling her breasts and her forehead resting on her hands so she wouldn't ruin her carefully backcombed hair. Her face was buried deep in a pillow and May couldn't make out her sister's muffled reply. *What?* – and again, as the muffle grew

277

louder but the detail still lost, as if Kitty were calling from another room – *What did you say?* With a great sigh Kitty pushed herself up, moving as if she were wearing a neck-brace, her arms taking all the strain so as not to disturb the alignment between head and shoulders. She turned her upper torso towards May.

I said – why do you think?

May looked at her – wide-eyed and blinking – needing more, and Kitty obliged by holding up one hand and pointing to her upswept hair before quickly lowering herself back into the pillow in a kind of controlled collapse. There was a pause before the beds started to shake, first one, then the other – the sisters laughing until their sides hurt, their pillows wet with tears and snot.

Kitty's hairdo trembling.

Stop . . . oh, please!

When they finally achieved a kind of stillness, she moved her hand lightly across the surface of the crystallised structure.

Is it all right?

May looked at the back of her sister's head, glistening under the moonlight. The impressive bouffant had caved in on one side and looked like a half-eaten candyfloss.

Yes, she said, *it's all right.*

And Kitty believed it, and slept at last – her vanity case packed and her wedding dress hanging against the curtains like a ghost – knowing that as long as she had May everything would be all right.

Now, for some reason, whenever she thinks of her wedding it's the bridesmaids' socks that stick in her mind – brilliant white nylon from the USA. Boy, did she love those socks. The honeymoon was a long weekend in Blackpool (doing nothing that they hadn't done before). Kitty in a short, pale blue jacket with matching

pillbox hat, Dave looking a bit like JFK to her Grace Kelly.
A good man.

This instrumental thought has played in her head like a
mantra over the years and she's often wondered at the
heaviness of it, how the weight of someone's goodness can
pin you down. Only now that he's said no, she's feeling
less pinned. At last he's given her something to kick against.

★

THE NURSE offered to move the patient to the day room
but Heath declined. The day room is bland and has no
windows, chairs line the walls, some with wheels and no
visible brake. It is a silent locutory, ill thought out and not
fit for purpose.

When they reach the bed Heath asks Jacob to give her
some time alone with Lomond. She takes care to smile and
squeeze her nephew's arm as she speaks, choosing her words
carefully, mindful of the way in which innocuous phrases
are frequently injurious to him. A wrong word can sting
him so easily, they're fired rather than spoken – like stones
from a catapult. When he leaves she sits beside Lomond
and watches him sleep. She feels reconciled and comforted
by proximity. He's clutching a brown glove, the elbow and
wrist bent so that it's almost tucked under his arm. Heath
is content to sit like this, listening to him breathe. Over
the years the sound of another person sleeping has become
strange.

His breath takes her away.

It pulls her from her one-ness and brings her into the
world.

LOMOND WAKES exhausted and returns to his dull paralysis.
His sister is speaking nonsense and she knows it. She stops

279

and repeats the same sounds again, buffing them up with a lazy motion until they take on the soft shine of milk. When her sounds fall into words he listens. She's bringing up history – stories that need to be passed on before it's too late and they're both gone. He watches her – her jaw set firm as she determines all she wants to say – and when she speaks her words jostle with each other, familiar and unnamed, and her gaze searches his face in a way that's different since his stroke. Before, the speaker's look was a ragged, uneven thing – the eyes glancing off the listener's gaze. *Before.* Now it's he who glances, faltering under the sustained scrutiny of others, his stone face telling lies.

His face is a quiz.

Guess how much I know? it says.

This much. There is no need for atonement.

Thirty-one

*W*HAT'S IN *a name? What's in a face? What's in a voice? Ask Truman Capote.*

I miss Wilson and his bon mots. What would he say if I told him I'd had breakfast with April and quite enjoyed it? The *if* in this question scares me a lot. I've come back to the flat to change and check the answer machine, but all it throws up is the sound of snow falling. I shiver.

At least there's nothing from *Mr Fish*.

The debris from last night's dinner is still lying in the kitchen, everything exactly as we left it, which makes me think that Wilson hasn't been home, but his coat has gone and I'm sure he didn't have it with him when he walked out. (I would have noticed, just as I am noticing now. Wilson bought an impressive twelve-hook coat-stand for the hall in the January sales and his coat is the only thing that ever hangs from it.) He must have come back for it. Suddenly I have this wild thought that he's driven up north to track Cameron down, but then two things occur to me – one, the car's still here, and two, he's not the jealous type. There's time to tidy up before I'm due to meet Heath at the hospital so I stack the dishwasher and clean the kitchen to a gleam. Wilson likes clean surfaces. When we first met I would always tidy up before he came round, but that soon wore off and it wasn't long before he started calling me Oscar, and I'd call him Felix.

Cute.

Now I want to woo him back. I want him to see how shiny these taps are. I rub the chrome with a dry J-cloth and when I check my reflection in the spouts I see Walter Matthau looking back at me, which seems encouraging. I'm confident I can put things right if I can just show him these taps.

I'M NOTICING detail – as though I've borrowed someone else's eyes. I dress for someone else (I'm not sure who), changing into a black skirt that looks plain but isn't. Two thin lines of black silk hoop round it, just above the hemline, and there's a tiny cream rose sewn between them on the left side. I find a grey wool coat that I'd forgotten about completely. It's very fitted, not just at the waist but all the way round my torso. I must have bought it on one of those rare but vivid days when for an hour or so I think I look like Katharine Hepburn (it's been said – once, a few years ago – in a bar on Lewis). I buff up my patent leather boots and nearly finish with a pink damask scarf, only changing for something dark at the very last minute. I'm feeling nervous as I drive up to the hospital. The traffic is heavy and a huge four-wheeler starts to cut in front of me. We both brake and look at each other. The other driver is a blonde, sharp-nosed woman who's telling me to fuck off. I smile and wave her in.

THE SMELL in this place is not the obvious 'hospital smell', it has a taste, a fusty reek that lags the corridors, permeating everything: skin, a plastic sandwich box, the petal of a rose. Luckily the building sits on a hill facing north so we can rely on a ferocious cleansing gust each time we leave. As I emerge from a stairwell a man is coming out of Dad's unit

282

and is walking towards me. There is something about him I like, his avuncular quality perhaps, but why would I notice? When he passes me he doesn't speak and I'm left feeling ignored, my pretty skirt and shiny boots unappreciated.

'Oh, Rosie . . . bang on time, dear, the doctor has just left.'

When I bend to kiss Heath she tightens her grip round my arm and speaks in a low voice.

'Your father is being irascible, don't flummox him.'

I sit on the bed and kiss him. He gives me a pat but nothing more. Heath is gathering herself in and seems keen to go.

'I think Lomond needs a nap. There's been quite a bit of coming and going since I got here and we've had a long talk. He's done in.'

She smiles, looking tired.

'What sort of comings and goings?'

'Oh, nurses, therapists . . . that sort of thing. Then there was the charming Dr Findley who was rather insistent, I'm afraid, and managed to upset your father very quickly. He'd arranged for another doctor to see him but it looked to me like it all came as a bit of a surprise to Lomond.'

We both look at Dad. He's crying. I don't recognise the sound he's making. If my eyes were closed and I heard that sound I wouldn't know it was him (only now I will). I've never seen him cry before and I find it harder to bear than anything else that's happened. I'd rather watch his brain die. In that situation there are things I could do. I'm sure I could hold him all the way through a comprehensible death.

But this.

Suddenly I'm crying too and saying stupid selfish things like *Don't, Dad, please.*

Heath puts her arm around me and comforts me while my dad sobs into a brown glove.

★

KITTY CHOSE not to examine why she was packing. The acknowledgement that she *was* packing, rather than 're-arranging her things' was enough to be getting on with. The placing of a few items of clothing in a suitcase had always felt like a harmless pleasure, her actions generating a sense of hope without hurting anyone. Because Dave so rarely left the house now, her sessions with the suitcase were sporadic. The case was stored in the cupboard on the upstairs landing, wedged vertically between the wall and the hot-water tank, so when it was pulled out and opened the contents were always concertinaed into one half of the case. She would re-fold the garments (which included some brand new underwear and a pale blue shift that felt like silk), and smooth out the layers of tissue paper that lined each tier. She enjoyed the look and feel of the paper, and the sound too, the dry crinkle of autumn leaves blowing about. Deciding what to pack had led Kitty to drawers and cupboards that she rarely visited, and she was frequently discovering forgotten objects, heavily coded things with no obvious associations – plastic rings, a shark's tooth, a small bag of brown and white marbles – kept for one reason or another, obscure now, but still holding a tiny pulse, the memory not quite dead.

Today had brought an unexpected opportunity. Her regular ten o'clock had been taken to Lourdes and Dave had the rare task of collecting some winnings from the bookie's. Normally she would have fitted in some time with Lomond or visited his house to add a further small preparation – taping down some frayed carpet, or removing a rug (she knew all about those spot-the-hazard home visits that the hospitals organised – the tyranny of them), but today was the day of Heath's visit, and the unfettered morning blazed as bright as the sun.

She pulled out the suitcase, opened it on the bed and tidied things up, then added her slippers, a towel, and a few toiletries. The case zipped up easily and sat primly on its feet like a dog hoping for a biscuit. When she was ready she carried it downstairs, where it waited on the front step while she tied a scarf round her neck and swept her hair back off her face, then she pulled out the retractable handle and walked down the street – enjoying her straight back and the noise of her bag at her heels.

And there was still no harm in it.

Only this time something felt different. Kitty had thought about leaving Dave so many times that it was hard to believe it was actually happening. She felt as though she was in a film. Not just taking the bus, but taking the bus to freedom, driving through grimy streets then disappearing over a green horizon, her head growing smaller as the world expanded – just a speck of dust in the cosmos.

WALKING UP Lomond's path was the best few steps she'd ever taken. Her mind was clear and she didn't ask herself anything. She was content just to be a woman pulling a suitcase. She unlocked the door and parked her case in the hall, sliding off her scarf the way she does (if only she knew) and switching on the power and the immersion heater. In the kitchen there was a smell of damp – a slight pungent whiff of winter. She unscrewed the window lock and opened it a few inches, then made tea and sat at the table, cradling her cup and waiting for the water tank to heat up. When there was enough hot water she climbed the stairs and ran a bath, pouring in some of her ginger and lime bath oil. The perfume gathered and lingered at the top of the tall house, its vapours curling through the eaves, drawing a line of pigeons from the nearby wood. The room was big and sparsely furnished, not like a bathroom, more like a room with a bath. She collected her suitcase from the hall and placed it on top of a wicker ottoman. Then she took off her clothes and draped them over a chair. Crossing such a large room was the furthest she had ever walked naked.

She stopped, and shivered, dipping her toe into a sudden shaft of sunlight. The glass in the window was clear, and at this height there was no need for a curtain or blind – it was as naked as she was – and although she knew it was too high for anyone to look through, Kitty couldn't quite dispel the thought that someone was watching her splendid white flesh flashing in the sun as she climbed into the bath. Holding onto the edges, she lowered herself down into the water. The sides were so deep her elbows rose above her shoulders and she had to let go suddenly. A hot pain twisted through her right shoulder and she slipped, crying out – a loud yelp that sent the birds flying as her hip landed on the bottom with a dull thud.

★

I FEEL cold. I roll off the sofa and crawl towards the radiator, then remember that I'm with Heath so I straighten up and walk properly, turning up the heat. I come back to the sofa and curl up again and put my head in her lap. She smells a bit, and I worry that her bones might snap under the weight of my head, so I move off and rest right next to her, hanging onto her arm like it's a pole on a fairground horse.

We've been talking about my mother.

It's not easy thinking about someone you never knew. When Heath started to tell me about Ethel it felt exciting. I asked her to stop for a minute so that I could take the picture out of my purse, then she resumed with the illustrated tale of my mother's life, or rather, her death – an odds-on event, apparently.

'You lived, she died. There was only one other possible outcome for that year – and that was that we might have lost you both.'

'Really?'

'Yes. When you came out you didn't start breathing right away. You were . . . floppy.'

'Floppy?'

It sounds like an endearing nickname. Why didn't anyone call me Floppy? *It would have made me feel wanted.*

I lean away from her a bit so I can see her. I don't want to miss a thing. She doesn't look at me but she picks up my hand and examines my fingernails. She's reliving something – moving on – but I want to know more about me.

'Do you think that means I was technically dead?' (It would be an interesting prefix, one I'd be happy to live with. It makes me feel more self-forgiving. I think I could forgive Floppy anything.)

'Well . . . maybe, but only for a moment, and not so's you'd notice.'

Not so's you'd notice? *The small matter of a dead baby?*

My revelation proves not to be quite as revelatory as I thought. Heath carries on, unshaken, her focus consigning me to a bit part with no lines – a faint blue blur in a basket, motionless, but only for a moment, and not so's you'd notice.

'I suppose there might have been one other possibility, that you might never have existed, but she still would have died. Poor Ethel . . . I suspect she always drank, but she managed to keep it hidden for a long time. I believe your father knew right from the start, but of course he always protected her. Nobody ever spoke about it. I always thought she just didn't know how to feel, that it was all an act somehow, unconvincing but genuine at the same time. I know that sounds impossible – what I mean is she didn't know she was acting.'

Heath puts my hand back on my lap and sits up straight, folding her arms. She pushes her head back, eyes closed, stretching her neck. I prise my hand round her elbow and hold onto her arm again. She continues.

'We knew she had cirrhosis of the liver and just assumed that somehow that caused the bleeding. She'd refused to go into hospital and wasn't even going to accept a midwife but Lomond told her he'd have her sectioned if she didn't agree. I think that's something he finds hard to live with, having to threaten her and then losing her like that, before he had any chance to explain. It was an act of love.'

She pauses, checking to see if I'm OK with this. My hair feels funny, cold and prickly as though I've just had a shock to the head, and I want to ask her, *Do you mean me? Do you mean he acted out of love for me?* But I can't talk because somewhere along the line we've switched mothers. I don't recognise the woman she's talking about. I'm searching the photograph again – checking every detail, every silver grain, just as I've always done, only this time I know what I'm looking for.

A sign.

Sallow skin, or yellow eyes – or teensy little liver-spiders threading across her cheeks.

I wish the picture was bigger, or in colour. All I can see is that she's beautiful. She looks vibrant and happy.

Or maybe just drunk?

'That was terrible . . . a really terrible time. I think she concealed her labour for as long as possible. Anyway . . . in the end her heart just stopped. The certificate said "heart failure caused by peripartum cardio-something-or-other" – myopathy, I think that was it. Seemingly the walls of her heart got damaged when she was carrying the twins.'

'The twins! My God.'

Heath extricates her arm from my grip.

'Is there any water?'

'Of course.'

I leap up, moving fast because I don't want her to stop talking. If we pause too long she might not be able to pick up where she left off, or she might not want to. She might change her mind. In the kitchen I think about Dad and all the things he might be crying about.

Quite a pick.

I look at Heath from the doorway and her eyes are closed. Maybe she's nodding off, but then she calls out in a loud voice, her eyes still shut.

'Do you remember a Dr Bird?'

'Dickie?'

'Oh!'

My voice is too close and it's given her a fright. She presses a hand on her chest and blows out as if she's trying to whistle.

'I thought you were in the kitchen.'

'Sorry.'

She drinks the water.

'So you remember him?'

'Yes, I think so. He was nice.'

'Well, can you believe we met him today?'

'What?'

'He came to see to your father, but Lomond refused to have anything to do with him. He just wouldn't respond. I felt quite sorry for the man.'

'Oh, God . . . hang on . . . I think I saw him coming out of the unit today. But how come you know him?'

'He came to the house once when I was there. I remember he wanted to see us having a meal, for some reason. The boys were impeccable but you refused to eat. I kept saying to Dr Bird, "It's not usually like this," and wondering what he thought.'

I am following this. I can remember. I'm on a knife edge – Jacob smiling at me across the table, he's raising his knife and saying, Rosie, do you want me to cut up your sausages?

We sit quietly for a while, surveying our own images of that meal. My thoughts Grimm, Heath's less so.

'He gave us an aide-memoire to fill out – a kind of grid thing – far too complicated to be useful.'

'How did it work?'

'I don't know. It was supposed to be a note of your speech habits and it was all coded. I can't really remember. There was *F* for frequency and *V* for volume so you could have a *V plus* for loud, *V minus* for a whisper, and *V* equals normal, then on the chart the rows represented people and the columns were for places . . . I remember that. It was all a waste of time. We'd be really careful to fill them in and keep them up to date and then no one ever looked at them.'

Heath paused and I could tell there was more to come.

'I've still got some somewhere if you wanted to see them.'

But I don't need to see them. I know the code already, and I know how those pluses and minuses fall. Anyone who cared to screw up their eyes and look at those charts would see it – the patterns of silence. The long quiet rows marked J for Jacob, white and straight – my brother's white fury.

Sometimes it's necessary to look at the world through slit eyes – to take the narrow view.

HEATH MOVES on through my silence – used to it – still not minding if I don't talk. She's telling me too much, one rich dish after another with no time to digest any of it. I want to think about my mother and where all this drinking and disease leaves my notions of her perfection. I used to believe she might come back, that she was lying in a glass coffin somewhere, like Snow White, waiting for a kiss.

She's still talking. She's telling me how I used to *beam* and how everybody loved my *beam* and this *beam* was more powerful than clever Jacob's linguistic acrobatics, and the more verbally elaborate he became the more I *beamed* – and that's something else to think about, my brother's verbosity and how I quietly rubbed his nose in its futility.

And then there's William. She says he was my voice, and now he's left me speechless and we both stop, right there – minding the gap. His missing is unspeakable.

Now we're on more familiar ground. The drugs. Heath never approved, and even though I passed my SCARED test (Screen for Child Anxiety-Related Emotional Disorders) – just skipped my way right through it – there was still the baby syrup, and then me feeling chuffed when I moved on to tablets. A miraculous compression in such a tiny orange pill, it was – amongst other things – glossy, biconvex, sugar-coated, a pharmaceutical glaze that was 10 per cent stomach ache and 90 per cent hypersomnia. I liked the sleepy-sleepy but not the sore tummy – so they switched it to 40 per cent insomnia, 30 per cent tired and still the 10 per cent sore tummy but with 20 per cent enuresis and Heath says thank God for the wet beds because when they suggested *another* drug for *that*, Lomond – finally – said – ENOUGH.

AND THAT'S when the headaches started. I think I was caught up in the tail end of a biologic revolution. It was my misfortune not to land up in the partial-blind-placebo-crossover group. I'm probably written up somewhere as a case study – but I can't take all the credit.

I couldn't have done it without my family.

IT TAKES a while for me to recognise the doorbell. He speaks as soon as I open the door.

'Christ, what is it?'

I realise I must look pretty bad for Jacob to notice something's up. I let him in, turning my face away quickly and leaving him to close the door. He follows me back into the living room where I snuggle up again on the sofa with Heath.

'What's happened?'

I have abdicated. I'm only small and I look at my brother and he looks maybe thirteen or fourteen but inside he's still a frustrated, oppositional ten-year-old who's afraid of snakes and ghosts.

I can't speak to him.

'Nothing's happened, Jacob, we're all fine. Rosie's just feeling a bit upset, that's all. Could you put the kettle on? I think we need some tea.'

The young words that come out of Aunty Heath's old mouth astonish me. The theory surrounding my silence is quite sophisticated and still unresolved (I suppose that will continue – as long as I keep shtum about the scissors). As Heath recalls it (her caveat, not mine), the psychiatrists said my mutism was elective, but nice Dr Bird always referred to me as a 'reluctant talker'. He said that sooner or later I'd just start talking. It's called spontaneous remission.

You mean she'll just get better?

Yes.

WE CAN'T really talk any more. Jacob will be listening through the wall. He keeps interrupting us, calling through from the kitchen to break us up – Where's the tea? Where's the cups? Then he comes back through with a tray and puts it down with a clatter, which is our cue to attend solely and entirely on him. He's looking very irritated and can't hold himself in any longer.

'Did you know that William's back – and he's brought a woman with him?'

Thirty-two

'**I** COULD have died in that bath.'

Kitty was picking some invisible fluff from her sling while May floated a few tiny white marshmallows on top of the steaming hot chocolate.

'There . . . just let that melt a bit. So, what did Dave say?'

'I haven't spoken to him yet.'

'You mean you haven't called him?'

'No, not yet.'

'You mean he doesn't know you've had an accident?'

'No.'

'Why haven't you called him?'

'Well, I can't use the phone, can I? I was going to ask you to do it.'

'And say what?'

'Well . . . just tell him what happened.'

'What, tell him you slipped in Mr Friel's bath?'

Kitty appeared to ignore the question, directing full concentration on her chocolate and how to use a long-handled spoon with her left hand. She had spent two hours waiting in casualty, still wearing the belt that William had buckled round her to stabilise her arm against her chest. He had emerged through the pungent vapours that filled Lomond's

293

bathroom and rescued her. It was hard to believe it, so she'd smiled and let everything wash over her, as though she was settling into a dream. When he unbuckled his belt and pulled it free with a loud *crack* she passed out. She came round moments later, clear-headed and covered up by a towel, with another cushioning her head and the bathwater completely drained away. As they waited for the ambulance William had insisted she take some painkillers, something she would not have done in these acute circumstances without medical sanction were it not for his surprisingly confident tone. He told her she had dislocated her shoulder and that he could probably manipulate her humerus back into the socket himself, if she'd let him have a go (he'd seen it done when someone fell from a honey tree in Ethiopia). She thought he might be joking, but she wasn't sure, so she declined his offer using a light tone, and he laughed too – and for Kitty, the strangeness of it wasn't her nakedness, or William's remarkable reappearance, but the being cared for. He had stayed with her all afternoon and seemed in no rush to be anywhere else.

MAY WAS worried. There was something about her sister's behaviour that couldn't just be put down to trauma and painkillers. She phoned Dave and told him that Kitty had slipped when they were out and was having a sleep at hers. It was just a little lie – the kind that caused her no trouble to tell – but her words didn't flow the way they should. They dropped from her mouth unevenly, like the first heavy drops from a rain cloud that was about to burst.

★

AND THEN he saw her face.

She swam past him in the back of an Audi – untouchable. Wilson watched from the pavement, just one in an amorphous

294

mass of wet pedestrians who were all tracking the car and resenting having to wait for it to pass. He'd been making good progress, having talked half the night with his friend Lucy and her husband Jake. Lucy was an old flame (a fact known only to them) whose consolatory nature shone like a lure, attracting the downhearted and the desolate. It wasn't the first time Wilson had spent a reparative night drinking their wine and eating a meal they called 'supper' as he gave account (sounding like a girl he always thought, but enough of a man not to care) of Rosie's erratic behaviour.

The Juicy Lakes (Rosie's collective noun for them) would listen, hold hands, hold his hand, and always, always, not judge, until finally – as if by deflection – his head would clear to reveal his own brassy unapologetic thoughts. *What do you think?* he'd say. *It's not for us to judge*, they'd say, watching him flounder and thrash about until he found something to hang on to – a judgement of his own. Something that showed him who's to blame.

Eventually, drunk and grateful, he had clambered onto the top bunk, where he succumbed to the exhaustion of survival, shushing himself against the sweet sleep of the four-year-old below, as Juicy Lucy (his non-collective noun for her) tucked him in. Breakfast was a bright, hopeful affair, where his previous life – a life without Rosie – opened out before him, and he resumed it, there and then, having found his way back to Kansas at last.

Only, her face in that car – pale and inscrutable, turned slightly toward the crowd.

What is it he recognises through the rain? He tries to read it as the car turns to the left, gliding out of sight like a bored shark. She was sitting in the back, and although he didn't see who was driving, Wilson assumed it was Jacob. There must have been someone else in the car, someone more prestigious than Rosie who merited the front seat.

He considered the direction they were driving in and guessed they were heading for the hospital.

Abandoned, he carries on. When he reaches campus he goes straight to the boardroom to make sure he bags the seat with the best view. He dumps his papers and helps himself to coffee and a giant yellow scone, then positions himself opposite the ornate high-back chair reserved for the external examiner, a diminutive woman from Lancaster who always puts him in mind of Miss Bartlett from *Room With a View*. Attributing fictional persona to members of the exam board was one of various techniques Wilson used to bring some colour into an otherwise dull gathering. Today's meeting was the best he could have hoped for – a long, detailed agenda that should carry him through the afternoon relatively undisturbed. As the room filled and the excitement caused by the giant yellow scones settled down, the academics took their places and began their meditative chewing. Wilson looked towards Miss Bartlett and beyond, gazing across the city and picking out the leaden rooftop under which sat Rosie – making her way without him.
I saw her today, I saw her face
It was a face I loved.

And he knew. He looked at his watch and counted back. He needed to put an exact time on it – the precise moment when everything he held dear in life had passed him by. A pale smudge in the back of an Audi. It had taken just a few seconds.

*

THERE WILL be a party on Wednesday to celebrate St Patrick's Day and Lomond is considering how to get out of it without attracting the attention of the more recently qualified (and hence, more vigilant) staff. These nurses (all graduates apparently) have been trained in psychotherapy, brief therapy, cognitive behaviour therapy and aromatherapy. They are always keen to cross-refer, particularly when it comes to matters of the *affect*. Their ability to apply a bandage, however, is less clear (and anyway, is that really their job?).

The unit is transforming into a green place. Leprechauns popping up everywhere, peeking out from behind the bedheads, climbing up the drip-stands, obscuring the windows in the swing doors. The shamrocks are miserable. They hang from the ceiling like dried peas on a string, curing in the desiccative heat. The huge green banner that is suspended above the support bars in the gym pronounces the place as HAPPY. Under it, the student occupational therapist unlocks Jimmy's left knee. His lower limbs appear to move independently, as if disconnected from the rest of his body. It is a gait not a hundred miles off what might be recognised as an Irish jig, at least in essence, if not pace. The student is wearing a green diddy hat that bends as implausibly as Jimmy's estranged legs. She's going to do a write-up of the party for her dissertation, in the hope that this will pull her through the placement.

Lomond looks at the large clock face. There is something about the shapes on it that cause anxiety. He's pulling slightly on his breath, wondering if it's too late for Kitty to come. He knows he can convey to her the horror of donning a conical party hat, of pulling a party popper – or worse, being the target of one. He looks through a faraway skylight and prays for a mid-week break in the weather. If it's fine she might wheel him out into the grounds to look at the crocuses.

'We're popular today, Lomond?'

Someone speaks to him and he looks round. Jacob is marching towards him, followed by Heath and Rosie. The women are linking arms and he sees that they are both the same height. It's not something that he's particularly noticed before, and he wonders if Heath has shrunk. He remembers marking the children's height against the door frame in the kitchen until eventually each stopped growing – Jacob edging to the top, then Willliam, then Rosie a clear eight inches below.

Coming in a poor third, I'd say.

Which he did say, and now regrets.

'Hello, Pa . . . we're back again. Has William been in?'

The question throws him, but he is getting used to that, and has learned to wait for more.

The fact that William hasn't visited yet is a puzzle to every one of them. Rosie is clearly excited and she and Jacob vie for Lomond's attention, so the story of the bags found at the house comes at him from two directions and the sequence of events (which included the discovery of a woman's suitcase and William's rucksack) is lost. Lomond struggles to follow it, not due to any kind of receptive dysphasia, but because the children (for so they seem) are babbling over one another, Rosie holding her own with Jacob in a way he has never witnessed before (or is that another *dys* – a *dysmemory* perhaps? What part of his brain can he trust?).

When all the facts are out and tagged it is evident that the only thing they really know for sure is that William is back – the rest is speculative. They have experienced the relief of William's homecomings before, the long exhalation of a breath that they didn't know they were holding – then the sun rising as it should, only bolder. But William with a woman? This is new, requiring speedy adjustments that formulate quickly in their heads. Whether or not this is a matter for celebration depends entirely on the girl, and it is the girl (in various guises) rather than William, who occupies their thoughts.

There is a hiatus when Jacob leaves to take Heath to the station. Rosie calls Lomond's house number again and again, wishing there was a ring-back sensor that would let her know when William and the girl (at some point during the last half-hour she had transmuted from woman to girl) were back in the house. Technologically it wouldn't be difficult. She filed the thought for further discussion with Wilson, then stroked her father's arm and threw him a cloudy-eyed look that reminded him of the little boy out of *The Yearling*.

'So. He's back, Dad. At last.'

And she rested her head on his shoulder and sighed. Were he able, he would have stroked her dirty blonde hair. He stared at his other hand, lying where it was last put. It was a stupid hand – a hand without a brain – more dead than Jimmy's low-tech ski-boot feet. Lomond was sick of looking at it. He preferred to keep it covered up, but the staff wouldn't let him.

Swathing himself in a Gordon Highlander rug when he felt like it was a right he no longer had.

★

THERE WAS something about the flat that unnerved Wilson. It was too tidy, cleaner than when he left it, and he wondered if she had hired someone, or gone through some kind of cathartic cleansing while he was away. Whatever the explanation, it felt as if Rosie had been very proactive. He'd expected to come back to a mess. This was typical of relationships (in his experience). Someone was always in the ascendancy while the other was curled up in a child's bunk bed feeling sorry for themselves. Suddenly it occurred to him that he might have been part of a big clear-out. He rushed to the bedroom and checked the wardrobe. His clothes were still there, neatly arranged in their reserved space, while her stuff bulged from overloaded hangers like a line of decapitated bodies. He rubbed his head vigorously, then checked the drawers and the bathroom cabinet, just to be sure. In the kitchen there were three assorted cups on the draining board and the teapot

299

was sitting on a tray. He felt the sides of it then lifted the lid. There was a large pile of teabags inside, too many for the pot. He smiled – she never could make tea – but when he emptied the pot he realised there were too many bags even for Rosie, even allowing for the likelihood that she'd just added new ones without taking out the used bags. He looked through each room again, sniffing like a dog, but the search turned up nothing.

SHE COULD smell the coffee even before she opened the door.

'Hello – o.'

He didn't feel ready, wasn't sure what he wanted to say. He'd longed for her all day, ever since he saw her in the car. It gave him a sore stomach, but when he heard her key in the lock and that silky hello he felt bloody angry. She appeared in the doorway, flushed and beautiful.

'Guess what . . . William's back!'

She stood still for a second, tilting her head and smiling, her brows arched in expectation of a reaction.

'Well – isn't it great?'

Thwarted, he agreed, of course he did, and as she hugged him he couldn't think of a way to get back to his own hurt. She dropped her coat across a chair, helped herself to coffee, and made toast, all the time talking about William's mysterious as-yet-unseen but definite return. She was light on her feet, her eyes bright. Her fingers were dancing, sending frantic messages across the room. She looked like a young girl, but he was the child, his feelings rendered small and insignificant.

'Do you have to talk with your mouth full?'

She stopped chewing and looked straight at him, not talking.

'Well . . . it doesn't look very nice.'

She looked away and started to clear up in silence.

'I'm only saying,' and he stopped there, feeling even smaller.

What a prat . . . I'm only saying I'm a prat. I feel like pulling your hair.

He'd seen this before, the way she took on a kind of sheen whenever William was home, even if they hardly saw each other – which they hardly ever did. *He* wanted to do that, he wanted to give her confidence and make her eyes go that funny way.

I'm only saying I'm jealous.

Why couldn't he say it? He could sing it, dance it, paint it across his forehead, write it down on a piece of paper and put it in the fridge, stand at a distance of thirty feet and use semaphore, get her to cup her hands over her ears and then send it to her in Morse code by tapping his index finger against her mastoid bone (she knows Morse code for God's sake – there's just no end to her).

Say it.

He could tease her, test her, quiz her – ask her to fill in the blanks.

Blank just a blank guy.

He could eat her half-eaten food, tongue on tongue, mouth-to-mouth regurgitation.

Say it, shitface. Tell her she's too careless with you, slapping you across the face with her joie de vivre, eating the last of the bread.

'Is there any bread left?' he asks.

'No. I ate the last piece. Sorry.'

'Hmm.'

She left him feeling wretched in the kitchen. He expected her to come back, but after a few moments he heard the bath running. He was so disappointed; she doesn't understand him. She needs to realise that sometimes you have to read between the lines.

Thirty-three

SOMEWHERE A celestial explosion has occurred, and under a blue twilight an astronomical swell travels down from the Norwegian sea. The northern surge breaches the stone walls and stirs up the waters of the pool. A pelagic creature rises to the surface, its blue back merging with the evening light, as if the sky has penetrated the sea. By morning the body is anchored in shards of frazil ice. It's spotted by a passing American, who reports it to the local aquarium, mistaking it for a dead seal.

★

CLOSED UNTIL FURTHER NOTICE DUE TO BEREAVEMENT.

When Heath read the note in the shop window she thought that old Mrs Fraser had died. The news alarmed her more than she might have expected, and her first thoughts were of Cameron, and the effect this might have on him. She assumed his mother was a stabilising influence, but quickly recognised this as a reflex thought, uncorroborated, and – having quickly recalled every mother she has known – unlikely. Nevertheless her absence would have an effect, and death invariably throws up something unexpected. It might be something small and unremarkable, but there is always something, even in circumstances of petrified grief where mourning gets stuck in a particular room, its very dust becoming sacred. Heath had sometimes wondered what went on in the Fraser house, how mother and son lived with such a bleak past. What would the interior be like? She imagined it chintzy, possibly with a secret basement that only Cameron could access. Who knows what things might be found there? She remained standing in front of the shop, vaguely aware of her reflection – how she looked like a ghost. She couldn't quite shake off the feeling that this death held some kind of significance for the Friels.

'Terrible, isn't it . . . such a shock.'

Another ghost appeared in the window and spoke to her.

'I can't believe it's happened to that family again.'

'Again?'

Heath turned and looked at the woman who had joined her. She was staring at the empty, well-scrubbed trays, shaking her head.

'The drowning.'

'What drowning?'

'Cameron Fraser. He drowned in the phibbies rock pool on Sunday night. Didn't you know?'

'Oh, God, no . . . I just assumed . . .'

Heath checked the door again, giving it a slight rattle as if it were only stiff rather than locked. She was hoping Cameron would appear at the tiny window and let her in.

The woman watched her, wary.

'It's shut.'

'Yes, of course, I had no idea. I just spoke to him a few days ago and he was . . .'

Heath realised she was speaking to someone she recognised but didn't know, about events that were probably best left unspoken. The woman waited, sensing that she might be about

303

to hear something interesting that she could add to the story. There was already intense speculation sweeping through the town about how such a strong young man who knew every local rock and eddy could drown in such still waters. The last reported sightings of him were throwing up a few surprises, and it seemed that everyone had an anecdote about Cameron's strangeness, as if all these small observations and encounters, even things that preceded the famous family drownings, made such a death explicable. It was the sort of thing that happened to people like that.

'What were you going to say? He was what?'

'Oh, nothing. It doesn't matter.'

The moment of possible revelation had passed and the woman walked away, disappointed. When Heath got home she took the empty Tupperware box out of her bag and put it back in the cupboard. Then she called Rosie and gave her the news.

★

WHEN LOMOND saw William and Kitty walking towards him he was confused, but it was not the usual, comfortable confusion that might or might not untangle itself. This confusion made demands on him. There was a lot to take in and his surviving brain had to work hard to make sense of it. Firstly, there was William, thin but substantial, moving slowly in that lopsided way. Then there was the coupling itself. Why were they together? It seemed established rather than a chance encounter (something about the way William carried her bag), and Kitty wasn't right – she was wearing a huge sling and there was a shadowing under her eyes, suggesting pain.

The uneven trace of his son was familiar and easy on the eye. His face had changed – aged by things he'd not yet spoken of – and he looked out of kilter. Lomond could see the effort he was making to fit in, and he knew it would only last so long. He wanted to make the most of it, and hoped that when the time came to say goodbye again all the bits of him – the hands and the feet and the mouth – would hold together long enough for him to stand up and kiss his boy.

★

THEY SAT by the window in an alcove they had discovered by accident when William was at the helm. He'd been wheeling Lomond toward the hospital café with Kitty in tow when she spotted the perfect nook, tucked away, with a view of a horse chestnut ripening under a surprisingly warm sun. They decided to park there for what remained of the afternoon. William had gone off, ostensibly to buy a couple of teas, but in truth, to be alone. She'd insisted that Lomond take the shady side, where shadows of leaves danced about him. Her chair was in bright light, as seemed to befit her, and sitting there, looking out, they could have been sitting in an ordinary house, with a garden and a tree. He kept glancing at her, the light catching the soft down around her lips. It was almost as though she was in bud – her soft catkin mouth. She was as pleasing as a freshly cut lawn.

'I had a teacher called Miss Chestnut.'

And of course, all the jokes about chests and nuts and being a Miss were left unsaid, and they both smiled in honour of an unsung life.

Being alone with Lomond was the only circumstance Kitty could bear after the humiliating events of the past two days. When William found her in the bath he did all he could to spare her any embarrassment. He was entirely nonplussed, as if it were not unusual to find a naked woman in his father's bath. She had managed to pull the plug, and as the water drained away it might have been the last amplified belch from the pipe that drew him upstairs (she would never know, since they would never discuss it). He simply draped a bath towel across her, then made a pillow with another and placed this gently behind her neck, his eyes fixed elsewhere throughout. Then he turned up the thermostat on the old radiator and called an ambulance. They both knew this was not a medical necessity, but *better safe than sorry* he said, and anyway, Kitty's wild-eyed look when he suggested she wrap her one functioning arm round his neck told him she'd had enough – to manoeuvre her would have been like trying to calm a rabbit in a trap.

William's sensitivity extended to not asking any awkward questions, and she believed his discretion would stretch as far as she wished it, and that whenever the bath incident arose he would follow her cue. In other words, no one else need know the exact circumstances of her accident. The family already knew she visited the house to organise Lomond's laundry. A simple slip on the stairs would provide a satisfactory account of her dislocated shoulder.

But what she had not reckoned on was Jacob's subsequent visit to the house and his discovery of her open suitcase and her toiletries in the bathroom. There were damp towels strewn about, and a pair of pink satin slippers had been placed neatly by the door. In a tangle of half-composed questions that sought to make sense of Kitty's account – *but how, but why, but didn't you?* – she eventually came clean about the bath, tagging on an unconvincing explanation about testing things out to best prepare the house for Lomond's return. Having exposed herself as a liar, the existence of other falsehoods was apparent to everyone, so much so that no further questions were asked.

ROSIE FOUND them hiding in the alcove, away from the party. She walked past them and returned with a chair.

'My God, you two are hard to find. I've been looking for you everywhere.'

Her eyes were small and unhappy.

'What is it, Rosie?'

Kitty touched her arm, but only briefly – uncertain now, after all that had happened. She felt as if she were still awaiting judgement.

'Someone we know has died.'

Rosie looked at Lomond.

'It's Cameron Fraser, Dad. He drowned . . . on Sunday night, they think. They don't really know what happened yet . . . he wasn't even in the open sea, they found his body in the phibbies pool.'

'Drowned!'

Kitty muffled her own mouth and Lomond closed his eyes.

'It's not even that deep, really . . . well, it is at the castle end, but Heath reckons there's a lot of seaweed and stuff growing beneath the surface . . . she thinks maybe he banged his head and got caught up in it but . . . you'd think he could have . . .'

She has to stop and hold herself in.

'You'd think . . . they think maybe his clothes bogged him down . . . his shoes . . .'

Her voice rises, declaring his shoes in a high squeal that climbs and disappears.

'His shoes were gone . . . maybe they . . . they might have . . .'

Kitty feels it, cries with her, and Lomond opens his eyes to witness what is being done here by this particular drowning, and he cannot help but think of his own, a warm, altogether kinder death – not like the Fraser boy's. He knows the place where Cameron must have been, and sees what he doesn't want to see; the lad's skin grazing across barnacled rock, his dark asphyxia clogged with brown seaweeds, dead man's rope slithering up his legs, pulling him down into water thick with bristle worms that scuttle towards him, their eyes greedy and coal-black.

His drowning would be nothing like that.

Rosie composes herself, pressing her nose with the sleeve of her coat, a gesture that prompts Kitty to pull out a packet of fresh tissues from her bag and distribute one to each. They sniff into them.

'Anyway . . . um . . . there's going to be a post-mortem, and the police have been investigating the circumstances. They're coming to see me later today, in fact . . .'

Sniff.

She looks at her watch.

'I'd better be going soon. It took so long to find you I need to get back.'

Lomond frowns and raises his shoulder, questioning her with an open palm.

'Mmmm?'

'I think they want to interview me because I spoke to Cameron on the phone the day he died. I suppose they check the records.'

They both look at her, waiting for more.

'He phoned me about something that day.'

She blows her nose with unexpected vigour then re-folds her tissue and presses it hard against her eyes, first one, then the other.

'I didn't know where he got my number from and I got a bit scared.'

Sniff.

Her tissue is in shreds. Kitty hands her another.

'Thank you.'

Sniff . . . sniff.

She pauses and reassembles herself, then looks at Lomond, her composure immediately breaking again. Words squeezed out between sobs and gulps.

'I said some really unkind things to him, Dad . . . just because . . . because I didn't want him to contact me . . . but . . . he didn't seem to be getting the message. I couldn't get through to him and I think . . . I think I might have said something horrible that tipped him . . . that maybe tipped him over. I think maybe it was my fault.'

He leans forward, grabs her arm and shakes his head. He's breathing loudly through his nose and his nostrils flare as if he's detected something acrid, then he suddenly relaxes and speaks, his voice as deep and thick as it ever was.

'No,' he says, his *o* short and shaped like a plum.

And Rosie and Kitty, neither of whom possesses a trace of fickleness, are instantly transformed into a duettino of delight.

'Oh!' they cry – and their sudden harmony disarms him, the sweetness of it squeezing his heart, two, maybe three beats skipped. He looks from one to the other, and seeing the way his tiny spoken word has transcended everything, he wonders how on earth he can leave them.

Thirty-four

I HAVEN'T had my shoes off outside for months. Not since Wilson and I had that weekend in Barcelona. It's funny how much you learn about each other when you're in a country where you can't speak the language. Me feeling empty in front of La Sagrada Familia, and Wilson incredulous, over-reacting to what I say, as usual.

Blowsy? You think Gaudi's a bit blowsy?

Now I'm barefoot and in front – a good fifty yards ahead of William. He's still on African time and walks at an African pace. I can't help pulling ahead. I'm carrying my boots and my feet are slightly numb in the cold sand, the couch grass and sea rocket stinging my toes. I turn my back to the sea and head towards the grassy hummocks where the turf is soft and springy. The moss is short, grazed neat by rabbits. I sit down on the ridge of a hollow and wait for William. He's wrapped up as though it's winter and I think he's developing a slight stoop. He's watching the waves, looking small under a big sky. A kestrel hovers, then climbs and climbs, taking in the dunes and the hinterland. I cast about, expecting Jacob to appear and break the moment – move things on. (There is a peace when it's just William and me, but also a missing. We are never entirely sure what to do.)

When William reaches me I open the rucksack and we share a ham and mustard sandwich, washing it down with coffee that tastes of tomato soup.

'Do you remember Jacob's moat?'

'Yes.'

His shoulders lurch upwards briefly. We think about it and laugh, a proper belly laugh that releases us onto our backs.

'You know . . . having you home changes everything.'

'Ahhh . . . pressure.'

'No! No pressure. Please, don't feel pressure. I thought you wanted to come home?'

'I do, for a while anyway. And I've told you . . . I'm happy to stay and help Kitty look after Dad if it means he'll get home sooner, but I do need to be back in Tigrai by New Year at the very latest.'

'But that's brilliant, that's nearly nine months! I can't remember you ever being home for that long.'

'It's not nine. Ethiopian New Year is on the eleventh of September, remember, and if things work out here I'll go back sooner.'

'God . . . what a date.'

(I'm thinking about all those Ethiopians who live in New York and I'm wondering how they celebrate New Year. It's the sort of thing we could do a piece on, maybe I could swing a transatlantic trip out of it?) I feel ridiculously optimistic, as if I've just taken a shot of whisky and someone's lining up another.

'Things will work out. I know it.'

We're still on our backs and I chum into him, holding on and resting my cheek against his arm.

'No, you don't know it. He might have another stroke. Anything could happen.'

I think about the anything.

'Or Kitty might leave.'

'Do you think she will?'

311

'I doubt it.'

'Won't her husband cause trouble?'

'I don't know. He might. That's why it's so important that you're there now, so we can get all the hassle over and done with before Dad gets home.'

Above us the wind pushes across a white sky.

'Do you think you'll get on?'

'Who . . . me and Kitty? I don't see why not.'

I don't see why not either, who wouldn't get on with William? Anyway, the house is big enough to sustain parallel lives. I can see them – passing on the landing, allocating shelves, sharing the occasional meal but other times not, Kitty making something in the kitchen and William carrying a tray to his room. They'll leave notes for each other. It will be a period of quiet preparation, they'll establish an atmosphere of harmony and order – hell, they'll probably join the Quakers.

'We'd better get back. It's a long walk, especially at the rate you go at . . . come on.'

I pull on my socks and boots and we help each other up. He stretches then retracts quickly and watches me as I pack up the rucksack.

'This must have been hard for you, Rosie . . . seeing Dad like that. I'm sorry I wasn't here.'

'It's been hard for all of us. I think Heath is heartbroken.'

'And you.'

It's not a question and that's when I feel it – a pain that's so sharp it knocks the breath out of me. He picks up the bag and offers his arm. I take it and we bump along unevenly. Everything subsides. I'm feeling peaceful now, as though I'm walking with a priest.

And then he goes and spoils it all by saying something stupid like . . .

'Jacob's really struggling, isn't he.'

'What?'

'Jacob, he's really struggling.'

'Do you think so?'

'Oh yeah . . . definitely. He's terrified.'

'Well, he doesn't show it.'

'That's because he doesn't know how. He probably doesn't even know how scared he is – but you can see it in his eyes.'

'I think you're confusing myopia with something else.'

'Aw, come on, Rosie, you need to cut him some slack.'

I can't believe he said that. William, who knows everything.

I can feel something moving here that's not supposed to move, like a dropped anchor shifting in the mud.

'ME cut HIM some slack? ME cut HIM! Did you know he was going to put Dad into Craigmalloch . . . did you? Believe it or not it was April who talked him out of it. I could hardly believe it, but anyway I don't know why you feel so sorry for him. You're wrong about him, you know . . . you're just so completely wrong. The only person Jacob cares about is Jacob. How can you *be* so wrong?'

But of course he's not wrong, he can't be – they grew from the same egg.

'Come on, Rosie, be reasonable . . .'

'Reasonable! Reasonable! Did you know that I was drugged?'

I spit it out, my voice dropping so low on the word *drugged* the sound distracts me (I hear it, but it doesn't sound like me).

'What?'

'Did you know?'

'No. What are you talking about?'

This.

'I was drugged for over a year – over a year – all because of him. They had me on God knows what . . . lithium probably, battery fluid to keep me going. It was a kind of experiment . . . everyone probing and prodding . . . and all the time he's sitting there like something out of Edgar Allan

Poe polishing his wee penknife and threatening to cut out my bloody tongue.'

All the velvet in my voice has gone – pared off with a blunt razor until I'm screeching in a kind of stubbly rasp. I speed up so he can't see my face but he's on my heels, trying to catch my arm again. I push him away and he loses his balance. I hear him yell and turn. He's fallen into a gorse bush, spreadeagled and intricately pinned, but I can see he's unscathed under all those clothes.

I could say so many terrible things – they're stacking up, a long list of previous that would make him gasp – but I don't because he still looks priestly, and he's still forgiving me for being unforgiving.

'You look ridiculous.'

'Well, I'm trapped in a cactus pear, what's your excuse?'

A couple and their dog are approaching from the right so I decide to leave him there till they pass. They're almost clear when the bush speaks. The dog goes berserk and snaps at William's protruding foot. He tries to free himself up for a kick but is so tightly bound now that it comes out more as a kind of electrical fit – weird enough to put the dog off. Nobody says anything and the man holding the lead presses a button on the handle (which is bigger than the dog) and yanks the dog backwards, then they all hurry off.

'Bye.'

Cowards.

'What's their problem?'

I look at William, hoping the bathos will work (it usually does), but he's got me on a hook – as though I'm the one caught in a whin bush.

'He wouldn't do it, you know. Jacob would never hurt you.'

I tut, not knowing what to say.

'It was just something he said. He was never going to do it.'

But I believed him. I still do. *Does nobody get that?*

'He was just a sick wee boy with a sick idea.'

I kneel down onto the sandy slope in front of the bush. William's face is right in the middle of it – his body has disappeared under the yellow pea-flowers. It feels like a scene from *Happy Days*. 'He blamed me for Mum.'

'No, he didn't. He blamed you for Dad.'

'Blamed me for Dad . . . what do you mean?'

'When Mum died it was you who got all the attention. Dad had effectively brought us up. He'd shielded us from the worst of Mum's excesses, then suddenly she's gone and you're here and Heath moves in and takes over because Dad's too busy protecting you, like nothing else matters . . . it was like we were some kind of bloody threat or something.'

'He must have been grieving.'

'Yes, I know, but so were we – we were grieving for both parents. At least I had Jacob, but who did he have? He couldn't lean on me. Christ, at that time I wouldn't even go to the toilet without him. I couldn't eat unless he was in the room. I used to have nightmares that he was just going to disappear if I took my eyes off him.'

I need to think about this and I really need to talk to Wilson and I really really need a drink.

I tip onto my side to get out of the wind and pull my knees up. After a few minutes the bush talks again.

'Rosie?'

'What?'

'Can you give me a hand?'

★

HEATH CONSIDERED herself exceptionally lucky in lots of ways. She believed in counting blessings, did so regularly, and refused to hanker for the life not lived, even when she caught a glimpse of it. She knows the dangers of *giving in,* how quickly the essential spirit of a human being can choke on self-pity. You have to keep an eye on its invasive power.

Today she was feeling slightly weak, so she sat at the table and laid out her good fortune like two silver spoons – her brother alive, and her nephew safely home from Africa. She tried to dispel her ghastly dreams and her visions of William killed, all the sweetness sucked out of him. He could so easily not have been at all. When the twins were born the obstetrician made a casual remark about the slightly smaller, secondborn starting out as a granular abrasion on a cell wall – just a wee scratch, but enough to separate the cell in a split second. The notion of William's life as always precarious has never left her and she has fretted ever since. She knows it is all just hysterical fancy.

Thank God.

Yet something persists, troubling her. He seems robust enough, a bit thin perhaps, and feeling the cold, and his appetite is small. He moves more slowly than she remembers (he'd always defied those wonky limbs with an easy agility, but maybe there's a strain in his asymmetry that catches up over time, the way things do). She finds some reassurance in reminding herself that he needs time to acclimatise to the cold and the hurried pace, and his father changed. William told her that he had prepared for the worst as he waited (for twenty hours) at Mekele airport. It had been twenty hours of orphanage – then the rain clouds lifted, allowing the Fokker 50 to land, and when he finally reached his living, breathing father, he was thrown. He felt hunger in his stomach, and had to still it with both hands.

Later, he felt bereft.

But he's doing so well!

Which made him feel bad about feeling so bad.

And Heath knows exactly what he means.

★

316

ROSIE AND William had given themselves the whole morning to shut up the summer house. They had both fancied it would be a peaceful, contemplative process, one of those sibling moments, a resurrection of the past – but it turned out not to be so. They had not anticipated Cameron's ghost – the way he hovered at the gatepost, whittling a stick and glancing up every time they passed a window or moved towards the door, his vain hope exposing their shortcomings. Children without virtue.

And now the strange boy is dead.

They tidied up in silence, rinsing a cup and bagging up the scant detritus of Rosie's half-baked plan – the few eggs she'd placed in the wire nest, the white bread (a slice toasted, just for the smell of it), a jar of withered grass – it didn't take long. Then they took the keys back to Heath and watched her growing smaller as they drove away, William twisting round to look through the back window and Rosie using the rear-view mirror. She stood waving them goodbye, and at the last moment she blew them a kiss, a kind of two-stage sequence, the fingers to the lips, then off, but only slightly. It was a shaky, old woman's kiss, and its eloquence pierced them both, like a needle through skin.

Rosie took the back road home. They passed herringbone fields whose borders were lined with neat dykes that drew the eye, draping the land from coast to coast in a net of boulders. Each stone chosen, some hewn, whilst others fell into a sweet fit – but every single one considered and placed, their patterns a thousand shades of modest grey. Seeing the dykes of Fife can change your life. They make you feel lucky to be alive.

Thirty-five

THERE ARE times when Rosie remembers who she was, when myth and reality flip over and she becomes the woman from the radio. Her voice is the voice of a real person – a loveable person. Somebody worth knowing.

Somebody known.

Somebody.

The sergeant has stars in his eyes but the constable's never heard of her, he's never strayed from Radio One, and he can't believe what he's seeing. Hard Nails Harry going all molten under the heat of a dame.

Her voice licking molasses from his balls.

Harry's magic blue suit has lost its power and he feels uncomfortable, as though he's intruding, asking cheeky questions. He's skimming the milk – giving her the *It's only routine* routine, standard procedure in cases like this. Harry's favourite word is *suspicious* – he loves its impact, the way it widens the eyes, or sends them downwards or sliding sideways without moving the head (as though you're not going to notice), twitching the foot and itching the nose. Blushing throats telling tales.

He loves the sound of it too – the Sean Connery shush.
Shush-pish-ush.

But he's not using it today. He's choosing his words carefully. He doesn't even say that they're investigating – they're just compiling a standard report for the procurator fiscal on a sudden, unexpected death. A neutral death. It sounds as though she was one of the last people Cameron Fraser spoke to and she's not saying much (*but oh, when she does . . .*) out of respect for the dead, Harry thinks, but there's a picture emerging – a stalker. She must get a lot of that, folk that think they've got a claim on her. He's thinking she can probably go about quite the thing and nobody will bother her until she speaks. It must have an effect. She's probably really quiet by necessity, if not by nature. When they finish the interview he asks her how her dad's doing. She flinches, then recovers and says *fine, thank you for asking,* and he clenches his teeth, wishing he'd bitten his tongue. Everyone's heard about what's happened to her dad – it's public knowledge – and the lassie who's covering for her on the radio has started to keep the listeners up to date, but even so, he knows he's crossed a line.

Bugger.

His walkie-talkie sounds like a dentist's suction-pump sucking up saliva. He knocks it then picks up his hat and tucks it under his arm. As they turn to leave she seems to relax a bit and asks him about the funeral. He sees it as a chance to redeem himself and show her he's not your average bobby, following the thick blue line. He tells her a bit about the post-mortem and shows off his knowledge of forensics, explaining how they establish death by drowning. He's talking about the dead man's teeth, how after a week they'll probably turn pink.

'Pink teeth?'

Rosie and the constable say it at exactly the same time. They look at each other briefly and give out a two-note laugh, then look at Harry again. He's explaining the way blood seeps into the necrotic pulp tissue, and as they listen they both pull back their lips and bare their own teeth in an empathetic clench. Cold blood oozing from dead teeth. Harry can see he's unsettled her again.

Bugger.

He nudges his young sidekick but the constable's grimace sticks. He notices that the lad has quite a bit of tooth decay and is tempted to tell him that if he were to drown – or experience some other kind of sudden death in a moist environment (strangulation in the bath, for instance) – his teeth would probably be too rotten to turn pink. Harry stares at the constable, opens his own mouth, and points to his own teeth.

'Cover the Sugar Puffs, there's a good lad.'

Bugger.

That's not the sort of remark he wanted to make in front of her.

Bugger.

He laughs to lighten things up a bit, then ushers out the constable, keen to leave now before he makes matters worse. As Rosie closes the door he looks back and she smiles. Her face is wan, as if she might faint, and he wants to tell her there's nothing to worry about, that the world's a better place without him.

Everybody knows that Cameron Fraser was a nutter. Who knows what he might have done?

Thirty-six

L OMOND IS waiting to be pushed into his case confer-
ence. He looks through the window, watching air.
Strange light illuminates the grass. A gardener appears; he's
walking in an odd way, only moving from the waist down,
pushing a wheelbarrow full of manure – old-fashioned
horse-shit that's light on the end of a fork. His long grey
hair and beaky nose make him look old, but Lomond's not
sure. The gardener is tall and his back is bent to lengthen
the drop of his already long arms so he can reach the
handles of the barrow. When he puts the barrow down and
walks away his back stays bent at exactly the same angle,
and his head maintains the same height. Lomond laughs
quietly, his chortle hitting against a closed, unexpectant
mouth.

'Have you got an itch, Lomond?'

'Nnno.'

'Are you sure?'

The nurse is smiling and pulling a gormless Stan Laurel
expression. His eyes keep flitting up and down in an exag-
gerated way, from Lomond's face to Lomond's hands. He's
telling him to look.

And when he does look, Lomond sees his left hand

scratching his right hand, and although he can't feel anything, they both know what it means.

'WELL NOW. This is quite a turnout. Shall we get started?'

The consultant managed to look pleased and irritated at the same time. The group had tipped over the edge, tumbling into noisy little sub-groups of twos and threes. April had changed her seat, crossing the tiny central circle to sit next to the social worker. They were discussing shoes. Rosie moved up one and squeezed Kitty's hand.

'You OK?'

Kitty took a deep breath.

'I think so.'

She smiled and looked across at Lomond, finding him looking back at her in a sleepy way that made her blush.

Still, that blush could be anything – the room was hot and it was a highly charged atmosphere, there was quite a bit of high colour all round. Kitty was sitting with her back to the window and felt fairly confident she was not much more than a silhouette, her facial features obscured. The thought relaxed her, and she pondered over how wonderful it would be to feel like this all the time. It was like a state of grace.

William was slouching with his arms folded and legs stretched out, his feet still undecided. He was scrutinising Mr Emslie's face, watching his mouth tighten as the meeting descended into a state of pleasant disorder. Someone started off a shush that rippled round the room like a Mexican wave, stalling only at April, who needed a bold tug and a few moments to let the effects settle. Mr Emslie spoke again.

'Excellent. Shall we start?'

'My husband's just parking the car.'

'Your husband?'

'Yes. He had to go round again, I'm afraid, so he just dropped me off.'

The social worker relaxed her pencil then pointed it at William.

'I'm sorry, I thought this was your husband?'

'Oh, no. That's my husband's brother.'

'Are you sure?'

April's shrill laugh transcended her small, even features, catching the attention of everyone.

'Oh, yes, quite sure! I always—'

Mr Emslie cut across her, just as anyone might.

'I think we'll carry on.'

'But my husband is the next of kin.'

'Is he?' said William, straightening himself up to his full height. He's smiling, which confuses April. She's casting about, flitting from person to person, her blue eyes touching lightly on each in the hope that someone else will confirm Jacob's status.

'Well, what I mean is . . . what I meant was . . .'

Rosie is watching her sister-in-law flounder like a drowning fish. She considers a riposte, something to redden the gills further, then decides to pick her up and throw her back into the sea.

'She means he's the firstborn . . . by nineteen minutes.'

April gasps and presses her hand against her chest.

'Yes . . . that's it! Thank you, Rosie.'

She gives Rosie a new look, a kind of misty-eyed gratitude that surprises them both. Rosie suddenly feels a bit bashful. She wants April to stop looking at her like that so she juts her jaw out and lets it slip slightly to one side, but April fails to take the hint, so Rosie frowns, and, without taking her eyes off April, lowers her chin until she's staring through her own skull. It's her best devil-look (but still not perfect, even after twenty-five years of practice). Suddenly the door opens, crashing into the back of the OT's chair.

'Christ!'

'Jacob!'

April gasps again, half rising, then settles herself with a loud dry swallow. Rosie has swivelled round to catch her brother's entrance, leaving her slack jaw behind. Her mouth gapes.

'Sorry I'm late. Bloody car. Had to park miles away.'

He's looking for a seat. Rosie closes her mouth, smiles, and pats the empty chair beside her.

'Come sit next to me and William.'

Jacob's already dark look darkens. He can't read her – doesn't trust her smile and her helpfulness. Wondering what game she's playing, he lowers himself into the chair as though he's been asked to sit on a landmine. There is a general shuffling about as the room accommodates the patient's next of kin. Mr Emslie finds the sight of long-bodied middle-aged twins sitting side by side mildly diverting. He is tall himself, and the usually sparse no-man's-land in the middle of the circle is peopled with legs criss-crossing like a pile of pick-up sticks. It is not entirely clear which knee is which, and the consultant is grateful for the ambiguity, such is the tedium of these interminable case conferences. He is a clinician, a damn fine one, and there is nothing clinical about this meeting. His work is done and the rest is a matter of detail. Over the next few months Mr Friel will complete his therapy and go home. His notes suggest the patient is an educated man, who will therefore determine his own course. He will choose to be reckless, or prudent, or both, in a random or systematic way – or not – depending, etc., etc.

There's really nothing to add, medically speaking.

LOMOND KNOWS he will never be alone again. Never sleep in an empty house. His most constant companion will be his next stroke. It will occupy the room, sitting in the corner

324

like Typhoid Mary. Then one night (he feels it will be night), she will stand up and move towards him. There will be a moment of brief recognition, the sudden strong smell of vanilla perhaps, or the taste of metal at the back of his throat. Some survivors report visions, epiphanies, the sound of their mother calling them in. Others remember an extraordinary silence – the big switch-off. No hiss. Whatever.

Of course, what might herald the final one is anybody's guess.

Unusually, the consultant leans forward and looks at the patient, who sits one along to his left. Lomond has been staring out of the window, weighed down by the realisation that this sort of assembly is likely to continue, intermittently, for some time to come. He can see that something is about to happen outside. There's a faint green veiling under an ivory sky, and spores of the youngest moss have been released, and are dancing in electric yellow light. His unimpaired peripheral vision catches the sudden movement of Mr Emslie's bold chin, which is now almost touching the starchy right breast of his key nurse.

'I believe you spoke on Wednesday, Mr Friel. That's quite a breakthrough. Is the speech therapist here?'

The nurse shook her head, tucking herself in for fear of a collision. Lomond looked directly at the consultant, then looked away, embarrassed by how clearly he saw the man, a naked melancholic going through the motions – so familiar with death that it did not really matter who was alive and who wasn't.

'Right, well . . . would you like to say anything now, while you have such a captive audience? After all, it's your meeting. No? Well, just shout when you have to, tell us when we're talking nonsense. Now . . . who's going to start?'

NOT ME. *I have already started. I'm way ahead of you. I've thought my way out of my own box. The lid was down and then there was*

*a loud creaking like a colossal weight of water or earth bearing down
and I slept and waited and was quite comfortable until the ache
started and I thought it was toothache because it was sharp and
diffuse at the same time and I couldn't figure out where it was
coming from and it seemed then that it was death itself and I felt
so disappointed that death was like a bad toothache just a miserable snivelling gnawing thing but then there was one of those golden
hiatuses where the pain suddenly stops and you're weightless and
you thank God only you know it's going to come back and when
it does you surrender without a fight and just let it consume you
and it did just that and I realised then that it wasn't death it was
toothache and the thought of having toothache while I'm dying was
unbearable because I knew it would be all consuming and I'd miss
everything and never know what death feels like after all that effort
and speculation and I felt cheated not by life or death but by a
rotten tooth and I must have been moaning or something not a
metaphysical lament just with the ache in my face and someone
lifted the lid of my box and I thought . . . why not just deal with
the toothache first?*

Then let's just see what happens.

HE LOOKS across at Kitty. She's sitting in a snowfall. Fresh
cotton landing as it falls, in great swathes, a generous folding
that muffles every sound. The last thin voice trails off into
silence as the light in the day room softens, dipping until it
is too dark to make anyone out. All they can do is watch
the snow falling under a March moon.

326

Acknowledgements

Thanks to Judy Moir and Poppy Hampson, and to Kevin MacNeil, Roddy Llewellyn, Linda Walker, Jean Gregor, Peter Gregor.

And of course, to Charis and Bill.